CATARINE
HANCOCK

CURSE
OF
STOLEN
FLAME

FIREBIRD

For little me, who dreamed of stories.
This is for her.

CONTENT WARNING:

Please note that this book contains explicit language, sexual content, fantasy violence, mentions of sexual, emotional, and physical abuse, murder and war.

ISTRERIA

Temprian
Sea

Alverinian Isles

Oslien Sea

To Ciryn, the Southern Continent

Ramdelle
Evalanian
Mountains
Pryllia
Harthwin
Silverglen
Mistbarrow
Bridgewood
Oakwryn Forest
Roulierne
Paselyn
Lakes

Wendrith

Tempra's
Point
Greymont
Dowshire
Alverin
Krisille
Greenroot Swamp
Dewport

Elyhiam
Laoruwen
Breyenth
Whiterest
Stillward
Duskhael
Craxor's Forest
Blight
Dark Blade Mountains
Blackrock Strait

Scaldryn
Sands
Drucanar

Haqari

Vrina
Eslai

CURSE OF STOLEN FLAME

by
Catarine Hancock

PROLOGUE

When the girl came upon the men in the woods, she did not expect them to be quite so large.

Men seemed so much bigger when they were dangerous, when one had to face them alone. When one was little more than a child.

She had her magic, she told herself as she stepped onto the path in front of them. She had her magic, and they did not. She'd spent days studying them, watching them from afar for any sign of wielding. But none of them possessed a single bit.

Still, as they stopped in their tracks to take her in, no more than a few yards from her, she had to fight the urge to turn and flee.

"What do we have here?" one of them asked, leering as his lips curled in a nasty sneer.

She bared her teeth and willed her eyes to brighten, revealing the magic she carried within her. "Stay away from my home," she snarled. They'd been terrorizing this road for days now, robbing traders, travelers and hunters alike. Robbing her home of much-needed supplies for winter.

She had had enough.

The men blinked, and then burst into laughter. It grated down her nerves, but her annoyance steadied her, surprisingly. "Stay away from my home," she repeated, louder this time. She raised her hands before her. Embers sparked at her fingertips.

"Is this really the best they could do?" A different man, the largest of the three, took a few more steps towards her, narrowing the gap between them until she had to tip her head back to look up at him. "Some skinny little thing with a flicker of fire magic in her blood?" he asked as he studied her, not even bothering to keep a hand on his weapon. A vile smile spread across his face.

Quick as an asp, he struck, his fist slamming into her cheek. She fell to the ground with a scream, her magic guttering. Still, she recovered, scrambling to her feet even as the man attacked again, this time hitting her square in the stomach. She buckled over, but remained standing, and lashed out wildly with a flame-covered hand.

The man danced out of reach, laughing. He lunged before she could catch her breath, gripping her around the throat and raising her off the ground. She kicked at him, her burning hands smoldering against his jacket, but the flames were weak. They singed the leather, but not deep enough, not strong enough.

She shouldn't have come. Should have left it to the guards, even though she knew they'd do nothing. And now her brashness would get her killed, and that would be a relief after what these men did to her. She could see the cruel promise in their eyes.

Please, she begged the gods, though they'd never listened before. *Please, help me.*

And as her vision began to darken, as the fire at her fingers began to die out completely, she felt something brush up against her very soul. Something ancient and burning, asking a wordless question. A silent request.

Yes, she answered, too afraid to care or think it through. *Yes.*

That ancient, fiery thing vanished, and for a heartbeat she thought she'd imagined it all. But then pure, undiluted power surged into her body. It was rage and hunger and death.

Fire.

One moment, she was nearly unconscious, sagging in the man's grip.

The next, she was an inferno, fire enveloping every inch of her. Before the man could shout or drop her, she'd engulfed him in flames, too.

And as the clothes melted from his body, as she incinerated him to ash and his companions ran screaming, a god began to watch.

CHAPTER I

The morning was cold, but the autumn bite was no match for Kindra's fire.

Her flames curled just under her skin as she moved through the forest, warming her against the fall morning chill. Winter was several weeks away yet, but already the Evalanian Mountains were a brilliant white, smothered with snow. Though the afternoons were still pleasant, the mornings and nights had fallen victim to the bitter winds and icy storms that blew in over the Pryllian border, coating Harthwin in glistening frost every morning.

That same frost crunched softly beneath Kindra's boots as she approached the bandits' camp she had been scouting for the last few days. She'd caught wind of their presence last week when Filip, one of Harthwin's best hunters, spied them setting up and reported it.

He hadn't reported it to *her*, of course. He'd told one of the village guards, who had then mentioned it loudly when she walked by the guardhouse later that day. Kindra rolled her eyes as she ducked behind a bramble bush. She'd been doing their job for them since she was thirteen, and still, people went to the guards with concerns about safety. Still, the villagers asked them for help when there were bandits or scouts from Pryllia or deserters coming too close for comfort. Still, they refused to outright acknowledge everything she did to keep them alive.

Even though they knew it was her.

Always, they saw the smoke rising as they traded at the market or chopped their wood.

Always, they smelled the scent of burnt flesh that followed her as she walked back into town.

The familiar surge of anger rushed to the surface, and Kindra took a deep breath to force it back down. There was no place for anger right now. It made her magic less controllable. More deadly.

Before her, the bandits' camp was quiet, the fire down to mere embers. If she focused on it, she could feel it sputtering, gasping for air. A part of her itched to feed it some of her magic and bring it back to life, but she ignored it. Later. That would come later.

One of the tent flaps opened, and a seedy young man stepped out. He couldn't have been more than five years her senior. His clothes were old, and the leather armor strapped across his torso was thin and cracked. He was dirty, his shaggy brown hair clumped and matted.

Kindra watched him as he fed some wood to the fire, feeling her magic flicker as the flames licked at the log and regained their strength. A moment later, a second man emerged from the tent, his own appearance just as worn and ragged. He joined his companion at the fire, pulling some stale bread out from the crate next to him. They talked quietly, and Kindra didn't bother straining to hear.

Every time, she hoped it would be different. That it would just be a relocating family passing through or a group of friends on an adventure. That it was a mistake or a misunderstanding.

But it never was. Nobody wanted to come this close to the Pryllian border for fun. It was the same reason why Harthwin hardly ever got new residents—nobody wanted to live within ten miles of one of Alverin's most vengeful neighbors.

Sure enough, the two men began to move about their camp, rifling through sacks and crates to expose what could only be stolen things: a silver necklace, a gold ring, a bejeweled dagger. Alarm and anger flared at the sight of a slashed open corset, still stained with blood. Kindra waited for her cue.

A few minutes later, it came:

"We could see what there is to find around Harthwin," one of the men suggested.

"We'll need to be careful," the other responded, "It's a Wielder town."

"Yeah, Earthwardens." A scoff. "As if any of them would have enough magic in their blood to do anything."

"No, there's a Firefury that lives there. Some girl. I've heard she protects the town all on her own."

Unable to help herself, Kindra smirked.

"Then we'll have to be sure the bitch doesn't catch us."

The smirk disappeared. She readied her flames and stepped out from her hiding place.

"Hello, boys," she drawled, strolling casually over to the fire. They jumped up from their seats, hands flying to their weapons.

"Who the fuck are you?" the first bandit spat.

She smiled, calling to the flames, and they surged up to greet her, wrapping around her arms. "Why, I'm the *bitch* herself, in the flesh." She cocked her head. "Now, what was it you were saying about Harthwin?"

She was upon them before they had a chance to reply.

An hour later, Kindra walked past the meager guardhouse on the way back into Harthwin smelling of smoke and burning wood. The men had escaped relatively unscathed. She'd been content to watch them flee with their tails between their legs and not have any more injuries or deaths on her conscience. They weren't coming back; not until she was long gone, so she'd taken the time to poke through their belongings. Bags filled with stolen jewelry and silverware, crates loaded with pilfered food—she stuffed the best-looking food into a sack, grabbed up some of the other goods, lit the entire camp on fire, and watched it burn to nothing. Once she'd put the fire out, she made her way back to Harthwin with her prizes.

It wasn't often that the people she dealt with had food or trinkets she could bring back with her, but when they did, she figured there was no harm in re-purposing the goods for the people of Harthwin. Better to give it to those who deserved it than to leave it behind as a pile of ash.

"Took care of those bandits for you," she snapped as she passed the two guards playing cards. "You're welcome."

They didn't reply, but they at least had the decency to look embarrassed, their faces reddening.

She stopped at the small earth temple they kept for Aspa, goddess of the forest, and Dovon, god of animals, dropping off the bag of food to the earth priestess, who took it from her with softly muttered thanks and averted eyes.

Kindra made her way through the small market next, trading the jewelry for food and a couple of blankets for the coming winter. As she walked, she picked up bits of news; a bit of a rarity in Harthwin, considering how isolated the village was: another border skirmish down by Breyenth; another group of Pryllian scouts caught too far past the border; debates on if the king would send any soldiers here; concerns about whether he would care about the eastern villages at all when everything finally boiled over and war was finally declared.

As usual, the vendors made their exchanges with her as quick as possible, hardly showing any gratitude for what she'd brought them or what she'd just protected them from.

As she walked away, she reminded herself that they *did* thank her in their own way. She and her mother always got more than what they bargained for at the market. When something broke at their house, the carpenter would repair it for free. A random basket of eggs, vegetables or cheese had shown up at their door more times than she could count. Those usually appeared right after she went into the woods and came back smelling like death.

But there was another consequence, one that was both a blessing and a curse: everyone left her alone.

Of course, she wasn't a total pariah, and her mother was well-liked by the entire village. When Kindra was younger, she'd had tons of friends who'd all marveled at her budding magic. But then she'd turned thirteen and started setting people on fire, and well, it was understandable that the other kids quit asking her to come play with them in the woods. Even though without her, Harthwin would have been robbed and pillaged down to nothing. Even though she had never hurt a soul who hadn't tried to hurt her or anybody in her village first.

Again, that bitter anger rose, and again, she choked it back down. She'd rather be this, uncaged and wild, even if her childhood best friend no longer lingered to talk when they ran into each other. She'd rather be this, frightening and avoided, than be forced to live a life where her magic wasn't able to *breathe*.

Her final stop was the metalsmith, an elderly man named Elric. He was an Earthwarden and used his small bit of earth magic to help craft fine blades and strong armor. He was also one of the only people in town who wasn't too frightened of her to strike up a conversation. He greeted her brightly when she walked in, and when she handed him the pair of daggers she'd brought back, he smiled and thanked her.

Kindra always looked forward to her visits with him. That's why she always saved them for last; it softened the blow of the fear and wariness everyone else felt towards her.

"Would you like these, too?" She held out the assortment of silverware. "You could melt them down, use the silver for something else."

He reached out and took the silverware from her hands. "Yes, I definitely could. Are you sure your mother won't want these? They're quite beautiful, if a little worn."

"No, she has a set already from a couple years ago," she replied hesitantly, preparing herself for the inevitable stiffening of the shoulders and loss of eye contact. That was what usually happened when she alluded to one of her... excursions.

But Elric simply nodded, moving to set the silverware on his workbench. "Then I shall use them to create something new," he said with a gentle smile. "Now, I've got something here for you in exchange." He began to move about his shop, his aged and wrinkled hands roving over various weapons and pieces of armor, searching.

"No need," Kindra said quickly, "I don't need anything."

"Nonsense. You deserve something for these lovely gifts." He paused, turning back towards her, and said without any fear or disdain, "You deserve something for all that you do for us."

For a moment, she was stunned into silence. Even he had never actually acknowledged what she did. She'd never expected him to. She'd been content with his kindness. That had always been enough.

He held her gaze for a few seconds longer, his eyes sad. Kindra waited to see if he'd say anything more, but then he returned to his search. When he faced her again, it was to hand her a dagger. As she looked down at it, her breath caught.

It was beautiful, as all his creations were. The blade was as sharp as ever, but it was the hilt that captured her attention. Crafted with a level of detail only Earthwardens could achieve, the bronze was engraved with sweeping, elegant flames. They circled the entire grip, snaking up to the pommel.

He had made it specifically for her. Something about that made her want to cry.

Kindra took the dagger, running her thumb over the flames. He handed her a sheath, and she attached it to her belt before slipping the dagger inside. "Thank you," she said after a moment. "I... thank you."

"It is the least I can do, Kindra," Elric replied. "Tell your mother I said hello."

She nodded and made her way out of the shop, both relieved he'd said nothing else and wishing he had at the same time.

Kindra meandered along the worn dirt road that led back to the cottage she shared with her mother. Beside her, the small river that ran alongside Harthwin babbled quietly. The crisp chill from that morning had faded into a comfortable, gentle warmth, and she stopped to remove her cloak. The sun always soothed her; she was less inclined to succumb to her bitterness when she could feel its calming rays.

She rounded a corner and her home appeared, tucked away amongst a grove of trees. It wasn't more than a few minutes away from their neighbors, but the towering oaks made it feel more secluded. Kindra appreciated that. It was nice to come home and be away from the wary eyes of the townsfolk.

The front door opened, and Sera Bedelyn appeared, wearing a stained apron. "Home already?" she asked as her daughter made her way up the cracked stone path to greet her. Sera surveyed her with sharp intensity. "Safe? Unharmed?"

"Didn't really put up a fight," Kindra offered by way of explanation. Her mother stepped aside to let her in, and she moved through the small, cozy room to set her basket on the table. "They fled."

She didn't miss the flash of relief in Sera's brown eyes as she shut the door behind her. "But they were bandits?" Her mother pressed, following her to the table.

"Yes," Kindra replied bluntly, punching down the swell of irritation. Her mother still hoped that every time Kindra ventured out to dispose of threats, she would discover there was no threat at all, that she'd come back with a new family or gaggle of friends in tow.

Kindra had given up on such foolish hopes long ago.

"Are you sure? Did you wait until you really knew?"

"They had bags filled with stolen shit, Mama," Kindra snapped, not bothering to hide her annoyance. "A blood-stained corset, for gods' sake. Besides, they were talking about Harthwin. We were their next target. I wasn't going to wait until they assaulted somebody on the way into town before doing something."

The silence between them was thick with tension. Kindra hated it. "I took some of the stuff that wasn't gross or too broken from their camp before I burned it. Traded it in town," she said after a heartbeat, not meeting her mother's gaze. She gestured to the basket.

After a pause, her mother nodded, reaching out to touch the blankets. "Wool?" Her voice was ripe with surprise.

Kindra mustered up a smile, relieved that they were changing the subject. "I know. Pretty lucky, right? Not often you see anything other than itchy pelts."

Sera gathered the blankets in her arms, pressing the soft fabric to her face. It was almost childish, but it made Kindra's heart warm. "How did Fenryl even get these? It's so hard to find this far away from the plains."

"Who knows, but we'll be warmer this winter because of his luck."

With a genuine smile, her mother went to place the blankets by the hearth, muttering a prayer of thanks to Dovon as she did. Kindra always found it odd that she chose to commune with the Earth deities, despite being part of a Firefury family. Perhaps it was due to her father being dead, or her mother not being a Wielder herself. It probably didn't help that Kindra had never shown much outward interest in the Fire deities—what was the point, after all, in a village with no fire temple?

Deep down, though, Kindra wondered if the reason Sera went to the earth temple every week to offer prayer was because that was what the rest of Harthwin did, and she wanted to feel like she belonged. It was an Earthwarden village, after all; apart from Kindra and the local Healer, the remaining Wielders were all blessed with earth magic. The Healer was revered, of course, because all Healers were, and Harthwin was blessed to have one. Kindra was...well. Kindra was Kindra.

"Could you give the fire a bit of a boost?" Her mother asked, snapping her out of her thoughts. Kindra had the flames roaring once more with the wave of a hand. Sera patted her shoulder in thanks as she carried the basket of food to the small kitchen in the back of the cottage. Kindra settled into the worn rocking chair by the fire, finally relaxing for the first time that day.

She leaned her head back, listening to the sound of her mother putting food away. She removed the sheath from her belt and pulled out the dagger Elric had given her, studying it. Without thinking, she drew a thread of flame from the fire and wrapped it around the blade, admiring how the metal gleamed. *You deserve something for all that you do for us.* Elric's words echoed in her head, and she smiled softly.

There was a knock on the door, and Kindra cast the flame back into the hearth as she moved to answer it, setting the dagger down on the table as she did so. A young courier stood before her when she opened the door. "Hello?"

"Is this the Bedelyn household?" the courier asked. In his hands was an envelope.

"Yes, what is it?"

"This is for you. From His and Her Majesty of Alverin, King and Queen Annalindis."

Kindra's mouth went dry. She stopped registering what he said after the words 'royal family.' *No,* she thought. *No, no, no.*

"Miss? The letter? Will you take it?"

Kindra snapped back into reality. The courier was holding out the envelope for her to take. Stiffly, she took it from his hands. "Thank you," she whispered, panic almost rendering her mute. She closed the door in the courier's face without waiting for a reply.

"Kindra?" Her mother came in from the kitchen. "Who was it?" Her eyes fell to the envelope, and she spotted the Royal Seal, pressed into wax. She froze. "It can't be."

Kindra could hardly breathe. "This can't be happening," she croaked. Her hands were shaking so badly she could hardly maintain her grip on the envelope. Her mother hurried to her side, gently prying the envelope from her hands. Without ceremony, she ripped it open and pulled out the letter within. Gnawing on her bottom lip, she read it. Kindra didn't need to. She knew what it said.

"They are coming in two weeks," Sera said, and Kindra sank to the ground. "Prince Jasper is coming. He has… they have heard of your talents, and he wishes to make you his bride. They believe you are a strong candidate to…" She trailed off, kneeling to join her daughter on the cottage floor. "It is… this is an honor, Kindra," she tried, but the tremble in her voice gave her away.

"I don't consider being the royal family's brood mare an honor," Kindra spat.

"It is the highest honor in Alverin to be chosen," Sera tried again. "They believe you could be able to break the curse—"

"I do not *care* about the curse!" Kindra screamed, her emotions—fear, shock, and anger, always anger—surging up inside, causing her to spark and ignite from her fingertips. "I do not care about the fucking curse," she repeated, ripping the letter from her mother's hands and standing up. "They can't do this to me. They can't take me away—I will not go. I cannot."

"Kindra, the decision has been made. They are coming. They will—if you were to refuse—the Annalindis family is capable of terrible things—"

"Of course they are," she spat, "That's why they got cursed in the first place. Because they are cruel and terrible and committed atrocities we can't even begin to understand—they brought this on themselves and now I am to be the one who pays for it? Who loses everything? No." She shook her head back and forth rapidly, her wild dark curls falling in her face, pacing about the room. "No. I can't—I would rather die, than this," she declared, her breath coming in shattered gasps. "I would rather die."

Her freedom, her *everything*—it was being ripped away from her. She couldn't breathe, couldn't think—

"Please, Kindra. Please try and see this in a positive light. I know it seems terrible. I do. But you have to understand," her mother pleaded, her eyes flashing with terror, "they will not take no for an answer."

Kindra stopped listening. Her ears rang; her vision blurred. Her skin was burning. She lunged for the front door, staggering outside and around the back of the house. She stumbled into the clearing where she'd first learned to use her magic; the grass had long since burned away, leaving a wide circle of dirt.

She was vaguely aware of her mother calling after her. Her knees gave out again and she collapsed, her fire erupting from her in a fierce, grief-stricken wave just as a scream tore out of her throat. It burned through the letter clenched in her fist, burned through her clothing, until she was nothing but a naked, raging girl engulfed in a ball of flames. She stayed like that, hunched over and burning, until her magic petered out. And then her mother was there, wrapping her in a cloak, guiding her back inside.

"It'll be okay," she whispered, settling Kindra into her bed, "It'll be all right."

But Kindra could hardly register the words, could hardly decipher them except to know that they were the biggest lie she'd ever been told. She could not even muster up the energy to cry. She was burned up; hollowed out. As exhaustion kicked in and she began to drift unconscious in her mother's arms, she thought of Elric and his dagger, his kind words and sad eyes.

Her last thought before falling asleep was that all she'd done for her home—for herself—had been for nothing.

CHAPTER 2

Kindra hated Prince Jasper the moment he stepped into the room.

It had been two weeks since the letter came. Two weeks of walking into the woods, finding a clearing and setting herself aflame to give the anger somewhere to go. Two weeks of her mother trying to get her to find even a sliver of a silver lining. Two weeks of harboring a fury so strong it threatened to burn her up from inside.

Since before Kindra had been born—before her mother had been born, even—the Annalindis family had been arranging marriages with Wielders of noticeable strength regardless of their social class. This was all in an effort to break the century-long curse that had been placed on them, stealing the magic from their once-powerful bloodline. When they'd run out of noble families to marry themselves to, they expanded their options, giving commoners a fantasy life they could dream about one day attaining. Very few ever did. Though not of noble blood, most of the Alverinians chosen for royal marriage still came from wealthier families. The poor were, as usual, not given much thought.

When she'd been a child and still had friends, the other girls used to ramble on and on about getting chosen to marry one of the princes. They'd whisper and giggle about the prospect of being taken from Harthwin, transported to the massive city of Wendrith and living their lives in the castle, surrounded by grandeur and more wealth than they could ever possibly need. They'd gather around the few depictions they had of the grand capital, the ornate castle and its sprawling grounds, and imagine all the ways they'd spend their time as princesses.

Kindra had never entertained that fantasy much. Her father had died fighting for the Annalindis family; as far as she was concerned, they'd essentially killed him themselves. Why would she want to marry one of them?

Over time, her disinterest morphed from misplaced anger about her father's death, into a fierce love for her freedom. She was poor—in Harthwin, they all were—but she was free to do what she wished with her life and her time. Her choice to marry, to have children, to use her magic—all of that was for her to decide. She cherished that freedom deeply.

The horrifying irony was not lost on her, that out of all the people in her village, she had been the one chosen.

There was nobody in Harthwin who could have wanted this less than Kindra.

So when Prince Jasper walked into their humble cottage, all the rage that had been brewing for the last fortnight finally found its target and sharpened into a scorching knife of hatred. So Kindra did not bow. She did not curtsy. She did not smile. She held her head high, as though *she* were royalty and the prince was common. He seemed to find this amusing rather than infuriating and met her fiery golden gaze with a gentle steel gray one, lips turning up slightly in a smile, his cheeks dimpling. Kindra felt sparks fighting to ignite at her fingertips in frustration and curled them into fists to suppress them.

"Are you Miss Kindra Bedelyn?" The guard by Prince Jasper's side asked, reading off a sheet of paper. The guard's eyes were a brilliant blue, a sharp contrast to his dark brown skin. If that hadn't given him away, the canister of water belted to him would have. A Wavebreaker.

I wish I wasn't, she thought to herself as her mother finally raised herself out of her bow to nod.

"Yes, this is my daughter Kindra, Your Highness," Sera said, forcing a smile. Kindra fought back a wave of nausea.

"And she has been blessed by the gods with the gift of magic?" The guard asked her mother, picking up rather quickly on the fact that Kindra was not happy to see them. Beside him, Prince Jasper's smirk only deepened.

"Yes, she is a Firefury. She is very talented—" Her mother started, but was interrupted by the guard.

"Age?" he asked.

"She is twenty-two, sir."

The guard ran his watery gaze over her. "Any conditions we should know of?"

Smoke began to filter from Kindra's closed fists.

"She's of peak health, I can assure you, sir," her mother stammered, surprised by the question. "She's very honored to have been given this opportunity." Another wave of nausea at the massive, horrible lie.

Kindra hated to see her mother pander like this, hated watching her suck up to a sniveling guard, hated hearing her offer such empty assurances. But she could feel the fear radiating from her mother and resisted the urge to reach out and squeeze her hand.

The guard peppered Sera with more questions: her education, her family, her wielding training. Kindra was so busy trying not to set the cottage on fire that she didn't process a single word. It was demeaning; being evaluated as if she were nothing more than an animal at auction, making sure she was going to be worth purchasing.

The prince also was hardly paying attention to the conversation between her mother and his guard. Instead, he was staring intently at her, his gray eyes alight with curiosity. He had yet to speak.

When their eyes met again, he cocked his head slightly and raised an eyebrow, as if he were challenging her, as if this whole humiliating conversation was a test. The thought twisted into her like a dagger, and she felt the flames swelling inside her, growing stronger and stronger, until—

"I think those are enough questions, Heinrich," Prince Jasper said, his voice smoother than Kindra had expected. The surprise ruptured her rising fury enough to quell the fire that had been building. "And please, Mrs. Bedelyn, there's no need to lie. It's glaringly obvious that Miss Kindra is horribly displeased by our presence."

"Your Highness," Sera began to form an apology, but Prince Jasper raised his hand to silence her.

"Don't apologize, please." He gave another easy smile. "It's understandable. We are about to ask quite a lot of you both, as I'm sure you know." He strode over to the table and sat down in one of the chairs. He crossed his legs at the knee and leaned back, assuming an alarmingly casual posture for a prince. "Shall we discuss?"

Her mother hurried over to join him, but Kindra did not move from where she stood by the front door. She wanted to run out of the cottage that moment, and escape from the torture that awaited her.

"Miss Kindra, please." Prince Jasper's voice cut through her thoughts. He gestured to an empty chair. "Would you join us? Please?"

Despite her best efforts to bite her tongue, Kindra huffed out a sharp laugh, finally speaking. "You use 'please' a lot for someone who's never had to ask for anything before. I'm amazed they even wasted time teaching you manners."

There was a moment of silence, in which Sera dawned a horrified expression, Heinrich frowned, and then Prince Jasper… laughed.

"The spirit matches the element, I see," he chuckled, cheek dimpling again. "Would you rather I have Heinrich here encase you in water? Hold the threat of drowning you where you stand over your head? Is that the kind of behavior you expected?" His eyes flashed with warning; he would do it if he had to.

"So that's why you have a Wavebreaker with you." Of course. Of course, they came prepared in case she was dangerous. She frowned at Heinrich. "Aren't Wavebreakers pacifists?"

"Heinrich is one of my most capable guards. Their supposed pacifism is an age-old stereotype that holds little truth these days. But they *are* rather effective at dealing with those who have more… fiery temperaments." He beamed, proud of his joke. Kindra curled her lip in a snarl.

"Shitty puns won't make me like you," she sneered, but she sat down at the table. Heinrich and her mother each gave a relieved sigh.

Prince Jasper hummed softly, glancing down at his hands, then looked up to meet her gaze again. This time, she detected a hint of steel in his eyes. A hardening of some sort, as though he were closing part of himself off. "Unfortunately, whether or not you like me has little bearing here, doesn't it?" His voice was soft, but the words slammed into her anyway.

"No," she muttered, her hands sparking again, "I suppose it doesn't." Beside her, her mother shifted anxiously in her seat.

"Right. Heinrich, if you would be so kind?"

"Yes, Your Highness." Heinrich returned to the paper he'd pulled out when he'd arrived, cleared his throat, and began to read. "Miss Kindra Bedelyn, it has come to the attention of Their Majesties, King and Queen

Annalindis of the Great Kingdom of Alverin, that you have been blessed by the gods with the ability to wield magic. As such, you have been summoned to the capital city of Wendrith. Soon after your arrival you will be wed to His Highness, Prince Jasper Annalindis, with the intention of bearing children with magical blood to restore the Annalindis bloodline to its former greatness and power."

Heinrich glanced up at her, trying to gauge her reaction, then continued, "As a magical citizen of Alverin, it is imperative that you use the powers bestowed upon you for the greater good and do your part in fighting for Alverin's survival. Your family will be compensated greatly and will be allowed to relocate to the capital if they so choose. You will reside in the castle with Prince Jasper. You will be expected to produce a child once every four years, at minimum, until you reach the age of thirty-five, unless the Head Healer deems you unable."

Another pause, then, "While the importance of your duty during these times cannot be overstated, let it be known that you are not above the law. To attempt to flee is treason—punishable by death. To attempt to terminate a pregnancy, or to succeed in terminating a pregnancy is treason—punishable by death. To plot against any member of the royal family, whether to assassinate, overthrow, or otherwise harm, is treason—punishable by death. To be romantically involved with any person other than Prince Jasper is treason—punishable by death. You will be allowed to participate in court, assist in planning festivals and balls, and have some involvement in the issues Alverin faces, but your main priority is and must always be to produce a magical heir and restore magic to the Annalindis bloodline. Do you understand?"

Kindra did not respond. Instead, she glared at the table, clenching her smoking fists so tightly her nails were cutting into her palms. Her breath came in shaky erratic bursts.

"Miss Kindra," Heinrich repeated, blue eyes widening with worry, "do you understand?"

Slowly, Kindra nodded. Her whole body burned. She felt like she was seconds away from setting the table on fire.

"Good. And you accept?"

The question threw her, and her head snapped up. "Oh, do I have a choice?"

"Well," Heinrich glanced at Prince Jasper nervously. "Um, the question is just a formality, really—"

"What if I said no? What if I refused you?" She stood, flames beginning to lick at her fingertips. Heinrich stood as well, visibly alarmed, his hand twisting off the lid of his canister.

"Kindra!" Her mother cried, grabbing at her arm, trying to pull her back into her seat.

Kindra shook her off, tears pricking in the corners of her eyes. She looked down at her hands, which were engulfed in flames now, then up at Prince Jasper, who hadn't moved from his relaxed position. A sneer formed on her lips. "What would happen, really? I suppose you'd just kill me, right? After all, wouldn't that be *treason*; refusing an order of the Crown?" Her voice grew sharp. "How many women have said no? How many women have you pieces of shit murdered—"

"Your Highness, perhaps she is not the one." Heinrich tugged at the prince's shoulder with one hand and pulled water from his canister with the other. The fear on his face brought a ping of satisfaction to Kindra, but she ignored it, the flames snaking their way up her arms, starting to nip at the sleeves of her tunic.

"You will have to kill me," she snarled, "*I am not going.*"

A sob fell from her mother's mouth, and she ignored that, too. But still, Prince Jasper made no move, not to attack her nor to flee. Finally, he spoke, and despite the scene in front of him, there was still a soft, calm expression on his face. Only his eyes, hard and cold, betrayed the tension he felt.

"Kindra, you do not scare me. And, despite your best efforts, we will not kill you."

She struggled not to falter. "What?"

"No, we won't kill you." He cocked his head to the side again just as he had earlier—another test was coming. "We will not kill you, but refusing an order of the Crown is treason, and punishable by death. In this situation, though, the question is, whose death will it be? Whose death will be worth something?" His gray eyes glinted, sharp like steel, and for the first time she saw the face of the prince she'd expected him to be. "Your mother's, perhaps?"

The flames sputtered out. "What?" Kindra said again, this time in a shocked whisper. Her mother whimpered.

"Yes, I suppose it would be your dear mother, who has been so lovely and kind, who would have to pay the price for your crime. You would be free to go, of course, as you wanted, but would it be worth it?"

Kindra collapsed back into her chair. "You—how dare you." The words held no weight.

"It would be a lovely life, Kindra, for you and your mother. No more harsh, starving winters. No more poverty. You would live in luxury and comfort—both of you. Is the thought of marrying me really so terrible that you would turn that down?"

What you offer me is a life in a cage, she wanted to scream at him. But he could not possibly understand.

She glared at him, studying his face. He was handsome, as she supposed all princes were, with blonde wavy hair and a sun-kissed complexion. And of course, there were the eyes, which were staring back, sharp and focused. A few minutes prior, she might have admitted that, no, it wouldn't be so terrible, but he had just threatened the life of her mother. "You are as horrible as I imagined you'd be," she hissed, "Threatening an innocent woman's life just to get what you want."

Prince Jasper set his jaw, but Kindra could have sworn he flinched; nothing more than a minuscule movement. "Well, I tried to be nice about it, but you didn't exactly make it easy." He stood, stretching his arms over his head. "At ease, Heinrich, she won't hurt us now." He patted the man's shoulder, who reluctantly let the water circling his fist drift back into its container. "We depart in three hours—want to get a head start on the journey before nightfall. That should be enough time to pack. You won't need much—you'll be fitted for new clothes once we get to your new home. Just bring anything of importance to you and whatever you might need for the journey. A month after your arrival, a carriage will return to bring your mother to the capital. A few weeks after her arrival, we will be wed."

He smiled broadly, but unlike earlier, this one lacked the same shine and charm. It seemed pained, almost. "It will be a wonderful occasion, I'm sure."

The prince headed towards the door, Heinrich following. Sera hurried to formally show them out, her face still streaked with tears. The door had just about closed behind them when Prince Jasper's hand caught it, and he stuck his head back in.

"Oh, and Kindra? Don't bother trying to run. I meant what I said. It's in you and your mother's best interest that you cooperate. I'm done saying please."

Then he vanished and the door slammed shut behind him.

CHAPTER 3

An hour later, Kindra sat on her bed, staring at Elric's dagger once more. Her mother stood next to an open trunk, rifling through the books and scrolls on her desk, holding each one up to ask if Kindra wanted to take it with her. Kindra absentmindedly shook her head for either yes or no at each one, barely taking the time to read the titles. Finally, Sera stopped and came over to her.

"You are angry, I know," she stated, "but one day, you will... you will see that this is not so terrible."

Kindra didn't look up. "We don't starve," she said softly. "We aren't that poor. Can you not see the horrible life I am being forced to go live? Do you not care that it's going to kill me from the inside out?" She glanced up at her mother then, eyes wide and pleading.

Her mother frowned. "Kindra, the prince... he will be kind to you—"

"He threatened to kill you, Mother."

"But he knew he wouldn't have to. I could see it on his face, the way he looked at you... you sparked something in him. Curiosity, at least, but maybe there is a chance for you to be truly happy—"

"There is not," Kindra spat, her voice shaking, offended that her mother would even suggest such a thing. "I could not love him. I *will* not. He is the very future I have spent my life fearing. I just want to be *free*. I want to be here, with you. With the people I know and love, the people I have known my whole life, have spent the last decade protecting. And you, you will be leaving them too, you realize that?"

"I know." Sera's voice was shaking, too, and she turned away and moved to the small bookshelf in the corner of the room. She picked up a wooden firebird from the shelf. Kindra's father had carved it when she was still a baby and was the one piece of him she had left, besides her magic. "But it… I believe, no, I *know*, that," Sera's voice grew stronger, "this will keep you safe, in the long run. You couldn't have protected us forever, Kindra. At some point, you would've found yourself in a situation where even your magic could not save you."

She handed the firebird to Kindra and cupped her daughter's face. "You gave up your childhood and burned it to ash for this village. And I know you may never admit it out loud, but it hurts you to have been so cruelly rejected for doing so. I know it does. Perhaps… perhaps it is time to move on to a place where your magic will be appreciated—revered, even, rather than feared." Sera looked as though she couldn't believe she was even saying those words.

Kindra couldn't believe it either, recoiling as if she'd been hit. "What would he think of that?" She thrust the wooden firebird into her mother's hand. "What would he say about this?"

"Please don't bring him into this, Kindra," her mother pleaded. "Your father would understand. He would have been so proud of you for what you've done here, for what you've learned to do all on your own. But he would have wanted you to be safe. He wouldn't have wanted you to die. He knew better than anyone that an order from the Crown must be followed."

"Followed to his death, right?" Kindra snapped. Sera flinched, and Kindra instantly regretted what she'd said. "I'm sorry," she murmured.

"It will keep you safe," she repeated, and moved to set the wooden firebird in her trunk.

"But what about happy?" Kindra felt tears threatening. "What about being happy?"

"My dear." Her mother reached out and grabbed her hands, holding them tight. "Sometimes happy and safe simply cannot coincide."

Kindra let her mother's arms encircle her as the tears finally fell.

Prince Jasper knocked just as the sun was beginning to set. As Heinrich and another guard helped load Kindra's single trunk into the carriage, he leaned casually against the door frame, watching as Kindra said her goodbyes to her mother. Around them, nearly a dozen other guards waited on their horses.

Having been emptied of tears earlier, Kindra didn't cry as she hugged her mother. She tried to ignore the dread pooling in her stomach as she walked out of her home towards the carriage, Prince Jasper at her side. As he opened the carriage door for her, she looked over her shoulder at her mother one last time.

"I'll see you in just a couple months," Sera said, teary-eyed despite the reassurance she was offering. At first, Kindra had thought it strange that she couldn't bring her mother with her. It felt so isolating. But the more she thought about it, she realized that isolation was likely the point. She would be entering this new life with no real allies at her side.

Kindra offered a tight-lipped smile, waved her hand in farewell, and stepped into the carriage. Prince Jasper climbed in after her, and seconds later, they lurched into motion.

As they traveled through the streets of Harthwin, they sat in tense silence. Kindra stared out the window as they passed the market stalls, the small earth temple and graveyard, the ivy-dressed statue of Morta, goddess of death, sitting among the tilted tombstones.

My whole life, she thought, *I'm leaving my whole life behind.* Some of the villagers had gathered along the road to see them off. None of them cheered or waved her farewell; they watched the traveling party with a guarded wariness—if not a little bit of dread.

They passed by Elric's shop, and tears welled up once more as she noticed he was standing in his doorway. Their eyes met, and she thought of his dagger, tucked away into her luggage, the one piece of gratitude anyone here ever gave her. His mouth curled up in that same sad smile, and she offered one back, lifting her hand in goodbye.

Thank you, he mouthed, and Kindra's lip wobbled. She nodded and looked away, blinking away tears. When she looked back out the window, his shop was out of sight, the carriage moving past the tiny guardhouse that marked the entrance into town.

"Are you all right?" Prince Jasper's voice cut through the quiet, coloring her melancholy with annoyance.

"I was until you opened your mouth, Your Highness," she bit out. *I hate you.*

The prince gave her a tight-lipped smile. "You can call me Jasper."

Kindra did not give a response as she watched Harthwin—and her freedom—disappear as the carriage crested a hill.

CHAPTER 4

By the third day of nearly non-stop traveling, cooped up in the carriage without the ability to do much more than light a small flame in her palm, Kindra felt like she would explode any moment. She'd rarely experienced the type of restlessness that could ensue when a Wielder went too long without using their magic. Her life in Harthwin had gifted her with ample free time to explore and develop her abilities. But now she felt like a too-full water-skin, her magic ready to burst at the seams.

In all honesty, the itch to engulf herself in flames had set in the very first night, but she'd hated the thought of having to ask Jasper. Their stops during the day to relieve themselves had been brief, and the guards were so wary of her when they stopped to sleep for the night she was afraid if she wielded without permission they'd try and kill her on the spot. And even with the guards, there was that stubborn pride. She refused to act as though she needed something from them.

But a day and a half later, she would've done just about anything to have just a single moment to expend her energy.

"Jasper," she said, eyes closed, her head resting against the carriage window.

He hummed in response.

"I need—we need—to stop the carriage."

"Why?"

"Because I have to—*need* to—light myself on fire."

"Wha—" Jasper started, and Kindra's eyes snapped open, her head turning to him. The gold of her eyes glimmered with an intense hunger; her mouth set in a thin line. Jasper shut his mouth and nodded, understanding immediately. "Right. Right. Wielders have to—gods, why didn't you say something earlier? We would've stopped." He pulled the rope, signaling the carriage to come to a halt.

Heinrich dismounted and hurried over to open the carriage door, a question poised on his lips, but Kindra was already climbing out, tearing her cloak off and tossing it back onto the seat.

"Lady Kindra, what are you—"

"Move," she snapped, bringing the heat that had been pooling inside her for the past two days to just under her skin. "Don't come near me unless you want to get burned." She broke into a run, sprinting until she was a safe enough distance from the traveling party, and then she held out her arms and let herself breathe.

Fire exploded from her palms and snaked quickly up her arms, stopping just past her elbows to avoid burning her sleeves. Kindra's head rolled back and her eyes closed, a sigh of relief escaping her lips.

"How extraordinary," Jasper's voice came from behind her. He must've approached once the initial burst of fire was over.

Kindra didn't indicate that she'd heard him; she simply reveled in the familiar warmth of her fire on her skin. It danced and wound around her like a flaming serpent, nibbling up the grass surrounding her. After a few minutes, she felt far more relaxed. Releasing a final deep breath, she reduced the flames to just her hands and turned around to face Jasper.

The look on his face was nothing short of complete wonder. It was almost child-like, so much so that it caught Kindra completely off guard and the flames in her hands flickered unsteadily. "What?"

"I've always found Firefuries to be some of the most entrancing Wielders," he admitted, the awe quickly turning into sheepishness. He paused. "You have an incredible gift."

"I didn't even do anything," she mumbled, the compliment unsettling her further.

"I would love to see what you could do in a battle," the prince mused, still studying her with that wide-eyed gaze.

Kindra blanched, the thought of her father flashing through her mind. Dead like so many others, forced to defend a royal family that deserved to be punished for its centuries of crimes. "I am no fighter," she said quickly.

Unfortunately, Jasper caught the lie in an instant. "That's not what we were told." His voice was soft, almost hesitant, gray eyes reflecting the fire Kindra still held.

Kindra shook her head, turning away from him once more. "I didn't have a choice," she conceded after a moment. A decade's worth of fights accented with death flashed through her head. Perhaps that was one respite a charmed life in Wendrith could give her, although guilt tugged at her for thinking it. Who would be left to defend her village now that she was gone? Horror pooled in her stomach at the thought. The useless guards, who were more content to drink and play cards than actually defend Harthwin? What could they do, now that they'd spent a decade letting her do their job for them?

The fear channeled itself into rage quickly. Yet another reason to despise Jasper and the royal family and their twisted marriage system. The havoc a group of criminals could wreak upon Harthwin now that she was gone—or, gods forbid, if war finally broke out in full and soldiers from Pryllia showed up, hungry to seek revenge for centuries of brutality and death...

How did word of her even reach Wendrith? She knew she'd had a reputation, those bandits from a few weeks ago confirmed that, but had stories about her really traveled so far?

"We heard that you defended Harthwin single-handedly," Jasper was saying, "that one time you even fended off a group of ten bandits—"

"And now they will be left defenseless," Kindra hissed, not bothering to turn and look at him. She feared she might light him aflame if she had to see his face. "You took me, and now they will be left with nothing but drunkards and fools to protect them." Her fire began to lick its way up her arms again, and she focused on it, shaping it into a sphere that she balanced between her hands.

For once—for *once*—Jasper had nothing to say. So she pressed on, still not looking at him, still channeling her fury into her ball of fire. "I have killed twenty-four people," she breathed, and she didn't have to look back to know that Jasper had just become substantially more afraid of her. She could practically feel the alarm rippling off of him. "Twenty-four people—for them. For Harthwin. For my—my mother. I am twenty-two years old." She laughed bitterly. "And I have killed more people than there are years I have been alive." Her stomach turned as the faces of each one flashed through her mind.

"The first time, it was a trio of robbers who had taken to attacking people on the road into the village. People had been asking the guards to do something, but they said it wasn't within the village limits, that it *wasn't their problem*." The fireball churned, flames stroking her fingertips. "So I went out to deal with it. They weren't even Wielders. I knew I could scare them off. Even then, I knew what my fire could do." She paused. Behind her, she didn't think Jasper was even breathing. "They saw me, and thought I was easy prey. I wasn't."

As the memory surged, the fireball began to press at the seams of her control, dripping flames onto the ground. She worked to steady her breathing, forcing it smaller and smaller, until it dissipated entirely. Balancing a single flame on her index finger, she confessed, "I didn't—I didn't intend to kill anybody. But I hadn't ever fought anyone. I'd just practiced on—on trees. The control I thought I had over my magic…it vanished when I was faced with three frightening men. When I was actually fighting against an opponent who wanted to kill me, or worse—" Her voice died for a moment as she remembered their sneering faces, remembered everything about the horrible encounter she wished so desperately to forget. She wasn't even sure why she was telling Jasper this at all, but some part of her needed him, desperately, to understand.

She continued, "I exploded. Literally. I erupted into a ball of flame. And by the time I had it back under control, they were all horribly burned, and one of them—one of them was just… ash. I had burned him alive." Finally, she turned to face the prince. His face was pale, and his mouth slightly agape. "The other two fled. I don't know if they lived or died. I was thirteen," she finished, and Jasper swore softly.

"I am—I am sorry," he finally whispered, "I didn't know… I didn't know you were—"

"What? A murderer?" she sneered, flames dying out at last. "Does that make you want to take me back? Don't want a killer as your wife?" She waved a hand at the road. "Then by all means, please, take me home."

"I didn't know you'd had to be so brave," Jasper said quickly, and Kindra scoffed, but he continued, "You are incredibly brave. I haven't even… I've never killed anyone before," he admitted. "I've trained my

whole life, of course, even served time at outposts, but I've never had to…"
He trailed off, shaking his head.

"It is terrible," Kindra admitted, her voice lacking the ire it had held for
him since they first met, "to kill somebody. Even if you are doing it to
defend your home. Your family. I remember—I remember each of their
faces, and the sounds they made as they died. I remember the-the smell of
burnt flesh—" She sucked in a breath, steeling herself once more. "But I
would have done it again and again to keep Harthwin safe. I would relive
every death a thousand times, justify each one to Morta herself, if it meant
my mother could sleep peacefully at night." Her lip curled, and the hatred
seeped back into her words. "And now I shall forever be haunted by the
people I have killed, knowing it has probably all been for nothing, since
you have forced me into this trap you call a marriage so I can produce
children that will be, like every other heir your family produces, *completely
magic-less.*"

Jasper's eyes flashed, indignance creeping back into his voice. "We
don't know that. You're one of the most powerful Wielders we've
discovered in a long time—the first Firefury to marry into our family in
decades. You're certainly stronger than either of my brothers' wives—"

"It will not work," she snapped. "It will fail, just as it has for the past
century. But you refuse to accept that, and my village will suffer for it."

"What if I could send some more guards there?" Jasper asked hopefully.
It made Kindra want to gag. "I could hand pick them myself. A wedding
gift, from the royal family to your village for giving us—"

"I was not an object to be given away!" Kindra shouted, and the guards
that had been standing nearby drew their swords or fell into wielding
stances. Even Jasper flinched back, body stiffening defensively. She did not
back down, but she did her best to keep her fire at bay. "I am not *property.*
I am my own person. I should have been able to choose!" Tears she
thought she'd finished crying blurred her vision. "I should have— I should
have been able to choose. You *took* me from them. You took me from my
home. This isn't fair, it's not fair…." Her voice died as nausea rolled over
her, the weight of everything her life was becoming pressing down, sucking
the breath from her—

Firm hands gripped her shoulders. "Calm down, Kindra." Jasper's voice was gentle, though she could hardly hear it over the sound of her hyperventilating. "You need to breathe, okay? Here, I'll do it with you."

She was vaguely aware of guards closing in, begging the prince to step away lest she explode into flames and cook him where he stood, but Jasper stayed where he was. "Look at me," he said, and when she didn't, he lightly grabbed her by the chin, forcing her to. "Look at me," he repeated, his voice sharpening. Their eyes met, gold clashing against silver. "Good. Now breathe in." He inhaled deeply through his nose, and Kindra, desperate to get a grip on herself so she wouldn't set him on fire and get herself killed, did, too. "And out." He exhaled slowly through his mouth, and she matched him. "Again," he ordered, voice still soft.

For several moments, they stood there, never breaking eye contact, simply breathing in, and out. Slowly, the inferno raging under Kindra's skin cooled, and her breathing steadied, her senses returning to her once more. When she felt like she was under control again, she jerked away from him immediately, shame burning her cheeks.

Jasper watched her warily. "I know that this isn't fair, Kindra," he said, "but I have little choice in the matter. This is… this is not the life I would have chosen for you, either, if I had been able to do anything about it." He looked back over his shoulder, at the guards still warily hovering nearby, and then back at her. "I think we should get moving again. We still have a lot of ground to cover before nightfall. But we'll make time on our stops now for you to expend some of your magic. You have my word." He dipped his head to her once, and then strode away.

Kindra hurried back to the carriage, climbing inside and moving as far away from where Jasper would sit as she could. When he entered, she pretended to be falling asleep. She did not thank him for helping her calm down, because it was his fault she'd had the panic attack in the first place. And she did not apologize for his hands, which were now wrapped in bandages, having been burned and blistered as he'd held her. She simply closed her eyes and focused on her breathing.

In and out.

CHAPTER 5

The next week of traveling dragged on. Their party passed through Bridgewood and entered the Oakwryn Forest, keeping to the well-traveled roads. They never stopped in any of the small towns or villages they passed by, only sending in a couple of guards if they needed to purchase any supplies. Kindra would have loved to have an actual bed in an inn to sleep on instead of her bedroll, but Jasper had explained to her it would only add more time to their journey, and they wanted to return to Wendrith as quickly as possible.

Kindra did her best to kill the time by sleeping through the day. But her sleep was filled with nightmares of Harthwin being raided and destroyed in her absence, and she often jerked awake in a panic, fire already sparking in her hands.

The first few times this happened, Jasper looked at her with concern but stayed silent. The fourth time it happened, he asked her if she was all right, to which he got nothing but a curled lip in response.

They had not spoken since the day of her panic attack. Kindra was determined to keep it that way, and Jasper seemed content to let her continue ignoring him. Every day, when they stopped for meals or to set up camp for the night, they gave her space to go expel her magic, just as he had promised. Jasper hadn't come up to her since the first time, but she always felt him watching her. She did her best to ignore it.

The fifth time she jolted awake from a nightmare, however, was different.

It hadn't been the usual terror. This time, it had been images of her marrying Jasper, her wedding dress hiding the chains wrapped around her. Locked in a bedroom, unable to use her magic. Trapped in bed, heavily pregnant, being pulled every which way by half a dozen other children. Wasting away, a husk of the person she'd once been.

When she erupted from her sleep this time, the first thing she saw was Jasper's face, which did *not* soothe her in the slightest. She scrambled back against the carriage wall, her chest heaving as she tried to root herself back into reality. Jasper's eyes went wide with worry. "Woah, Kindra, it's okay. It was just a dream. You're here."

That's the problem, she wanted to scream. But she focused on her breathing, begrudgingly using the trick he'd taught her because it worked and in that moment she hated the frightened, wild way she felt more than she hated him.

He watched her carefully as she calmed herself. When her breathing steadied, she began to turn away from him, embarrassed that he'd seen her in such a panicked state. Again.

"What was the nightmare about?" he asked, his voice taking on that same soft tone he'd used when he'd calmed her down the first time. "If you don't mind telling me," he added.

Kindra debated ignoring him. But she could feel his eyes on her, unwavering, and sighed in resignation, turning back to face him. "It was about marrying you."

He covered up the glimmer of hurt that crossed his face so quickly Kindra almost thought she'd imagined it. "Are they all about that?"

She looked away. "No," she responded, "just that one."

Silence stretched between them for a few moments. Kindra prayed the conversation was over. But then—

"I'm sorry I threatened to kill your mother."

It took her by such surprise she actually laughed, her head swiveling back to him. "What?"

"It was cruel, and I shouldn't have done it. I'm sorry."

"But you would have done it, wouldn't you?"

Now it was his turn to be surprised. "Wh—"

"You can apologize and feel guilty for it all you want," she cut him off, "but you would have done it, right? If I'd continued to say no. If I'd run, you would have killed her."

"I don't—" he started, then stopped. She could see him gathering his thoughts. He started again, "I knew I wouldn't have to. It was a… it was a calculated move. To make sure nobody ended up getting hurt. But it was still cruel, and I am sorry for it."

"But you would have killed her," Kindra repeated, voice blunt. "If your *calculated move* hadn't worked, you wouldn't have let me call your bluff. You would have killed her, right in front of me." She shook her head. "Sorry, my ass."

Jasper clenched his jaw, frustration steeling his gray eyes. "I don't know if I would have killed her. I didn't *want* to, I know that. Not all of the Annalindis family gets off on unnecessary violence," he finished, rather pathetically.

"Yes, the man who threatened to kill somebody's mother because she told him no is actually a pacifist!" she scoffed. "Give me a fucking break."

"Look, I'm trying here, okay?" He splayed his hands before him imploringly. "I don't want to spend the rest of my life married to somebody who hates me. I'm *sorry*, Kindra."

"If you didn't want to spend your life married to someone who hates you, you should have *left me alone*," she hissed, fire beginning to brew within her.

"I honestly don't even know why you wanted to stay there so badly; everybody was so damn afraid of you—"

Kindra jerked back as if he'd slapped her in the face. "How *dare* you." She reached past him and yanked on the rope to get them to stop the carriage. "You don't know anything about me or my life. How would you know how they felt about me?"

The carriage began to slow, and she moved to the door, opening it and jumping out before they'd even come to a complete stop.

"I know because it was one of the villagers who wrote to us about you!"

Kindra froze. "What?"

Jasper scrambled out of the carriage after her. Heinrich dismounted from his horse and hurried over, looking alarmed, but halted when Jasper held up a hand. "That was how we heard about you. Didn't you think it was weird how we found out about you; some Firefury tucked away by the Pryllian border?"

"You're lying to me."

"I'm not, I swear. I have the letter; I could show you it right now—"

"Then do it." She spun to face him. "Show it to me."

He hesitated, then nodded, gesturing at Heinrich. The Wavebreaker went to his horse and pulled out an envelope from the saddlebag and came over and handed it to her.

She pulled the letter out, and when she read the first sentence and the name of the sender, her world started to spin.

To the Council of Alverin,,

My name is Elric Afayn. I am an Earthwarden from the humble village of Harthwin, near the Pryllian border. I am writing to let you know of a potential marriage candidate for His Highness Prince Jasper Annalindis. Her name is Kindra Bedelyn, and she is a Firefury of extraordinary power.

For the past decade, she has used her magic to defend our home. She has killed, bled, and burned for her people, who, I regret to say, have shown her almost no kindness in return. She is excluded, avoided, and feared, though she has only ever aimed to protect us. She has never hurt a soul in Harthwin, but you wouldn't know it from the way my fellow villagers behave.

On and on the letter went. Elric outlined all her history: how she'd taught herself, the various enemies she'd gone up against, the way she'd been treated. She'd never had any inkling that he'd known all of this. She hadn't even thought he'd been paying that much attention.

She is a stubborn, hot-headed girl, as most Firefuries are, the letter concluded. *Her pride will never allow her to admit that she is angered and hurt by their behavior. And as much as I appreciate what she does for us and fear what might occur in her absence, I cannot stand by and allow her to die for this town. So I am writing to you, in hopes that you will see this and consider her for a Royal marriage. She is meant for much greater things than a life fighting for people who can't even say thank you. She possesses a great, mighty gift, and I believe that she could be powerful enough to break the curse.*

For the glory of Alverin,

Elric Afayn

"I don't—I don't understand," she whimpered when she finished, dropping the letter on the ground. "He—why would he do this?"

"Because he cares about you. Because he saw the writing on the wall. Because he didn't want your mother to have to send out a search party to find your body when one of your altercations went wrong." Jasper stepped forward and reached out to her. "It was only a matter of time, Kindra. Even you had to have known that. He was trying to do what was best for you."

She jolted away from him. "He didn't know what was best for me," she spat, and was disgusted to find she was crying. "None of you know what is best for me. I was happy—"

"Were you? Were you really?" Jasper's voice was tight with exasperation, rising into a yell. "Tell me truthfully, did it really fill you with joy to have all of your friends shun you? Did it warm your heart to have people unable to look at you, unwilling to fucking thank you for *saving their lives?* Did you enjoy being seen as the town pariah, the local freak?" Each word landed like a physical blow.

She was crying in earnest now, body shaking with sobs, the fire in her sputtering out. She didn't know if she was sad or angry or shocked or some kind of combination of all three. But she did know one thing, and it killed her, felt so sick and oily to admit:

Jasper was right.

She *hadn't* been happy. She was angry and hurt and bitter; she'd spent most of her life swallowing those feelings down. And she hated him for pointing it out, for being so brutally honest.

"Your life with me in Wendrith will make you happier than you could ever imagine, happier than you could have ever been in Harthwin," he insisted. "I *know* it will."

And just like that, the blind arrogance in his voice reminded Kindra of just exactly who Jasper was: a prince—an Annalindis—who had never known sacrifice or hardship in his entire life, with the audacity to act as if he knew her at all. Her shock and grief faded into the background as her fury surged forward.

"You are unbelievable," she hissed. "Of course you think you *know* because you think you know *everything.* But you don't. You don't know a damn thing about me. I don't care that they were all afraid of me, Jasper. It was my choice to protect them, and I made that choice every day knowing how they'd react. It was *my choice,* which is what you are incapable of wrapping your head around! You think you're so smart, but you can't understand why taking away my right to choose anything about my life anymore makes me *fucking angry!*" She stalked over to him, halting a mere foot away, and snarled, seething, "You want to know why I have nightmares about marrying you? Because I *hate you,* Jasper. I hate you for what you stand for and for what you have taken from me and for the fact that you think you're my savior because of it."

Jasper's face fell. "Right," he sighed, stepping back. "Of course. Of course you do." He gave her one final, pleading look. "Well, hate me all you want. I guess I'll just have to get used to it." Then he was gone, storming away.

Kindra stood there, feeling more unmoored and defeated than she ever had. It all made sense now: the dagger Elric gave her, the last conversation they had, the farewell from the carriage. He'd known. He'd *set it up*.

The one person left in town who'd ever shown her kindness besides her mother had been the catalyst for her worst nightmare.

She grabbed the letter from the ground but couldn't bring herself to burn it. Instead, she crushed the pages in her fist and climbed back into the carriage. As she did, she noticed Jasper mounting a horse. He didn't look at her.

For the next three days, he rode on horseback next to Heinrich. He did not speak to her. He hardly glanced in her direction.

Kindra stayed in the carriage and felt terribly, terribly alone.

CHAPTER 6

Despite her discontent with her situation, even Kindra could not deny that Wendrith was a marvel.

Alverin's capital was built along the towering cliffs overlooking the Temprian Sea: a near impenetrable fortress. Kindra had read about it once, and as the city loomed ever closer, she recalled what the book had said.

The sharp slopes gave it a permanent uphill advantage, and the steep cliff-side made assault from sea almost pointless; even the most powerful squadron of Wavebreakers couldn't create waves high enough to crest the walls. It was a pinnacle of defense design. The buildings, too, were built with the power of Wielders in mind, constructed with thick stone that could withstand a Windspinner or Earthwarden assault. And it was all surrounded by massive stone walls armed with turrets and battlements.

It made sense that the city had never once been lost to another kingdom, why no army had ever gotten close. The closest Wendrith ever came to falling was during Eija's Rebellion, over a hundred years ago. That had ended as all attacks on Alverin did: with slit throats and decapitated heads, and the royal family's power unscathed.

Or so they thought, until they realized the seemingly unimportant seventeen-year-old rebel they'd killed had the most powerful last words in history.

As their traveling party got closer to Wendrith's walls, Kindra felt a burst of respect for the young girl who had forever altered Alverin's future and dealt the power-hungry and cruel royal family such a humbling blow. Eija had been a Cursebringer, a Wielder of a rare form of Darkened magic. She could cast curses at the expense of her own life force. The larger the curse, the greater the toll. When faced with certain death after the defeat of the rebellion, she used her last moments to banish magic from all future members of the Annalindis bloodline.

King Iyron hadn't believed it, of course. Not until a year later, when Prince Edward and his wife had their first son. The baby had opened his eyes, revealing them to be a muted, ordinary blue rather than the fierce gold all Annalindis heirs had. It was then that they knew Eija's curse was very, very real.

Kindra shifted in her seat, yawning. They'd been up since dawn, the guards ushering her out of her tent and back into the carriage without giving her more than a few minutes to relieve herself and throw on a cloak. If there was one thing she was looking forward to at the castle, it was the prospect of a nice, hot bath followed by a *very* long nap.

It was clear the rest of the traveling party was eager to finish their journey as well. From her view out the window, she could see guards chatting animatedly, more talkative than they'd been for most of the two-week trip. Even Heinrich, who wore a near constant face of anxiety, was smiling as he rode alongside Jasper, looking more relaxed than he had the whole time she'd known him.

She envied them. While they grew more excited with every passing moment, she grew more terrified.

They were soon passing through the clusters of farms outside the capital, the landscape a sea of sprawling fields and pastures. It was a bit warmer here than it had been in Harthwin; the harvest was still occurring in full force. She spotted some sheep, and her heart panged, thinking of the wool blanket she got her mother just a few weeks ago. *Well, she'll be able to get all the wool she wants here*, she thought.

The city walls loomed closer and closer, and Kindra had to crane her neck to try and see the top. She'd never seen anything so large. They were grander than even the tallest oaks in Harthwin, and probably ten times as thick, built to withstand war of magical proportions. Though she'd seen drawings of the city before, nothing could have prepared her for how huge it was in person.

A shadow fell over the party then, and Kindra's breath caught as they approached the main city gate. At the apex of the gate sat a gold depiction of Scaldor, the god of fire. The Annalindises were—well, used to be—a family of Firefuries so powerful that one of them alone could raze an entire town in a matter of minutes. It was said that the first rulers of Alverin had been God-blessed, that Scaldor himself had come to them and gifted them some of his power, and that power had trickled down through generation after generation.

Until the curse.

Now, Scaldor's presence was more mocking than anything. The statue of the god was cloaked in fire, and it exploded from him in every direction, engulfing the entire top portion of the gate in swirling, metallic flame. The statue's face was contorted with angry determination, his mouth open in a battle cry.

For so long, the Annalindis family had used their God-blessed power to bring other kingdoms to their knees and ensure Alverin would never fall. They had embodied all that Scaldor was; from the flames that consumed him to his affinity for war and destruction.

And then Eija Cursebringer took it away with no more than a few words.

The loss of magic that powerful was catastrophic for the kingdom, and Kindra knew that the worst was yet to come. Alverin had centuries of violence to atone for. There'd been smaller, not-quite wars here and there over the last few decades once the truth of the curse got out. They were mostly skirmishes along the borders, sabotaged trade routes, or small campaigns that Alverin easily quashed, like the one that had killed her father. But Kindra was no fool, and she doubted the king was, either. Their neighbors were just getting started, and with the tensions that had been building over the last few years, all-out war with one of their neighboring kingdoms was inevitable. Though she could understand why the other kingdoms wanted revenge, she just hated that innocent civilians would suffer for it.

The carriage came to a halt suddenly, and Kindra stiffened as the door opened and Jasper stepped in. He hardly spared her a glance as he shut the door behind him and settled into the bench across from her. It had been four days since they last spoke.

She was not going to be the one to break that silence now. She gave him a scorching glare, and then turned her attention back to the window.

Jasper, unfortunately, seemed to be finished giving her the cold shoulder. "We're about to enter Wendrith," he said, and Kindra almost laughed at the pointless statement.

"Clearly," she replied, not looking at him. Then, because she was suspicious, she asked, "Why are you in here?

"Well," he began, clearly surprised she was talking to him, "if the people see me, riding next to the carriage... not in it... they will make assumptions."

"They'll assume you've brought back a bride?"

"Yes." The carriage jolted back into motion.

"But you did, didn't you?" She shot him an angry glance. He avoided her gaze.

"Yes, but..." he sighed, struggling to find the words. "They get rather... um, excited, about the prospect of another wedding, and um..." He cleared his throat, then said, "I didn't want you to have to be subjected to some of the things they might say. That's all."

"What things might they say that would be so upsetting to me?"

"Well for one, they'll be very eager to find out when we're going to... start having children." Jasper winced slightly as he said it.

Kindra clenched her fist. They were passing through the gate now. Her heart ached as they did. Only the gods knew if she ever would go beyond the city walls again. "Yes, I suppose there will be plenty of children, won't there?" she muttered.

He shifted in his seat, and it made Kindra feel better to see him so uncomfortable. At least he wasn't some lewd, awful man who had no qualms about just taking what he wanted from her.

So far. He's shown no indication of being that way so far, she reminded herself.

"Look, Kindra." His voice was soft, pleading. "I wouldn't... I know what the marriage contract states. But I'm not... I wouldn't... I don't want to force you. To do anything."

She turned towards him. "And what if I never consent?"

He shrugged. "I don't know. I don't want to think about that. That's why I want you to like me. For us to like each other." He smiled at her. "I want to prove to you that I will be good. I will treat you well. I won't lie, the rest of my family can be..." He sighed again, the smile falling from his face. "My older brothers take after my father. They're arrogant, angry men.

Their wives are nice enough, but they can still be petty and mean. My mother is only half-present. And my father..." He grimaced and looked away. "You know what my father is like."

Kindra did know what King Leofric was like, and it was a good thing he wasn't a Wielder. He'd have razed the entire continent by now if he had been. "Your sister," she asked, "Helena. We never heard much of her in Harthwin. What is she like?"

A loving glow lit up his face. "Helena is my best friend. She's about the only truly kind person in the family. Well, her and her wife, Emeline." He grinned. "I think you'd have a blast with them."

"Maybe," was all Kindra said, the rest of her thoughts dissipating as they emerged on the other side of the gate, and Wendrith sprawled out before them.

The first thing Kindra noticed was the pipes.

One of the many inventions borne with the help of magic was indoor plumbing, something Kindra had never experienced. Only the major cities in Alverin had it. Along the city streets were grates and vents leading down to what she guessed were the sewers. Metal pipes ran up the sides of buildings, alongside bridges arching over canals, under staircases, carrying clean water to even the poorest households within the city walls.

Jasper smiled, noting her amazement. "I have missed plumbing greatly these past few weeks."

Kindra decided not to give him the satisfaction of knowing that she was also looking forward to experiencing it. *Growing up here would have been so different,* she thought as they moved through the city.

"How is it cleaned?" she asked, giving into her curiosity.

"Wavebeakers in the sanitation centers. There are a few dozen of them all over Wendrith." Elemental Wielders could always feel the wellbeing of their element; an Earthwarden could tell how a plant was faring just as Kindra could feel the strength of a fire, or in this case, Wavebreakers could sense if water was clean or not.

Before she could say anything more, she was distracted by the gathering crowd lining the streets as they began the long ascent up to the castle.

Judging by the clothes of the people—clean but worn—she could tell they were still among the commoners, not yet passing through the neighborhoods housing the upper class and the nobility. But while the citizens outside their carriage didn't look rich, they all looked healthy. Well-fed. Content. They cheered and waved at the party, knowing from the seal on the guards' uniforms that an Annalindis was passing through.

Her surprise must have been obvious, because Jasper explained to her gently, as if knowing it would be a touchy subject, "We try our hardest to make sure the people of Wendrith are well taken care of. I know..." He swallowed, then continued, emboldened, "I know that was not the life you had in Harthwin, and I know you find it hard to believe that the cruel Annalindis family would care so much about any of its people, much less the lowly commoners. But we are trying to do better, Kindra. We may have once been blinded by our greed, but if the curse has taught us one thing, it's that our kingdom is only as strong as our weakest citizen—our poorest family, our sickest babe. The last hundred years has made us recognize that." He finished his spiel with a nervous smile.

Kindra stared at him for several heartbeats. "How long did you rehearse that?" she finally said, raising her eyebrows.

Jasper sputtered. "I— well, I didn't—" Kindra frowned in disbelief, and he sighed, his cheeks reddening. "I'm just trying to show you that marrying me isn't the death sentence you think it is, Kindra." She rolled her eyes, but he barreled on, "Yes, my father would abandon all the plans to expand infrastructure and resources throughout the kingdom in a *second* if he could have magic and happily return to a life of war and bloodshed, and yes, my brothers are some of the biggest assholes I know, but *I'm* not. Helena is not. My mother, for all her other problems, is not."

"Well, if you have to say you're *not* an asshole, chances are..." Kindra trailed off as Jasper threw his hands up in the air in exasperation, the second crack in his careful composure she'd seen in just as many weeks. And perhaps it was the exhaustion from traveling, or the excitement at the thought of getting to draw a bath without taking half a dozen trips out to the well, but Kindra let out a quiet chuckle at the showcase of his frustration.

"You're impossible!" he exclaimed, but a relieved smile was flowering on his face too, and for a moment—just one—the heavy, angry tension that had lived between them since they'd met lightened. He was just a man, and Kindra was just a woman.

And then, as quick as it had left, the tension slammed back into place, and she was reminded of why she was here, in this grand city with running water and no empty stomachs, and the desire to laugh died. The smile slid from her face, and Jasper's did too, because he knew he'd lost her.

Kindra turned away from him, opting to stare out the window as they passed through a second, much smaller gate into the neighborhood of the rich. Here, the residences were farther apart and grander, but she knew they had their main, large manors outside the city walls where their lands could sprawl for acres. Jasper offered no more commentary.

As they moved past the extravagant homes, she wondered how many of the families that resided in them could say they had a tie to the Annalindis family. They'd been seeking out commoners for marriages for the last few generations because of that very issue. Centuries of only marrying other high-class families within the kingdom would have posed a problem eventually, whether or not there was a curse. Besides, the few noble marriages they did have in the last century proved the curse could not care less about status or class when they, too, failed to produce a magical heir.

They came upon one last gate, this one as ornate as it was sturdy, providing entry through another otherwise impenetrable stone wall. Kindra didn't need to look to know that the castle lay on the other side, but she did anyway.

The royal castle was stunning from a distance, but nothing could have prepared her for how beautiful it was up close. Built out of dark, smooth stone, it was a colossal feat of architecture. Kindra once again found herself straining her neck to try and take in all of its grandeur. Turrets, both slim and broad, broke away from the main castle to stretch up towards the sky for what looked like miles. There looked to be four levels, guards lining the walls along each one. Again, as they came up to the main entrance—a giant door perched at the top of a giant staircase—she noted the triumphant golden flames of Scaldor. They were woven into the adornment of every doorway, every window, every tower; his fire seemed to engulf the castle in a permanent embrace. She thought once more of the curse and knew those flames mocked the Annalindis family and all of Alverin more than anything.

The carriage continued around the side of the castle, entering a hidden courtyard. There, another host of guards, as well as a group of servants, awaited them.

Heinrich was the first to reach them, dismounting from his house and handing the reins to one of the servants. Several more servants stepped forward as the other members of their party practically leapt off their mounts, eager to be rid of the animals now that their journey had come to an end.

The carriage slowed to a halt, and Kindra felt her throat threaten to close as fear sunk in. She was here, in Wendrith, miles upon miles from her home, to marry Jasper Annalindis, Prince of Alverin. The reality of her situation slammed into her, more so than it had even over the last few weeks, and the carriage suddenly felt very, very small.

"Kindra." Jasper's voice snapped her out of her panic, if only for a second. He had one hand on the carriage door, ready to exit. "Deep breaths, okay? It's going to be fine. You have the day to rest. You don't have to worry about meeting any of my family until tomorrow—" Suddenly, a sweet, lilting voice called out his name, and Kindra watched as, for the first time since she'd met him, a real, unrestrained smile bloomed on his face. "Well, you don't have to worry about meeting *most* of my family," he amended, and stepped out of the carriage, leaving the door open behind him.

Kindra watched as he strode over to a beautiful young woman dressed in a simple but finely made gold gown. She had blonde hair like Jasper, and it fell over her shoulders in loose, golden waves. She reached out to embrace Jasper, only to pull back a moment later, her nose crinkling in disgust.

"Good gods, you smell like shit!" She jerked her head away, faking a gag. "Forget catching up until you've bathed." Her attention turned to the carriage then, and a teasing smirk blossomed on her lips. "Don't tell me you managed to bring home the one shy Firefury in the kingdom, brother?"

"She's not shy," Jasper rebutted, "This is just… a lot of change for her, Helena." *Oh.*

This was *the* Helena Annalindis. Princess of Alverin. Jasper's older sister, and best friend.

"Oh, please. Based on the stories we've heard about her while waiting for you to arrive, I doubt anything could scare her."

Kindra scoured Helena's words but found nothing mocking in them. Instead, she found a healthy dose of respect. It was that which got her moving, stepping out of the carriage and into the sun.

Before she had even steadied herself, Helena surged forward, clasping Kindra's hands in her own. "Oh my! Aren't you just stunning! And look at your eyes. I don't think I've ever seen a Firefury with eyes *that* gold before."

Gods, Kindra thought as she scrambled to gather herself. S*he talks a mile a minute.*

"Helena," Jasper chastised, though it was warm with fondness. "Give her a second."

"Right, right!" The princess blushed, though she didn't let go of Kindra's hands. "I'm sorry, I've just been so excited for your arrival, it's all Emeline—that's my wife—and I can talk about!" Kindra opened her mouth to speak, but Helena stepped back, dipping down in a small curtsy, and continued, "I'm Helena, though I'm sure you've already figured that out. Technically, it's Princess Helena, but since we're going to be sisters, you don't have to deal with all the uppity titles and fancy bullshit. To you, I'll always just be Helena."

"R-right," Kindra stammered out, shocked that she was finally getting a word in, "Well, it's an honor to meet you, Prin— er, Helena. I'm—"

"Kindra Bedelyn, yes, I know!" Helena smiled even wider, and it was the genuine enthusiasm and kindness in it that had Kindra smiling back, albeit hesitantly.

Behind her, Jasper cleared his throat. "Helena, if you would be so kind as to continue this introduction on the way to Kindra's chambers?"

"Yes, of course!" Helena moved to Kindra's side, linking their arms together and guiding her towards the door to the castle. "We'll see you later, Jasper!" All they got in response was a laugh.

Ahead, the guards opened the doors for them, and Kindra swallowed nervously, terror rising in her and pushing down any feelings of comfort she'd found seconds prior.

Helena squeezed her arm comfortingly. "Welcome home," she whispered.

Kindra knew she meant for the words to soothe her, but as they entered the castle, that couldn't have felt further from the truth.

CHAPTER 7

The first thing Kindra noticed when she stepped into the castle was that it was deceptively bright.

Despite the exterior being built from that dark, black stone, the interior stone was a pale gray. As they progressed from the small entry hallway and into the main pathways of the castle, it grew even brighter, the outside walls lined with large windows that allowed sunlight to illuminate all it touched. The windows were framed by red velvet curtains trimmed with gold: the Annalindis family colors. The black marble floors were covered in plush rugs. She had expected the castle to be dark and intimidating, not this. This was... inviting.

Helena chattered as they walked, but Kindra found it hard to pay attention to what she was saying, too busy trying to steady her breathing and take in her surroundings. Already she was lost; all it took was a few turns and a couple flights of stairs to render her completely disoriented. Still, she forced herself to nod along and tune in every other sentence to make sure she wasn't being asked a question. Other than that, all Helena was saying was going in one ear and out the other.

"...the first Annalindis rulers wanted the castle to be scary on the outside, but cozy on the inside," Helena was saying as Kindra checked back into the conversation, "I mean, obviously, a giant castle fit with catapults can only be so cozy, but still. I think they did a pretty good job, what do you think?"

"Um," Kindra stammered, "yeah. Sure." She searched for a better thing to say, and settled lamely on, "It's really nice."

Helena hardly noticed her lackluster response, barreling on, "I think you're really going to love your chambers. I looked them over myself before you arrived! Lots of natural light, a bathing room, a giant closet, and even a balcony, which is large enough for you to do some basic wielding on—"

"Wait," Kindra interrupted, "I can still wield here?"

Helena blinked at her, shocked by the question, and stopped walking, turning to face Kindra directly. "Of course," she responded, frowning slightly. "Did you think you wouldn't be able to?"

"Well, honestly... no, I didn't think I'd be able to. At least not without supervision," she confessed, cheeks heating with embarrassment.

"You can wield whenever you want, Kindra." Helena's voice had shifted, and she now sounded as if she were speaking to a frightened and confused child, which, much to Kindra's chagrin, was basically true. "I mean, don't go flinging fireballs around at the dinner table, but we strongly encourage daily wielding here. My family... we aren't Wielders at the moment, but we still know the harm that restraining one's magic can cause."

Some of the terror that had been pressing in on Kindra since the day she got that letter eased, and she found it easier to breathe. "Okay, that's... that's nice, then. I just thought... because I'm a Firefury, that it might be too dangerous. For me. Or other people."

"I'll admit, you may not be able to do anything elaborate unless you get into a training ground. But this castle is built from stone for a reason. The Annalindis family is Scaldor-blessed, remember?" She smiled, but it didn't meet her eyes. "Well, was, at least."

They began to walk again, and Kindra's anxiety subsided a bit. "Do you... does it make you sad, to not be a Wielder?"

For a moment, Helena didn't respond, and Kindra opened her mouth to apologize, afraid she'd overstepped. But then, Helena said, "Yes and no. Yes, because it's frightening to be cursed, and to see the impact it's had on my kingdom. No, because all I have ever known is this life as a non-Wielder. I don't know what it feels like to have such power as you do, or my ancestors did. I think, many days, I am content not to," she finished softly, and Kindra felt as though she'd just been told a secret. She couldn't fight the fact that that it made her feel good, like she really could be friends with the princess.

Before Kindra could say anything else, they came to a stop before a set of white doors. "Here we are!" Helena chirped, any trace of seriousness gone. "I'll leave you here. A couple of servants will be stopping by shortly; they're yours, so feel free to ask them to do whatever you want—bathe you, dress you, bring you food, anything." Kindra's mouth fell open at that statement. "You can take your meals in your room for the rest of the day if you wish, but if you'd like to have some company tonight for dinner, Emeline and I will be dining in our rooms. Feel free to join us. But we also completely understand that you're probably exhausted from your journey and won't take offense if you decide to stay in for the evening."

"Will Prince Jasper be joining you?" The words left Kindra's mouth before she could vet them for any taste of spite or disdain, and unfortunately, they came out riddled with both.

Helena only smirked, eyes alight with mischief. "No," she replied, "I can imagine you're pretty sick of him, aren't you?" She laughed. "No, he will not be there, I can promise you that."

Kindra nodded. "I will think about it," she said, "I need a bath and a nap first, though."

"Of course, of course." Helena stepped forward and turned the handle on one of the doors. "Well, I wish you a peaceful afternoon, Kindra. Enjoy your rooms!" She ushered Kindra through the doorway and quietly closed the door behind her, leaving Kindra, for the first time in weeks, blissfully alone.

The room was ridiculous.

It was at least twice the size of her old cottage in Harthwin, and that was just the main bed chamber. The walls were the same pale gray stone, the floors a matching gray marble, covered in plush white and beige fur rugs. The far-right wall was almost entirely filled with floor-to-ceiling windows. There was a set of glass doors in the middle of that wall that led, as Helena promised, to a large balcony. Pale gold curtains framed that wall, parted to let the mid-morning sun dapple the room with light. A few feet from the windows were a round dining table and chairs.

The rest of the walls were adorned with paintings of various landscapes, no doubt parts of Alverin, and beautiful, detailed tapestries. There was a line of tall bookshelves along the same wall as the door through which Kindra had just entered, and a small sitting area beside them. Next to that was a fireplace, a fire already lit. A plush cream sofa and matching armchair sat in front of it. On the left wall sat a large wardrobe and another set of doors, behind which Kindra assumed was the bathing room. Finally, along the wall opposite her was a large desk, and her bed, which was massive.

She moved across the room—which was so big, gods, it was just *so big*— towards the bed, hands outstretched as though she were in a trance. She ran her fingers over the lavish cream-colored quilt and gasped at how soft and smooth it was. Her hands moved up to the half dozen pillows, which were covered in silk cases. The thick wooden bedframe was almost the same color as the bedding, decorated with gold detailing. Atop the four bedposts stretched a sheer, gauzy off-white canopy, flowing down to create curtains that could provide her some additional privacy while she slept if she wanted.

The bed was so—light. Delicate, even. Looking around the room, she saw that the other furnishings were as well. There was no piece of furniture that was dark. The softly colored furnishings, along with the bright natural light, made the spacious room less intimidating. It was, in a weird way, homey.

Kindra was still admiring the room when there was a knock on her door, followed by the quiet entrance of two young women. They looked to be about her age, and they stood at attention as she stared at them.

"Who—" she began, but then remembered Helena's parting words. *Servants. These are my servants.* She stopped herself mid-sentence and started again. "Are you my... servants?" Just saying the word felt strange.

They bobbed into curtsies. "Yes, Lady Kindra," the one on the right said. Her hair and eyes were a plain brown, but the healthy glow of her brown skin reminded Kindra of the Healer from Harthwin. The other servant was a Windspinner, given away by her pale silver eyes. She had hair that was so blonde it was almost white.

"What are your names?" she asked.

"I'm Cerulle, and this is Sala," the Windspinner responded, and they both curtsied again. Kindra bit back the urge to tell them to stop.

"Nice to... meet you." She found herself unsure of what to say. What *did* you say to people meant to serve at your beck and call?

A stretch of awkward silence passed, before Sala said, "Do you require anything of us, my Lady? A bath, perhaps?"

Kindra began to bristle at the insinuation that she was dirty, but there was nothing snide hidden behind Sala's offer. They weren't there to make her feel less than, or to remind her of her background. They were just there to serve her. And, in this case, give her a bath that she desperately wanted, and needed.

"Y-yes," she stammered, struggling to put any bit of authority into her voice, "that would be very nice, thank you."

"Right this way, then." Sala gestured to the door that led to the bathing room, and Cerulle rushed ahead to open it for them.

Kindra could not have prepared herself for what lay behind it.

Like her bedroom, the bathing room was also flooded with light. The walls were made of smooth cream marble tile. The wall opposite her had a large window, in front of which sat the most enormous tub she'd ever seen. Shelves filled with soaps and other cleaning tonics stood next to it. Along the far-left wall was a huge vanity, complete with a sink and mirror, and next to that was a toilet.

"I've never—" Kindra spun around in a circle. "I've never seen a room like this before. We didn't even have toilets in Harthwin."

"I felt the same when I arrived here from Mistbarrow," Sala said, and Kindra started. Mistbarrow was only a few days' travel from Harthwin. "I couldn't believe it really existed."

"How long have you lived here?"

"About ten years. My family moved here because they were afraid living so close to Pryllia."

"I know that fear well," Kindra admitted, her discomfort easing slightly knowing Sala had lived, at least for a while, near her home. That she, too, knew what living out there was like. "And you, Cerulle? Where are you from?"

"A small village outside Roulierne, my Lady," the silver-eyed girl replied as she moved over to the tub. Indeed, she had a slight accent, reminiscent of a merchant that had once passed through Harthwin many years ago: a bit nasal, her words flowing together like syrup. "I came here to attend Grydmarth."

"The Academy?" Kindra asked, slightly distracted as Cerulle turned one of the nozzles on the tub and water started flowing from the faucet. Grydmarth Academy was the top school in Alverin, for Wielders and non-Wielders alike. There had been a time long ago when Kindra had dreamed of leaving Harthwin to go there. "Isn't that for battle training?" The Wielder nodded, reaching out to test the temperature of the water with her hand. "But you're—"

"A servant?" Her lips parted in an amused grin.

Kindra studied her, noting the graceful air with which she moved, the sleek muscles of her lower legs peeking out from under her gray dress. She recalled what little she knew about Windspinners. "You're a bodyguard."

Cerulle's smile widened, and Sala let out a small giggle.

"Yes, you could say I am a bodyguard. I'm meant to be by your side, or at least within arm's reach at all times. Here to serve you in whatever way you require, of course, but my primary duty is to protect you." Cerulle gestured to Sala, who had come up behind Kindra and gently pulled her hair out of the dirty, matted bun it had been in for the last several days. "Sala is a Healer. Also a strategic appointment. She will always be close by, as well, in case of any…" She paused, deciding on what word to say, then settled for, "incidents."

Kindra allowed Sala to help her in removing her clothes, feeling only slightly uncomfortable about being undressed and bathed by other people. Her curiosity helped her push through any awkwardness.

"So you're not really servants, then," she said as she pulled her dirty set of undergarments off. She handed them to Sala, frowning at the grime that coated them. She'd only had a few sets of clothes to wear while traveling, and without a proper chance to adequately bathe, it didn't matter how many times she tried to wash herself or her clothes in streams. She was just plain filthy.

"We are still servants, my Lady, but we aren't *only* servants," Sala corrected, placing her hand on Kindra's elbow and guiding the naked young woman over to the bath.

Kindra eased her way into the tub and could not hold back her moan of contentment. It was perhaps the most amazing thing she'd ever felt. She released a bit of her magic, heating the water up to the point of steaming.

"Yeah, I could get used to this," she sighed, dipping her head back to allow her hair to be thoroughly soaked.

A burst of guilt coursed through her at her enjoyment. Was she really so easily placated by the lure of a hot bath and the innovation of running water? Was a plush bed and bubbly princess all it took to sway her?

Cerulle began slowly untangling her dark curls with a comb, and Kindra pushed aside her internal debate, resolving to sort it out later. Right now, she just wanted to be clean. That's all it was. She wasn't betraying her morals; she was just tired and dirty. Of course she was going to enjoy this. She would have enjoyed any bath, any bed.

At least, that's what she settled on telling herself.

Sala lathered up a bar of soap onto a washcloth, reached out and took one of Kindra's arms, and began to scrub away the weeks' worth of dirt as Cerulle washed her hair. Kindra had honestly thought she'd done a fairly good job at keeping herself clean on the way here: they'd had some soap she'd been able to use every few days to bathe. But a handful of rushed baths in a creek and her unwillingness to strip entirely down out of fear of being ogled, had clearly not been as effective as she'd hoped, she realized as she watched the water begin to turn a pale brown.

The bath was slightly uncomfortable. Kindra hadn't had another person clean her since she'd been a child and that person had been her mother. When they had her stand, she fought back the desire to squirm away as they ran their washcloths over her backside and inner thighs, instead focusing intently on how clean she now felt.

After one final rinse, they helped her step out of the tub, drying her off with fluffy towels. She gawked as they presented her with a new set of undergarments that were finer than any clothing she'd ever worn.

"Your dressing room is fairly empty right now, my Lady," Sala informed her, nodding to a door on the right wall. "You will be fitted properly tomorrow. There are couple of sets of casual wear, in case you'd like to attend dinner tonight with Princess Helena, as well as a few different choices in sleepwear."

"Thank you," Kindra managed, and moved through the door. She was not surprised to find it was another giant room, filled with shelves and wardrobes and a mirror that took up almost an entire wall. It was, as Sala said, mostly empty, which made the size of it seem all the more ridiculous.

She looked through the drawers until she found some of the sleepwear. Unlike in Harthwin, where the nightgowns she'd worn had been plain and modest, these were as intricate and colorful as fancy gowns, and twice as revealing. She selected a deep red one, surprised at how revealing it was with its light, flowing fabric and lacy detailing. It came down to just above her knees, held up by thin straps, and displayed far more of her cleavage than she'd like.

"Gods above," she muttered as she studied herself in the mirror, "I might as well be naked."

"It is traditional Alverinian fashion," Cerulle said. "Before the curse, the Annalindis family, with their history of being Firefuries, wore lighter fabrics year-round, due to their—and your—ability to warm themselves with their magic. It was a symbol of their power, to walk about in a blizzard with their bodies bared to the elements. You will be fitted with the older attire in mind." She smiled kindly. "You're the first Firefury to be in the Annalindis family for almost a hundred years."

Kindra flinched at the reminder that she was to soon be an Annalindis. Kindra Annalindis was going to be her name. No longer a common girl from Harthwin, but a Princess of Alverin. A wave of nausea rolled through her, the bliss of her bath immediately forgotten.

"My lady? Is something wrong?" Sala asked, brow furrowed with concern.

"I think... I think I'd like to take a nap." Her voice came out barely above a whisper. "Alone, please."

The two young women did not question her further, dipping their heads in understanding. "Of course. We will be only a cord pull away, should you need us." Within seconds, they had exited her chambers, closing the doors quietly behind them.

Kindra walked numbly out of the bathing room and over to her bed. Her giant, obscene bed, in her giant, obscene room, in this giant, obscene castle. For a moment, she simply stared at it.

Loneliness stabbed through her, as sharp and brutal as a steel blade. The realization that she hadn't seen her mother in two weeks, when for her entire life she had seen her every single day, slammed down on her. Tears gathered in her eyes.

She blinked them away before they could fall, pulling the covers back and crawling into bed. She could not cry here, could not be weak. She could also admit that it could be worse. Her rooms were beautiful and comfortable. Her wielding would not be restricted. Helena was kind, and Cerulle and Sala seemed sweet. But as exhaustion overtook her and she began to drift off, Kindra could not forget why she was here, and no amount of luxury or smiling faces would make up for the horrible sacrifice she'd been forced to make.

CHAPTER 8

Kindra awoke sometime later. For a second, she forgot where she was, and she jolted up in bed, her eyes darting around the room until she remembered.

She was in Wendrith. In the castle. In her personal chambers. Kindra simultaneously relaxed and tensed at the recollection.

Judging by the low angel of the soft light filtering through the windows, she'd slept most of the afternoon away. At some point, they'd brought her chest of belongings in, putting it near the door. She started slightly at the intrusion, disturbed at how she'd not been woken by it, and hoped that people entering her rooms while she slept was not going to be a regular occurrence here.

Kindra slipped out from under the covers, still awed by how soft they were, and stretched. She wouldn't lie—that had been possibly the best nap she'd ever taken. She felt much better than she had earlier.

Her stomach rumbled, reminding her that while she may have bathed and slept, she hadn't eaten anything since that morning. She recalled Helena's invitation to join her for dinner. What time was it? She reached out and pulled on the cord that hung next to her bed, one of several throughout the room that allowed her to call for servants.

Just a couple of heartbeats later, the door swung open and Cerulle walked in. "How was your nap, my Lady?" she said by way of greeting.

"It was refreshing," Kindra replied. "I was wondering if dinner happened to be soon?"

Cerulle smiled, dipping her head in a nod. "Within the hour. Would you like to accept Princess Helena's invitation to dine with her and her wife?"

Kindra mulled it over for a moment longer. When her stomach grumbled again, she caved. "Yes. That would be nice."

"Wonderful. Then I shall send a runner to inform them that you will be attending. In the meantime, shall Sala come help you get dressed?"

Again, she started to bristle at the suggestion that she needed help with *everything*, but the thought of her refusing assistance and then being unable to dress herself or make herself look presentable made her cringe. She was not so prideful that she couldn't admit when she was in over her head, and in this castle, she very much was. This was not Harthwin, where her ratty tunics and threadbare leggings were enough. Even Sala and Cerulle were dressed elegantly, their uniforms—off-white, knee-length dresses—made of finer material than any family in Harthwin could afford.

Kindra nodded to Cerulle. "Yes, I'd appreciate that, thank you."

In a matter of seconds, the Windspinner disappeared from the room and Sala took her place. Kindra rose from her bed, and the two of them made their way into the dressing room.

Sala moved to one of the wardrobe chests, opening it and pulling out a pale gold gown. It was the same cut as the one Helena had been wearing— light, flowing fabric that came in at the waist and fell to the floor, with sheer, loose sleeves that just barely covered her shoulders. Kindra pulled her nightgown off and Sala stepped forward to help her into the gown.

It was surprisingly comfortable; light and breathable, even as Sala began to tighten the laces at the back. Kindra inspected the delicate beading across the waist as she did so, then lifted her head to observe herself in the mirror.

The pale gold brought out the more vibrant gold of her eyes, and the color of her freckled, tanned skin: a deeper golden brown than normal thanks to the summer sun. Her hair, a brown so dark it was nearly black, was a mass of curls falling across her shoulders and back.

But despite the unruliness of her hair, and the shadows under her eyes from weeks of poor sleep, Kindra thought she looked rather nice.

"You look beautiful, my Lady," Sala complimented.

"Thank you," Kindra replied, blushing slightly.

Sala beamed, and moved to twist some of Kindra's hair back, pinning it on either side with a bejeweled clip and leaving the rest of it down. She presented her with a pair of simple flats, and then led her from the dressing room back to the bathing room, where she sat Kindra down at the vanity.

The Healer grabbed one of the many jars of concoctions Kindra could not begin to identify, dabbing some oil on to her hands. She ran her slick fingers through Kindra's hair, smoothing the curls. Then she touched her fingertips to Kindra's face. There was a warm buzz across Kindra's skin, and Sala's eyes flashed gold as she smoothed away any blemishes and under-eye fatigue. Just the gentle touch of Sala's magic made her complexion flawless. Kindra couldn't help but hum appreciatively.

"All done," Sala said, and the two of them made their way out of the bathing room. In the bed chamber, Cerulle was waiting for them.

"I'll escort you to the princess's chambers," Cerulle informed her, "if you're ready."

Kindra took a steadying breath. Dinner with Helena and Emeline was nothing to be frightened of, she told herself. Just a meal with royalty, which was what she was now. Or at least, what she would be soon enough.

At her nod, Cerulle turned, and together, they made their way into the hallway.

Kindra became only slightly more oriented with her surroundings as they walked to Helena and Emeline's chambers. She gathered from glancing out the windows that she was on the third floor of the castle, and that, based on the view from the windows nearest her rooms, she was on the east side. This pulled a small smile from her; she enjoyed the thought that the first thing she'd feel every morning would be the touch of Cyrie, the goddess of the sun.

The hallways were alive with people; they passed several servants pushing carts of food, carrying extravagant clothing, or running messages. She noticed that many of them were Windspinners, gray and silver eyes gleaming in the evening light, their bodies lean and strong. It must be a defense strategy, then; place some of the most adept defensive Wielders in the position of maid or servant, and guarantee that there will always be security nearby.

Most of them didn't acknowledge Cerulle or Kindra at all, but a few nodded their heads in greeting to Cerulle. Fewer still registered Kindra's presence and made the connection about who she was. She did not particularly enjoy it when that happened, and it made her body stiff with discomfort.

"More will recognize you after tomorrow," Cerulle said, misreading why Kindra was so tense. "They will know to address you properly then."

"I would prefer it if they didn't notice me at all," Kindra murmured in response, and Cerulle's face, which was sharp and pointed, softened with understanding.

"You will get used to it. It's a shock for most, especially because many princesses of the last fifty years were not raised in nobility. But they all adjusted. Queen Cordilya came from a village similar to yours. And look at her now! She's the epitome of royalty."

Indeed, Queen Cordilya was, if what Kindra had heard about her was true. She was notoriously soft-spoken—the single known Oracle in Alverin was apparently a woman of few words.

Kindra was certainly not that.

They rounded a corner and came upon a small squadron of guards posted by a set of large, white doors.

"Lady Kindra, here to dine with Princess Helena and Princess Emeline," Cerulle announced.

The guards looked her over with a sense of scrutiny that made her want to squirm, then nodded and moved to let her in. Kindra turned to say farewell to Cerulle, but the Windspinner was already gone.

She was on her own.

So she squared her shoulders and stepped through the doors.

CHAPTER 9

Upon entering Helena and Emeline's chambers, Kindra realized immediately that her quarters didn't even come close to how grand the castle could be.

She was standing in a small foyer. On each wall was an archway that led to a different area of Helena's chambers. To her right she could see an entire library, complete with a fireplace and plush sofas, as well as a desk adorned with piles of papers and scrolls. On her left was a dining room, which was mysteriously empty. Directly before her was an arched doorway that led to what she could only assume was the main sitting room, and beyond that, the bed chamber. Soft chatter drifted from beyond that archway.

A servant greeted her, dipping down into a bow. Kindra cringed inwardly. How would she ever get used to that?

"Her Highness is just through there, my Lady," the servant said, gesturing to the center arch. Kindra nodded her thanks as she walked into the room.

The sitting room alone was as large as her entire bedchamber, complete with not one but four different sitting areas. Like Kindra's room, the one wall was entirely lined with windows that stretched all the way up to the ceiling. The sky was a swirl of orange and pink beyond the glass. The walls and floors were light as well, the furniture mostly cream, pale gold, or, oddly enough, a deep turquoise.

Despite the grandeur of it all, though, it felt lived in. There were blankets and throw pillows on every seat, stacks of books on the surfaces. To use Helena's own word, it felt cozy.

A squeal cut through Kindra's thoughts, and she turned to see Helena hurrying over from where she'd been sitting on a sofa near a white marble fireplace.

"I'm so glad you decided to come!" The princess grasped Kindra's hands, beaming. "You look lovely. Emeline, come here!"

A woman rose from the same sofa, her hair as black as night. It rippled like a sleek curtain as she stood, falling down to her waist and swaying with her hips as she walked. She was clad in a sapphire off-the-shoulder gown, the gauzy sleeves billowing out around her. As she got closer, Kindra could see the startling ice blue of her eyes, a sign of her water magic, appearing all the more brilliant against the warm brown of her skin.

"So, this is who's given Jasper such a hard time these past few weeks?" she drawled, her voice a low, rich harmony to Helena's bright melodic tone. Emeline gave a crescent-moon grin. "You'll fit in with us just fine, if what we've heard about the screaming matches is true."

Kindra blushed, embarrassed that this was her first impression. "It wasn't—"

Emeline threw her head back and laughed. Beside her, Helena's eyes danced. "Oh, don't bother. Heinrich already came and told us all about it this afternoon."

At the mention of the nervous Wavebreaker, Kindra grimaced. She hadn't appreciated the way he had looked at her like she was some sort of feral animal, always afraid she'd snap and burn down everything around her.

Helena, as if she had read her thoughts, waved a hand dismissively. "Heinrich's not so bad once you get to know him, Kindra. His overwhelming, constant level of concern for everything is almost charming, sometimes." She turned back to the sofa, placing her hand on Emeline's waist as she did so. "He's one of Jasper's best friends, and the head of his guard." The three of them made their way over to the sitting area, Emeline and Helena taking their places on the couch again, and Kindra sliding into a plush armchair.

"He's in charge of Jasper's protection?" Kindra found that hard to believe. A Wavebreaker, and a nervous one at that, responsible for the safety of a prince?

"I know what you're thinking—the anxious Wavebreaker might not be the best for the job," Helena said, and at Kindra's sheepish shrug, she laughed. "Believe me when I say he has *more* than earned that position. Jasper trusts nobody else with his safety more than Heinrich."

Kindra hummed, considering that maybe she'd gotten off on the wrong foot with the guardsman. After all, she could understand being fiercely protective of the people she cared about. "So does every member of your family have a personal squad of guards?" she asked.

"Our," Helena corrected softly. Kindra cocked her head slightly, brow furrowing. "Our family," the princess repeated, "You're part of it now."

Kindra tried to stifle her reaction. She really did. But her hands tightened on the armrests of the chair anyway, and her face twitched slightly as she tried to fight the flinch.

Emeline frowned. "What's the matter?"

Kindra shook her head quickly, choosing to focus her gaze on the fireplace. The fire flickering there was getting low. She could feel its wheezing gasps in her veins. She took a deep, fortifying breath, and as she exhaled, she brought the flames back to life. Helena let out a soft squeak of delight.

"It has been a long journey. Lots of changes," was all she said, turning back to them and offering a tight smile. Neither of them looked convinced. Desperate to change the subject, she asked, "So what's for dinner?"

The two ladies exchanged a glance, and then Helena replied, "Roast lamb and vegetables, seasoned potatoes, rolls, and some chocolate cake for dessert."

In response, Kindra's stomach growled rather loudly. Emeline barked a laugh, and to her relief, the tension eased.

"I will send a message for them to hurry up, then," Helena chuckled, and nodded at the servant posted by the doorway.

"How are you finding your chambers, Kindra?" Emeline inquired, grabbing a glass of wine from the end table and taking a sip.

"Big," Kindra said, then added, "and beautiful, of course. But they're very… different from what I had in Harthwin."

"They're yours until you decide otherwise," Helena informed her. "If you choose to move into Jasper's quarters, it'll be a suite just like this—"

"I think I'll be just fine in my chambers," she blurted, and mentally kicked herself for not watching her tongue.

The golden-haired princess only smirked though and moved over to a nearby bar cart to pour herself a drink. "Not liking my little brother too much, eh?"

"Hard to like somebody you hardly know," Kindra replied, turning her focus to the fire again.

"You'll get to know him. You'll have lots of time leading up to the wedding to do just that." Helena made her way back to the couch, sitting down and pressing close to her wife.

She seemed to have a habit of saying what she thought were reassuring things that were actually not reassuring at all.

Kindra didn't respond, and after a moment she felt a hand on her arm. When she looked over, she found Helena leaning forward, her soft gray eyes intense. "He is a kind person, I assure you," she said, entirely serious. "There is a reason I am close to him and not my other brothers."

Anxiety pooled in Kindra's stomach at the mention of the two older brothers. This was the second time in a day she'd been warned about them, and that didn't sit well with her. "Are they really so cruel?"

Emeline laughed dryly. "It *is* the Annalindis family, Kindra. There's a curse for a reason." Helena shot the Wavebreaker a sharp look. "What? I think it's best if she's warned before she has to deal with them."

"Is it that bad?" Kindra breathed, suddenly feeling panicked. "How did they treat you?"

"It's mostly mind games and not-so-subtle jabs, honestly. But after a few weeks of that, I just wanted to battle it out in a sparring match and be done with it. That is, of course, what they want. They *want* you to snap, so then everything they say about you—that you're a poor, stupid, classless girl from some sad little village—will be right." Emeline's blue eyes gleamed. "If even a fraction of what Heinrich said is true, then I *know* you're going to want to snap."

"So how did you handle it?"

"Went to the training ground every day, flung water around for a couple hours and got the anger out. It was mostly jealousy, anyway. Hel and I made quite the stir when we announced our intent to marry." Emeline gave Helena a fond look. "I'm a baker's daughter, not worth the dirt on her shoe—that's what some people said. But she never wavered in her decision. Neither of us did."

Kindra felt a small tug of longing in her chest at the soft glow that fell over both of them when they looked at each other. In another world, perhaps she would have found something like that: a genuine connection and love. Doubtful, seeing as she most likely would've never left Harthwin, and there hadn't been anyone there who'd ever thought of her that way. But a part of her had always wondered if she'd ever meet somebody who would find her power beautiful rather than terrifying. Somebody who would embrace her love of freedom instead of trying to restrain her.

A useless hope to have now.

She distracted herself from that depressing string of thoughts by focusing on what Emeline had said. "You really have access to a training ground? Every day?" She didn't bother to tamp down the eagerness in her voice.

"Oh, yes. They never denied me when I asked, once the engagement was official. So they certainly won't say no to you."

"I told you," Helena chastised lightly. "Did you not believe me?"

"It just seemed too good to be true," Kindra admitted, shrugging apologetically. "I'm sorry, I—I just don't know what my life is going to be now. How it will look anymore. I don't know how to… to *do* any of this." She gestured helplessly at herself, the room around them, the grandeur of it all.

"Oh Kindra," Helena said, "I have known nothing *but* this for my whole life, and some days, I hardly have a clue."

Dinner arrived a short time later and was unsurprisingly the best food Kindra had ever had. She struggled to hold back several sighs of delight, trading them for enthusiastic compliments. She figured that was the classier reaction. But she was quickly realizing that she didn't need to put on a front for Helena and Emeline. The two women were unfiltered and authentic, only putting on what Emeline referred to as their "royal masks" when servants came in and out with more food and drink. When it was just the three of them in the dining room though, it felt far less like a dinner with royalty and much more like a meal with friends. Kindra found herself loosening up, answering questions about her upbringing without hostility or wariness, and *laughing*, truly laughing for the first time in weeks.

"So, how exactly did you two meet?" Kindra asked as they waited for dessert.

"My father is the owner of a bakery in the middle district of Wendrith. We're from Dewport, down near Breyenth, originally, and moved here when I was five for a better life," Emeline began, "We had a rough first few years here, but now, it's one of the more popular bakeries in the city—"

"And by that, she means the *most* popular," Helena interjected with a grin. "That's how we met. He made my birthday cake when I turned thirteen and came to personally deliver it himself. And he just happened to bring his daughter with him."

"Hel invited me to attend her extravagant birthday ball. Lent me a dress and everything for the occasion. I thought she was just doing something nice to thank my father for the cake or to get points with her high-class friends for being charitable."

"But the truth was I was lonely. I didn't have any close friends, just other girls my age to pass the time with, but they were all either mean, or worse—boring." Helena frowned, then smiled once more and looked at her wife fondly. "But Emeline was neither of those things."

"She had no idea what I was, actually," Emeline quipped. "I hardly said a word to her before she extended the invitation, I was so scared. I don't think I said more than a few sentences the entire night either."

"That's true—except when Anya Mireldis made that comment to me—"

"Oh, gods, yes, I almost forgot! Hard to keep track of all the times that bitch and I've gone head-to-head." Emeline rolled her eyes. "She came up to you, and said something shitty about your dress, right? I can't even remember now."

"Honestly, neither do I," Helena admitted, laughing. "I'm sure it was something that wouldn't even faze me now, but at thirteen, if someone so much as looked at me wrong, I was a mess."

Kindra smiled, recalling how she'd been at that age—so quick to ignite and melt down. *You're still like that*, a voice in her head whispered, and she quickly silenced it.

"Anyway," the princess continued, "Emeline had been standing next to me the whole night, utterly silent. But when Anya made her little jab, she looked her up and down, and simply said, *Interesting*." She dissolved into a fit of giggles. "Anya had no idea what to say to that, though to be fair, I did drag us away before she could try and assault Em with thorns."

Kindra found herself laughing, too. She could see it in her head: a young Emeline looking some Alverin noble in the face and demolishing their confidence with one simple, effective word.

"After that night, I found myself traveling into the city to go to her family's bakery and see her. And coming up with more excuses to order their delicious cakes and pastries. Emeline became a regular fixture in my life seemingly overnight. She was my breath of fresh air, my reprieve from everything else around here." Helena reached over and grabbed Emeline's hand. "She still is."

Something in Kindra's chest pulled again at that. A feeling she didn't want to put a name to.

"When we were sixteen, our friendship turned into something more. Neither of us can really pinpoint the exact moment things changed. We just grew from one type of love into another. And we kept it quiet, for the first few months—Jasper didn't even know. But he figured it out eventually."

"How'd he react?" Kindra asked, surprisingly curious.

"Honestly? I think he was jealous. He'd never really looked forward to the arranged marriage in his future. He's always been a romantic at heart—something his status was never really compatible with." Helena gave Kindra a sympathetic look. "For what it's worth."

It isn't worth a damn thing, Kindra thought to herself. "When did you get married?"

"When we were twenty, I went before my parents and asked for their blessing. They'd known about our relationship for a few years at that point—and knew it was serious, too, despite their misgivings about Emeline's class. If I were a son instead of a daughter, they never would have allowed it to continue that long—the marriage process for men in this family is much more complicated, as you know. But any child I might bear—if the baby could even survive the pregnancy or birth—would be undoubtedly magic-less, just like me. So for the past century, the daughters of the royal family have essentially been given free rein to marry whomever they please. Father wasn't super happy about it, of course, because I went and picked a *water-wielding commoner*, but what point would there be in saying no?" She laughed, but nothing felt funny. "If it won't aid in breaking the curse and bringing him more power, he doesn't really give a shit."

A heavy silence fell over them for a few seconds, shattered by Emeline. "We were married pretty quickly after that. And then I got to sit back and watch all the nobility that had practically spat on me for years—especially once our engagement was announced—realize they no longer outranked me." A wicked smile bloomed across her lips. "Now *that* was satisfying."

Kindra opened her mouth to reply but was interrupted by dessert being brought in: thick slices of chocolate cake, as promised. She had thought she'd barely have any room left to eat it, having cleaned her plate earlier, but a newfound hunger sprang to life as it was set in front of her.

For a few minutes, the conversation was paused as they each devoured their cake. Kindra thought it couldn't have gotten any better than the dinner, but she was wrong. She looked up from her sweet, cakey bliss and noticed Emeline giving her a small smile. Then the pieces clicked into place.

"Is this…?"

Emeline nodded. "Yep. Papa brings an assortment of treats to the castle at least once every couple weeks. Has for the last decade."

"I bet that pays well," Kindra commented.

"Oh, it did, before he demanded they stop paying him." At Kindra's surprise, Emeline clarified: "The bakery is doing so well now he doesn't need it. He'd rather they'd spend it on people who need it more. And it's kind of just an excuse to see me, at this point."

Kindra's heart twinged. A wave of longing for her mother washed over her, and she swallowed it down with another bite of cake. "Do you not get to see him often?" she asked.

Emeline shrugged. "I try, but it's not so easy to just go into the city, anymore. Have to bring my guards with me, which kind of ruins the intimacy of visiting family, even if they just stay posted outside." She gave Kindra a knowing look. "I can't imagine that level of hovering will go over well with you."

"It won't," she admitted, and was unashamed to say so. "I'm very used to being alone and in full control of my whereabouts."

"I was too," Emeline said, then corrected: "Well, am. I still find my ways, of course. I'd go crazy if I didn't."

"I hope you'll be willing to share some of those secrets, then," Kindra laughed, but deep down she knew she'd need any help she could get.

"Oh, don't you worry," Emeline replied with a wink, "I'll let you in on all my tricks."

With their meal finished, the table was cleared, and drinks refilled one last time. Kindra sipped slowly on a glass of sweet-smelling wine; she'd never had much of an opportunity to drink in Harthwin, so she thought it would be smart to tread carefully. It was getting late, too; much later than she'd planned to stay. *Time flies when you're having fun, I suppose,* she thought, and was surprised to find the sentiment didn't have as much bitterness around it as she expected. Perhaps it was the wine.

But it wasn't the wine that was making her so tired. Even after her nap, she still felt heavy with exhaustion, having not yet slept off the weeks of traveling. Despite Helena and Emeline's best efforts to keep the conversation lively, Kindra's eyelids began to droop, and her responses to their questions and stories became less and less enthusiastic.

Helena caught on quickly. "Well, I think it's time to call it a night, don't you agree, Em?" she said, clapping her hands and standing. "Kindra needs her rest for tomorrow."

Kindra stood, stifling a yawn as she did so. The princess came around the table and embraced her warmly. "I'm so glad you decided to dine with us tonight. The three of us will be thick as thieves in no time, I can tell!" Her smile was a beam of glowing light, and Kindra couldn't help but bask in it.

Emeline gave her a hug and a conspiratorial grin. "I'll keep you sane here," she vowed. Kindra was too tired to properly express how grateful she was for that offer.

She made her way into the foyer as though she were in a daze. For the first time since she'd left Harthwin, she felt hope. Hope that maybe, even though she'd be stuck in an arranged marriage, she'd at least have friends to pass the time with.

At least she wouldn't be so alone.

The thought of friendship—something she hadn't had since she was a child—made her smile. She was still smiling as she bid Helena and Emeline good night, and made her way out of their chambers, stepping into the dimly lit castle hallway, where she expected a guard would be waiting to escort her to her room.

Only there was no guard.

Instead, Kindra stepped into the hallway and ran straight into Jasper.

CHAPTER 10

"What are you doing here?" The words flew out of Kindra's mouth before she could stop them.

Jasper only smirked, leaning casually against the wall, hands in his pockets. He was dressed in casual finery: brown pants with a loose white shirt, the top few buttons left undone.

Kindra definitely did not take note of that.

His eyes traveled over her slowly, and she fought against the urge to recoil from his stare.

"I'm here to walk you back to your quarters," he finally said.

"Where's Cerulle?" she demanded.

"Busy."

"Bullshit."

He chuckled. "Fine. I told her to let me be your escort."

"Why."

His eyebrows raised at her tone. "If I didn't know any better, I'd say you were getting used to your new royal authority rather quickly." His gray eyes danced in the low light provided by the fire lamps along the walls.

Kindra's cheeks heated, and she finally lurched into motion, skirting around him. "I'm not getting used to anything."

"Of course not," Jasper replied, easily falling into step beside her. Kindra huffed angrily, and he chuckled again. "You've always been like this."

"Been like what?" She tried to pick up her pace, but she realized as they turned a corner that she had no idea how to get back to her rooms, a problem made worse now that it was night and the halls were darker, softly lit only by the sconces.

"Powerful," he stated simply. Before Kindra had time to even register that he'd complimented her, he added, "And lost, it seems. Allow me." Shooting her a victorious smirk, he began to guide them back to her rooms.

"Did you enjoy your evening with Helena and Emeline?" he asked as they walked, dipping his head to the guards patrolling the corridors. A few remained near them: probably members of Jasper's personal guard.

"Yes, I did." Kindra was still pleasantly surprised by the turn her evening had taken. "They're very kind."

"I told you you'd find them to your liking."

She gritted her teeth.

"I'm sorry," Jasper apologized quickly, sensing her irritation, "I forgot you don't like that."

"Maybe start remembering," she snapped, and several guards' heads swiveled towards them. "And tell your guards to relax while you're at it. I'm not a feral animal, for gods' sake." A bit of hurt crept into her voice, and her face flushed again.

To her surprise, Jasper did just that, gesturing for them to be given some space. "I'm sorry," he repeated. "I really seem to have a knack for upsetting you, don't I?"

Kindra only grunted in response, too busy getting control over her emotions to speak.

Gently, he placed a hand on her elbow, bringing them to a halt. "I didn't know that you felt like you were being treated as though you're some untamed beast, Kindra." His eyes were wide and earnest. He was being honest. "Tell me, what can I do?"

"There is nothing you can do." She averted her gaze to the floor, trying to turn away and continue walking, but he kept his hold on her, forcing her to remain still.

"There must be." His voice was soft. Desperate, even.

She shrugged herself free of his grip. "I don't know if there is, Jasper. I've been looked at like that my whole life."

"You deserve—"

"Better? Yeah, I've gathered that you feel that way." Kindra started to walk again, and he had no choice but to walk with her.

"I feel that way because it's true. Your magic is beautiful. Something to be marveled, not feared."

"My magic destroys." She was being contrary at this point, she knew that. She would have normally been the first to acknowledge the beauty of her fire. It made her skin itch, the way she was talking. This whole conversation made her skin itch. It was too intimate, too personal. She sped her pace up, praying at some point the doors to her chambers would appear and she could hide herself behind them.

"Your magic protects," Jasper countered, matching her stride for stride. And gods, she hated how nice it felt, to hear somebody else say those words and mean them. She'd spent years repeating them to herself after skirmishes and ambushes, when she'd stumble home with the scent of charred flesh stinging in her nose.

She needed this conversation to be over.

"How far are we from my room?" She tried to keep her voice light and casual.

"Just around the corner. Tired?"

Kindra nodded, relieved that she'd maneuvered them into safer territory. "I still haven't recovered from the travel here. I think I'll be fine after a good night's sleep, though." Unintentionally, she yawned.

"I'm sure you will. You'll need your energy for tomorrow. You'll be formally introduced to my family and the court."

She sucked in a breath. "I know."

"Are you scared?"

"No." She spoke too quickly, and though she knew Jasper caught onto the lie immediately, he didn't call her out on it.

"I'm scared," he confessed softly.

She snorted. "Why?" They made a turn and she saw the doors to her chambers ahead of them. *Thank the gods.* "I can handle it."

They reached her doors, and the two guards posted outside moved to open them.

"Oh, I don't doubt that," Jasper said as they came to a halt. His voice lowered to a near whisper, too quiet for the guards to hear. "I'm afraid they won't know how to handle *you*, Kindra. And my family isn't exactly rational when faced with something they don't know how to control."

Before she could reply, he reached for her hand and brought it to his lips, kissing it lightly. Kindra went still as a statue at the brush of his mouth against her skin.

"Sleep well," he murmured as he pulled away, dropping her hand. "I'll see you tomorrow."

He was gone before she could muster up a reply, still processing the feel of his lips.

Still thinking about the weight of his words, and the warning behind them.

CHAPTER II

Kindra awoke the next morning to the rising sun, its soft morning rays caressing her face and gently pulling her from sleep. She started to jolt upright, momentarily forgetting where she was again, but the surge of panic vanished as quickly as it had come. Soon she would no longer be jarred by her new surroundings. She couldn't decide exactly how that made her feel.

She got out of bed slowly, still marveling at the intricate beauty of her rooms. The ceiling, which she had failed to notice yesterday but now took in, was breathtaking, decorated with golden, swirling suns. In the center, a glowing portrait of Cyrie was painted; her eyes closed and hands splayed as though she were soaking up the daylight just as Kindra so often did. It was, she realized, the first depiction of the goddess that she'd seen outside of a book. The fire deities hadn't been spoken of often in Harthwin; there had been no temples or shrines dedicated to them in the tiny village.

Her thoughts were disrupted by Cerulle and Sala entering her chambers, each rolling a rack filled with an array of clothing. Kindra spotted trousers, blouses, simple day dresses and extravagant gowns amongst the mounds of fabric. *How did they get my measurements?* She thought, and realized with pang of alarm that they very well might have looked through her chest to measure the clothing that was in there. Not a perfect method, but one that would do in a pinch when a fast turnaround was needed.

"Good morning Lady Kindra," Sala greeted her. "I'm glad to see you are awake. We have much to do this morning before your presentation to the king and queen."

Right. Kindra stilled for just a second before swallowing her anxiety down. Today was not a day to be cowed by anything.

"So, what's first?" she asked, working to keep her voice steady, "A bath?"

Sala shook her head, smiling. "Not yet, my lady. First is breakfast." As if they'd been waiting for those magic words, the doors opened again and another set of servants wheeled in a cart laden with food: round, fluffy biscuits, steaming sausages, bowls of fruit and oatmeal, pitchers of milk and juice. Kindra's mouth watered.

"Is this... is this all for me?" *How could one person eat this much?*

"No, you're going to have to share, unfortunately."

At the sound of Jasper's voice, Kindra twisted her fists into the sheets. She turned to see him stroll casually into her chambers as if they were his. Donned in a similar outfit to what he wore last night, he was the picture of casual elegance.

He was also the last person she wanted to see right now.

"What do you want?" she snapped.

He plopped down in a chair at the dining table as the servants moved the food from the cart to the table, along with two table settings. She noted they were on opposite sides of the table, a fact she was grateful for. "Why, what I want is to have a lovely breakfast with my darling bride-to-be." His eyes traveled over her, and his mouth quirked up in a wicked smirk. "Who looks very good in red, I must say."

"Don't," she warned, and he shrugged, turning to his attention to the food. She itched, as if she could physically feel the remnants of his gaze on her exposed skin, and she was suddenly very aware of the tiny excuse for a nightgown she was wearing: the same red one she'd first changed into when she'd arrived at the castle.

"Can I—can I have a robe, please?" she asked Cerulle quietly as she moved by with yet *another* heap of clothing.

"Of course, my Lady." The Windspinner vanished into the bathing room and returned within seconds holding a long, off-white, silk robe. Kindra took it from her with a nod of thanks and threw it on. Only when she'd tied it shut securely did she stand up and move to join Jasper at the table.

She did not speak a word to him as she spooned food onto her plate and filled her glass with juice. It was orange in color, and when she sipped it, its tangy flavor filled her mouth. She made a small noise of delight.

"It's juice from the orange fruit," Jasper informed her, almost as if he knew that she wouldn't ask even though she was curious. "We ship them up from Dewport. Not quite the right climate to grow the fruit here."

"Mmm," was all Kindra said in response, drinking again.

"I wanted to go over the... logistics, I suppose, of today, actually," Jasper said around a mouthful of sausage. Kindra frowned.

"So," he continued, swallowing, "at noon, we are to make our first appearance as *Alverin's new hope.*" He rolled his eyes, and she fought to keep her lips from twitching up into a smile.

"Is that what they're calling us?" she asked, spreading some jam onto a biscuit. She popped it into her mouth, and it seemed to melt on her tongue.

"Oh, for a few years, yes. And then we'll have an heir, that will be, like every other heir my family produces, *completely magic-less.*" She stiffened and shot him a glare, and he grinned. "Are you so surprised I remembered what you said to me all those weeks ago?"

"I'm surprised you have room in that giant head of yours for anyone's sentiments other than your own," she fired back. Somewhere across the room, somebody sucked in a nervous breath, and she was reminded that they were not alone.

Jasper's eyes danced, like steel in the sun. "Oh, Kindra," he practically purred, and she elected to ignore the way the words zipped down her spine, "I will always have room for the wonderful things you say in my *giant head.*"

She opened her mouth to retort once more, but he barreled on, "Gregory asked if you needed a, uh..." He trailed off, wincing, as if he could already tell what he was about to say wouldn't go over well.

"Who is Gregory and what does he think I need," she demanded more than asked.

Jasper huffed out a laugh. "You—" He coughed, cleared his throat. "Never mind. Gregory is the etiquette master. He thought you may need etiquette lessons." He took a bite of oatmeal.

Kindra felt heat begin to simmer just underneath her skin.

"I told him no, of course," he continued. "You have no problem holding your head high and acting like you're better than everyone around you. No lessons necessary on that, though it may be good to have somebody show you how to curtsy."

She flinched, and he ate another spoonful of oatmeal. "I don't think that way," she bit out.

He leaned back in his chair, studying her from across the table. "Don't you, though?" His voice had taken on that soft, gentle tone she'd grown to hate. A servant bustling out of her bathing room stopped and took in the tense scene with wide eyes.

She dropped a slab of butter into her oatmeal, refusing to answer.

"Your silence speaks louder than any words, Kindra."

"Then enlighten me, O Wise and All-Knowing Prince," she sneered, looking up from her meal to shoot him a hateful glare. She knew her eyes were burning bright right now; she could tell by the small flash of alarm that crossed his face. "Tell me what my silence says."

Jasper held her gaze for a moment, his own eyes blazing with frustration, then glanced over to where the servant—now joined by another—was still standing, as if frozen in place. Watching. Listening. He stood, placing his napkin on the table. "Well, I bid you good morning, Kindra. I think it may be best to have Cerulle and Sala give you today's schedule instead, seeing as we can't ever seem to have a productive conversation." There was a bite of anger in his tone.

"If our conversations are unproductive, the blame lies on your shoulders," Kindra snapped, standing as well—she was no longer hungry. No, she felt sick, really. Sick at the thought that this was to be her life now, forever tied to this arrogant, presumptuous snot of a man.

She could tell he wanted to say more, could sense that he was barely holding himself back. But people were watching them, and she didn't have any doubt that they reported to somebody—a spymaster, maybe, or the king himself.

"I will see you outside the throne room doors at ten 'til noon," was all he said before excusing himself and storming from her chambers.

Only when he was gone did she relax, leaning against the table. For a moment, she was filled with deep, aching sadness, but she channeled that quickly into rage, the feeling she was much more familiar with. Her mouth filled with the smoking taste of flames.

She wished she could expel it in a way that wouldn't draw so much attention. But if she were to do so right now, when she was already the subject of so many nervous stares, she worried that could get her in trouble. If not now, then in the future.

If she showed herself to be even a hint of the untamed animal they clearly thought her to be, they may not let her wield at all. At least, not the way she wanted—needed—to.

And that would be a fate worse than death.

Kindra took several deep breaths, her eyes closed. Once she finally felt settled, she stood to her full height and called for Sala.

"Yes, my Lady?" The gentle Healer's voice was tight with nerves.

"I'm through with breakfast, Sala." She gave her best attempt at a reassuring smile. "It was delicious, thank you. I'd like to begin getting ready for this afternoon, please."

For a second, the two young women simply stared at each other. Sala's eyes bore into hers, as though she were searching for the answer to a question she dared not to ask.

"Of course," she said, breaking eye contact with a small smile. "This way."

And she led Kindra into the bathing room.

Kindra hardly recognized herself in the mirror.

Over the past two hours, she'd been transformed. First, a tailor came and officially took her measurements, then hurried off to make last minute alterations to whatever clothes needed them. That had been an experience. The woman had measured her fingers. Her *fingers*! For gloves and rings, she'd said. Kindra had barely restrained from laughing at the absurdity.

Then, she'd been scrubbed raw and slathered with various sweet-smelling creams. Her hair had been washed and styled to sit upon her head in a pile of curls, a few meticulously chosen strays left dangling to frame her face. Her nails had been trimmed. Her eyebrows had been plucked—though not much, due to Kindra's protests—and her skin had been dusted with a glimmering powder that made her appear as though she were sparkling when the light hit her just right. Her eyes had been lined with kohl, her cheeks turned a dusty pink by rouge, and her lips painted dark red.

And then there was the gown.

It matched the color of her lips—a rich, deep red, accented by thin, delicate golden swirls. The bodice clung to her like a glove, thanks to the corset, and the skirt fell to the floor in a pool of soft chiffon. It had no sleeves, leaving her neck and shoulders entirely bare.

She had never before felt like she did not belong in her own skin, but she felt that way now.

"Just some final touches left," Cerulle informed her as she fastened a glittering necklace around her neck. Kindra peered at it. *Are those rubies?* Sala slipped bracelets of a similar style onto her wrists, then fastened two of the red gems to her ears.

Finally, the two women stepped back, finished. They smiled, clearly pleased with themselves.

"How do you feel, my Lady?" Sala inquired.

Like I'm in a body that is not mine, she wanted to say. *Like a stranger.*

"Different," was all she said instead, and she hoped she made it sound like a positive thing.

She didn't know what she hated more: the way her shoes pinched at her toes, the way the corset boning dug into her sides, or the way Jasper looked at her when she arrived outside the throne room at ten before noon.

Gone was the gleam of annoyance and disdain from their exchange at breakfast.

No, she could only find awe in his gaze, now. Awe and… something else. Something nobody had ever looked at her with before.

She decided right then that she hated that most of all, that no amount of painful squeezing and pinching from her attire would come close to the way that look made her feel.

Like she was being stripped bare.

Jasper dipped his head as she approached him, Cerulle and Sala at her side. They had both changed as well, trading out their usual dresses for sleek, black, long sleeve tunics and leggings. Their tunics were embroidered with golden thread in a similar fashion to her gown.

Jasper was bedecked in a fine jacket the same colors as her gown: deep red with threaded gold detailing. His black pants were tucked into polished knee-high boots. His hair was brushed back, though a stray curly lock still flopped across his forehead. Atop his head sat a small golden crown of gilded flame.

He looked every bit the prince he was, so used to wearing such finery it may as well have been a second skin. Kindra felt like a child playing dress-up.

"Kindra, you look..." For a moment, he appeared lost for words, his eyes still surveying her. He recovered quickly, though, finishing his thought, "You look beautiful."

She nodded her thanks, and then, for the sake of getting through this as painlessly as possible, she said, "You look very nice."

He smiled, relieved. "Thank you."

They stood in silence, the tension from this morning still between them.

Kindra looked around the hall. It was a huge foyer with tall, arching ceilings, a space meant to accommodate many people. But apart from the guards posted at regular intervals, it was empty.

"Where is everyone?" she asked, unable to fight her curiosity—and trepidation.

"Inside," Jasper replied, gesturing to the grand set of doors before her. "I'm sure you noticed yesterday that you didn't see any nobility in the halls. That's because they were forbidden to set foot on the third floor, where your rooms are. They are not to see you a second before my parents do."

Kindra hadn't noticed the lack of nobility, actually, but didn't say so. "The servants saw me," she countered, "and I'm sure the nobility gathered at the windows to watch me arrive, if this is such a big deal."

"You would be shocked to learn what rules these people are not willing to break." Jasper's cryptic reply was soft, meant for her ears only. "And what rules they find themselves unable to care about at all."

A chill fell over her, so strong even her fire could not push back its bite. Once again, his warning from the night before rang through her mind.

At that moment, the doors began to open, pulled inward by hands Kindra could not see. She could hear the excited titter of the people inside falling away to silence as they eagerly waited to see their new princess.

Fresh panic surged through her, and she struggled to get a solid breath down.

"Jasper," she whispered, fear making her forget their fight from this morning, forget all the fights they'd had over the past few weeks. She only wanted comfort in this moment, reassurance that she was not in this alone, that he was, like he said last night, scared right alongside her. "I said I wasn't scared last night. I'm scared now."

Jasper took her arm, gently wrapping it around his. As the doors opened wide enough to make the two of them visible, he looked down at her, with eyes as terrified has her own.

He didn't say anything to assuage her fears. He probably couldn't come up with anything to soothe himself, much less her.

Instead, he took a deep, trembling breath, and Kindra mirrored him. Then, he gave her a grim smile and softly tugged her into motion.

And into the throne room they went.

CHAPTER 12

The throne room was as dark as the Annalindis's family history.

It was such a stark contrast to the rest of the castle that Kindra almost did a double take upon entering, her terror quelled momentarily by shock. It, unlike every other part of the castle she'd seen, actually matched the exterior: black walls and floors with gold accents. And Scaldor—Scaldor was *everywhere*. The god and his fire were in the mural on the ceiling that domed so high above her head, on the columns throughout the massive space, even the stained-glass windows, which lined every wall except for the one with the entrance.

Kindra thought it seemed excessive, but then again, he did give them their power. The least they could have done, she considered, was decorate a castle with his face. Still, she found it painful to look at, given the circumstances, and she wasn't even cursed.

They walked down a long red carpet that led to the steps before the throne. Her grip on Jasper's arm tightened with every step they took. Her heart was hammering so hard she thought it might burst from her chest. Her magic was no better, coiling in her veins like a serpent gearing up to strike. *Calm,* she told herself, *you have to stay calm.*

All around her, members of the court gathered, peering over shoulders and around golden columns to get the best view. It made her skin crawl, and she focused on staring straight ahead, refusing to be overwhelmed by the immense crowd staring at her, or by the bits and pieces of whispers she could make out.

Staring ahead, however, was almost worse.

King Leofric Annalindis did not have Jasper's soft gaze or Helena's glow. In fact, Kindra found herself wondering how either of them could be related to the harsh, domineering man before her at all. His hair, receding at the temples, was blonde, though it was riddled with streaks of gray. His face was sharp and hard, but *there*—that was Jasper's nose, she was sure of it—though the king's jaw was wider, his brow more defined.

The throne he sat upon was cut from the same black stone as the room's wall and floors, and was decorated with golden flames in a way that suggested it was engulfed by them. Kindra wondered how infuriating it felt to sit in a seat representative of such magical power and have none of it.

But King Leofric did not need magic to be powerful; she understood that very quickly. She could see it on his face as they grew closer, the sharpness and danger that lurked there.

Beside him sat Queen Cordilya. That, Kindra could tell, was who Jasper and Helena got most of their looks from. She was beautiful, her long light brown hair falling over her shoulders. Her skin, though beginning to wrinkle and show signs of her age, was aglow.

But it was her eyes that struck Kindra. They were gray, like Helena's and Jasper's, but they were utterly empty.

The queen was Alverin's sole Oracle, able to receive prophetic visions and messages. A powerful and highly coveted type of Wielder. In a position so close to the king... Kindra took in her vacant stare and wondered if perhaps King Leofric had abused that privilege a little too much.

They reached the foot of the stairs. Jasper took his arm from her and bowed deeply. Kindra followed.

"Your Majesties," a voice announced—Heinrich, who must have entered behind them with Cerulle and Sala, "His Highness Prince Jasper Annalindis, and his betrothed, Lady Kindra Bedelyn."

A moment passed. They remained in their bows. Then, "You may rise."

If a silent King Leofric was frightening, his voice made him downright terrifying. It was utterly devoid of any warmth or kindness, so different from Jasper's smooth timbre or Helena's bubbly tone. It was so *cold*.

They stood, and Kindra pressed her palms into the skirts of her gown, hoping it would absorb some of the sweat. The whole room was utterly silent, as if everyone was holding their breath.

The king's gaze settled on her. She resisted the urge to squirm or look away.

"You are a Firefury, yes?" he asked.

She nodded. "Yes, Your Majesty."

"They say you are quite good for somebody with no formal training."

Kindra heard the insult behind those words. She prayed there was no bitterness in her voice as she replied, "Thank you, Your Majesty. I did the best I could."

"Well, we are all eager to see what your *best* is." The king smiled at her, but it was not kind. It looked more like he was baring his teeth.

There was a sharp intake of breath beside her. *Jasper.*

"Father, Mother, how have you been in my time away?" he started, and she did not miss the slight waiver in his voice nor, she was sure, did the king. "I have missed you dearly and cannot wait to regale you with stories from my travels. We saw so much—"

"You can regale us later, Jasper," King Leofric dismissed him with a wave of his hand and she saw Jasper barely halt his flinch. Somewhere in the room, somebody failed to disguise their snicker.

Kindra began to feel like something was very wrong. She risked a look around the room. The crowd was still huddled behind the columns; it was as though they refused to cross the threshold into the main space.

Among them, closest to the throne, were Antone and Sebastian, who clearly took after their father in looks. Beside them stood their wives— Celeste and Myala, Kindra recalled—both images of beauty and grace in their own right. And just next to them were Helena and Emeline. Kindra met both of their stares. Dread filled her heart when she saw fear in both of their gazes. *What's happening?* She tried to silently communicate. *Help me.*

Next to her, Jasper tried again, this time addressing his older brothers. But they did not deign to give him a response, as stone-faced as their father. Perhaps in a different situation, Kindra would have felt bad for him, embarrassed even, but she was too busy subtly assessing what was happening to feel anything for him at all.

Just then, Emeline's hand moved. The movement was so small that Kindra almost didn't catch it. But her index finger twitched ever so slightly, pointing to the guards. Kindra snuck a glance, and immediately went rigid. Their movements were so subtle that she would have missed it otherwise: the slight widening of their stance, their hands sliding higher inch by inch. These were Wielders, and they were preparing to do *something*.

What the fuck is going on? She readied her magic, preparing as best she could without drawing too much attention to herself.

"Enough of this," King Leofric snapped suddenly, cutting off Jasper mid-sentence. "I grow weary of your babbling, son." He waved a hand. "Go on, show them what they want to see."

Kindra felt the Earthwardens' vines before she saw them.

"What do you me—" Jasper started, only to cut into a scream as a wall of flame sprung up in front of him, swallowing the vines before they could touch the prince.

Cries of alarm and amazement rippled through the room as Kindra encircled her and Jasper with a ring of fire. Her flames stretched high above them, nearly singeing the ceiling. While Jasper sputtered in shock beside her, she paced in a circle, hands burning, waiting for the next strike.

The vines that surged towards them slammed against her fire and fell away burning. Even as the blows came more steadily, she held fast, hardly wavering. All the while, her mind whirled with a million different explanations for this attack, and too few ideas for what to do about it.

"What is this?" Jasper shouted over the crackling blaze. Sweat beaded his brow, and his eyes were wide with panic. It was not particularly reassuring that he had no idea what was going on. "Father, what are you doing?"

After another moment, Kindra heard the heavy clapping of hands—the king, signaling the attack had come to an end. She lowered the flames slowly, and once she saw that the guards were relaxed, no longer wielding vines at her face, she extinguished them entirely. Her hands, though, remained encased in fire, ready to set the whole room aflame at a moment's notice if necessary.

King Leofric was standing, continuing his lazy applause. The rest of the room followed suit, oohing and aahing as if they'd witnessed some amazing entertainment and not an assault on a member of the royal family and his future wife. Helena and Emeline, she noticed, did not join the others. They were clutching each other's hands tightly. Helena was on the verge of tears. Emeline looked downright furious.

"Well, look at that," the king drawled, walking down the steps towards them. Still, he clapped, a nasty grin on his face. "Perhaps they weren't lying about you after all."

Kindra remained silent. She was afraid if she began to speak, she would either scream or cry or both.

"When they told me they'd found a Firefury of worthy skill, I didn't believe them, I must confess," he continued, "You see, my idea of *worthy* is different from most people's. I am, after all, an Annalindis. And we *are* Scaldor-blessed."

Were, she thought as she tried to relax, snuffing out the fire in her hands. She forced herself to stand tall, to look him in the eye. *I am not afraid of you.* She tried to make herself believe it.

King Leofric came to a halt right in front of her. She could see each hair on his head, the dangerous glint of his dark eyes. Her insides twinged. "There's a reason no Firefury has married into the Annalindis family in decades. We hadn't found one *worthy enough.* But you?" His smile deepened, twisting into something ugly. "You might actually come close, girl." He looked at his son, who was standing open-mouthed. "Take good care of her."

Then he moved away, back up to his throne, where his wife still sat. Eyes still vacant. Expression still empty. As if she hadn't noticed anything out of the ordinary happening at all. The king turned and addressed the room. "You have seen for yourself the power of Alverin's new hope. May you spread it to all that fire once again burns in these halls, and it is strong and bright." With that, he sat down, and the room exploded into chatter and activity. Many surged towards Kindra and Jasper, but Helena and Emeline reached them first. Emeline quickly looped her arm through Kindra's, the shock of her water-cooled skin a welcome reprieve against the hot magic still roiling under Kindra's. Helena did the same with Jasper, herding her stunned brother towards the door.

"Let's go," she said softly, and together she and her wife steered the trembling couple out of the throne room, leaving behind a sneering king, nosy courtiers, and a singed, still-smoking circle in the carpet.

CHAPTER 13

The four of them made their way rapidly to the third floor, desperate to get away from prying eyes and ears. Kindra's chambers, it turned out, were the closest, and they hurried inside. "Make yourself scarce," Helena had all but snapped at Cerulle and Sala before shutting the door in their faces.

"What. The. *Fuck*," Jasper blurted as soon as the doors were both closed and locked. He whirled around and glared accusingly at his sister. "Did you know he was going to do that?"

Helena flinched, then glared back. "No. No, Jasper, of course I didn't. We knew he was going to do something, he always does, but—"

"Wait," Kindra interrupted, "what do you mean, you knew he was going to do something?"

The princess opened, then closed her mouth, clearly at a loss for words. It was Emeline who spoke instead. "It's called Novon's Trial."

"I'm sorry, what is that?"

"Novon Annalindis was the first King of Alverin," Helena answered, finding her voice. "When he was searching for a woman to make his queen, he devised a competition of sorts. Women from around the kingdom came to present their gifts, wielding or not, for consideration. It lasted for weeks. Every day, dozens of women came, each hoping that their few minutes before him would be enough to convince him to propose marriage."

"Queen Scalya came on the second day of the fifth week," the princess continued. "King Novon already knew of her. He'd fought with her in battle and had seen her power on full display. They say that King Novon knew she was his future queen even then and hoped she'd show up at his Trial so he could ask for her hand." She paused and gave a small chuckle.

"Obviously, she came. Then, for her talent, she encircled every person in the room in an identical ring of fire, and told him that if he chose her, she would do the same to their enemies, and the circles would grow smaller every time they wronged the kingdom of Alverin."

Kindra was starting to suspect that the Annalindis family had been unhinged for a very long time.

"The point of all that is it's a tradition done every time a betrothed is introduced to the king and queen. They have to… present their talents, somehow."

"And you didn't think to, I don't know, tell me?" Kindra asked, voice climbing into a yell.

"Well, it's usually not—not whatever that was!" Helena exclaimed. "Usually you don't *need* to be warned. It's normally very underwhelming."

"So why was it different this time?" Kindra knew the answer before she'd even finished the question, and Jasper voiced it for her.

"Because you're a Firefury." He was leaning against the backs of one of the sofas, rubbing his face with his hands, still half-crazed and shaken. He gave a rough shake of his head. "Of course. I don't know why I was so surprised he pulled a stunt like this."

"He wanted to see how I'd react under pressure. He didn't want some showy display—he wanted something *real*," she said.

"Exactly. You're the first Firefury to marry into this family in almost a *century*, Kindra, because no Annalindis royal has found another one that comes close to the power we had before the curse." Jasper's voice was very quiet, but the intensity in it was jarring.

"So, what, my magic rivals the great power of your bloodline? Are there really no other options? No noble houses? Is that what you're telling me?" She started to giggle, because the whole thing was funny, really. It was just absurd.

But Jasper, Helena and Emeline weren't laughing. "That's exactly what we're telling you, Kindra," Helena said, deadly serious.

Kindra shook her head, pacing to the other side of the room. "That's crazy. You realize that, right? I'm not—I'm from *Harthwin*, for the gods' sake. I taught myself how to do this—I don't even really know what I'm doing—"

"Please, Kindra, don't sell yourself short," Jasper said softly.

"I'm not, I just—surely there are other options."

"Kindra, there *aren't*. There are no Firefury noble families, because we killed them all off, centuries ago, to make sure the only Firefury noble bloodline was ours. We didn't want any competition, which worked wonderfully after the curse, because by that point the only other Firefury nobility were in other kingdoms, who all *hate* us." He crossed the room in a few strides, stopping mere inches from her. "You are literally my father's—my entire family's—best chance."

The intense emotions of the day—gods, it was still early afternoon—began to weigh on Kindra, and she stumbled over to a chair, collapsing into it. The corset of her gown, mildly singed, felt far too tight all of a sudden, and the calm she'd been desperately clinging to since this morning finally started to crumble into despair.

"Kindra, it's going to be okay," Helena said, kneeling in front of her and clasping her hands. "I know this is a lot, and I'm sorry, really, for how it went today. If we'd known we would have told you, I promise. I just figured he'd have you toss around a fireball, or something—"

"I can't do this," Kindra gasped, breaths coming in short, shallow bursts. "I cannot fucking do this. You people are insane."

"Hey, look at me." That was Jasper, kneeling down next to his sister. His hand gently gripped her chin, forcing her to look at him. "Breathe, remember? Like we did before."

But Kindra was not so easily calmed this time. She pushed them both away and staggered across the room, chest heaving. If not for the magic she'd expelled in the throne room, she'd likely be on fire right now. Even still, heat burned under her skin. "Do you understand how—how fucked up this is? To do this to me? It's not just ridiculous, it's *cruel*. A month ago, I was just a girl, living a normal life—"

"To be fair, nothing about your life before this was normal," Jasper quipped weakly, and Kindra curled her lip at him. She felt the familiar tug of anger and gave herself over to it.

"What happens when I can't break the curse? When—when we have a-a child," she choked out, almost gagging, "and they aren't a Wielder? You think your father is going to let that go? After *that*? No. No." She shook her head, pacing furiously. "He will kill me. And you won't get off easily, either."

"Kindra—" Helena started.

"Look at me and honestly say you think he won't, Helena." She was met with silence. "That's what I thought," she spat. "I don't want this. Any of it."

"We know," Jasper grumbled, but he was shifting uncomfortably. The heavy truth—that his father would kill her, and probably punish him, if the curse wasn't broken—was settling in. They were all quiet for a moment. Then he looked at Kindra curiously. "You protected me without hesitating. Why?"

"What do you mean, why?" Kindra asked, brow furrowing.

"Just this morning you looked at me like you wanted to kill me yourself. Yet your first priority was not to shield yourself, but me. Why?"

She shrugged, momentarily at a loss for words. "I don't know," she admitted finally. "It just… seemed like the right thing to do."

Jasper said nothing in response, rubbing his hands over his face for what seemed like the dozenth time. Kindra suspected it was a nervous habit.

"Okay, so what happens now?" Helena's voice was small, and it made Kindra queasy. She'd only known the princess for a short time, but she could already tell that she was a force of nature in her own right; bold and bright like Cyrie herself. To hear her sound unsure, *afraid*, was deeply unsettling.

"Well, we've got a while before we really have to worry about the curse. Like, at least nine months, right?" Emeline attempted a smirk, but it lacked its usual spark.

"Em, please," Helena pleaded, but Emeline stood and walked over to them, the smirk fading into a more serious expression.

"No, I'm serious. We have time. I mean, the wedding is still, what, two months away? And then you figure that even if you two decide to like each other, it's probably going to take a few months before… you know…" She coughed. "So even if it goes like *that*—which, given the way you two behave, is unlikely—you have probably a year and a half before Leofric realizes you can't break the curse and probably arranges for your accidental untimely death. We can figure something out."

They sat with that for a few minutes. Kindra paced. Jasper rubbed his face. Helena finger-combed her hair. And Emeline observed, her blue eyes sharp.

"I mean," Helena said, breaking the silence, "do we actually believe he would kill—"

"Yes," Jasper cut her off. "He hates to be embarrassed. And if he makes a big spectacle out of our marriage, only for it to result in more magic-less children... Yes, he'd kill her for that. He's killed people for less." He crossed his arms. "He'd probably kill me too."

Kindra started. "Jasper, you're his son."

"Come on, you saw how he treated me in there, in front of the entire court. I don't think he'd be that upset about it." It was so matter of fact, the way he said it. And, surprisingly, Kindra felt sympathy for him. She and her mother fought as much as any mother and daughter, and she'd disappointed her at times, but her mother loved her deeply. Kindra had never doubted that. She couldn't begin to imagine having a parent that was so apathetic about her existence.

Perhaps Jasper's life here was not as cushy and perfect as she'd thought it was. Maybe she'd misjudged him, even just a bit.

"So this has been his belief all along—his big gamble," Helena said. "He hasn't given a shit about who the rest of us marry because he's convinced himself that only another Firefury—one of great power, at that—will break the curse, and that's why nobody's succeeded yet."

A beat of silence.

Kindra sighed. "Well, fuck."

"Yeah," Jasper replied, "fuck, indeed."

At least they could agree on that.

Jasper left not much later, claiming he wanted to rest his eyes. But Kindra was the opposite: she was filled with pent up energy, desperate to expel it. As soon as the doors shut behind Jasper, she turned to Helena and Emeline. "I need to get out of this dress," she proclaimed, and hurried into the dressing room without seeing if they were following.

They did, of course, if only because they knew she'd be unable to undress herself. While she removed her jewelry and took down her hair,

Helena unlaced her corset with rapid precision. Kindra didn't realize how used she'd gotten to the tightness of it until she took her first deep breath in hours without it.

A bolt of pain raced down her side, and she twisted to see what the source was. "I don't know how well I'll be able to wield in something like this. Look at this." Along her sides were reddened and scraped patches of skin from where the corset boning had dug in, most likely from the rapid movements wielding required, which the rigid and restrictive structure of her gown did not easily permit.

Emeline sucked in a breath. "You should have Sala look at that. Some of those look bad."

Kindra nodded, then shimmied out of the dress completely. She'd already shed her modesty about being undressed in front of others; it was clear that was to be a staple of her life here and the sooner she got over it, the better. There was plenty else to be distressed about. Clad only in her undergarments, she moved about the room, opening drawers and chests. She found embroidered tunics, billowing gowns, and more of those lacy nightclothes, but she could not find what she was looking for.

"What are you searching for?" Helena asked.

"Something I can move in," Kindra replied as she dug through yet another drawer, only to find it filled only with different styles of *gloves*. She groaned in frustration, then turned to Emeline. "You said you have access to a training ground, a place I can wield."

Emeline blinked, surprised. "Yes, but—I mean, wouldn't you rather rest, after today?"

"No," was Kindra's blunt response.

There was a stretch of tense silence while she tore through the dressing room. "Kindra, we should maybe talk about—" Helena started, but Kindra shook her head rapidly, cutting her off.

"No. We've talked enough. I want to *do* something."

"Like what?" Emeline pressed.

Kindra shrugged. "I just want to be ready. For anything." *To fight my way out of here*, she finished in her head.

"You need to be careful," Helena warned. "Show too much power and suddenly you go from being his greatest prize to his biggest threat."

"Well, I imagine I'm a bit away from that. Your ancestors used to burn whole cities down single-handedly. The most I've done is—"

"Fight off an entire group of bandits on your own? Scorch a raider's camp down to ash and hardly break a sweat? Create a wall of flames so high it almost touches the ceiling of the throne room, and still be teeming with magic afterward?" Helena crossed the room and grabbed Kindra's hands, forcing her to meet her eyes. "Kindra, I know you know you're strong, but you still greatly underestimate yourself. My father wasn't just trying to get under your skin when he commented on your lack of formal training—he was being honest. Those aren't uncommon feats for Firefuries who've gone through Grydmarth or spent years on the battlefield, but for you? Somebody who taught herself in the woods behind her home? It isn't just rare. It's practically *impossible*."

Kindra shook her head again. "I just did what I had to do to—to stay alive. To protect Harthwin."

"And I don't doubt that that's a big reason why you're as powerful as you are. But still, the power you so effortlessly possess is… Kindra, that has not been seen here in a long time."

Kindra opened and closed her mouth, struck stupid. Then she shook her head furiously, wrenching her hands from Helena's and turning back to her search. "I don't want to talk about this right now."

"I just want you to understand—"

"I said *I don't want to talk about it*," she snapped, and Helena's eyes bulged in surprise. Kindra took a deep breath, centering herself, then added, "Please. I just—can't, right now."

"Okay," Helena said softly, "okay." She moved back to stand beside Emeline, who reached out and squeezed her waist comfortingly.

Finally, Kindra stumbled upon a drawer filled with just what she was looking for: leggings and tops meant for training. She pulled out a black set and pulled them on. They were an interesting material: a solid, but breathable black mesh-like fabric that clung to her body like a glove, fitted with sheaths and buckles to attach weapons. The top was sleeveless but high-necked, covering her more vulnerable torso and chest but leaving her arms unrestrained.

"What is this?" she asked, running her hands over the fabric again.

"It's nerushmyr. First invented in Laoruwen some centuries ago," Emeline answered. "It's become the standard uniform for training, and all soldiers wear a suit of it under their armor. It's essentially fireproof."

Kindra whirled around to face her. "It's fireproof?"

The Wavebreaker smiled. "Yes. So its creation was a blessing, as I'm sure you can understand. No more getting your clothes burnt off and having to run around naked during a battle."

Kindra chuckled at the thought, hands still wandering over the material. Tentatively, she called a small flame to her fingers and ran it over the nerushmyr. She felt a bit of warmth where the fire touched, but it didn't burn or singe, or even smoke. Awed, she couldn't fight the broad grin that blossomed across her face. "You have no idea how many clothes I've destroyed over the last decade," she said, then looked to Emeline. "Can you take me?"

"Of course. It's a haul though; the ring's on the other side of the castle grounds," Emeline said, handing her a pair of black boots from one of the chests—also nerushmyr, with thick leather soles.

"That's all right with me. I suppose I could use a tour." Kindra tugged the boots on.

Emeline looked at her wife. "Want to come with?"

Helena shook her head. "I need to do some work. I've got a mountain of paperwork on my desk that I've been putting off for too long." She smiled. "You two have fun, though." She pressed a quick kiss to Emeline's lips, waved Kindra goodbye, and slipped out.

Kindra grabbed a ribbon and messily braided her hair back out of her face. Her eyes were still lined with kohl, her lips still that deep red, though the makeup was all a bit smudged now. Her eyes gleamed, pools of molten gold.

"You look fierce, princess," Emeline commented, and for the first time the title didn't chaff on Kindra's nerves. "You ready?"

She didn't hesitate before she nodded. "Lead the way."

CHAPTER 14

Kindra drew a lot more attention now than she had the first time she'd walked through the castle corridors. As if her performance in the throne room wasn't enough to get people talking, her stalking alongside Emeline in her nerushmyr and half-smeared makeup had people stopping in their tracks.

But she didn't balk. She held her head as high as Emeline did and took their slack-jawed stares in stride. Sala hurried along behind them. The Healer had been posted outside Kindra's doors when they'd left, and Kindra had invited her to come along, in case of any training accidents. A small group of guards—Emeline's, she assumed, since she hadn't heard anything about her own yet—also kept close by, though not within range of hearing their conversation if they spoke quietly.

"So, obviously this floor is where the royal family, as well as the highest-ranked officials, reside," Emeline said, dutifully playing the role of tour guide, "Courtiers and other guests stay on the second floor. Typically only the nobility closest to the crown stays for long periods in the castle. That, or the ones who visit from other cities. Most courtiers prefer to reside in their own residences in the noble district, popping in for a few days at a time or simply taking a carriage back and forth."

They turned a corner, and Emeline pointed to a heavily decorated set of doors along one wall. "Each floor has access to the Great Library, which takes up space on all four floors of the castle."

Kindra gaped. "How many books are in there?"

She shrugged. "Who knows? Thousands? Millions? All I know is there's a massive fireplace, huge windows, and the comfiest sofas. I spend most of the winter days curled up in there."

"That sounds nice," Kindra sighed, and in the back of her mind, she felt the small joy of having something to look forward to.

They arrived at a large staircase and made their way down it, all the way to the ground floor. "The first floor holds the throne room, as well as the main kitchens, ballroom, dining room, parlors, and council rooms. There's also access to the inner courtyards, and the catacombs."

"Catacombs?"

Emeline nodded. "Yep. Miles of 'em, stretched out beneath the castle and all of Wendrith. It's where the Annalindis family is buried. And there are several escape routes that cut down through the cliff sides and out to sea as well."

Escape routes. Kindra took that information and stored it away, though she had no idea how she'd navigate that labyrinth if she was desperately trying to flee the kingdom at the same time. Emeline gave her a pointed look. She knew exactly what she was telling her.

The ground floor of the castle was much more crowded than the higher levels. Down here, people had to part to make way for them, dipping their heads in acknowledgment as they did. Kindra heard some of their whispers: *cursebreaker* and *savior* were the words she could pick out most often. Neither made her feel very good.

I won't be saving anybody but myself, she wanted to retort.

Emeline kept her voice low as they walked through the crowded hallways. "You're basically royalty now, even though you're not yet married, so you don't have to acknowledge or entertain anyone or anything. They are obligated to do so with you, but that doesn't mean they'll always do it kindly. You're not an Annalindis by blood, and you're also not noble-born, so they can be as blatant about their dislike of you as they want, so long as they do it with a smile and a bow."

As if on cue, a pair of almost identical young women gave Kindra a once-over, their pale silver eyes resting a beat too long on her face. As she and Emeline passed them, their sneers twisted into tight-lipped smiles, and they gave what could barely be considered a bow. The moment they thought they were out of earshot, their hisses— "Did you see her cosmetics?" and "So messy"—floated down the corridor.

Emeline clicked her tongue. "The Halis twins have never been known for their discretion or class, despite the station of their birth." Her voice was louder than it needed to be and somewhere behind them came an enraged gasp.

Emeline flashed Kindra a satisfied smirk, and she laughed. "They'll have to say much worse to get under my skin, anyway."

Emeline's smile faded, and she gave a beleaguered sigh. "And they will, once they figure that out."

Kindra didn't doubt that.

Finally, they came upon a large set of doors that opened up to the castle gardens. Kindra hadn't seen them yet; her balcony overlooked the sprawling streets of Wendrith instead.

Even in the chilled grip of autumn, the gardens were still beautiful. Instead of lush greens, it was a sea of reds, oranges and yellows, many of the trees and bushes already shedding their leaves. Seating areas and benches were spread about, as well as an array of statues. At the center stood a huge fountain, sporting a depiction of Cyrie and her sister, Cylina, the goddess of the moon, locked in the heat of battle. Cyrie was carved out of white stone and gold, while the stone Cylina was crafted from was deep black with veins of silver. It was the first sign of a deity other than those worshipped by Firefuries.

Kindra paused as they walked by it, studying it further.

"Beautiful, isn't it?" Emeline said, stopping as well.

"Yes," Kindra replied, "though it's an interesting part of the deities' history to put on a giant fountain."

"Is it really?" Emeline tilted her head. "The Day the Sky Split—when Cyrie and Cylina fought for who would rule the skies. And Cyrie came out on top, in the end. We spend more hours a day with the sun than in true darkness with the moon. Fitting, I think, to have it in the middle of the Annalindis family's garden."

"A reminder of Cyrie's strength," Kindra murmured. By extension, it was a reminder of the Annalindis's strength as well.

"And of her mercy. Cyrie could have taken all the skies for herself, but didn't, instead giving her sister almost half. Almost. Cyrie kept just a little bit more for herself, as a token of her victory, and a reminder to Cylina."

"I always wondered what made her do that," Kindra mused. "The books I read growing up never really said."

Emeline shrugged. "Nobody knows for sure. Some say it was out of love for her sister. All siblings fight nastily, only to turn around and be best friends again the next day. Some historians believe this was a case of that. Except it wasn't two mortal sisters; it was two goddesses who controlled aspects of our world, and their fights had major consequences, no matter how easily they were forgotten by the deities themselves. Others say it was because Cyrie recognized the important balance the world had through her and Cylina sharing the skies, and in the end she knew not to upset that."

"Not upset it too much, at least."

Emeline chuckled. "Right. Anyway, the mercy bit is ironic, considering I doubt this family has ever really shown it to any of their opponents."

Kindra hummed. "Are there depictions of any other deities besides Cyrie and Scaldor on the castle grounds? A temple? Something that acknowledges them?"

"There's only a fire temple here on the grounds, but that's understandable. If you want to go see another elemental temple, you'd have to venture out into the city. There are loads of them in Wendrith. There are even some smaller temples for individual deities, not just ones dedicated to the element as a whole." She gave Kindra a curious look. "Do you not worship Scaldor and Cyrie?"

"No, I do, at least I think so. But… Harthwin is an Earthwarden village. There was just an earth temple there, and it only had one priestess. The Healer didn't even have an official House, just her cottage that she lived in and worked out of. My mother's not a Wielder, so she just followed what the other non-Wielders did, which was worshipping the earth deities. I've never even been to a fire temple. I don't really know what worshipping them actually means."

Emeline gave a look that was too close to pity for comfort. "Well, we have another stop on the way to the training ground, then."

The fire temple was, as expected, completely extravagant.

As Kindra made her way up the *solid gold* steps with Emeline, she thought about the shabby earth temple in Harthwin. It had been little more than rough-cut stone shrouded in green leafy vines, which remained bright and lush year-round thanks to the earth priestess's magic. With all the Earthwardens there, they could've made it more extravagant, could have carved the stone to fine, smooth edges and sharp corners, could have engraved it with the legends of the deities.

But they chose not to. She'd asked her mother about it once when she was younger. Her mother had simply said that's how they believed the earth deities would most prefer to be worshipped: with the focus not on elaborate presentation, but on the deeds they did in their names. So time was instead put into making sure the village always had a large enough harvest to make it through the winter or ensuring everyone had a solid roof over their heads.

Kindra took in the arched, golden ceilings of the temple. The walls were covered in detailed paintings and stained glass, all showing some moment of Scaldor and Cyrie's history, and dotted with flaming sconces. The space was filled with worshippers. Fire priests and priestesses were also prevalent, some roaming around to talk with people, while others were seated, their eyes closed in meditation.

But to Kindra, the temple felt anything but holy.

She did not feel Scaldor or Cyrie here—and she was well-acquainted with both. She could feel Scaldor in her rage, her focus when she fought. She could feel Cyrie in her moments of calm when she admired her magic for its beauty instead of its brute power. Where Scaldor was burning flame, Cyrie was soothing warmth. They'd walked beside her for her whole life, had whispered in her ear for as long as she could remember.

But when she reached for them here, in this temple, she found herself grasping at nothing.

It was deeply unsettling. She did not worship the earth deities, but even she could sense them, in a way, at the earth temple in Harthwin, shoddy and run-down as it may have been.

"Pretty amazing first fire temple for you, right?" Emeline whispered. Kindra thought her voice held the tiniest note of sarcasm.

"Yeah," Kindra replied, spinning in a circle to take it all in. She hoped Emeline thought the weak response was due to awe.

They stayed for a few more minutes, and Kindra was relieved when they finally left.

"What do you think?" Emeline asked as they walked. They were nearing the training grounds now; Kindra could see the large building stretching up just above the tree line, and they were passing more and more guards, donned in nerushmyr like Kindra.

"I think…" Kindra chose her words very carefully. "I think it's a very… grand tribute to them. To Scaldor and Cyrie, I mean."

Emeline raised an eyebrow. "Just say it, Kindra. I guarantee you I feel the same way."

She shrugged. "They put all this wealth into this temple, thinking it would carry favor, when they could have used that gold to help people in need. It just seems like their priorities are skewed." She paused, then added, "The deities have always cared more about what you do in their name for others than about what you build in tribute to them. At least, that's what I was taught."

The Wavebreaker hummed. "I was taught the same." She clicked her tongue. "Must be a poor person thing."

Kindra barked a laugh. "Not sure if it's that or just simply not being born into a royal dynasty."

Emeline scoffed. "You haven't met most of the nobles here yet. After you do, you'll realize it's not just a royalty thing; it's a *wealthy* thing. These people wouldn't know true discomfort if it slapped them in the face. They've never gone hungry; they've never felt the fear of not having a roof over their head. Never had to worry about not having thick enough blankets to last through a cold winter night or access to clean water to drink or bathe. They don't grow their own food; they don't clean their own houses. I wouldn't be surprised if half of them had people around to wipe the shit from their asses for them."

She said it all with a smirk on her face, but Kindra saw in her eyes how much she meant it. The anger was wrapped around every word.

"Even though you're a princess now, you still feel it, don't you?" Kindra asked.

"I do," Emeline admitted. "In the way they look at me, the way they speak to me…"

They'd been so lost in conversation that neither of them had noticed they were right outside the training ground now. Kindra stared up at the large stone building. It was shaped like an arena, and she could hear the noise of sparring drifting out of the dozens of open windows and stone archways that decorated the structure.

"I've spent my whole life being looked at like some kind of wild creature," Kindra confessed. "Harthwin made sure we were taken care of because of what I did, but the stares never changed. And when I was coming here, the way the guards—the way Heinrich—it was like that, but worse. I was brought here because of how amazing my abilities are, apparently, but even still, the looks don't change."

"But at least they call you cursebreaker at the same time, right?" Emeline joked, but her eyes were gentle, and Kindra knew she understood. If there was one person in this castle who would understand any of what Kindra was experiencing, it was her.

"Hate to think of what they'll say when I fail to break any curses."

"Well, I suppose we'd just better make sure you're ready for whatever they're going to throw at you, right?" Emeline squeezed her shoulder, then gestured to the training building. "After you."

CHAPTER 15

The training grounds were alive with the sounds of sparring and exercise. Kindra and Emeline walked through torch-lit halls that were lined with benches and gear stands on one side, and archways on the other. The archways led to the giant training ground, where Kindra could see several sparring matches occurring.

In one corner, a pair of Earthwardens flung vines at each other, twisting them like long, wily snakes. In another, a Windspinner went up against a non-wielding guard, who used a large shield to fend off heavy gusts. And in another corner: "Firefury," Kindra breathed, coming to an abrupt halt. Her heart seemed to stop, its beats skipping frantically. "That's... that's another Firefury."

She couldn't take her eyes off the Firefury down in the ring, training alone. Clad in nerushmyr like Kindra's, the Wielder had a feminine figure, though Kindra could tell she was hardened with muscle from all the way across the ring. Her braided hair—a deep, burnt orange—fell well past her shoulders and danced as she moved. She shot spears of flame at hanging targets, her steps smooth and focused. And she didn't miss a single one, not even when she let loose three fiery darts at once. Each one slammed home. Kindra's chest burned, and it took her a moment to place the feeling: excitement. For the first time in weeks, perhaps even in years, Kindra was excited. How long had she dreamed of this exact moment? And how long ago had she resigned herself to it being an impossibility?

Emeline came up to stand beside her. "You've never seen another Firefury before, have you?" she observed, voice soft.

Kindra shook her head. "No, no I haven't. I mean, my father was one, but I don't remember him." She broke out of her stupor, but her words still stumbled over themselves. "I have to get down there—I have to— Who is that?"

Emeline smiled knowingly, saying nothing, and moved through the archway and down the stairs. Kindra followed her eagerly, heart thundering in her chest. They stepped onto the sand floor of the ring. Some people stopped to look at the two of them. They regarded Kindra with a sense of curiosity, a bit of apprehension, but Emeline they regarded with respect.

Kindra recalled how Emeline had said she'd come here every day to blow off steam when she first married into the Annalindis family. She glanced at the Wavebreaker now, and noted for the first time the lean, trained muscles of her arms, left bare in her delicate cream gown. She also noticed how the tension seemed to bleed from her body as she stopped to talk with some of the guards.

This is her safe space, Kindra realized. *This is one of the only places aside from behind closed doors with Helena where she can really be herself.*

Kindra tried to be as patient as possible while Emeline caught up with her friends, but she was fidgeting in place, unable to look away from the orange-haired Firefury across the ring. The woman was now wrapped in a large fiery serpent. Kindra struggled to keep her mouth from falling open as she watched the Firefury move the serpent around herself with only one hand.

"Okay, sorry," Emeline apologized, turning back to her. "Haven't been by in a week or so. They wanted to catch up." She eyed the flaming serpent now snaking its way through the air. "Tess is really showing off today, isn't she?"

"When isn't she?" quipped a guard behind them, wiping sweat off his brow with a towel. "It's why nobody wants to train with her." A few of the other men laughed.

"Oh, shut it," Emeline snapped, annoyed, "We all know it's because none of you have the courage to ask her to spar since she whooped your ass last month, Terryn."

The group of men—some of them barely more than boys—all looked decently abashed, laughing halfheartedly and looking anywhere but Emeline. Terryn, however, ignored her entirely, looking instead to Kindra. "You're Jasper's bride, aren't you? Kindra, right?" He moved over to stand in front of her. He had eyes the same color as moss. An arrogant smirk stretched across his face. He stuck out his hand. "I'm Terryn."

She gave him a tight-lipped smile. "Pleasure," she said, sticking out her hand as well. He took it in his and pressed a wet kiss to the back. Kindra schooled her face into careful neutrality, fighting the urge to cringe.

Terryn looked her up and down. "Didn't know there were such beautiful women hiding in those tiny villages."

"Us beautiful women are everywhere," Kindra replied with a sweet smile, yanking her hand from his grasp and wiping his slobber off on her leg. "It's just that none of us find charm in your leering."

Emeline cackled. This time, Terryn looked properly embarrassed, cheeks blushing a deep red. "Just trying to compliment you," he grumbled, stalking back to his friends.

Kindra turned her attention back to the Firefury—Tess—and saw she had stopped practicing. She was instead making her way across the ring to them. Kindra's heart jumped again, her annoyance dissipating and her anticipation returning.

"Terryn put his foot in his mouth again, didn't he?" she said as she got closer. Kindra took in the strong muscles, the confident, sauntering gait with which Tess walked.

And then she saw the burn scars.

Kindra was no stranger to the brutality of fire. She had inflicted it upon dozens of people, watched as their skin burned and blackened and charred. She herself had been burned many times, back when she was still learning how to control her magic.

The scars on Tess were not the result of a training moment gone wrong.

The left side of her face was a mass of twisted, bumpy pink and white skin that stretched from her forehead down to her neck, narrowly missing her mouth and left eye. Her left ear was badly scarred, some of the hair on that side of her head permanently seared off, leaving behind pink, mottled scalp. Though her mouth was untouched, the skin at the left corner was tighter, causing her lips to curl up in a constant half smirk. The scarring went beneath the high collar of her nerushmyr, traveling down her left arm and hand. All healed burns.

The right side of Tess's face was unmarred, revealing pale white skin and an arched orange eyebrow. She didn't have a left one. Her eyes were a searing deep orange that matched her hair, and they sparked with mischief as they came to rest on Kindra.

"Of course, is that so surprising?" Emeline stepped forward, arms held out. Tess stepped into them and they embraced, laughing.

"Good to see you, Wavebreaker," Tess said, a wicked smirk crossing her face. "When am I getting another shot at you in the ring?"

"Not for a long while. You almost burnt my eyebrows off last time," Emeline retorted, her own mischievous grin appearing.

Tess stuck her bottom lip out in a pout. "Aw, you don't want to match with me?" Emeline tipped her head back and laughed.

Kindra simply watched, not bothering to wipe her expression of wonder from her face. A Firefury, right in front of her, for the first time in her life. Her magic strained at her skin, like it was reaching for the kindred Wielder just a mere yard away from her.

Finally, their laughter died out, and Tess faced her. "Well, hello, Kindra Bedelyn," she drawled, "Or should I call you *cursebreaker*? Perhaps savior of the realm would be better? The hope of Alverin?" Again, her lips twisted up into that humorous smile.

"Please, just call me Kindra. I'm not ready for all those ridiculous titles," she replied, forcing what she hoped was an easy smile. *Nor am I deserving of them.*

Tess hummed, giving her a once over. "You sure do look the part, though," she said softly, as though she were only talking to herself.

Kindra looked away, uncomfortable under Tess's searing gaze. "Kindra was wanting to train," Emeline jumped in, saving the conversation. "After this morning, she was hoping she could blow off some steam."

"Ah, yes, His Majesty's big surprise," Tess rolled her eyes and began walking backwards to her corner of the ring. She gave Kindra a reassuring smile. "Heard you handled it like a champ. Blew everyone away."

"You weren't there?" Emeline asked, raising her eyebrows. "But the Council—"

"The Council can go fuck themselves. I was busy doing more important things." She shrugged at Kindra. "Sorry."

"No apology necessary," Kindra replied. "If I'd had the option of not going—"

"Tess, you can't just disobey an order from the Council," Emeline interrupted hotly. "They aren't just suggestions, you know. You can get in serious trouble."

"Oh, I'm quaking with fright! A half a dozen old men are *so* scary, Emeline!" Tess scoffed. Kindra watched the two of them go back and forth, her gaze darting between them. Just a moment prior, they'd been embracing and laughing together, and now they were arguing like siblings.

"Tess, they explicitly stated that any off-duty castle staff were to attend. The fucking gardeners were there, for gods' sake," Emeline retorted, her voice taut with frustration. Her next words were quiet, but no less intense. "If you keep playing these games with him, he's going to run out of patience eventually. He'll figure out that you weren't there, if he hasn't already."

Who is 'he'? Kindra thought, startled by the sudden switch from talking about the Council to just one person.

"And then what? He'll suspend me from duty? Please! I'd love to have a couple weeks off. Maybe he'll really do me a favor and discharge me entirely, and I can finally get the hell out of this city."

There was a lot being left unsaid here, and Kindra knew better than to butt into the conversation to ask about it. She could inquire about it later.

Emeline took a deep breath, trying to calm down. "Look, I know you think that you can openly disrespect the Council just because your—"

The last bit of humor drained from Tess's eyes in an instant. "Don't you dare."

Silence fell over them. Kindra was practically afraid to breathe. Tess and Emeline were locked in a staring match to end all staring matches. Then Emeline broke the stare. "I'm sorry. I just—don't want to see you hurt. More than you already have been."

Tess nodded stiffly. "I know. But there are worse things he could catch me doing than skipping the reveal and subsequent ambush of our newest princess." She met Emeline's eyes again, and something passed between them that Kindra was not privy to understanding. "Much worse."

"Just be careful, Tess. That's all I'm asking." Emeline looked at Kindra, blue eyes apologetic. "Sorry you had to see that, Kindra. We tend to get into it like this." She sighed and ran her fingers through her hair. "I'm gonna go. Let you two get familiar, do your Firefury thing. But I'll be back in a couple hours, yeah? We've got dinner tonight with the whole family."

"Whole family?" Kindra croaked. "Like, everyone?"

"Yeah. Everyone. But you'll have Hel and me, and, whether you like it or not, Jasper."

"Good thing I'm getting all my energy out now, I guess. Though maybe I should keep some on reserve in case the king tries to drown me while waiting for dessert."

Emeline couldn't help but crack a smile at that. "I'd say you don't have to worry, but I don't know what to expect anymore." She lifted her hand in a wave. "I'll be back." She shot Tess another indecipherable look as she left.

Kindra faced Tess. The other woman tilted her head to the side, giving her another one of those burning looks. "So," she started, "I imagine you've got some questions now, don't you?"

CHAPTER 16

"What exactly is the Council?" The words flew from Kindra's mouth before she could stop them, her curiosity getting the better of her.

Tess moved away from her, creating a bit of distance. She stretched her arms behind her head, loosening up her muscles. Kindra copied her, feeling the tightness leave her body as she did.

"The Council," Tess finally answered, "are the assholes who manage everything the king doesn't have time for. Or interest in."

"So, just about everything?"

Tess laughed. "You're catching on quick. Yes, that's basically everything. Besides war and the curse, of course. The king basically signs off on whatever they send him. They need his seal of approval, but he generally has no arguments against what they suggest."

Kindra let a string of fire wrap itself around her wrist. "They can't be doing too bad, though. I mean, the whole city has clean, running water. I saw people when I arrived. Nobody looked destitute or starved."

Tess brought forth a ball of flame, and it danced in her palm. "Their interest ends at the big cities. The trading hubs. The… beacons of Alverin. It's all an effort to show the other kingdoms that we're doing so great, even with a curse that sapped us of our firepower. Literally." She gave Kindra a pointed look. "You know that, being from Harthwin."

Kindra decided not to comment on that. "The curse didn't take away magic from other families though, just the royal family," she pointed out. "There are plenty of powerful Wielders still in Alverin. In this very castle."

Tess hummed softly. "So it seems," she said cryptically. And then her face changed, all interest in the topic at hand disappearing. "Well, are we doing this?"

Kindra's heart began to pound. "I've never dueled another Firefury," she admitted, "so go easy on me."

"Of course. Just until you get your bearings, though." The fire in Tess's hands grew. "First things first: battling within one element is about willpower. It's about control. You can fling fireballs at an Earthwarden all day, and what can they do about it? Nothing. But when you're fighting another Firefury, your mind must be sharp, on constant guard. Because if you slip up," she warned, the fire jumping suddenly from one hand to the other, "then your fire becomes *theirs*."

"How can you get it back?" Kindra asked.

"In the heat of battle, I'd advise against trying to win back fire you've lost. Just make more and get your shit together, which is easier said than done. The feeling of your own magic being ripped out of your control, and used against you... it's jarring at best, and paralyzing at worst." Tess's face twisted, the burned side twitching involuntarily.

"Do it," Kindra said. "I need to know how it feels."

Tess nodded. "Alright, hit me."

Kindra breathed in, the thin line of fire around her wrist growing so that it engulfed her entire hand. Then she raised it, and with one thrust, sent a blast of it shooting towards Tess.

What happened next didn't seem real: One second, her fire was flying towards Tess's face. The next, the other Wielder had harnessed it under her control and sent it flying right back at her. Kindra reached out one hand, then both, as she realized she could not redirect it away from her or bring it to a stop. Panic—a panic that was unlike anything she'd ever felt—coursed through her body, and she stumbled backwards, falling.

The flames dissipated into nothing just a few feet from her, leaving her panting and shaking on the ground. Tess walked over, offering her hand to help Kindra back up. "Terrifying, isn't it?" she asked.

Kindra only nodded as she took Tess's outstretched hand and stood, the fear she'd felt not yet gone. "How... how do I protect myself from that?" she inquired once she'd found her voice again.

"Training. Lots of training. And not just the physical stuff. You must have the mental strength to make sure your magic stays yours—something you've never had to worry about before. So if you want to master this, make it so it's as easy as breathing, as the rest of wielding is to you, you've gotta fully commit. I'm talking practicing deep breathing, stilling your mind, staying calm even when your betrothed makes you want to scream— yes, I have heard about that—all of it, okay?" She took a step closer, so she was mere inches from Kindra. "If you're anything like me, Kindra, which I think you are, you'll want to be as prepared as you can be when they come for you. And the only way that's possible is to make your mind, your control, unbreakable."

Kindra raised her eyebrows. "You're the first person besides me who's said 'when' instead of 'if.'" She was struggling to keep her voice light.

"Firefuries have never been known for their idealism. Even I can't fault the Annalindis family for that." She stepped back, then made her way back across the ring. "Again," she called. "We go until you can't anymore."

Kindra gathered fire in her palms once more, sending it racing towards Tess. She tried to keep a grip on the flames with her mind, but Tess was still able to wrest control from her without much effort. Instead of sending it back to Kindra, though, she simply extinguished it off to the side.

Over and over again, they did this. And slowly, over the course of the hour, it became a bit harder for Tess to ensnare Kindra's fire, the fight for control becoming longer, if only by one fraction of a second at a time. Kindra's attacks became smarter, too, no longer large indiscriminate blasts of flame, but pointed burning darts or twisting fiery snakes. She found that the more she thought about how she'd use her magic, the way she'd shape and move it, the more difficult it became for Tess to manipulate it. And though she was covered in sweat and her muscles were screaming, she was smiling, reveling in her new discoveries, joyous in the fact that for the first time in her life, she wasn't so alone. She finally had somebody she could share her magic with.

Finally, Kindra shot a thin arrow of fire. She sent it whistling through the air, directly towards Tess's face. The other Firefury only narrowly avoided it, ducking at the last minute and letting it slam into the wall behind her.

Kindra froze.

Tess grinned. "You sneaky bitch," she laughed, clapping her hands. "You almost had me there."

"I did?" Kindra couldn't fight the huge smile spreading across her face. "I did!" She threw her fist victoriously in the air, whooping.

"I think that's enough for today," Tess decided, walking over to the side of the ring and grabbing a cloth from a bucket of water. She tossed Kindra one, and they wiped sweat from their faces. Kindra was certain that her makeup, already smudged from this morning, was streaming down her face by this point, if not gone entirely. But she didn't care if she looked a mess. Her cheeks were cramping from smiling so much.

"Tomorrow, then?" she asked, already desperate to go again, even though she was exhausted.

Tess smiled. "Sure. I have the afternoon patrol block most days, so I'm free in the mornings until after midday." She reached out and squeezed Kindra's shoulder. "Good job today. I didn't really believe what people were saying, about you being so powerful and all. But I believe it now. When I'm done with you..." Her smile grew devious. "You're going to be unstoppable." She looked over Kindra's shoulder, raising her hand to wave. "Hope you enjoyed the show!" Her voice was teasing, and Kindra spun around to see who she was talking to.

"Oh, we did," Jasper replied, his eyes meeting Kindra's as the smile melted off her face. Emeline stood beside him, looking only slightly apologetic. Softly, he repeated, "I definitely did."

Kindra did her best to stay calm as she walked with Jasper and Emeline out of the training grounds, practicing her deep breathing and mental fortitude and all that. Tess had bid them farewell, looking rather eager to escape the ever-present tension between the prince and his betrothed.

"So, you just learned how to do that today?" Jasper asked, trying to start a conversation.

Kindra only gave him a curt nod in response. She'd felt exposed when she'd turned to see him standing there, and betrayed when she'd realized Tess had known he'd been watching for gods know how long, and that Emeline had decided to bring him—or allow him, knowing Jasper—along. He was a constant reminder that despite the new friends she was making and the training she was finally receiving, her purpose here had nothing to do with either of those things.

"That's amazing. I've read that it takes Wielders years to get a handle on that skill—the control it takes, the mental dexterity you have to build up… and you managed to do it successfully in just a couple hours." The same admiration that had been in his voice the first time he'd seen her wield those weeks ago was back again, and Kindra grimaced.

"You know, I'd love to get down in the ring with you," he continued, barreling on despite Kindra's lack of interest. "I haven't sparred with a Firefury in months—not since graduating Grydmarth. I don't want to get too out of practice, considering—" Emeline coughed then, and he abruptly cut off. Kindra took note of that with mild suspicion.

"You wouldn't stand a chance against me," she retorted, giving him a bored look. Only then, when she finally glanced in his direction, did she notice how nervous he looked. His eyes were darting around, looking everywhere but her. As if he were desperately trying to distract both her and himself from something else. Even Emeline appeared, for the first time, less amused by their interactions and more wary, which made the seed of suspicion inside her begin to take root.

Kindra stopped dead in her tracks, wheeling around to face Jasper head on. "What's going on?"

"What do you mean?" He laughed, but it was fluttery and anxious, betraying him.

She caught his gaze again and held it. "You're nervous. Both of you are. What's happened?"

Jasper and Emeline exchanged a look, communicating silently. That was something she'd noticed happened a lot between the three of them—Jasper, Helena and Emeline—and it made her uncomfortable every time. Finally, Jasper turned back to her and said delicately, "It's Pryllia."

Her stomach twisted. "What's going on in Pryllia?"

Jasper swallowed and looked around anxiously. Gently, he grabbed her by the shoulder, steering them off the path and into a small alcove of trees. Sala, who'd been following slightly behind, hovered nearby, but out of earshot. Once they were alone, he said, "Pryllian forces have been spotted gathering along the border."

Kindra frowned. "I mean, their scouts have been coming into Alverin for years," she replied. "I've fought them off several times."

Emeline smiled grimly. "These aren't scouts, Kindra."

"Oh," was all she could manage to say. Then, she choked out, "My mother—"

"We are monitoring the situation, and if necessary, the party organized to retrieve your mother will depart early," Jasper told her.

"Now. They could depart now." Panic swelled in Kindra, wild and unruly.

He ran a hand through his hair, and he looked genuinely apologetic. "I'm sorry, Kindra, but with this update, we need to use a lot of our immediate resources elsewhere. The soonest we could send them is in three weeks, maybe two."

"Where along the border?" Kindra forced the words out, trying to keep them devoid of emotion and failing. "How—how far from Harthwin are they?"

"So far, they've only been spotted farther north. They'd probably be five, six days away at their fastest pace. It may be too out of their way—we imagine they'd want to get as far inland as possible, as quickly as they can, and not take any detours."

War. This was war. Finally, after years of brewing, it was happening. And what horrid fucking timing.

"When did you find this out?" Accusation crept into her voice. Dread was pooling in her gut.

Jasper held his hands up defensively. "Just now—I was in the Council meeting this afternoon. I got out less than an hour ago. I swear, I haven't been sitting on this, Kindra. I know how important Harthwin is to you. How important your mother is."

She held his stare for a moment and decided she believed him. "How long do you think it'll be before they attack? Before war breaks out?"

"They haven't sent any messages officially declaring war yet, but the Council and my father don't think they will. We suspect it will be a sudden attack—and soon. A few months at most. We've begun gathering a force to meet them, to try and stop them from getting too far, but..." He trailed off and sighed in frustration. "We've been focusing on Breyenth."

Kindra felt the world begin to spin around her. "Do you think they planned this? Made it seem like Breyenth was going to attack first so most of the military would be stationed in the southwestern part of the kingdom?"

Briefly, the concerned, worried look on Jasper's face cleared. "Yes," he replied, "that's exactly what we think. Pryllia's been too quiet for years now, but Breyenth… I mean, we've practically been at war with them for decades, with all the border skirmishes between us." Kindra grimaced, remembering her father. "The only thing missing has been an official declaration of war."

"Well, I think you should've considered the possibility that everybody hates Alverin so much they'd be willing to work together to bring us down."

Jasper opened, then closed his mouth, at a loss for words, and Kindra took the opportunity to end the conversation, turning away and beginning the walk back to the castle. The others had no choice but to follow mutely behind her.

Kindra kept her head high and put all her strength into not being sick.

CHAPTER 17

Kindra and Sala returned to her chambers to find Cerulle waiting at the door for them.

"Lady Kindra," Cerulle greeted her with a smile, opening the door for her. "How were the training grounds?"

"Enlightening," she replied. She strode into her rooms. "Apparently, I'm to dine with the whole family tonight. I suppose I should start preparing."

"Preparing your body or your mind?" Sala quipped, following her into the bathing room.

Kindra huffed a laugh, yanking off her boots and peeling the nerushmyr off her body. "Both, if this morning is any indicator." She pulled her hair out of its braid, then turned toward the bath, which Cerulle was already in the process of filling. She began to move towards it but was interrupted by Sala reaching out and gently gripping her arm.

"Let me see to these, first, my Lady," the Healer said, grazing her fingers over the scrapes from the corset on Kindra's side. She'd almost forgotten about them, but now, as Sala touched them, they sent sharp darts of pain up and down her torso. Kindra let out a small grunt of discomfort. Sala hummed in response, her brown eyes beginning to gleam as she brushed over the wounds again. Kindra felt a burst of warmth, then a pinch of tightness, and she looked down to see her skin heal where it had been torn, the redness fading as if it had never even been there. As the warm feeling faded, so did all remnants of the pain she'd felt.

"Wow," she remarked, "thank you, Sala."

"It is what I am here for, Lady Kindra," Sala replied, dipping her head and stepping back.

Healed, Kindra slid into the bath, once again heating the water herself. As Cerulle and Sala scrubbed her hair and skin, she closed her eyes, losing herself in thought.

Pryllian forces at the border, readying to strike. And Alverin had had no idea until now, when it was quite possibly too late. Kindra could almost laugh at the ridiculousness of it all. How arrogant must they be to think that kingdoms would not unite in an effort to destroy them? As if there was any other way to take them down but to join together. Alverin had made sure of that by spending centuries carving chunks of land from each kingdom, leaving them with less than half of their original territory. The only ones left untouched were Drucanar, protected by the blistering Scaldryn Sands and Dark Blade Mountains, and Eslai, the island nation who hardly paid anybody on Istreria any mind. But Alverin's neighbors—Breyenth and Laoruwen to the west and Pryllia in the northeast—had borne the brunt of Alverin's aggression ever since they came into being. Kindra doubted there'd been an era of peace that lasted longer than a few decades in their joint history.

So of course they'd be willing to ally together if it meant they could exact their revenge and wipe the threat of Alverin out for good.

How the fuck could they have not seen that coming? Kindra wondered.

Her pondering gave way to worrying about her mother. Surely, if what Jasper had told her was true, then she wasn't in any immediate danger. But the rest of Harthwin… what would they do?

She itched to be back there. If she was, then they'd at least have somebody to protect them. Even though she couldn't do much against an army, she could buy them time to escape before she met her end.

But that didn't sit well with her either. Hadn't she given them enough, over these years? Must she die for them, too?

If not for this marriage, that would be my fate. The realization did not settle easily in Kindra's heart. Nor did the fact that she felt a jolt of gratitude for everything that had transpired in the last few weeks.

Was she becoming complacent already?

No, she thought, silencing that voice. *It's not complacency to be glad I'm alive.*

Cerulle gestured for her to stand, and Kindra did, silent as she and Sala washed the lower half of her body. Already, the experience that had made her squirm just yesterday no longer did. Things were changing. She wasn't entirely sure how she felt about it. She didn't love it here, but she didn't hate it, either.

Sala handed her a towel, and she dried herself off, slipping on her robe. The two women sat her down at the vanity, combing out her hair and leaving it to dry as they rubbed thick, sweet-smelling creams on her face and neck.

"What do you wish to wear this evening?" Sala asked, turning to go towards the dressing room, Cerulle following suit.

"Gods, I don't know, what options do I have?" Kindra replied, studying her face in her mirror. Now clean of sweat and smeared makeup, she looked dewy and refreshed. She peered at one of the jars, wondering what exactly they were putting on her.

"Maybe you should come and see for yourself. It may be hard to list them all for you."

Kindra got to her feet and hurried into the dressing room, her mouth falling open as she entered. It had seemed overwhelming before, but now, it was even more so. The closets were bursting with all sorts of tunics and gowns, and she knew that if she opened the drawers, they would be as well.

"How do I...how do I even start to figure out what to wear?" she breathed, stupefied. She slowly turned in a circle, taking it all in. "These clothes are beautiful, but... I just have no idea how this works." She bit her lip. "I suppose there's no time like the present to start learning."

"If you would like some help in choosing, we can be of some assistance," Sala offered.

"Thank you," Kindra said, feeling the pressure ease a bit. She moved over to one of the bursting racks, reaching out and running her hand over a gauzy pale pink gown. "What would you recommend for dinner tonight? How formal?"

"Definitely nice, but nothing like what you wore earlier today," Cerulle answered, her voice steady and authoritative. She moved to stand next to Kindra and began taking out gowns she thought were appropriate. One was a brilliant gold that matched Kindra's eyes, and the flowing fabric shimmered slightly in the light. It had long, billowing sleeves that gathered at the wrists, and the neckline dipped in a low V that didn't seem to be too scandalous.

"That one would work, I think," she said to the Windspinner.

Cerulle nodded. "I agree." She gave Kindra soft smile and added, "It matches your eyes perfectly."

Kindra trailed her fingers down the skirt. "Sounds good to me, then."

They went back to the bathing room, finishing up her hair. They twisted it out of her face but left it down, pinning it back with golden sun pins. Sala added a thin line of brown paint right above her eyelashes and dusted her cheeks with rouge, leaving her lips bare. Cerulle fastened a simple gold necklace around her neck, the small pendant a diamond. All that was left now was to get dressed, which the three of them accomplished in just a few minutes.

Ready to go, her dress laced just tight enough, Kindra made her way to the sitting area by the fireplace and settled into one of the armchairs to wait. "Where is dinner?" she asked Cerulle as she and Sala came over to her.

"The family dining room," Cerulle answered, "in His Majesty's chambers. The family dines there when they eat together, and sometimes are joined by selected advisers or courtiers, when the king and queen invite them."

Kindra did not like the thought of being in King Leofric's chambers at all. "Right," she said, "and when will you be escorting me there?"

Sala and Cerulle exchanged a look. "Well, actually," Sala began haltingly, and Kindra knew what was coming next, "we will not be escorting you tonight."

"Jasper will be, won't he?"

"Yes, my Lady," Sala replied, and she looked genuinely apologetic about the situation.

Kindra sighed. "I suppose I'd better get used to that."

There was a knock on the door then, and the man himself stepped into the room. Kindra closed her eyes and inhaled deeply, then stood to face him.

"Good evening, Kindra," Jasper greeted her, a slight smirk on his face. He was dressed in black pants and boots and a red jacket, a less extravagant version of his morning attire. His eyes scanned her head to toe, and she fought against the urge to squirm or look away or punch him in the face. "You look lovely," he said.

"Thank you," she returned stiffly, walking over to him. She tried to appear as calm as possible, as if she was completely unaffected by the prospect of dining with the king of Alverin. Jasper, she observed as she got closer to him, was not making such an attempt. She could see the individual beads of sweat on his brow. She blinked up at him. "All right?"

Jasper glanced at Cerulle and Sala, who smartly dipped their heads and quickly exited the room. Kindra was alarmed to see them go—she was now alone with Jasper for the first time. Yes, they'd technically been by themselves when they were in the carriage on the way here, but there'd been guards just a few feet away on either side of them, peering in through the windows. Now, they were behind closed doors. Kindra wanted to leave as soon as possible.

"I am nervous, yes," he admitted once the door shut behind Kindra's servants. "I would be nervous regardless, but considering what happened this morning, and now the news of what's going on in Pryllia…"

"I'm sure it will be fine." She found herself wanting to soothe him and told herself it was only because his anxious energy did nothing to quell her own. "I'm on his good side right now, aren't I? Surely that means we're safe, at least for tonight."

"Father is not the one I'm concerned about at the moment," Jasper said. "Antone and Sebastian are top generals in the army."

"And they found out this afternoon that they've been completely fooled," Kindra concluded for him. "So they may be a bit on edge." She reached out and placed her hand on his arm, squeezing it lightly. Jasper stared at the point of contact, something unreadable crossing his face. "I can handle a family dinner, Jasper. So can you, I'm sure."

"This is no ordinary family dinner, Kindra. In case you haven't figured it out yet, we are not an ordinary family."

"And I am no ordinary woman," she returned, startled at how confident the words sounded, how she believed them.

Jasper relaxed a bit. He smiled at her, cheeks dimpling, the worry fading from his expression. "Indeed," he murmured, their eyes locking. Kindra's heart did something strange in response. "I definitely agree with that." He offered her his arm. "Shall we?"

She took it without argument and offered him a small smile. Together, they made their way out of her chambers.

And deep in Kindra's heart, she felt a little bit like that might have been the start of something.

The start of a truce, an understanding, however tumultuous and fragile.

CHAPTER 18

The doors to King Leofric's chambers were down a long, heavily guarded and windowless hallway.

The silence around them was thick with tension. The guards regarded Kindra and Jasper stonily as they walked by, and she met each one of their gazes, returning the cold stares with one of her own.

"Jasper!" A man's voice sounded behind them. It was similar to Jasper's, but harder. More stern.

They turned to find Antone, the eldest son, striding towards them, his wife Celeste trailing slightly behind. Now that they were under less duress than they'd been this morning, Kindra was finally able to get a good look at them.

Antone was, as she'd noticed earlier, almost Leofric's mirror, and she imagined this is what the king had looked like twenty years ago. The only difference was his eyes; they were gray like Queen Cordilya's. And they were hard, like the very stone this castle was built out of.

Celeste was lithe and slender, her black braided hair pulled up into a bun. Her ebony skin shimmered in the light; she'd dusted her cheekbones and exposed shoulders with gold powder, much like they'd done to Kindra that morning. Her off-the-shoulder gown, too, was gold, though it was a deeper, metallic shade, cut from silk.

"Ah, Antone, Celeste," Jasper greeted them with a tight smile. "How are you this evening?"

"Well, thank you," Antone replied, barely bothering to look at his little brother before turning to Kindra. "Quite the performance this morning, Lady Kindra. I wanted to introduce myself after but Helena and Emeline rushed you out before I could." He reached out his hand for hers.

"Thank you, Your Highness." Kindra allowed him to press a quick kiss to the back of her hand. "It's nice to meet you, finally." She turned to Celeste, and flashed what she hoped was a friendly grin. "It's wonderful to meet you as well, Princess Celeste."

Celeste returned the smile, though it was thin. Her dark silver eyes flashed as she dipped her head in a nod. "A pleasure."

Jasper gave what Kindra was beginning to identify as his nervous smile and gestured to the doors. "Let's go in, shall we? Don't want to keep Mother and Father waiting."

"Absolutely not. I wouldn't be surprised if Sebastian and Myala have already arrived." Antone frowned, disapproval coloring his features. "Though I doubt Helena and Emeline have made an appearance yet, knowing them."

"They'll be here," Jasper shot back, rather aggressively. Antone raised an eyebrow, his lip curling, and Celeste looked anywhere but the two of them. Jasper coughed awkwardly, then tugged Kindra forward.

The guards opened the doors, and the four of them entered a massive foyer. It was like Helena's and Emeline's chambers, the arches on either side leading to grander versions of a study and dining room. Through the center arch, Kindra could see a large meeting space with a huge oak table covered in maps and papers and beyond that, more doorways that led to what she assumed was the sitting room and the king's bed chambers.

The floor was black, the walls a dark gray stone. Statues, tapestries and paintings depicting Alverin's bloody history decorated every inch of the foyer and the rooms beyond, as well as large portraits of Alverin's past kings and queens. It was dark, lit with numerous sconces along the walls and dangling chandeliers but no natural light coming from any windows. Kindra squinted slightly, adjusting to the change in brightness.

"We are in the very center of the castle," Jasper murmured in her ear as they walked through the foyer, headed for the sitting room. "No walls of windows here. Safety reasons."

Kindra nodded but didn't respond. They were walking through the meeting room now, and here the ceilings stretched to over twenty feet tall. A few small windows, barely big enough to fit a child, were scattered around the top section of the walls. A large iron chandelier dangled over the table, lines of wax trailing down the metal from the thick candles.

She began to feel slightly suffocated, as though she were trapped underground.

Beside her, Jasper was stiff, his steps uneven.

"Breathe," she hissed softly, making sure Antone and Celeste couldn't overhear.

He squeezed her arm and inhaled deeply, then exhaled, then repeated the process again. His body began to relax, and by the time they reached the door to the sitting room, he had eased back into his casual, easy stride. "Thank you," he whispered, and then he opened the door.

Sebastian and Myala were, indeed, already there, seated on a couch together. Sebastian looked as though somebody had taken a still-wet portrait of young Leofric and smudged it with a rag; his features weren't as hard, softened from Queen Cordilya's bloodline. His eyes though—they were the same as Leofric's: a sharp, glaring brown. Myala was beautiful, her chestnut hair pinned back from her face by a few small braids and flower pins, gentle curls falling past her shoulders. She wore a short-sleeved, off-white gown that was decorated with delicate gold beading. She was short and curvy, Kindra observed as she got up from the couch to greet them; her head came no higher than Kindra's shoulder. And, she realized with a start, Myala was pregnant, her belly ever so slightly swelling beneath her dress.

"It's so lovely to finally meet you, Lady Kindra," Myala said, her voice high and tinkling like bells. "You were so remarkable this morning, one of the best Novon's Trials we've ever witnessed!"

"You've only seen one other," came a low, dry feminine voice, and Kindra relaxed substantially as Emeline strode into view, Helena on her tail.

Myala's face flushed and the sickeningly sweet smile she'd donned slid away. "Well, it was far better than yours, so I'm not lying." Her bell-like voice began to sound more like metal scraping against metal.

"I didn't say you were, My-my," Emeline retorted, rolling her eyes, already exasperated with the whole exchange.

"I told you not to call me that," Myala snapped, but Emeline did not deign to give a response, turning instead to a table cluttered with liquor bottles and pouring herself a generous glass. Kindra bit back a grin. Jasper, however, looked pained.

"Darling, you know better than to engage with her." Sebastian came up behind his wife and gently guided her back to the couch. His eyes were soft—they only went soft when looking at her, Kindra noted as she watched them sharpen back into daggers as he glared at Emeline's back. He rubbed his hand soothingly down Myala's spine, his other coming to rest fondly on her swollen belly.

"You're late," Antone shot at his younger sister, who had settled into one of the armchairs. Emeline came to perch on the arm.

"No later than you," Helena responded, indignant, "We walked in right behind you. Besides," she gestured to the room, "they aren't even here yet, so why does it matter? They're the ones who are late."

Antone did not have anything to say to that, and he and Celeste went to sit on the couch with Sebastian and Myala. Helena smirked, satisfied. She turned her attention to Jasper and Kindra. "Welcome to the family, Kindra!" She tried to give one of her signature beaming grins, but it lacked its usual sunny glow.

"Yes, aren't we just delightful?" Emeline added under her breath, taking a sip of her drink.

Kindra laughed then, which earned her a spiteful look from Myala and a disappointed one from Celeste. Well, fine. They were never going to be her friends, anyway. "Where are the king and queen?" she asked, walking over to sit in the armchair across from them. Jasper followed, seeming smaller by the second. He was shrinking in on himself, like he wished the shadows lurking in the corners of the room would reach out and swallow him.

So very different from the arrogant prince she'd first met in her cottage.

He hates them, she thought sadly as she watched him feebly fend off a teasing remark from Sebastian. What must it have been like to grow up here, if he was so deeply affected by their presence?

"Father is in another Council meeting, but he should be out soon. And Mother won't arrive until she has to, as always," Antone replied, butting into their conversation.

"Another meeting?" Jasper responded, looking alarmed. "Has there been an update?"

"Perhaps if you had chosen the military route instead of wasting your time with your books, you would be privy to such information," Antone jeered, and Jasper huffed, wounded.

"If this concerns Pryllia, I would like to know," Kindra interrupted, not bothering to be particularly polite, already sick of Antone's pompousness and stupid games. "My village is very close to the border. The lives of many I care about are at stake, so I'd appreciate it if you could set aside petty sibling squabbles and tell me."

A thick silence fell across the room. Pure shock flitted across the crown prince's face at her tone, and she saw Jasper's face pale. A thrill ran through her. *Look at me, the dumb village girl, stunning Alverin's future king into silence.* Perhaps if she were smarter, she would feel fear.

"Um, there is no update, necessarily, they're just… trying to get ahead of it," Antone stammered. Kindra wondered if anybody had ever called him on his shit before. Nobody, except his father.

Kindra nodded, then looked up at Jasper. "I'd like to be kept in the know about any new information you might receive about this, if possible. I worry for my mother and Harthwin's safety. I'm sure you can understand."

Jasper gave her a soft smile, his expression flitting between shock, terror and a fierce pride. "Of course, Kindra. You have my word." The two of them looked over to Antone, whose eyes were narrowed as he studied them, face slightly red with embarrassment and mouth drawn taut with frustration. Then he nodded stiffly, and turned back to his brother and their wives, loudly resuming their conversation. He did not glance their way or speak to them again, not even to poke fun at Jasper or shoot snide remarks at Emeline and Helena.

Kindra had a feeling she'd just made a new enemy.

But if it gave Jasper a reprieve, she didn't mind it all that much.

The king and queen swept into the room just shy of a half hour later. Kindra was sipping on some wine, courtesy of Jasper, when they did, and as the royal pair entered, she felt the urge to down her glass in one gulp. They all rose to greet them, bowing.

King Leofric swept his stern gaze over them, pausing momentarily on Kindra. Her skin crawled, and she was grateful when his eyes left her.

Queen Cordilya did not look at any of them, her distant stare settling somewhere on the wall above them. Nobody else seemed to find this unusual, though Helena did look particularly sad when she greeted her mother and barely got a nod in return.

The queen sat down in a plush chair near a fireplace on the other side of the room, staring into the flames. She did not notice when Helena brought her a glass of wine, nor did she so much as look at her daughter when Helena knelt to speak with her. Kindra felt a pinch of longing for her own mother. How many times had she wished she would have been left alone or given some peace when she'd been growing up? It felt strange to miss her mother's nagging and worrying, but she would have far preferred it to the heartbreaking abyss between Helena and Queen Cordilya.

"She wasn't always like that, you know," Jasper murmured softly in her ear. Distantly, Kindra could hear the voices of his brothers, talking with the king. She looked over at him.

"She wasn't?"

He shrugged, gaze trained on his sister, still desperately trying to get a response out of Cordilya. "She has always been shy, yes, but she used to talk to us… laugh with us, see us. Then one day a few years ago, she just…" He trailed off, lost for words. "It was like the light inside her was snuffed out." Grief flashed across his face.

"Do you know why?"

Jasper shook his head. "No. We have suspicions, though. It was obviously something with her magic. She must have received a vision, and it was so horrible it tore through her mind. We have no idea what that could have been, though." Kindra followed the direction of his gaze. He was staring directly at his father.

A chill ran down her spine. She took another sip of her drink. "Do you think he…"

"No, oddly enough," he replied. "My father is a lot of things, but he really loves my mother. Even now."

Indeed, she noticed the moments of tenderness King Leofric seemed to only have for his wife throughout the rest of the evening. As dinner was announced and they made their way into the dining room, he came over to her seat to escort her, one hand clutching hers and the other resting gently on the small of her back. In that moment, as Cordilya's eyes met his, there was a flash of something: Life? Recognition? Love? Kindra couldn't exactly tell, but it was something that contrasted with the usual blankness.

What did she see that was so horrible it did this to her?

Once they were all seated, the servants brought out steaming plates of food. Jasper piled his plate high with roast vegetables, seared pork, and rolls so fresh from the oven, they were still steaming. Kindra, though too nervous to have much of an appetite, helped herself to a good amount of food as well.

Nobody dared take a bite before the king began to eat. Jasper focused so intently on his dinner that it would've been comical if it weren't so sad, while the rest of the table resumed their previous conversations. She was seated between Jasper and Celeste, Antone on Celeste's other side. Across from them sat Sebastian and Myala, and Emeline and Helena. The king sat at one end, next to his two eldest sons, and the queen sat at the other end, next to Helena and Jasper.

Celeste peppered her with questions about her upbringing in Harthwin, wanting to know everything. What was it like to grow up in a small village? What was her education like? Did she really have no formal training? Did she ever starve? Kindra gave all the proper answers: It was fine; she had been educated by her mother and the elderly woman who operated as a teacher for the kids; no, she'd had no formal training; and no, she never truly starved, though sometimes they did go hungry for a meal or two. She searched for somebody to get her out of this interrogation, but Helena and Emeline were lost in their own conversation, and Jasper was too busy shoveling food in his mouth to be of any help.

"I saw you, once," a soft, silken voice said suddenly, and the room went utterly silent.

Kindra turned to face Queen Cordilya. Judging by the looks on everyone's faces, it had been a long time since she had spoken. Even the king looked shocked.

Kindra blinked. "I-I'm sorry, Your Majesty?"

The queen regarded her silently, and for a second Kindra thought she wouldn't speak again.

"You wore a crown of fire upon your head," Cordilya said cryptically. The whole room seemed to hold its breath. But she merely returned to picking at her food and did not speak again.

CHAPTER 19

The walk back to Kindra's rooms after dinner was silent. Jasper was tense by her side. She'd thought that once they were out of the king's chambers, he would relax, relieved that the ordeal was over with. But instead he didn't even look at her as they walked. When she tried to start a conversation, he didn't reply.

After a couple minutes of this, Kindra began to worry.

Had she done something wrong and upset him? Was he angry with her? Perhaps she'd overstepped when she'd snapped at Antone, but she'd only been trying to get information about her home. And, to her surprise, she'd been defending Jasper, too.

Did she do something wrong when speaking with the king? No, that couldn't be it. Leofric had hardly said two words to her the whole evening. His mind had clearly been elsewhere—the situation with Pryllia, no doubt.

Or was it the queen? Her cryptic, strange words had stuck with Kindra all night. Everyone had clearly been shaken. When had she last spoken before tonight? And what did she mean: she saw her? Had Kindra been in one of her visions? Even worse, had *she* been the vision that broke the queen?

She risked a glance at Jasper, trying to read his expression. But his face was blank, his brow just slightly furrowed, his eyes storming.

Kindra started to feel afraid, something she hadn't felt about him in weeks. Wary, yes. Angry, often. Annoyed, almost constantly. But not afraid.

She was a fool to believe that he wasn't actually the harsh man he'd been when he'd retrieved her. He'd let her relax, get a bit more comfortable with the idea that this was to be her life. But regardless of how he flinched around his brothers and father, he was still one of them.

When they got to her doors, she hoped he would just leave her. But instead, he nodded curtly to Cerulle and Sala. "Leave us," he directed, his voice soft.

Kindra brought her magic to just under the surface of her skin as they stepped into the room. She moved away from him as soon as the door was shut, and was across the room within seconds, bringing a fire to life in the fireplace, ready to wield it in a moment's notice.

"Kindra," Jasper started, reaching a hand out to her as he addressed her for the first time since dinner.

"Don't touch me," she snapped. His brow furrowed in confusion, and then his eyes widened and his jaw went slack as he understood.

"Oh, Kindra—I wasn't—gods, no, I would *never*—" His words fell over themselves in a nervous cascade.

"Then what was that in the hallway?" she shot back. She hated how hurt she sounded.

"I wasn't—Kindra, I was just *thinking!*" His eyes, wide like saucers, were so wounded at the insinuation that she relaxed, her magic quieting.

He crossed the room to her in a few strides and cupped her face in his hands. It was the most intimate they'd ever been; his face was mere inches from hers. The heat that gathered in her cheeks was not because of her magic. She went still, unable to even breathe.

For a moment, Kindra feared—no, it wasn't quite fear anymore, was it?—that he might kiss her. But he simply held her gaze, and said, "I get in my head sometimes when I'm thinking about something. I just—I pull into myself and can't really maintain conversations around me. I was just pondering what my mother said, that's all. Trust that I would never lay a hand on you like that. I'm disappointed in myself to have made you think I'd ever do such a thing."

Kindra swallowed, then pulled back from his grasp. "Well, I still don't know what to expect here. Your brothers are awful."

Jasper huffed a small laugh, not looking away from her even as he lowered his hands. "Yes, they truly are. But they got a taste of their own medicine, tonight, thanks to you."

She shrugged, turning away, uncomfortable under his stare. "I just wanted to know if there was an update on Harthwin, that's all." She'd been polite enough about it, considering Antone's rudeness. Gods, there were so many rules here, and most of them were unspoken. How could she have known if she was being disrespectful? Were they not having a discussion?

"People behave around them almost the same as they do our father; fearful and timid," he said. "It's they who will continue the Annalindis legacy, anyhow, so I suppose it's all good practice."

Kindra turned back towards him. "How come?"

He frowned, surprised by her question. "What do you mean? Antone is the crown prince, and Sebastian is next in line. The odds of neither of them ascending to the throne are slim. I don't stand a chance at being crowned King."

"What about Helena? Does she?"

Jasper snorted. "Hel would sooner flee to Drucanar than be queen. She told me years ago that if it ever fell to her, she'd reject it and pass it down to me. Which is a shame," he admitted, "as she and Em would be far greater rulers than me."

"Why do you think you wouldn't be a good ruler?" The question was out of her mouth before she could stop it. It had been the look on his face that had pushed her to ask it—the shameful acceptance she saw there.

"Because I am weak, Kindra," he replied, voice cracking slightly. "I don't say such cruel things about myself to get your pity or to make you feel obligated to convince me otherwise—I know I am weak. I have known for a very long time. To rule a kingdom, much less one in such turmoil, it requires a strength I do not have." He shrugged. "You heard Antone. I could have followed in his and Sebastian's footsteps. I could have chosen to be a more active member of our military, be a general like them. I am a finer swordsman than either of my brothers, but my father cares so little about me that when I opted for more scholarly pursuits, he did not even fight me on it. I exist to play a role—the bookish, charming Annalindis, the youngest son who will never do anything of importance except maybe fight in whatever war we're about to find ourselves in."

"Maybe that will change, now that you are set to marry me," Kindra suggested softly, mind whirling. How did they even get here? Just this morning, they were at each other's throats at the breakfast table; just a few weeks prior she had vowed to hate him for all time. And yet here she was, heart twisting as she took in his exhausted, broken expression, feeling the urge to soothe him.

"I am inconsequential. If you'd been of marrying age a decade ago, he would have hitched you to Antone or Sebastian. The only person he cares about in this marriage is you."

"Then maybe I can make things easier for you with your brothers—"

"I don't need your protection," he snapped, and Kindra's sympathy evaporated like steam. "I have learned how to live with this."

"Have you?" she countered. Again, she was amazed at how quickly he angered her. "Because tonight you were a *shell* of the person I thought you were, Jasper. Where is the arrogant prick who took me from my home? Who threatened the life of my mother?"

"That man is fake!" Jasper shouted, and Kindra didn't even flinch, she was so incensed. "He is *fake*. It was me playing at being what my father wishes I was, okay? I thought you'd be glad to know I'm not really like that! I thought you'd be relieved!"

"Relieved to know what? That you shrink into nothing every time your brothers so much as look at you? That you're mad your father doesn't give you enough attention?" She knew that wasn't what it really was and felt a sharp twist of regret as she watched the words land, Jasper reeling back as if he'd been hit.

"You know what? Fuck you, Kindra," he spat, his pain and fury etched raw on his face. "I am trying to reach you, to connect with you, because we are *stuck together*, whether you like it or not, but you make it damn near impossible to find any sort of common ground for more than five fucking minutes."

"You're the one who's responding to me offering to help you as if I spat on you! I got them to leave you alone, is that so bad?"

"I don't need you to protect me," he repeated. "I'm not one of your helpless villagers—"

The reminder of her defenseless home sent her over the edge, and she wanted to slap him square across the face. "You dare to throw them in my face?" she roared. She knew that servants were listening outside the doors, because there was no privacy in this place, and she didn't care. "You *dare* to remind me of the people you forced me to leave defenseless in a time like this?"

Jasper began to realize his misstep. "I'm sorry, I shouldn't have—"

"So many apologies, after the fact!" Kindra laughed, but it was a humorless sound.

"I'm sorry I stole you from your home, Kindra. I'm sorry I threatened to kill your mother. I'm sorry for forcing you to give up your body to bear children you don't want. I'm sorry I constantly act like I know more about you than you do, even though I've only known you for two weeks. I'm sorry, I'm sorry, I'm sorry, Kindra, please forgive me! It's my apathetic father and my mean older brothers, that's why I behave like this, that's all!"

She saw each sentence pierce him brutally, but she felt no remorse. She was shaking with rage, barely suppressing her fire. "Have you considered that the reason I am so impossible to *reach* is because you are impossible to be with? That every time I find myself starting to hate you just a bit less, you say something so cruel I have to start all over? That maybe this inability to *connect*," she sneered, "isn't as much my fault as it is *yours*?"

Jasper didn't respond. He was pale, fists clenched at his sides.

Kindra waved her hand at the door. "Get out."

He didn't move. "Kindra—"

"Get. *OUT!*" she screamed, patience finally snapping entirely. Flames leapt from the fireplace and into her hands, burning the sleeves of her gown. Jasper stumbled backwards, alarm in his eyes, and Kindra felt ashamed to see it, even among all her fury. That he thought she would hurt him with her magic, even now, seemed so absurd it made her choke on a sob. *Of course I wouldn't hurt you,* she wanted to say, *for I am not like you. I am not cruel.*

The doors slammed shut behind him and she fell to her knees, barely able to extinguish the fire in her palms. Brutal sobs racked her body so hard her ribs strained with each one. She felt as if her heart had whiplash from being tossed back and forth so much; she'd gone from feeling fondness for Jasper to hating him within moments. He was so careless. He felt so insignificant that he believed anything he did was inconsequential. But it was consequential for her. And she desperately wished he could see that, if only to spare her from this exhausting cycle.

She vaguely heard the doors opening and closing. Seconds later, warm, gentle hands were wrapped around hers. Sala.

"Come, Lady Kindra," the Healer said softly. "Let's get you out of this dress."

Kindra couldn't respond. She was crying uncontrollably, the dam she'd worked so hard to hold finally breaking. She curled in on herself, sobbing harder.

A second set of hands, this one on her shoulders. "Here, let's help you up," came Cerulle's voice. Together, they lifted Kindra to her feet and moved her into the dressing room, where she finally got enough of a hold on herself to stand on her own.

She looked at herself in the mirror, eyes red-rimmed and swollen from crying, the sleeves of her gown scorched to the elbow. "I ruined the dress," she blubbered, feeling rather stupid. "I'm sor-sorry."

"Don't worry about the dress," Sala soothed, unlacing it and sliding it off her shoulders.

"It was beautiful," Kindra whispered, and hiccupped with another sob.

"It was," Cerulle agreed, pulling out a nightgown from a drawer, "but there will be many other beautiful dresses for you to wear."

"Yes," she murmured, and then, because she felt she had to, she added, "He was being very mean."

Her servants exchanged a glance. "Prince Jasper does not know the weight of his words, sometimes," Sala said, choosing her words carefully; Kindra knew that she'd heard most of the fight. They both had. "You are not the first person he has upset like this. He and Helena have fought countless times over similar things."

"When will he learn to be careful?" Her voice sounded so small.

Cerulle helped her into a nightgown. "I have found that caution is a rare trait among most men."

There was silence, except for the sound of Kindra sniffling and fabric rustling. "I miss my mother," she said suddenly, because why not? They'd lifted her, sobbing hysterically, off the floor; she doubted they'd ever see her much lower than that. And she needed to say it, needed to admit it. She was tired of acting like her mother's absence wasn't an ever-present ache in her chest.

"So do I," Sala replied, taking the pins from her hair.

"And so do I," Cerulle chimed in, removing the jewels from Kindra's ears and neck.

Kindra merely nodded. When they were finished, they guided her to her bed, folded the blankets back and helped her slip under them.

Kindra settled into the pillows, sleep already pressing down on her. "Thank you," she said, reaching out and squeezing their hands. "I'm sorry for my... display."

Cerulle squeezed her hand firmly in return. "Lady Kindra, you have no need to apologize. There are few here who are truly in your corner; fewer still who will never stray from it. But we are two you may always count on, even when you are sobbing on your floor. Even," she gave a small smile, "when you send a prince crying from your rooms."

"Oh," Kindra breathed, "he was crying?"

Sala shrugged, a mischievous grin blooming on her lips as well. "I do believe there were tears in his eyes, yes."

Kindra could only manage a soft hum as sleep tugged her into darkness, unable to fight her satisfaction.

CHAPTER 20

She did not speak to Jasper for an entire week.

On the first day, Helena came to visit her. The princess tried desperately to make amends on behalf of her brother, joining Kindra for breakfast in the morning.

"He's so sorry, Kindra," she insisted. "He didn't mean it—"

"Didn't he, though?" Kindra replied, too tired from a night of fitful sleep to snap at her. "I think he meant it very much." She took a sip of her tea; they were sitting at her dining table. She didn't have much of an appetite, nibbling at her food like a bird.

"Jasper says things he doesn't mean quite often, really. He's so kind, he just tends to put his foot in his mouth—"

"It's not my fault that he is insecure and ashamed of the fact that I am more capable of defending him from his vulture brothers than he is." Now she was snapping, annoyed out of exhaustion.

"Oh, because you have always conducted yourself so perfectly?" Helena fired back, and Kindra was so startled by the hard edge her voice suddenly carried that she flinched.

"I only—" she began, but Helena cut her off, speaking with sharp authority. Gone was the gentle woman who'd pleaded for forgiveness for Jasper. Before her now was an angry older sister sticking up for her little brother.

"You might think that Jasper's *attention* issues" —Kindra flinched again— "are miniscule compared to the struggles you have faced. And perhaps they are. But he has spent most of his life aiming to please a man who has always viewed him as an afterthought while being the punching bag of two brothers who delight in intimidation and bullying." Helena paused to take a small bite of food. Kindra didn't dare speak. Swallowing, Helena continued, "So yes, what he said was hurtful. He knows that. But what you said was hurtful too, and you're deluding yourself if you think he has no right to be upset about it."

Kindra was speechless, her face heated with shame. "This has just been—"

"Very hard, I know." There was sympathy in Helena's gaze, but it faded as she continued, "Believe me, we *all* know. Jasper more than anyone. And he has received your vitriol and disdain for him and this whole situation with much more understanding that anybody else in this castle would provide, me included."

"I suppose that's true," Kindra murmured, so embarrassed she could cry. Getting reprimanded by the princess was not something she'd ever wanted to experience, especially after Emeline told her Helena was a force to be reckoned with when angry. And gods above, was she. She'd left no room for argument at all.

Helena sighed, the fight bleeding out of her now that she'd made her point. "I'm not trying to minimize how you feel about this, Kindra. But a little grace would go a long way, or your life here is going to be miserable forever."

Kindra, sufficiently reprimanded, nodded in agreement and picked at her food silently until Helena graciously changed the subject.

Jasper did not come apologize that day. Or the next. Or the next. Or the next.

And with every passing moment he remained out of her sight, the kernel of fear that had taken root in her stomach that night grew larger. Fear that he would not come apologize, and their marriage was already doomed, their fragile, meager relationship already ruined beyond repair. Fear that he would instead decide to be crueler, that the charming, gentle side she'd just begun to see would vanish forever.

Fear that she had scared him away entirely.

She worried that he'd go to King Leofric and declare her dangerous— a threat. And what would happen if he did? They wouldn't let her go—no, nothing could be that simple. They'd lock her up, probably. Dangerous or not, the king had made it clear that he expected her to break the curse, and she doubted he'd change his mind because of something as minor as her threatening Jasper's safety.

She would never have tried to burn him. Even as angry and distraught as she'd been, she'd known she wouldn't lay one flaming hand upon him.

But he didn't know that. He'd only seen her screaming, flames leaping from the fireplace.

Of course, she could apologize to him. But she couldn't bring herself to do that, either. Partly because she was afraid of being rejected, but also because, despite Helena's scolding, she was not quite ready to show him any grace for what he'd said. He'd done a lot more than just saying rude things.

She could admit that she'd also spoken unkindly, that she'd diminished and mocked his own struggles, and she'd apologize for it, but not before Jasper did.

Be it foolish pride or stubborn arrogance, she just could not bring herself to go to him first.

She had taken to dining by herself in her rooms or with Helena and Emeline, both of whom mercifully did not bring up Jasper. Helena was happy to act as though their conversation had never happened. In her free time, she took walks with Emeline or, if the Wavebreaker was unavailable, with Sala or Cerulle, exploring the castle and the surrounding grounds.

She also had training sessions with Tess each day, which were quite often the only few waking hours of distraction Kindra got from her twisting thoughts. But by the fourth day, when her anxiety had rendered her barely able to eat or concentrate, even the exhilaration of wielding could not distract her.

Her control was slipping; Tess was once again able to yank her fire away with ease. The first time it happened, Kindra had brushed it off as an accident. But she couldn't focus her mind enough; her thoughts were scattered, erratic. Even the hour a day she spent trying to practice deep breathing and calmness couldn't save her. When Tess bested her again, she growled in frustration and held up a hand to stop.

Tess jogged over to Kindra as she bent over, resting her hands on her knees, panting. "Are you okay?" Tess asked. "You're not doing as well as you have been."

For a moment, she debated saying nothing. But she was tired of bottling it up. "We had a fight," she forced out, "Jasper and I. Four days ago. And he hasn't sought me out since."

"Ah," was all Tess said at first. Then, "Maybe he's waiting for you to seek him out."

"I will not go to him," Kindra shot back. "It was his fault, so he should apologize to me."

"Yes, but he is a prince, used to being treated in a certain way." Tess shrugged and reached out a hand to help Kindra upright.

Kindra frowned as she took it, standing tall. "I don't think he is, really. He's not—he hasn't had the best upbringing." Shame coursed through her as she remembered how she'd completely dismissed that truth.

Tess rolled her eyes. "Oh, spare me." She turned and walked over to the water basin, and Kindra followed.

The urge to defend Jasper crashed over her like a tidal wave. "I'm not denying his privilege. He's rich and comfortable and always has been. But his family—my family now, I guess—they are horrible, Tess, which I know you know. But—except for Helena and Emeline—they've been horrible to him. And his mother, before she…" She waved a hand, unsure of what to say about the queen and her emptiness. "Anyway, all the riches in the world can't buy you a loving family, that's all." She wiped her face down with a rag. "Besides, I don't think I made things any better. I wasn't exactly nice."

Tess studied her for a long moment. "You are kinder than I am to grant him that understanding."

"I think I have to be, if this marriage is going to be remotely pleasant." Helena had been right about that. Kindra met her orange gaze. "Besides, surely you do understand, at least a bit. You're close with Helena and Emeline—"

"Emeline," Tess corrected sharply, "I'm close with Emeline." At her bewildered stare, the Firefury shrugged. "They may be married, but they're not one entity. One doesn't have to be attached to them both."

"You don't like Helena?" Kindra found it hard to believe, but then again, she'd only known the princess for a week.

"Helena and I are not… the most compatible. I think I may be a little too vocal about my disdain for her family."

Kindra grabbed onto to the subject change gratefully, sitting down on the bench next to the basin. "Emeline seems to be plenty critical of the Annalindis family, though, and Helena doesn't seem to mind."

Tess grimaced, settling next to her. "She does mind. But she also loves Emeline too much to say anything about it. And she understands why Em would be so critical—she spent the first several years of her life in poverty, and the nobility have made a massive effort to not let her forget it. Antone and Sebastian were some of the worst offenders. So she can't say Em is wrong because she's not."

"But it hurts to have to admit she's right," Kindra finished for her, and Tess nodded.

"And with me, well." She gave another shrug. "It already sucks enough that your wife doesn't like your family, and that she's not wrong to hate them, so why make it worse by being friends with somebody else who also frequently expresses how awful they are? I get it."

"Hmm," Kindra said. "I mean, you could just not say those things around her."

Tess barked out a laugh. "Oh, we also just don't get along. We haven't from the time we were children."

"You've known her that long?"

Tess smiled bitterly. "Indeed I have. I've lived on the grounds since—" Her voice faltered. "Since I was eight."

"If I can ask, how did you come to live here?" Kindra asked softly, recalling the spiff Tess and Emeline had had when she'd first come to the training grounds, how they'd switched between referring to the Council and then one singular person.

Tess gnawed on her lower lip, looking down at the ground. For a moment, Kindra didn't think she'd answer, but then she began to speak.

"I was found on a farm outside Greymont by Councilman Avis when I was four years old. He said he found me while helping clean up after a storm, back when he was still of lower rank and did a few good deeds a year to keep up his reputation. He told me that lightning had struck my home and burned it to the ground, killing everyone inside but me." She paused, then gestured to her burns. "It's how I got these."

Kindra swallowed down her horror. "Do you remember any of that?" Kindra asked.

"I remember some things. I have memories of a family, people who looked like me. A sister, I think. I don't remember ever being alone." Tess frowned. "But it's all very scattered. I don't know. I don't really remember the storm or the fire or even being burned. Sometimes I have what I think are flashbacks in dreams—nightmares. But I can understand why my mind might block that out. Regardless, Avis took me in, raised me. He's a Windspinner, never married. I was his heir, for a time." She shuddered. "I'm glad his bloodline will be ending with him."

"Was he cruel?"

"At first, no. And that's part of why I hate him so much. He doted on me for the first few years. Until we moved here, and he was appointed to the Council. He became cruel then. But those first years... I loved him, Kindra, as any girl would love her father. He *was* my father, for all I knew, until he told me the truth when I was old enough to understand. And it really seemed like he loved me. I think he did."

"Why did he change?"

"I wasn't useful. We arrived here, and within weeks I was in intense wielding training. My magic came to me very young—younger than most, so I think he thought he'd discovered... well, I don't know what he thought. But I do know he wanted the king to pick me to marry Jasper, and his cruelty started coming out when he realized that wasn't going to happen, despite his high rank and all his pandering."

"You would've been worthy, though. You're certainly powerful enough."

"I'm not powerful as much as I am well-trained, honestly. My fire appeared early but wasn't very strong until I was in my late teens. I'm strong now, yes, but it took years of brutal training to get here. I was never like you." Her face shuttered closed, but Kindra caught the flash of envy before it disappeared. "Besides, the king would rather his cursebreaker be pretty."

"Oh, Tess," she murmured, reaching out to squeeze her hand. Tess allowed it but didn't squeeze back, staring intently at the ground.

"Avis proposed an arranged marriage between Jasper and me when I was ten. We'd barely lived here for more than a year. I liked it well enough at that point. Jasper and I had fun together, keeping ourselves busy, and Emeline was just starting to come around more often. Helena was fiercely protective of her—it was years before we were able to really call ourselves friends because of it." She looked up and rolled her eyes. "She didn't like me. I was always up to no good, she said, always getting into trouble, and she didn't want to be part of it. She would scold Jasper for going along with my 'schemes.' Little did she know, a lot of them were his ideas."

Kindra laughed a bit at that. Her heart twinged at the thought of him, but she refused to let her mind stray, not when Tess was opening up to her.

"When the king rejected the marriage proposal with some nasty remarks about my magical strength, behavior, and, of course, my scars, Avis completely turned on me. The kind father figure I'd known for years vanished overnight. He tossed me aside, barely paid me any mind, would physically push me away when I came to him. I spent years confused and heartbroken. I begged for him to treat me the way he used to, offered countless apologies even though I didn't know what I was apologizing for. I didn't know about the failed marriage arrangement until I turned fifteen and finally forced it out of him."

Tess chuckled. "I remember standing there thinking that it was all so stupid. He had loved me before the marriage idea, certainly he could love me after, right? But that was when he told me that the only reason he hadn't left me to die when I was four is because he'd known I was a Firefury. That ever since adopting me he'd been planning for this. And then he pointed at my burn scars and said that if only I wasn't so 'godsdamned deformed' it would have worked, and that he should have left me in the rubble when he saw how fucked up I was, Firefury or not."

Fury coursed through Kindra's veins. Tears pricked at the corners of her eyes. "I'm so sorry," she whispered. "Tess, I'm so, so sorry. You didn't deserve that. You didn't deserve to be a pawn."

"I know." Tess's voice was hard and cold. "And I knew it then, too. The second I turned sixteen, I abdicated my title as his heir—something he was furious about, despite everything, and changed my last name from Avis to Orindyn, effectively disowning myself."

"A commoner last name," Kindra said with a soft smile.

"Yes," she replied, and smiled slightly as well. "I thought it was the perfect way to tell him to go fuck himself. I stripped myself of all noble rank. And then I got into Grydmarth, graduated top of my class, and got appointed to the Royal Guard, one of the most elite Wielder positions in the damn kingdom."

She laughed loudly then, but it was forced, laced with bitterness. "And now, he is my fucking boss, because he is the Councilman of Defense. He revels in the fact that I tried to escape him but couldn't. He throws the fact that he saved my life in my face at every turn, undermines every suggestion I make, encourages others to disrespect me. I am one of the most competent people in this castle—my rank at Grydmarth proves it—and yet I am treated as though I am a foolish child. They hardly let me do more than grounds patrol. I have to beg—actually beg—to be of more use."

"Surely he can't just do that. Wouldn't the king—"

"What—intervene?" Tess cackled. "No, Leofric loves little games like this. He delights in it even more than Avis does."

A beat of silence stretched between them. Kindra took in everything Tess had told her. Her heart ached for her friend. "I don't know how you bear it," she murmured, "Staying here with these people. Why don't you leave?"

"Because there is still good work to be done here. And besides," Tess admitted quietly, "I just don't know where else I would go."

This time, when Kindra squeezed Tess's hand, Tess squeezed back.

Two days later, with Helena off visiting the farms that surrounded Wendrith, Kindra and Emeline had lunch together.

"What's Helena doing out there?" Kindra asked, spreading jam over a slice of bread. She'd spent the week apart from Jasper asking questions. She wanted to know who did what, when, and why; the ins and outs of the royal family and their advisers and the role she was to play in all of it. She did not want there to be any surprises; she was not going to allow herself to be caught unaware.

"Harvest survey," Emeline responded, slicing into a large red apple. "She does a lot of the outreach for the royal family. Gets out there and sees things for herself. Antone and Sebastian are too busy with readying the army, especially in the last few years, and frankly, they think it's beneath them. Jasper does a fair amount of visiting with the citizens as well, when he's not busy reading some ancient text or studying. I go with her when I can, but…" She seemed to mull over her next words before confessing, shooting her a pointed look as she did, "Well, since you and Jasper still aren't speaking, you don't have anybody else here you can rely on."

"I can rely on Sala and Cerulle," Kindra countered, choosing to ignore the comment about Jasper.

Emeline nodded. "That's true, but you can't spend all day with your servants."

She bit her tongue. She could, actually, spend all day with them. They were kind and steady and more than willing to answer her endless questions. Sala, in particular, was a joy to be around. She reminded Kindra of home. Their walks together had become a constant exchange of stories, both of them sharing their experiences growing up along the Pryllian border. It grounded her, gave her an anchor to latch on to when she felt completely lost, which was often.

But she didn't feel like arguing with anybody anymore, so she just took another bite of bread. "Fair enough."

"Speaking of Jasper," Emeline said cautiously, "how are you feeling?"

Not this again. Kindra shrugged. "I'm fine," she lied.

Emeline studied her closely, blue eyes sharp. "That sounds like a load of shit to me."

"Well, then I'm as fine as I can be, considering he hasn't spoken to me in a week."

"You know, Helena and I were hoping the little chat she had with you might offer some… perspective." Emeline cocked her head. "Were we foolish to think so?"

Great. Another admonishment.

"I won't go to him, Emeline," Kindra said stormily, already defensive. "I realize I'm not entirely innocent here, but to equate our behavior is ridiculous. I didn't take him from his home. I didn't threaten to kill his mother."

Emeline was quiet for a moment. Then she said, "I've known Jasper for a long time. Despite how Helena tried to keep me to herself at the start, I honestly considered him my friend before I did her—if only because I couldn't believe she wanted to spend time with me. He is… he does the best he can."

Kindra grimaced, petulant. "That doesn't mean I can't be upset."

"It also doesn't mean you can throw his very real pain back in his face like it means nothing," Emeline rebuked her. Kindra groaned; she was so tired of this conversation. "He's a good person, Kindra. I honestly don't know if you could've done better—"

"I could have," Kindra snapped, standing abruptly. "I could have not been forced to marry him. But here we are. So if he's as good as you and Helena swear he is, then he will learn to watch what he says—*as will I*," she added quickly when Emeline made to interrupt her, "and if he doesn't, then I will spend my life in luxurious solitude, with no hope for companionship, because gods know I can't do shit about it."

"Are you really so lonely?" Emeline asked softly. Kindra only stared at her. "You fill your days with activities," she explained. "You seem to have taken a liking to Tess, and Hel and I thought…"

"You all have been very kind," she conceded, "and I am grateful. Though, Emeline, perhaps it has simply been too long for you to remember. But you of all people should know just how lonely this is."

Emeline was briefly stunned into silence, and Kindra left before the princess could reply.

CHAPTER 21

Jasper finally showed himself that evening.

Kindra was hunched over her trunk of belongings from Harthwin, finally unpacking it, when the knock came. She knew in her gut that it was him even before she opened the door and saw him standing there.

He was holding a bouquet of flowers. It, along with his sheepish posture and expression, caused her stomach to flip with something between fear and excitement.

"May I come in?" he asked, eyes scanning her nervously.

She sighed, schooling her expression into one of indifference. "I guess." She stepped aside, waving him in. Cerulle, who was sitting outside the door, met her eyes and nodded slightly, reassuring Kindra that she wasn't going anywhere.

Kindra turned and walked back to her trunk, returning to her task. She tried to slow her pounding heart as she heard the door shut gently behind Jasper as he entered.

"I brought you flowers," he said, rather pathetically.

"Okay," she responded, not turning to look at him. She pulled out a stack of books—her favorite stories, the leather spines cracked and worn from years of love.

"Um, okay," Jasper stammered, clearly having expected different behavior from her. "I wanted to apologize. For what I said."

"Okay," Kindra repeated. There was silence. She stopped her unpacking with a sigh and looked up at him. "Well?"

His eyes widened. "I thought you'd be a lot… I thought you'd be different, than this. I had a whole speech prepared—"

"Ah, yes, one of your infamous rehearsed spiels meant to placate me," she snipped, unable to help herself. But then she took a deep breath, reigning herself in. *Grace, Kindra. Understanding.* "Just, out with it. I'm tired of this."

"Tired of what?"

Tired of not knowing where we stand. Tired of being afraid you may have turned your back on me. Tired of feeling torn between hating you and wanting to be near you.

"Tired of fighting," she said, voice heavy.

"Gods, me too." He kneeled down beside her, still clutching the flowers. "I'm really sorry, Kindra. It was cruel of me to bring up Harthwin."

She said nothing, only watched him. When he realized she wasn't going to reply, he continued, "I know that I've said and done some pretty shitty things to you, and I'm not considering how that has affected you, even with my apologies and attempts to mend things after. I get... frustrated when you don't see my good intentions—because they *are* good, Kindra, please believe me on that, even if my delivery isn't always the best."

He looked down, cheeks flushed with shame. "The truth is that I was jealous. I *am* jealous. I'm jealous of how easily you can speak your mind and how unafraid you are to protect those around you. It's like second nature to you. But instead of telling you how good it felt to see you hold your ground against my brothers, I let my insecurity take over. I lashed out, and I tried to make you hurt like I hurt. Because you're right—I am small, when they're around. And in that moment I just wanted you to feel small, too."

He blinked rapidly, his gray eyes rimmed with silver. "I really want you to be happy, despite everything that stands in the way of that. And I know," he took a deep breath, "that I am one of those obstacles. I know that you would rather be anywhere but here with me. I have to accept that. And maybe the only way for you to have a shot at being happy here is if I stay out of your way as much as possible, so I have fewer chances to put my foot in my mouth and say something utterly ridiculous that hurts you." A beat, then, "That wasn't really what I'd planned to say, in case you're wondering."

The rawness in his voice stirred a deep ache in her. And she realized then that she didn't want him to stay away from her, that the anxiety she'd felt over the last few days had not only been because of the unresolved anger between them, but also because she had grown used to his presence. She had, despite everything, come to find some sort of comfort in it.

She had missed him.

"I don't want you to stay away from me," she said roughly, and shock flashed across his face. She swallowed thickly, surprised to find she was fighting back tears, too. *Gods, what is happening to me?*

"Oh," was all Jasper could say.

"You just have to be more careful. And," Kindra paused, choking down her stupid pride, because it was her turn to apologize now, "I have to be more careful, too. I'm sorry for what I said. Truly." His eyes widened; he clearly was not expecting an apology from her, and that actually made her feel worse. "I just—I've been having a hard time adjusting to all of this. And I am angry about it still, but I know there's nothing I can do to change it… so…" She gave a small half-smile. "There's no point in wishing for something else. I *am* stuck with you. You're stuck with me."

She looked down at her hands, still resting on the rim of her trunk. "I don't think I'd be any happier here if we were estranged. I'd rather… I'd rather figure out how to lo—" She stopped short, rapidly correcting herself, "like you. And at least be amicable towards one another."

He nodded eagerly. "Yes, yes, that's what I want, too. More than anything."

"I just can't do the back and forth anymore, Jasper. I can't keep bouncing between liking you and cursing your name. It's exhausting."

His lips twitched in a slight smirk. "But you like me?"

She scowled, but she was fighting back a grin. "Shut up. You know what I mean."

His smirk vanished and he reached out to grab her hands, dropping the flowers on the floor. Her cheeks flushed with heat at the contact. "I do know what you mean. I'm so tired of it, too. I'm used to feeling like I'm just shouting into an abyss." He lifted a hand and brushed his fingers across her cheek. "But you're not an abyss," he murmured, a strange, almost reverent look on his face.

"Obviously not," she tried to joke, but her heart was in her throat and she was very aware of the sparks his touch was leaving in its wake. "I thought I'd scared you away," she whispered, needing to voice her fears, for him to chase them away.

His brow furrowed. "Oh Kindra, you could never scare me away." His hand came to cup her face, his other still clutching her own. "Even at your angriest, I still find you beautiful." He said it softly, more to himself than her, like it was some new realization that was just now hitting him.

Kindra's head began to spin with the closeness of him. She might have been shaking.

In that moment, she both wanted him to kiss her and to be as far from her as possible.

"Why did it take so long? For you to come back to me?" It was a miracle she could even speak. Her voice was a breathy, tattered thing. Everything about this was too much. His proximity, his openness, his touch. The way he looked at her. The way she craved and hated all of it at the same time. "It's been *days*." A mere week, and yet it had felt as long as a year to her.

"I was worried you wouldn't want to see me. I wanted to give you space. And… I wanted to make sure I had sorted myself out enough to not fuck up again when trying to apologize." They were locked in a staring contest, neither of them looking away. His thumb brushed softly against her lower lip. She worried her heart might explode. *Stop touching me. Keep touching me. Kiss me. Get away from me. Do it again.* Her thoughts were a jumbled mess. "Do you forgive me?" He leaned closer, his nose nearly brushing hers.

"I'll have to think about it," she breathed, her lips brushing against his thumb as she spoke and sending a shock down her spine. "I haven't decided." Her hand, seemingly of a mind of its own, came up to rest on his chest, lightly clutching his collar.

"Mm," he murmured, breaking eye contact to stare intensely at her mouth. "Well, do let me know what your verdict is, Your Highness."

"Do you forgive me?" She had to know. She had to.

Jasper's lips quirked up in a soft smile. "Kindra, I forgave you before I even left your rooms."

Gods.

The small space between them was stretched tight with anticipation. For a second, Jasper looked as if he really might do it: close the gap between them and press his mouth to hers. And in that fleeting second, Kindra wanted him to, all doubts and frustrations aside.

But then she came back to her senses. His remorse was genuine; she knew that. But the words he'd said in his anger still smarted whenever she thought of them.

Plus, a small part of her hated to think that she'd be placated this easily. Could this be all it would take for her to forgive him—to allow him to touch her this way?

She pulled back, clearing her throat awkwardly. Jasper pulled away, too, looking down at his now empty hands. He looked embarrassed; she knew that she wore a similar expression.

"I'm sorry," she started, wanting him to understand, somehow. "I just—I'm not—"

"It's okay," he assured her quickly. "I don't have any expectations from you, not like that."

Kindra opened her mouth to say something more but thought better of it. Jasper, looking desperate to change the subject, glanced at her half-empty trunk. "What's in there?"

She latched onto the subject change like a lifeline. "Things from Harthwin," she explained. "Though none of it really fits in here." She ran her hand over a thread-bare blanket: it had been hers since she was born. "I don't even know where to put it all. It sticks out like a sore thumb against all this luxury."

Jasper smiled softly. "I have one of those, too," he confessed, nodding to the blanket. "I couldn't sleep without it until I was fourteen." At her surprised expression, he held his hands up defensively. "I know it's embarrassing, but it was comforting to me."

"It's not embarrassing," she replied, gently taking hers out of the trunk and setting it on her bed. "I used to go everywhere with mine. Couldn't let go of it. My mother finally got me to stop taking it out in public when I was eight, but I still carried it all around the cottage with me until I was twelve or so." She paused. "I kind of stopped needing it, after I started…"

"Yeah, I understand." Kindra knew his interruption was an act of mercy; she was grateful for it. "Mine is still in my room. I'll show it to you, when you—" He cut himself off. "Um, I mean—never mind." His eyes moved to Elric's dagger, the one thing she'd left untouched. It still hurt too much. "Wow, that's a beautiful dagger." He reached for it, then hesitated. "Can I?"

She nodded mutely, her eyes stinging slightly. "Elric gave it to me before I left," she told him numbly. *Before I knew he'd betrayed me.* But the thought lacked its old malice.

Jasper turned the dagger over in his hands, marveling at the engravings and fine metalwork. Suddenly, he brought it closer to his face, thumb pressing down on a fiery sun. The sun sank in and released a tube from the hilt of the dagger.

"What?" Kindra leaned in too, curiosity getting the better of her. "What is that?"

"I think," he mused, "that it's a container for something." He looked at her, gray eyes sparking with excitement, and scrambled to his feet. He ran over to the lamp on her nightstand.

"Jasper, what are you doing?" She got up and followed him, brow furrowed in confusion.

"I think it's supposed to hold oil!" He blew out the flame, and carefully removed the oil bowl. "Gods, this is going to be so remarkable if I'm right, Kindra."

Slowly, he poured some of the liquid into the tube, then slid it back into the dagger's hilt. Then he grabbed her hand and dragged her out onto her balcony.

"I'm still not really sure what's going on," Kindra said, as he held the dagger by the hilt so it was facing down.

He held up a finger. "Watch. The oil is slowly coating the blade." He was practically radiating with energy; she was seeing a whole new side of him. Sure enough, the blade was taking on a slight sheen as the oil drizzled down it—not too much, but just enough to make it slick and shiny.

Jasper laughed, amazed. "Here." He reached for her hand again, and she let him take it, and he placed the dagger in her palm, wrapping her fingers around it. "Now, use your magic and ignite it."

Kindra did as he requested, sending a small burst of flame from her hand and down the hilt of the dagger. Immediately, the blade caught fire. Hesitantly, she let go of her control over the flames, and the dagger continued to burn. A smile sprung to her face unwittingly. She latched onto the fire once more, honing its shape into something precise and sharp.

"Amazing," Jasper remarked softly. She turned to look at him, and they beamed at each other, the thrill of their discovery melting away any last bit of tension that remained between them from the last few days. "He designed this weapon specifically with your magic in mind."

She didn't respond, partially because the thought of Elric painstakingly crafting something for her made her throat tight. But she was also too transfixed by her dagger to reply. Hesitantly, she swung it, as if she were facing an enemy. A lot of concentration was required to keep the flames in the shape she'd wanted; it was far easier to let the oil do the job of maintaining the fire. Then, with a pinch of giddiness, an idea formed in her head. She knew it wouldn't be possible for more than a moment or two, but she wanted to try it.

She formed the flames into a long, narrow shape, spilling off the end of the dagger. Then, she swung the dagger, putting all her energy into keeping that fiery thread, and it snapped in the direction of her swing like—

"A whip," Jasper blurted, bouncing up and down on his feet like an excited child. He was a true scholar, thrilled by innovation and creativity. "A fire whip!"

Her head ached slightly at the force of her focus, and she relaxed, allowing the flames to recede back to their natural shape along the blade. "It's hard," she commented, "to make it hold its shape and use it at the same time. It would take a lot of practice to master it."

"Imagine a sword like this," Jasper gushed, "Built for a Firefury such as you, so you can fight with something other than your magic."

"I don't want to fight with something other than my magic," she said quickly, feeling anxious at the thought.

"Well, of course not. I suppose you'd still be using it, to shape the flames on the sword as you wish—"

"I'm fine with just my magic," she insisted, rather petulantly. "I don't need a sword, or a whip, or—this." She extinguished the flaming dagger with a single breath, and handed it back to Jasper, who regarded her warily. She knew he was considering his every word.

"It's still incredible, though." He turned the dagger in his hands, carefully avoiding the blade, which was still hot. "This Elric fellow is quite impressive."

Kindra merely grunted in response, striding off the balcony back into her rooms. Jasper followed. Cautiously, he said, "I think you should consider it—using this. Learning how to work it into your wielding. I'm not telling you what to do," he added quickly as she turned to shoot him a glare, "I am just making a suggestion. For no reason, frankly, other than my own curiosity."

She looked at the dagger again, held delicately in his hands. "I do not need the help of weapons," she muttered. "I *am* one."

His eyes widened. "I don't dare suggest you need help, Kindra," he said soothingly. "I just—" He stopped himself, started again, "If I had magic, I would—gods, the things I would try! I would experiment with every possible way to enhance my wielding. I would spend hours figuring out all the possibilities, because it seems, from an outside perspective, that they are *endless*. There is always more being discovered. And I just wish I could take part in it myself, really. So I just think you should think about it. That's all."

She studied him for a moment, taking in the passion—and envy and grief—on his face. "You want to have magic so you can... do experiments?"

Jasper blushed. "Well, that's not the only reason." He shrugged. "That wasn't a very Annalindis answer of me, was it?"

Kindra shook her head. "Not exactly what I expected, no."

"Oh, then let me try again." He cleared his throat, then declared, taking on the stern, cold tone of his father, "If I had magic, I would use it to raze my enemies to the ground, and then I would dance upon their ashen remains!" He raised an eyebrow. "Is that better?"

The laugh was rolling out of her before she could stop it. But it was real—not the half chuckle she'd given him on the carriage ride through Wendrith, but a real, full laugh. Jasper seemed completely shocked by it, which only made her laugh harder. Then he broke into a broad grin, his cheeks dimpling, and he laughed too.

They were still chuckling when there was a knock on the door, and it opened a moment later to reveal a pair of guards—Jasper's, if she recognized them correctly.

"Your Highness," one of them said, "you are needed in the War Chamber." *What a ridiculously ominous name for a room,* Kindra thought.

But Jasper went stiff at her side immediately, all humor vanishing. "What's going on?"

The guard's eyes slid to her, narrowing slightly. They were green like chips of emerald. "There's been a development. You are to come immediately."

"Is it Pryllia? Have they made their move?" Kindra asked nervously.

The guard regarded her coldly. "Respectfully, this is not of your concern, Lady Kindra."

She bristled, and Jasper did as well. "She is to know of any new development along the Pryllian border, Tomas," Jasper snapped, and she was stunned by the bite in his voice.

"I need to be there," she insisted, a thousand scenarios running through her head, each one more horrible than the last. Her breathing hitched. Jasper grabbed her hand, giving it a comforting squeeze.

Tomas shook his head, still not budging. "She is not permitted—"

"Where are you from, Tomas?" she asked sharply.

Tomas blinked. "I'm from here, Lady Kindra."

"In that case," she snapped, "you don't know how it feels to be hundreds of miles away from your home when an army could be marching towards it."

She took a step towards the door. When the other guard moved to block her path, she shot her a scorching glare that had her halting mid-step. "I'm going to the damn meeting. They'll have to slam the door in my face to keep me out."

The two guards blinked, clearly at a loss for what to do. Jasper waved at the door. "Well, are you taking us to the War Chamber or not?" A tiny thrill zipped through Kindra at his demanding tone.

Tomas stammered, then sighed. "Yes, fine. But," He gave Kindra a hard look, "I am not going to take the blame when this goes poorly."

"This is entirely my idea," she assured him. "I wouldn't want you to take responsibility for it." Though she was doing her best to seem confident, anxiety was pooling in her gut. Surely, they'd let her in. It was her home. They wouldn't bar her from a meeting about her home, would they?

Tomas relaxed a bit at her reassurance and fell into position in front of them alongside the other guard.

Quickly, they led them out of her rooms and down to the War Chamber. The walk there was tense and silent, which did nothing to quell her worries. Though Jasper's hand was steady in her own, his palm was growing sweaty, and one glance at him out of the corner of her eye revealed that he was starting to look very nervous. She didn't want to know if it was about the meeting itself or trying to get her in.

Finally, after descending several flights of stairs and winding through corridors, they rounded a corner to see the entrance to the War Chamber. Kindra sucked in a deep breath.

"Here goes nothing," she murmured as they approached the door, and one of the guards posted by it slipped in, likely to alert those inside of their arrival.

They were going to let her in. They had to.

The door swung open. Kindra readied herself for whatever was coming: be it the king's acceptance or his wrath.

But it wasn't the king that stormed out to meet them.

It was Antone.

"You are out of your fucking minds," the crown prince snarled as he stalked towards them. If looks could kill, she and Jasper would both be dead. "Who gave you the *fucking right*—"

"It's her home, Antone," Jasper argued, voice wavering only slightly.

"Oh, was this your idea of a romantic gesture?" Antone sneered. "Bring her to a highly confidential meeting?" He grabbed a fistful of Jasper's collar, jerking his brother out of her grip and shoving him against the wall. The guards watched, faces impassive, like they'd seen this a million times. "I should break your nose for your presumptuousness."

Kindra started, her fingertips sparking. "Let go of him," she demanded.

"Is she your guard dog, little brother?" Antone hissed down at Jasper, who glared at him with hateful eyes. "Still haven't learned how to stick up for yourself, have you?" Jasper pushed back at him, and he relented, releasing him and turning his spiteful gaze on Kindra. His lip curled. "You are not permitted in the War Chamber."

"Why not?" she shot back, her anger threatening to get the better of her. "You're talking about my home in there!"

"We're talking about a lot of people's homes in there," Antone retorted, "but you don't see all of Mistbarrow breaking down the door."

"They're not here. *I* am. I can advocate for them—"

"We do not need your fucking *advocacy*, or whatever you want to believe your self-righteous bullshit is," he spat. He pointed down the hallway, away from the War Chamber. "Go back to your rooms. Let us handle this."

"Oh, because you've handled it so well so far?"

Antone was suddenly mere inches from her. She felt his hot breath on her face, and it took everything in her not to flinch away. "Let me make myself *very* fucking clear: you are not yet a princess. You do not officially hold any title. This tantrum you're throwing would get any other person thrown in the dungeons. But because our King, for whatever reason, is interested in you, I will not give that order."

Jasper tried to interject, yanking on Antone's arm, and the crown prince spun on his brother. "And *you*," His voice began to climb into a yell, "who's only here because Father requested it, not because you have any military experience to warrant it, have the fucking *gall* to bring your betrothed—who has *no* experience, *no* rank, *no* permissions, *nothing!*—to an emergency meeting that only the highest-ranking among us are called to? Are you fucking *insane?*"

Kindra began to realize that she'd made a grave misstep. This had been a bad idea. Tomas had been right to try and dissuade her. She'd thought, foolishly, that when she'd won her little face-off with Antone at dinner a few weeks ago she'd quieted him for good.

But Antone was still the crown prince, the next King of Alverin. Losing one small argument to her was not going to make him relinquish his authority.

"Antone, she just wanted to know if anything was going to impact her home. Can you understand that?" Jasper all but pleaded.

Antone scoffed. "You know, the one thing you've always had going for you is that you're smart, Jasper. But this is just moronic. Why would you throw all common sense and regulation out of the window because some woman asks you to?" He took a deep, stabilizing breath, and pinched the bridge of his nose.

When he spoke again, his voice was deadly calm. "It does not matter that it's her home. She has to be granted entry into these meetings by the king—and that is *not* going to happen today."

"I'm the cursebreaker—" she started, using her last possible card, and Antone laughed bitterly.

"Don't bother." He leaned in close to her again, and whispered, "We both know you won't be breaking any fucking curses."

She recoiled, shocked speechless that he'd say that so freely. Antone pulled back, smirking.

"Guards," he ordered, "escort our *cursebreaker* back to her rooms, and ensure that she stays there. Give her a book to read or something. And Jasper," he barked, "make your way into the War Chamber. Father will be here shortly." His lips curved in a wicked smile. "I can't wait to see what he says about this debacle. You should just be grateful he wasn't here to witness it." He turned on his heel and strode back to the War Chamber, not looking to see if Jasper was following.

The guards started to walk towards her, and when she took a step after Antone, angry that he was getting the last word, they blocked her path. Unlike Jasper's guards, they were not cowed by her burning gaze. One of them was even a Firefury, and his gleaming yellow eyes never left her.

"Kindra, I'm sorry," Jasper apologized, defeated. "I thought—"

"It's okay," she said, still glaring after Antone. "It was my idea. I should've known better."

One of the guards—the Firefury—gently took her by the arm, and she jerked away. "Do not touch me," she snapped, "I can walk myself back." Mercifully, the guard didn't try again. She faced Jasper. "I'm sorry if this gets you into any trouble. Tell them it was all my idea; that I forced you into it or something. I don't—" she swallowed, "I don't want you getting hurt."

He smiled at her, but it wasn't reassuring. "It's nothing I won't be able to handle."

"*Jasper!*" Antone thundered from the War Chamber.

Her betrothed looked over his shoulder at the room. The guards began walking forward, slowly guiding Kindra away. "I'll come, after it's over," Jasper promised, and when Antone yelled again, he turned and walked quickly into the War Chamber, the door slamming closed behind him.

CHAPTER 22

The guards did not say a word as they escorted her back to her rooms.

She did her best to hold her head high as she walked, to not look like she'd just been screamed at by the crown prince. She wasn't sure how many people managed to walk away from one of those encounters in one piece, so she supposed she should be grateful screaming is all he'd done.

He did say that if it weren't for the king's interest, he would have thrown her in the dungeons. So though she was enraged—more than that, humiliated—by how he'd treated her, she knew she'd been lucky today.

She only hoped that she didn't just make Jasper's already strained relationship with his family even worse.

When they got to her rooms, Cerulle and Sala, wide-eyed, opened the doors for her. The guards hovered behind her, and she shot them a sour look. "What, are you going to lock me in?" she snapped, uncertain that they wouldn't

The Firefury cocked his head. "Do we need to?" he replied.

She balled her hands into fists, grinding her teeth together. Humiliating. This was all so humiliating. "No," she bit out, and stormed into her rooms.

The doors slammed behind her, and through them, Kindra could hear muffled, agitated conversation.

Fear shot through her. Were they actually going to lock her in? She wasn't stupid; she wouldn't try to force her way into the meeting now that she'd been rejected. But the guards didn't know that.

She wrenched open the door. Cerulle and Sala were gone, replaced by not one, not two, but six guards, who turned and regarded her with compassionless expressions.

"Where are Cerulle and Sala?" she demanded.

"They've been released for the day," one of the guards replied. "We will be watching your chambers instead." Then, as if he wanted to rub salt in the wound, he added, "Let us know if you need anything, Lady Kindra."

She huffed angrily and shut the door.

So she was not going to be leaving her chambers for the rest of the day. That much was obvious. Technically, they weren't locking her in, but they may as well have.

Rather than sit and fume over something she couldn't control, she decided to keep herself busy. She finished unpacking her trunk. When the guards brought her dinner, she ate it, forcing food down her throat but not really tasting it. She even tried to calm her mind with one of her breathing sessions, but she gave *that* up not even fifteen minutes in and instead opted to pace about her rooms.

Lots of pacing.

When Emeline strode into her rooms a couple hours later, Kindra was so relieved to see another human who wasn't a guard she nearly cried.

"Kindra," Emeline began before she could even greet her, and her relief vanished.

"I know, Emeline," Kindra all but shouted, exasperation and shame fueling her outburst. "Spare me the lecture, please. Gods know I've gotten enough of them in the last week."

Emeline's mouth hardened into a firm line, her eyes storming. The last time they'd spoken, Kindra had snapped at her and stormed out of the room. The princess was probably debating whether or not she should tear into her for doing it again.

When she spoke, her voice was low and serious. "I was going to ask if you were doing all right, that's all."

"Oh," was all Kindra could say in response, embarrassment heating her cheeks. Then, "Sorry."

"You should be," Emeline replied curtly. Kindra stared at the floor. Emeline's next words were gentler. "We are not your enemies, Kindra."

Silence hung between them for a few heartbeats, before Kindra admitted, "It doesn't feel that way right now. I feel… I feel very…"

"Lonely? Isolated?" Emeline guessed, and Kindra nodded. Emeline sighed, some of the tension leaving her body. She eased herself onto the sofa. Kindra remained hovering near the fireplace. "I've decided to forgive you for how you spoke to me earlier today," she declared, voice jarringly authoritative. At Kindra's shocked expression, she continued, "That's not some royal declaration. I'm deciding to forgive you because you are my friend."

"Am I?"

"Yes, Kindra."

"I thought friends were supposed to be more understanding," Kindra grumbled, so tired of being talked to as if she was a stupid child.

"Have I not been?"

"You've spent an awful lot of time telling me to just get over it. All of you have."

"That's not what we intended—"

"Well that's how it *feels*, Emeline," Kindra shot back hotly.

Again, silence stretched between them.

"Then you will have to forgive us. We only want this transition to be as easy as possible for you. Maybe we don't know what it's like to be in your shoes, but we do know how cruel the people in this castle can be. We can help you settle in here and get used to your new life. That's all we've been trying to do." Emeline paused. "There's—there's no going back, Kindra."

"I know," Kindra whispered.

Emeline nodded. "Then all is forgiven?"

The assumption in Emeline's voice grated on Kindra's nerves. There was more to be said—more she wanted to say, at least, even if Emeline felt otherwise.

But she was so exhausted. And she knew Emeline was telling the truth: they were only trying to help her adjust to this life as best they could, even if they sometimes dismissed Kindra's feelings in the process.

But that discussion was for another day. Several days, if she was being honest, because their perspective wasn't likely to change any faster than hers.

"Fine," Kindra muttered, then repeated more firmly. "Fine. All is forgiven." She shrugged. "Jasper and I have made up, anyhow."

Emeline smiled. "Well, thank the gods."

Kindra frowned. "He's not getting strung up at the gallows for what happened, is he?"

"No, no. The king was probably pissed, though."

She shuddered. "The gallows aren't much worse than that."

Emeline chuckled. "No, I suppose not." The princess studied her for a moment. "You shouldn't give up this part of yourself, by the way."

"What part?"

"The part of you that pushed you to try to get into that meeting. Your sense of right and wrong." With something akin to hope flashing in her eyes, she continued, "There's a way to hold onto that here. You just have to learn how to play the game."

"And what part of myself will I sacrifice in order to do that?"

"Probably the part that makes you scream at crown princes, unfortunately."

Kindra laughed. "Unfortunate, indeed," she murmured.

Emeline departed soon after, the peace between them restored, and Kindra was left with a dark cloud of worry around her.

She couldn't help but think of her mother. Was she safe? Was Harthwin still standing? All the horrible possibilities danced in her mind, laughing. *And you aren't there,* they cackled. *You're tucked away in a castle, doing nothing.*

She snarled, running her hands through her hair, begging her mind to be silent. Her magic thrummed, desperate and aching to be expelled, to be useful in some way. But she was trapped here. Her power couldn't help Harthwin from hundreds of miles away.

I have to get into those meetings.

That was the only way she could try to help Harthwin and Mistbarrow and all the other villages along the border. She had to get into the War Chamber. There had to be some way to get the king's permission. She'd beg him, if she had to, though the thought made her stomach turn.

After distracting herself by changing into her nightgown and wrapping herself in a blanket, she settled onto the sofa. The clock on the mantle was approaching eleven. Outside, the night sky was clear, her balcony bathed in silver light from the full moon. The fire in the fireplace was getting low, and she lazily waved it back to life.

Kindra relaxed, settling into the plump cushions, studying the flowers now standing in a vase on the end table. Her eyelids drooped, and she struggled to force them back open. All the stress from the last few hours— few days—was bleeding from her body, and she became acutely aware of how exhausted she was.

Jasper will wake me, she reminded herself as her eyes slipped closed again. *I can rest my eyes, just for a bit…*

CHAPTER 23

A gentle hand shook her.

Kindra jolted awake with a start. Jasper was sitting on the sofa, his hand on her shoulder, a soft, tired smile on his face. She scanned him quickly, checking for any bruises. But he was unharmed, physically, at least. As she sat up sleepily, she wondered how long he'd been sitting there, watching her sleep. The thought did not disturb her as much as it once would have.

She looked at the clock. It was just past midnight. "Did you just now get out?"

Jasper nodded. "Yes, it was a long night." His mouth stretched open in a wide yawn, and he blinked blearily, scrubbing a hand across his face.

"What happened? Are you all right?"

"Yes. Father was—well," he chuckled drily, "We will get to that in a second. There were bigger problems at tonight's meeting than us. The Whisperer in Mistbarrow is dead."

Kindra was suddenly wide awake. "What?"

"She has been for a week now. We didn't know until tonight—that was what the meeting was for. We were worried they'd started to move, and we would be in the dark until news reached Bridgewood. But we're lucky— gods, we're so fucking lucky."

"So they haven't attacked yet?" Hope began to bloom in her chest, a fragile, fluttering thing.

Jasper shook his head. "No—and there's a new Whisperer posted at Mistbarrow now, courtesy of Bridgewood. There are normally three posted there, so they had one they could spare. But, Kindra…" He swallowed thickly. "I am glad that you weren't there tonight. My father was particularly... aggressive. My brothers, too. Threats were made. People were... people were hurt."

"What do you mean?" Kindra sucked in a nervous breath. "Did he hurt you, Jasper? You told him it was my fault, right?"

Jasper placed a hand over hers. "I assure you, Kindra, I am fine. What occurred between you and Antone was nothing compared to..." He trailed off briefly before continuing. "You know of the Council, I assume, and what their duties are."

"Vaguely. Tess told me about them."

"There are six of them. They decide many things together, but each of them individually oversees different parts of the city and kingdom. Councilman Avis—Tess's... whatever—is the head of Wendrith's defense, including the Royal and City guard, for example. Councilman Terbis oversees our agriculture and livestock, the food and water supply throughout the kingdom. And Councilman Epira..." He paused, looking pained. "Councilman Epira manages our communication, our trade. His domain is the Hall of Mirrors."

"He's in charge of the Whisperers," Kindra murmured, already sensing where this was headed.

"The Whisperer from Mistbarrow only reports in every few months or if there's an emergency. And when we heard of the army amassing at the border—well, that's an emergency. But the Whisperer didn't send any message. And instead of finding that strange or concerning, Councilman Epira did nothing."

"He didn't think anything of it? He didn't try to reach her?"

Jasper shook his head. "No, he did not. He was as shocked as the rest of us at the news. And to be the one person who should have already known—who could have prevented the chaos that was tonight, or at least lessened it—that's not something that sits well with my father."

Kindra couldn't say she blamed King Leofric for being angry. "What did he do?"

"Accused Epira of disloyalty, of working with Pryllia. Screamed at him for failing to do his job. And then he smashed a wine bottle over his head."

Alarm shot through her. "Gods, did he kill him?" She *was* glad now that she hadn't been there.

"No, but I'm sure Epira wishes he had." He looked away, to the fire still burning in the fireplace. "You know, my grandfather, Peter Annalindis, was ruling when it became public that the curse did indeed exist. We'd done a good job of keeping it secret. We stopped fighting wars, stopped murdering everyone who stood in our way. My great and great-great grandparents paid millions to all the kingdoms we'd terrorized for centuries. They hoped it would be enough to atone for all we'd done, to keep them from coming for revenge, exposing that we were no longer blessed with the power of a god." He chuckled darkly. "But the kingdoms wanted their land back. And of course, we said no. I always thought that was strange—my family acts like we did such a good deed, but we didn't give back anything we took from them, not really. No way for us to bring back the millions of people our armies have killed. And the one thing we could give back—their lands—we wouldn't do."

He sighed. "I mean, logistically, the argument my family made to keep it made sense, I guess. A lot of that land has been ours for centuries. There are generations of Alverinian families settled there. Some of it is only developed because of us. But... I understand why the other kingdoms wanted it back. And I understand why our refusal would make any amount of financial gift or trade deal basically worthless in the eyes of people we've destroyed and stolen from time and time again."

He cleared his throat. "Anyway, all that to say, my grandfather became fearful and mistrustful once it became public knowledge that we were cursed, and my father has followed in his footsteps. Especially over the last several years, as tensions have started rising again. We did a lot of damage to our neighbors, and a big part of that was making them almost entirely dependent upon us for a lot of resources. They've had to work furtively in preparing for this. And my father has always been worried about a war that we don't see coming. He has talked about it all my life. So Epira has no excuse for his lack of awareness. It's just pure Alverin arrogance. But my father has never believed, for one second, that this kingdom is safe."

"I suppose that's good, at least, that he doesn't think we are invincible, like some of the others in the War Chamber," Kindra tried weakly, but Jasper just shook his head.

"He still thinks we're superior to all of them. He doesn't think we have anything to apologize for. He's the one who stopped the yearly payments to our neighbors, the second after his coronation. He's shrunk trade agreements, shattered any relationships we were developing with other leaders—which were tentative in the first place. He's practically invited them to do this. He wants them to because he dreams of being the king that leads Alverin back into war and re-establishes us as the most powerful kingdom on the continent."

"And when those around him are foolish…"

"That hurts his chances of victory," Jasper finished, and smiled sadly. "We really are terrible."

"You're not." The words were like a reflex.

He met her eyes, and for a moment they simply stared at each other. Her cheeks heated as she recalled the last time they'd looked at each other so intensely. He swallowed, and she knew that he was thinking about it, too. "I'm glad you think that," he murmured. Their knees were touching.

Kindra's skin itched, the way it always did under the heat of his gaze. She looked away. "So, what is the plan now?"

Jasper leaned back into the sofa, his leg still pressed against hers. "A pretty sizable chunk of our army is on the way to the Pryllian border now. Should be there within the next week."

"Did you… did he say anything? About me getting to come?"

"Oh, yes." Jasper smiled. "He said it would be unprecedented for you to attend."

"Why are you smiling?" Kindra asked. "Isn't that basically a no?"

He shot her a smirk. "When Antone told him about what had happened—quite dramatically, I'll say—he expected for you to be barred from all future meetings, and probably me as well, for good measure. But that didn't happen. Honestly, my father seemed kind of pleased to hear about it." He laughed softly. "All he said was that comment about it being unprecedented and moved on. Antone was furious." He grew serious again. "My father never dances around what he means unless he wants to. If he wanted to say no, he would have."

"I have to prove to him that I should be in there," she said, understanding. Jasper nodded. Determination settled over her. "So I'll prove it to him."

He reached over and grabbed her hand, intertwining his fingers with hers. She both cherished and despised the comfort it brought her. "I have no doubt that you will," he replied, a gentle smile blooming on his lips.

And they were back to staring at each other again.

"I'm glad we're friends again," Kindra blurted, unable to peel her eyes away from his.

Jasper laughed breathily. "So am I, Kindra."

Just like before, that heated, fragile tension was building between them. As if pulled by some invisible force, she found herself leaning towards him, the blanket falling down to gather at her waist. His eyes darted from hers, briefly, dancing over her shoulders and chest, left exposed by her nightgown. He inhaled sharply. When he looked back up, his gray gaze burned like molten steel.

"You are more beautiful than I ever dreamed you would be," he breathed, and his words wrapped around her like an embrace. "I don't—I don't deserve you."

"You don't," she agreed, even as she moved closer and closer to him. Despite everything that had happened today, it was just one day. It mattered so little in the grand scheme of things.

Jasper blinked, surprised by her honesty. She smiled, feeling bold, and reached up to lightly touch his lips with her fingers. "Not yet, at least," she finished, reveling in how still he was beneath her touch, the slight tickle of his breath against her fingertips.

"Becoming worthy of you will be of utmost importance for me, Your Highness." His mouth brushed her fingers with every word. The sensual use of her future title sent a zap of lightning down her spine.

"I look forward to seeing you endeavor to do so." Oh, how she was starting to enjoy this little game they played, this dangerous line they both seemed to love almost crossing.

"I'm sure you do." Jasper grabbed her hand, pulling it from his mouth and to the side, exposing the underside of her wrist. He placed a soft kiss there. Kindra could have ignited.

His eyes danced with a challenge. She saw plainly what he wanted— what she wanted, too. And perhaps, if things were different; if she were here with him of her own accord, if he had not made her cry just days ago, if they were different people, she would have given it to him at that moment.

But things weren't different. And though it was all better than she expected—the castle, many of the people, and, shockingly, him—it still was a situation that made her sick when she thought about it too much.

He sensed the shift in her, the walls going back up. Delicately, he set her hand down. "You should get some rest," he said, giving her other hand one final squeeze before unlacing his fingers from hers. She tugged the blanket back up around herself. "The guards are gone, by the way," he added. "King's orders."

He left her on the couch after placing a chaste kiss on the back of her hand, leaving her to stew about just what she was getting into with him before drifting back to sleep in front of the dying fire.

CHAPTER 24

The next day, Kindra strode into the training grounds with a mission. The king wanted her to prove herself? Fine. She'd prove herself.

Tess was stretching her legs when Kindra entered the ring.

"I want to spar with you," Kindra announced as she walked up. "We've just been doing exercises since I arrived. I want the real thing."

Tess blinked, then smiled. "All right. If you feel ready."

"I don't have time to wait until I feel ready," Kindra responded, stretching her arms over and behind her head.

The other Wielder grimaced. "I don't suppose any of us do."

The pair moved to a clear spot in the giant ring. On the other side, Terryn was busy sparring with a Windspinner, wielding giant masses of greenery to block against heavy gusts of wind. A small crowd was gathered around them. Most were guards, but Kindra spotted a few among them who must be nobility; their nerushmyr was plain or decorated with colors associated with their families rather than the Annalindis crest.

"We go until first burn," Tess declared, gesturing to the trio of young men sitting off to the side. "There are Healers here."

Kindra nodded, adrenaline pounding through her veins. Her magic thrummed to life. She sucked in a deep, grounding breath, and then—

Tess came at her like one of the fire-breathing beasts of legend.

Kindra thought she was prepared, having spent so much time sparring with her over the last week. But soldier Tess was very different from teacher Tess, and if she didn't figure out how to adapt to the difference *right now*, this match would be over embarrassingly fast.

She barely managed to block Tess's first blast with one of her own. The air between them exploded into flames. Kindra staggered back a step, the force of their magic colliding temporarily unbalancing her. But she regained her stability, taking an open stance Tess had shown her a few days ago, one that would allow her to be grounded but also agile, able to dodge and move around a battlefield with ease.

Tess did not give her time to make her own strike. As soon as the fire started to clear, she shot half a dozen arrows of flame at her, one after the other. Kindra swung her arm out and deflected four of the six with a shield of fire, but the other two changed course, dodging around her defense. She reached for them, sweat already beading on her forehead as she fought against Tess's iron grip of control. When the other Wielder did not relent, the arrows heading straight toward her, she swung out her other fist, sending a wide blade of fire surging towards Tess low to the ground. Tess was caught off guard by it—only barely, but enough that she had to divert her focus towards dodging it. Kindra felt her hold over the darts weaken; she seized control and sent them flying to the ground.

Now, she was on the offensive. She charged forward a few steps, sending blasts at Tess from all heights and angles; some she sent in low, others she shot to the ceiling and then brought down, others she made swoop in from the sides.

Tess deflected them all, either by dodging or blocking them or wrenching control away from Kindra. And she still managed to respond with her own attacks; broad balls of inferno that had Kindra rolling across the ground to escape, slender snakes of flame that made her dance on her toes as she desperately tried to wrench them from Tess's grasp.

She couldn't tell how long they'd been doing this—maybe it had been minutes, maybe it had been hours. Her muscles screamed with every move she made. Sweat dripped down her face, into her mouth, her eyes. Nevertheless, her magic was singing. It was more alive than it had ever been, and perhaps she was, too.

It was like a dance, she realized as she spun on the ball of one foot, shooting her other leg out in a sweeping kick that shot a swath of fire at her opponent. She and Tess were dancing.

She watched Tess dodge, ducking low. She sent a slither of flame across the ground, so small it was hidden amongst the burning bits of ground beneath them.

Tess didn't see it.

Kindra's heart swelled as she realized the other Firefury had missed it, too focused on preparing her next move. Before Tess could attack, Kindra doubled the slither in size and sent it darting for her wrist.

Tess saw it then. She swore and leapt out of the way, reaching for the flame with a fist. Kindra felt the tug of Tess's magic against her own. Strong as she was, Tess was still stronger, at least when it came to this.

Kindra had to distract her. Wildly, she shot a ball of fire at her from the other direction, large and unavoidable.

Her friend looked at her briefly then, and before she turned away, her lips curved up in the slightest of smirks. Kindra grinned back, her smile sharp as a blade as Tess moved to block the fireball, allowing Kindra to maintain control of her tiny little sliver of flame and reach up to lightly tap against her arm.

Tess yelped; Kindra let her seize the fireball and dissolve it into nothing. She leaned forward, her hands on her knees, panting. Distantly, she heard Tess call for a Healer.

Only when her heart began to slow did she look back up.

They had attracted an audience.

Terryn and his opponent must have either finished or halted their match, for they now stood off to the side, along with the crowd they'd gathered. There were others, too; some watched from the seats above the ring, having trickled in during their fight.

All of the spectators wore an expression of astonishment.

Kindra looked away from them, directing her attention back to Tess, whose arm was already healed. The red-haired woman was leaned forward, same as Kindra, face wet with sweat. And she was beaming at her.

"You are something else," she laughed between deep gulps of air. "Holy *shit.*"

Kindra gathered her strength and walked over, her legs angrily protesting with every step. "You're something else, too," she replied, reaching out a hand and pulling Tess upright.

"I've never seen brute power quite like that before." Tess's orange eyes were wide, amazed. "If it had been anybody else, that last move wouldn't have worked. I could've easily handled both attacks. But the size of that—and you weren't even trying, were you?"

Kindra blushed, feeling sheepish. "No, I just knew I had to distract you." She paused. "How long were we sparring?"

Tess laughed again, like she couldn't quite believe what she had just witnessed. "Nearly twenty minutes, the Healer said. Everybody stopped what they were doing and came to watch about five minutes in—most matches don't last more than ten."

"I can see why. I'm exhausted."

She stepped closer to Kindra, so the crowd had no chance of overhearing them. "You know, I hate to say this, because I hate the man, but—Leofric was actually onto something with all his bullshit about you being worthy. You—gods above, Kindra. You have a lot left to learn, and it could use some refinement, but damn. Most Firefuries can only dream of casting blows of that size like they're nothing."

Kindra's head spun a bit at that, and she struggled to keep her smile on her face. Suddenly, she wanted to get out of the conversation.

So she turned around and faced the crowd. "You," she declared, pointing her finger at Terryn, who paled. "I want to spar with you, tomorrow. Are you up for it?"

"Um," the Earthwarden stammered, lacking his usual cockiness, "maybe not—"

"War is coming to Alverin," she snapped, raking her stare over them. "You all know this. So if you are too cowardly to face me, an untrained Firefury from the outskirts of our kingdom, what will you do when an entire army marches upon us?"

"I'll spar with you, cursebreaker," the Windspinner that Terryn had been fighting said. The title chilled her to the bone. "It would be an honor."

She steadied herself, gave him a curt nod. "Good. Who else? I could do four or five a day, perhaps, with breaks in between."

A few others started volunteering. A Wavebreaker from a noble house; an Earthwarden from the guard; even Terryn ended up caving.

"Put me on the list, too," Tess said, clapping her on the shoulder. "I want a rematch."

And as Kindra left the training grounds that day, her hair plastered to her face with sweat and smelling of smoke, a smile crept onto her face.

A smile that persisted despite what she heard in her wake: the whispers calling her the cursebreaker, the hushed voices calling her a future queen.

How's that, Your Majesty? She thought smugly as she made her way back to her rooms.

How's that for proof?

CHAPTER 25

That evening, Jasper and Kindra dined together, just the two of them. Kindra had been nervous about it at first, because the last time they shared a meal together, it had ended with Jasper storming out and Kindra's pride wounded. She'd been worried that this would end similarly.

But they were different now. Or at least, they were trying to be.

So far, the meal had been surprisingly pleasant. Of course, the food was incredible, the roasted meats and vegetables as delicious as ever.

It was Jasper that surprised her. Specifically, it was the fact that she was actually enjoying his company.

She knew they'd been steadily growing closer despite their arguments— especially after last night. But now, with a truce between them and a better understanding, some of the fraught tension had eased, although the tension they'd felt when they'd been mere inches away from kissing each other remained.

That, rather unfortunately, was not going anywhere.

"I heard you beat Tess in a match today," Jasper said, breaking the comfortable silence that had stretched between them as they ate.

"Yes," she replied, slicing into a piece of pork. "Just barely, though."

"The guards were talking about it earlier," Jasper informed her, shooting her a grin. "None of them could shut up about it, in fact. They also couldn't stop talking about how you demanded to spar with half the Royal Guard."

Kindra shrugged, swallowing her mouthful. "I figure it's as good a way to prove myself to the king as any. And it'll be good for me." She offered up a dry smirk. "Haven't had many opportunities to just spar with people, you know?"

"It seems you and I are the opposite in that regard," Jasper mused, leaning back in his chair. He sipped on his goblet of wine. The setting sun cast an orange glow over him; Kindra desperately tried to ignore the way it highlighted his cheekbones and sharp jaw. "I spent a lot of time sparring and not nearly enough doing the real thing."

"You went to Grydmarth, right?" she asked. At his nod, she continued, "What was that like?"

He shrugged. "Fine, I suppose. Some parts of it were wonderful: the library, the sword masters, and, of course, getting to live off the castle grounds." His lips quirked upward in a smile that lacked warmth. "But a lot of it was not to my liking. Antone and Sebastian fared much better there."

"Why's that?"

"Grydmarth is, ultimately, meant to churn out people for a fierce army. Future generals, like my brothers, powerful fighters for the frontlines..." He gestured to himself. "And I am not either of those things." He didn't seem to be self-deprecating as he spoke. Just matter of fact.

"You're a master swordsman, though," she blurted, remembering what she'd overheard some of the guards saying about him while at the training grounds and what Jasper himself had said about his skills.

Jasper's mouth twitched again in a smile—this time a real one, and her cheeks burned.

"Is that what they call me?" When Kindra didn't answer, he nodded. "I am, yes. Received the highest score in my class at Grydmarth for it—higher than anybody in the last decade, actually." He couldn't keep the hint of pride out of his voice at that.

"So, why are you not more active in the army, like your brothers?" Her disdain for the older princes, Antone in particular, overpowered her trepidation surrounding Jasper, and she added, "You are clearly a superior fighter."

And superior in just about every other regard, too, she was discovering.

Jasper's mouth opened in shock, delight dancing across his features. "Such flattery, Kindra! I'm honored." Though his voice was light, it wasn't mocking. Kindra's face flushed again.

Jasper continued, his smile fading, "To answer your question, I'm not more actively involved with the army because my brothers do not want me there, and my dear father doesn't care enough to contradict them. Antone and Sebastian do well enough—neither of them excelled in anything, but they're decent strategists, and with the sharper minds of the other generals around them, they haven't totally doomed us. Yet."

"It's a shame," Kindra admitted, "that they don't involve you more, and only seem to call you in when it's an emergency."

He nodded in agreement. "It is. Though they mock my affinity for books, that kind of intelligence is useful in a war room. I think, deep down, they know that, and that's why they still bring me in during dire situations. They also lack the ability to interact with most people without looking down their noses at them, making them fairly useless when dealing with the general population. That's why Helena and I handle most of the forward-facing affairs instead." He shrugged and took another sip of his wine. "They also really hate that I'm a better swordsman than the two of them combined."

She smiled, not doubting that for a second. "Did you ever spar with them?"

Jasper laughed. "Oh, yes, many times. They loved sparring with me when I was young and scrawny—half of the time they'd forgo the swords and just pummel me with their fists." Something dark crossed his face, but it was gone in a heartbeat.

"Jasper, that's awful," Kindra said. Once again, her heart softened with understanding for him. After Antone's behavior towards him yesterday, she wasn't at all surprised to learn that Jasper had grown up being a punching bag for his brothers.

"Of course it was, but that's why I'm the swordmaster of the family, and they are not." He grinned with satisfaction. "The first time I beat Antone in a match, he and Sebastian had been gone for several months at Grydmarth. I spent every waking moment they were away training with the Royal Guard. When they waltzed into the ring demanding to fight with their little brother, they were very unprepared. It only took a couple rounds before both of them stormed away, and we never sparred again." A pause. "Honestly, that's about the only time I can remember my father being proud of me."

Before Kindra could respond, he gestured to her. "And you? What was your training like? I know you learned the ways of your magic on your own, but what about your schooling?"

She scrutinized his voice for any trace of scorn, any suggestion that her upbringing was inferior to his. When she found none, she replied, "There was an older woman in Harthwin who had once studied at one of the academies—the one in Dewport, I think."

"Ah, yes, Miralt Academy." Jasper nodded for her to continue.

"Right. Well, I don't know how she ended up in Harthwin, but she's been our equivalent of a teacher for as long as I've been alive. She made sure all of us could read and write and taught us about the history of Alverin." She smiled sheepishly. "She also did her best to teach us some mathematics as well, but I never took to that too much."

"You are not alone in that," Jasper replied. "I struggled with it too." He regarded her with a keen interest that made Kindra fidget in her seat. "So, history, mathematics, what else? Any literature?"

Kindra narrowed her eyes. "What is this, an interrogation?"

He shook his head rapidly. "No, no. I apologize. I'm just curious, that's all. Forgive me if I seem overeager."

She relaxed a bit. "Fine," she relented. "I got to read some literature. But we didn't have a library. It was just Ms. Padalyn's—that's the teacher— her personal collection. She tried to find ways to get more books for us, but unless she made the journey to Mistbarrow or Bridgewood, it was hard to come by new titles. I acquired a few books of my own over the years, but only a dozen or so."

Jasper nodded thoughtfully. "I am glad that you had access to what seems to be a quality education."

Again, an opportunity to mock her, but he sounded entirely serious. Still, Kindra didn't quite trust it. "I'm sure you're relieved to be marrying somebody literate."

"Of course I am." He gave her an exasperated look. "Aren't you relieved to be literate as well?"

He had her there. She took a long sip of her wine. "Sure I am. Makes life a lot easier."

They sat in silence for a moment. It was not quite awkward, but not quite easy, either.

Jasper broke it. "I wish you would trust that I don't think you're beneath me because of your background."

"I never said that," she said defensively.

"You don't have to say it, Kindra."

She worried her bottom lip. She had been quite obvious with her distrust. "Why would I?" She shrugged. "I have no official schooling. I don't hold a certificate from one of the academies. I was taught by an old woman in my tiny village of not even a hundred people. The farthest I'd traveled before you showed up was to Mistbarrow." Jasper opened his mouth to interrupt but closed it when she held up a hand.

"So, with all these marks against me, why *wouldn't* I expect you—a prince who graduated with distinction from the greatest academy in Alverin; somebody who has traveled hundreds of miles across our kingdom, who has had access to all the knowledge and training anyone could ask for—why would I *not* expect you to look down on me?" She cocked her head as she looked at him. "*I* know that I am smart and capable, despite what some people may say are shortcomings. But why would I expect you to know it?"

Jasper considered her words, regarding her thoughtfully. When he finally spoke, his words were soft, but serious. "I know we've already talked about this, but I really do not put myself in your shoes as much as I ought to."

"You don't," Kindra agreed, then conceded, "But it goes both ways. I also don't consider you as much as I should."

"Oh?"

She nodded. She'd avoided saying this last night when she apologized, but it was necessary. Before she lost her courage, she said, "It was easier to believe that because you are royalty, your life has been devoid of hardship. And in all the material ways, it has been." Jasper nodded his agreement. "But you…"

She looked down at her plate, pushing around the few remaining bites with her fork. "You have had your own struggles, just as I have had mine. And I've realized that we actually have more in common that I initially thought—or wanted to believe."

She glanced back up at him, and found that he was smiling at her, that delicate, reverent look back on his face. She fidgeted under his gaze. He raised his glass in a toast, just for them. "Well, here's to considering each other, Kindra."

She raised her glass in response. "I'll drink to that."

CHAPTER 26

Over the next week, Kindra sparred with nearly two dozen people, some more than once. None of the matches went as long as her match with Tess had, so she had much more energy that she'd initially expected.

She'd fought Terryn thrice, emerging victorious every time, although he'd come close during the third match. He was a formidable opponent. They all were, but she found many of them lacked a real desire to win. They wanted to beat her, of course, but they didn't know the desperation with which she fought each match. They hadn't faced the same things she had while growing up, they didn't have anything to prove to the king; they'd proven themselves already, and that was why they were here, in the Royal Guard.

But several did best her. Ryle, the Windspinner who first accepted her challenge, did. He fought with a type of ruthlessness she thought bordered on psychotic: he'd cut off her air supply until she was on the edge of unconsciousness during their match. Jasper—who, of course, was there as often as possible—had nearly lost his mind because of it.

"Are you insane? Were you trying to kill her?" he'd shouted, Tess and Emeline barely holding him back.

Ryle had denied it profusely, dark gray eyes wide with alarm. "She has to learn how to fight Windspinners," he'd argued. "We pose a bigger threat to her than any other elemental."

Kindra had sided with him once she'd regained her breath. Jasper had brooded for the rest of the day because of it. She'd snapped at him for it that night over dinner. It was the closest they'd come to a fight in days, but it didn't boil over. Kindra had acknowledged his protectiveness and had even swallowed her pride enough to thank him for it.

And Jasper did not get angry at anybody who defeated her anymore.

Tess also beat her in their rematch. It wasn't nearly as long as their first, but it came close. Tess was adapting to her, figuring out her fighting style and modifying hers accordingly. Kindra might have more power, but Tess was a far smarter fighter, and it showed. Despite her initial victory, she doubted she would beat the guardswoman again anytime soon—and was glad of it, if it meant fewer comments about the strength of her magic.

Emeline even sparred with her, to Kindra's surprise and delight. She was fast on her feet and entirely unpredictable: a storm turned to flesh. Their match was a draw. Kindra had been drenched to the bone, her skin littered with a dozen cuts from the shards of ice Emeline loved to use, and Emeline was covered in an equal amount of burns, the end of her long, braided hair singed.

The Earthwardens were the easiest to fight. She could rely on sheer power to overwhelm them, and she'd grown used to battling them during her time in Harthwin, as they were the most common Elemental Wielder.

The Wavebreakers were harder: she had to be smarter, faster to outmaneuver them, or else she'd find herself too wet to light a single spark.

But the Windspinners were practically impossible. They could suffocate her from yards away, could send her flying across the ring with a wave of one hand. They snuffed out much of her fire with ease.

She lost to all of them.

It was for this reason Jasper once again broached the subject of her using physical weapons alongside her magic.

"I think it would be good to have a backup plan, Kindra," he argued. They were walking in the gardens. The air was crisp, but the sun was shining, still offering some warmth to them. It was midafternoon. They had just eaten lunch together after Kindra bathed off the sweat from the morning's sparring session.

She'd fought five matches and won three of them. The two she'd lost to were both Windspinners, but her continuous defeat by them didn't frustrate her as much as it made her more determined to figure out a way to best them.

Kindra sighed, shaking her head. "I don't even know how to use a sword. I don't see how that would help me."

"You could learn!" Jasper's voice was strained, teeming with exasperation. It grated mildly on Kindra's nerves. Despite how much easier their relationship had become over the last week, she still didn't like it when he told her what to do. Even though that wasn't necessarily what he was doing, she still bristled at every piece of advice or idea he offered. "It could prove useful to have something else to fall back on if your magic fails you." He felt her stiffen and squeezed her arm where it was looped through his. "Oh, gods above, Kindra, you know I don't mean it like that."

She gave a soft *hmm* in response, swallowing down the spike of annoyance.

"Look." Jasper stopped and turned to face her. "You think beating a Windspinner is hard in a sparring match? Try doing it when they're *actually* trying to kill you. There's a reason they make up the bulk of the Royal Guard. Ryle is intense in the ring, sure. But he was in my class at Grydmarth, and what you're seeing in these matches is *nothing* compared to what he's really capable of. I've seen him kill people before, when we had to serve along the border for a year. They didn't stand a fucking chance. It was over in seconds. I'm not insulting you when I say I think you should learn how to fight with more than just your magic. I'm saying that when a Windspinner cuts off your air supply and you can't produce a single ember, you could at least have a dagger on you so you could chuck it at their stomach and give yourself a fighting chance."

And despite all her stubbornness, Kindra found she couldn't argue against that.

"Fine," she conceded, and Jasper's face lit up victoriously. She turned away, and they resumed walking, arms still linked. "I'll wear Elric's dagger tomorrow. I haven't a clue how to use it, though, so I doubt it will be much help."

"I'll teach you," he offered, and when she raised an eyebrow, he said, "Master swordsman, remember?"

After thinking about it for a moment, she agreed. "Okay, you can teach me. Perhaps we can have night sessions, so I have a bit of a break during the afternoon to relax."

Jasper clearly hadn't expected her to be so open to him teaching her. He blinked, at a loss for words momentarily. Then he said, "Sure. Yes. That could work. We could train every other day. You deserve to have more than just afternoons off. You'll run yourself ragged."

She nodded. "Every other night, then."

And that was that.

Kindra strode into the training grounds the next day with Elric's dagger strapped to her thigh. Jasper was already there, standing with Tess and Ryle, which was odd. His expression was even odder: his mouth was drawn tight with worry, and his eyes had a panicked, wild look in them.

There was a fairly large crowd in the seats around the huge ring. She didn't pay much attention to it; she'd acquired a bit of an audience over the last week. While most of the people she'd sparred with so far had been members of the guard, she'd also gone up against a couple Wielders of noble rank. She'd started hearing talk from courtiers about who was daring enough to get into the ring with her and even people suggesting they start placing bets. It was irritating and trivial, but she welcomed any chance to improve her skills, so she wasn't going to say no to anybody, even when it was some snotty, privileged heir.

Besides, completely obliterating them was far too satisfying.

"I wore the dagger, as promised." She gestured to her leg. "Why do you look so sick?"

Jasper stared past her, over her shoulder. "I think you got what you wanted, Kindra," he said, voice thin.

She turned around, and her heart plummeted to her stomach.

King Leofric, along with all six members of the Council, were sitting in the stands, right in the front row.

"Oh, shit," was all she could say. Then, weakly, "I thought it would've taken a bit longer." She wished to have had more time to get better. More time to figure out how to beat a Windspinner.

"You should probably go say hello," Tess said. Even her voice was tense, lacking its usual dry humor. Her eyes kept darting anxiously to the king and the Council. Kindra knew that she was looking at one Councilman in particular.

Kindra steeled herself and silently uttered a prayer to Yvangil, the god of luck. She'd never given that deity much thought before, but now she begged him for even the smallest of blessings as she made her way over to stand beneath King Leofric.

She bowed low, hands pressed flat against her sides to hide their shaking. "Your Majesty," she called up, "I'm honored to see you here today." She nodded to the Council, acknowledging each of them in turn. "I am honored to see you here as well, Councilmen."

King Leofric smiled, and once again she was struck with how terrifying it was. "We simply had to come and see our fierce little Firefury at work. Word travels fast around the castle, Lady Kindra." His grin turned lupine. "You've bested quite a few of my guards and courtiers in combat these last couple of days. It's sent quite the message about your power."

He knows what I want. She realized, and now she was really praying to Yvangil and Scaldor and Cyrie, and every deity she could think of. "I have been bested myself quite a few times as well, Your Majesty," she replied, very aware of how quiet it was; she'd never heard the ring be so quiet. She tried for humility. "I'm just doing what I can to improve my skills and prove my worthiness to you. I have quite a bit to learn, as this is my first time receiving any kind of formal training."

"Yes, Guardswoman Avis has been teaching you, hasn't she?" One of the Councilmen was speaking. Kindra looked at him, took in his silver-streaked brown hair and rodent-like face. She didn't need to see the gray of his eyes to know who he was: Lord Avis, Tess's estranged caregiver.

"Guardswoman *Orindyn* has been, yes. She's been most helpful," she replied before she could stop herself. His face twitched, his eyes narrowing with fury.

The king's grin only grew. "I have a request, Lady Kindra, if you would be so kind." He folded his hands in his lap, looking almost casual.

"Yes, Your Majesty?" Her heart stuttered in her chest.

"You've proven by now that you're more than capable of defeating Earthwardens. You've held your own against some of our best Wavebreakers, and you've defeated one of the Royal Guard's most notorious Firefuries." Her stomach sank. "But you've yet to emerge victorious against a Windspinner." He cocked his head to the side, his gaze sharp as knives. "I want to see you defeat one, today."

CHAPTER 27

Kindra's mouth ran dry as she processed King Leofric's request. No, request was the wrong word.

Demand was more accurate.

The king leaned forward, that wolfish smile still on his face. "Well? Do you think you can, *cursebreaker?*"

"I—" She stopped short, biting back her initial response, which would have been, *I will do my best.* She forced herself to be calm and fought the waver out of her voice as she met the king's gaze. "Yes, Your Majesty. I can. Who shall my opponent be?"

She knew his pick before he said it. "Lieutenant Ryle Mistron had you incapacitated within two minutes, I heard. I think a rematch is called for; don't you think?"

Kindra could not bring herself to speak. Though she'd agreed with Ryle's reasoning for being so aggressive in their match, it had still been terrifying. She simply nodded and bowed again. Then she turned on her heel and walked back to where Jasper, Tess and her opponent were waiting.

Jasper grabbed her hands. "You have to be fast," he whispered very quickly. "That's how you win. Don't give him the chance to suffocate you. Keep him on his toes—they have to be grounded on their feet to wield, so just keep him moving. You have the strength. Hit him with everything you have. And the dagger—if you have to throw it, do so with a grip on the blade, not the hilt. The hilt is heavier because of the oil holder. It's all in the wrist. Just—try to avoid hitting any organs." He squeezed her hands, gave her a smile that didn't quite reach his eyes. "Show him just how powerful you are."

I'll try. She moved away from him, out to the center of the ring, right in front of King Leofric. She faced Ryle, who gave her an apologetic look before falling into an open wielding stance.

That single look made Kindra's focus snap into place, her nerves going from wild to eerily calm. Fury ignited inside her. Ryle was assuming she was going to lose. He was already sorry for the humiliation her defeat would bring.

Tess stood off to the side. "On my count," she called. "Until one is incapacitated or yields."

Kindra knew she wouldn't be yielding voluntarily. *He will have to choke me unconscious.*

When Tess yelled, "Three," Kindra struck first, an indiscriminate wall of flame flying across the ring.

Ryle cut through it with a knife of hard wind. Kindra jumped out of its path, and broke into a run, hands outstretched as she let her magic stream out of her.

Jasper had been right: if she was fast enough, and if she didn't let up, Ryle did not have a chance to do anything other than block her fire or send sharp gusts of air towards her that she easily dodged.

Sweat already gleamed on his olive skin, his shoulder length black hair damp with it. She had surrounded him in a ring of fire. He thrust his arms out on either side, and from his body came a surge of cold, brittle air, extinguishing half of the flames and shrinking the remaining ones down to mere inconveniences.

Kindra swore as he raced towards her, leaping straight over a swath of burning ground. He shot out his hand, clenching his fingers into a fist, and yanked on the air around her. She felt her lungs constrict as she began to lose her air supply. *No.* She started to move again, kicking out a foot and sending a shot of fire towards him. He swerved out of its path, and as he did so, he lost his control, the air surging back into her body. Gasping, she continued her onslaught: move, fire, move, fire. He moved with her, ducking and blocking as he did. His brow was furrowed with concentration, and bewilderment—he clearly hadn't expected her to last this long. It had been, what? Five minutes, now? She felt a trickle of pride, but it was momentary.

Kindra's stamina was faltering—her body's, not her magic's. She'd been sprinting nearly nonstop since they'd started, and with the strain of wielding at the same time, her muscles were aching already. If she could just stop for a moment, anchor herself, she could probably finish him off with one blow, if she could make it big enough—

Suddenly, her feet were not on the ground, and she was flying through the air. Ryle had managed to get ahead of her and had swung a low current of air towards her, tripping her. He'd then brought the current underneath her, catapulting her across the ring. A scream ripped out from her involuntarily, cut off abruptly as she slammed into the ground. Something cracked—a rib, maybe? Her vision went black at the corners.

Distantly, she heard Jasper yelling her name. "*Get up!*" he shouted. Some others from the crowd joined in. Others called for Ryle to finish her.

Blood filled her mouth—something was definitely broken, then. She coughed on it, scrabbling in the dirt, trying to get her hands and knees under her.

She looked up. Ryle was strolling casually across the ring towards her. He had a few burns on his face and arms. A few of them were bad enough that they bled, dripping red down his forearms. So she'd gotten him, too, at least.

"Do you yield?" he asked, stopping about ten feet away.

Kindra drew herself into a kneeling position, then started to stand. Her hand came to rest on her thigh—against her dagger.

Blood dribbled down her chin; her right side was absolutely screaming with agony. "Never," she croaked, fighting tooth and nail to make her voice heard across the ring.

People cheered.

Ryle sighed, looking deeply sorry. "Okay," he said, and then snatched the air from her lungs.

Kindra fell back to her knees. She gasped at nothing. One hand came up and clawed at her throat. Her vision blacked out entirely for a moment, her head swam.

She willed her eyesight to come back, forced herself to zero in on Ryle, standing so relaxed just feet away, so sure of his victory.

She pulled the dagger from its sheath. Her chest constricted, her heart thundering dangerously. *Throw it by the blade. It's all in the wrist.* She gripped the blade in her hand, trembling with the effort. Her vision went black again, then returned, blurry.

She was so close to passing out. Seconds away.

Kindra focused her eyes as best she could on his shoulder. She figured her throw would go wide, so she aimed for his chest.

She mustered all her strength into her arm and threw the dagger as hard as she could before slumping forward to the ground.

Ryle let out a stunned, pained shout, and suddenly she could breathe again. Vaguely, she was aware that spectators were wild with cheering in the stands.

Head spinning, she pulled herself to her feet, gulping down air. Nausea threatened to overwhelm her, but she forced it back as she staggered over to where the Windspinner was crouched on the ground, her dagger buried three inches into his right shoulder. The dagger had flown wide, as she'd expected.

She summoned her flames, surrounded him with them, so close they licked at his skin. They were weak but did the job. He screamed.

"Do you yield?" she choked out. He didn't respond. She brought the fire in closer, and he screamed again. "Godsdammit, YIELD!" she screamed—or rather, begged. *I need this. You don't understand. I need this.*

And then, after painstakingly long seconds, Ryle nodded vigorously, still clutching his wounded shoulder. "I yield," he rasped.

Instantly, she extinguished the flames. Healers were already sprinting towards them. One of them was Sala, who raced towards her with outstretched hands. Jasper and Tess followed.

Jasper's face—she couldn't look at him. Instead, she stumbled towards King Leofric and the Council.

He was clapping, that petrifying grin back on his face. The Councilmen were clapping as well, but they didn't look nearly as delighted as he did. Some of them looked furious—Councilman Avis was one of those, and she saw fear written on more than one of their faces as well.

Good, she thought, satisfied.

She stopped before the king, swaying slightly on her feet. Pain and adrenaline made her reckless; she dipped low in a clumsy, smart-assed curtsy, her side smarting as she did so. "I hope you've been thoroughly entertained, Your Majesty," she slurred, tongue weighed down by blood and agony.

For a second—a mere flash—he looked murderous, and she figured she'd just signed her death warrant. But he only nodded. "Oh, yes, Lady Kindra. It is a true privilege to witness a Firefury with such power as yourself in action. I have *wonderful* hopes for your *contributions* to this kingdom."

She read the meaning in between his words plain as day. "Yes," she agreed, knees threatening to give out. "So do I."

He stood, as did the Council. "See a Healer," he ordered. He glanced past her, voice turning cold, "If only so my youngest doesn't have a heart attack."

The second he began to walk away, Sala, Jasper and Tess were there. Helena and Emeline were running over as well, having been watching from the stands.

"My lady," Sala started, hands reaching for her. Jasper was speechless, his skin blanched white, eyes wide with terror.

Kindra swayed again. "I think," she said, already falling, "I need to lay down."

She was unconscious before she even hit the ground.

CHAPTER 28

The pain was gone when Kindra woke up, replaced with the dull ache of exhaustion.

As she crawled back to consciousness, she became more aware of where she was. She felt the plush mattress beneath her, the silk of her bed sheets. She heard the low crackling of the fireplace and the voices of several people.

"She cannot start this with him," somebody was saying, voice song-like even in anger. Helena.

"She's not starting anything with him, Hel, she's just trying to do what she can to protect her home." That was Jasper.

"He's going to treat this like another game—"

"I don't think he will," Emeline's raspy timbre butted in. "I think he respects her, after today."

"Em, you cannot be serious—" Helena's voice was getting higher with every word.

Kindra made some kind of noise—a mix between a groan and a whimper, and they fell silent.

She opened her eyes and took in the scene before her.

She was in her room, tucked into her bed. Sitting in a chair at her side was Sala, who was dozing, her head drooping onto her chest. Her brown skin was waxen, her cheeks gaunt—Sala must have expended a lot of energy when healing her.

And across the room, by the fireplace, stood Helena, Emeline and Jasper, where they'd clearly been in intense conversation. They'd frozen where they stood, staring at her with wide eyes.

"How—" She tried to speak, but her throat was paper dry, choking off her voice as she fell into a coughing fit. This woke Sala, who scrambled to pour her a glass of water as the others rushed over.

"Kindra," Jasper said her name like a prayer. He reached her first, crawling onto the bed towards her as she gulped down water. He looked a mess: his hair was disheveled, pulled in a hundred directions. He had discarded his jacket, leaving him in just his shirt and trousers. The top few buttons of his shirt were undone.

He brushed his fingers against her cheeks, her forehead. She let him, too tired to jerk away, even though she was uncomfortably aware of Helena and Emeline's eyes on them.

"How do you feel?" he asked.

She pulled the glass away from her mouth. "Tired," she answered, and he gave her a watery smile.

"I'm sure you are." He tried to laugh, but it came out as a battered exhale instead.

Kindra studied him, then the others. They all wore similar expressions. She glanced at the windows. Outside, it was growing dark, the sun having just set, leaving the sky a smear of pink and purple.

"How bad." She didn't bother to phrase it as a question.

Helena shook her head. "Don't worry about that. You're all right, that's all that matters. Sala did her duty beautifully."

"How bad, Helena."

The princess swallowed thickly. "It was bad, Kindra. You—when you collapsed—when Sala got you out of the nerushmyr... your whole side was—"

"It was practically black," Jasper whispered. He looked haunted.

Kindra nodded slowly. "I thought—I thought I cracked a rib, when I hit the ground."

Emeline snorted. "*A* rib? Kindra, you *broke three*. It's a damn miracle you didn't have a punctured lung."

Gods. "Well, Ryle was quite the opponent." She paused. "Speaking of him, is—"

"He's fine," Helena soothed her worries. "The Healers patched him up good as new. He's resting now but will be back on duty in a couple days."

She nodded again, feeling very fragile. "And I'm—I'm okay?"

"You're okay, my Lady," Sala said, voice thin and weak. She reached out and rested her hand on Kindra's. It was clammy and cold, so unlike the warm touch she was used to. "I wasn't strong enough—to mend everything entirely. You will be sore, but nothing more."

Kindra squeezed her Healer's hand. "Sala, thank you. A little soreness is nothing I can't handle. I didn't have you to soothe away my every ache and twinge in Harthwin, remember?"

The young woman smiled, some color returning to her pallid cheeks. "No, I suppose you did not."

Kindra looked at Jasper, who still looked shaken. She reached out and gently laid a hand on his arm. "I'm sorry if I scared you." She glanced at Helena and Emeline as well. "All of you."

Emeline sighed, sitting on the foot of the bed. "I'm going to be honest, there was a minute when we thought you were fucking dead, Kindra. Healers can only do so much. There's some damage even the most powerful of them can't mend."

"I-I know," Kindra whispered, staring down at the blankets.

"Hel wants to lecture you," she continued, ignoring her wife's attempt to silence her, "about all sorts of things. She wants you to stop sparring." Kindra flinched. "Yeah, that's what I thought," Emeline said. "I told her there was zero chance of that happening. I mean, you just beat a Windspinner, and one of our best, at that. We can't stop you now. But she's concerned about what message you've sent the king, what this might have started." Emeline sighed. "What likely started the day you tried to get into the War Chamber."

"I wasn't trying—" Kindra looked up, eyes wide.

Emeline's blue gaze was sympathetic. "To start anything. We know. The king asked you to prove yourself, so you did."

"It's just that the more attention he gives you and the more respect you manage to earn, the more furious he will be," Helena interrupted, speaking quickly. "When—you know."

Kindra leaned her head back into the pillows. "Yeah. I know." She gazed up at the ceiling, focusing intently on Cyrie's glowing face. Exhaustion weighed her down, pulling her deeper into the bed.

"Let's leave her to rest." Sala stood and began to gently shepherd the rest of them out. "I'm going to go fetch you some dinner, Lady Kindra."

Kindra grabbed Jasper's hand before he got up. "Stay. Just for a minute," she whispered. He settled back down on the bed. Emeline and Helena said their goodbyes, promising to stop by tomorrow, and then they and Sala were gone, leaving Kindra and Jasper alone.

"Are you all right?" she asked as soon as the door shut.

He chuckled. "You should not be the one asking that question, Kindra."

"Still. Are you?"

He traced circles on her hand with his thumb. "Yes," was his answer when he finally spoke. "But I wasn't. From the moment I walked in and saw my father sitting there to the second you woke up, I wasn't all right."

"I appreciate you not trying to stop me."

"I can't imagine it would have gone over well with you or my father if I'd tried. Besides, I knew what it meant, him being there. The chance it gave you."

"Yes, well, we'll see what good it did me, in the end," she sighed, heavy with resignation. "If what Helena said is true, and this is just a game to him—"

"If you were anybody else, it would be. He'd move the goal posts until you ended up getting yourself killed, because your life would be meaningless to him. But you proved yourself today, in front of most of the court, as well. And those that weren't there have already heard all about it." He rolled his eyes, shaking his head. "You've gained their admiration very quickly."

Or their fear. "That's nice, I suppose."

Jasper started to speak, then closed his mouth, clearly considering his next words very carefully. "I don't... I don't want you to think that I only sit there and worry, as I watch you train," he began, speaking very slowly. "I also love to see you use your magic. I think it's magnificent. You have no idea how you look. It's like... I can't really describe it. When you threw that dagger at Ryle and then limped, bloodied, over to him, and still—*still*—you surrounded him with fire, demanding his surrender... I know you don't like it, but even I understood then why people are saying you're Scaldor-blessed."

Oh. That was new. She hadn't heard *that* yet.

"They all believe I'm going to break it, don't they?" She felt very frightened all of a sudden.

Jasper squeezed her hand. "Let's—let's not worry about that right now, okay?" He smiled thinly. "We still have to get married. And actually have a—"

"Let's not worry about *that*, please." She shifted awkwardly, face burning. As comfortable around Jasper as she was getting, the thought of *that* still made her stomach turn with fear.

A beat of uncomfortable silence stretched between them, broken by a knock on her door, followed by the entrance of Sala, who held a tray laden with steaming food.

"I brought two meals, in case His Highness was staying for dinner." She set the tray down on the bed. On it were two bowls of a thick, hearty vegetable stew, along with a loaf of freshly baked bread and a slab of butter.

"Would you like me to eat with you?" Jasper asked.

"That would be nice, thank you," Kindra mumbled, her stomach rumbling as she took in the food.

Sala placed a kind of table across her lap, then set the tray atop it. She poured the both of them glasses of water, then curtsied. "If you need anything, I will be just outside."

"Where's Cerulle?"

Sala blinked. "She's posted outside as well, my Lady."

"I think just Cerulle is fine for tonight, Sala," Kindra decided. "You can go rest. If I need something Cerulle can't handle on her own, we'll be sure to call for you."

The Healer's shoulders slumped with exhausted relief. "Thank you, my Lady."

Alone with Jasper once more, Kindra focused on her bowl of stew. She reached for her spoon, only to be halted by Jasper's hand.

"Let me." He grabbed the spoon and dipped it into the stew.

"I can feed myself," she protested, moving to take it from him, but he shook his head.

"I know. But how long has it been since you've let somebody take care of you?"

She frowned. "Cerulle and Sala take care of me."

"That's their job. How long has it been since you've let somebody care for you simply because they wanted to?"

Years. It had been years since she'd let somebody feed her like this. Even her own mother had learned not to try since she became a teenager, except for one time at seventeen when she'd been so ill she could hardly move her mouth to chew. Even the village Healer's magic hadn't been enough to help her.

Grumbling, she opened her mouth. Jasper grinned, victorious, and brought the spoonful to her lips.

The stew was delicious, of course, warming her to her bones. She accepted the next bite from Jasper much more willingly, and before she knew it, he'd fed her the whole bowl.

Still hungry, she reached out and dug into the bread, dragging it through the remains of the soup as Jasper finally fed himself.

After they were both finished, he took the table off the bed and the tray of dishes to the door, handing them to Cerulle. Then he came back to the bed and settled down next to her once more.

Kindra was feeling sleep beckon, and she snuggled down into the blankets, yawning. Jasper watched her, fondness sketched plainly across his face.

"Thank you for feeding me," she murmured.

"Thank you for letting me." His eyes darted away, flitting around the room once before settling back on her. "I didn't know if you'd ever let me do that," he admitted. "I didn't know if you'd ever even let me touch you unless you had to."

She was too tired to flinch, but her chest twisted. "Well, you didn't exactly make the best first impression. Why…why didn't you act like this? When you came to get me?"

"You would've thought it was a ruse. And I thought it would make it easier to get you to come without resistance if I acted like an asshole." He winced under Kindra's sharp glare. "Sorry."

Her spark of anger died. "It's all right. I guess I understand. And it worked."

"I hated doing it," he whispered. "And I hated the fact that you believed it even more. My father, my brothers—they thought I should keep it up at least until we were married, if not forever, because of how important you are, how necessary it is that you're compliant and obedient." He winced again. "Their words, not mine. And I think they were hoping I'd finally become less *soft*, as they've often called me. But I couldn't do it. I couldn't even last three days." He shook his head. "That doesn't make me a good person, I know. But even though I've had to give up my ability to choose who I marry, I can't… I can't give up the chance to make that marriage a happy one."

Kindra said nothing. She didn't know what there was to say, really. "Thank you," she repeated, when she finally spoke, her eyes drifting shut. "You are a good person, Jasper."

Jasper didn't respond, just took her hand and squeezed it lightly as she slipped into sleep.

When she awoke the next morning, he was gone. But there was a head-shaped dent in the pillow next to her, and the surface of her blankets were ruffled in a way that suggested somebody had spent the night sleeping atop them.

CHAPTER 29

It was nearly two days before Kindra could move without wincing. She refused Sala's help, ordering her to regain her strength. "It's nothing I can't handle, seriously," she'd insisted, but gods, she'd grown to appreciate how the Healer usually melted away any aches she'd felt after training.

Kindra spent her time relaxing, allowing herself to recover naturally, the way she'd had to all those years in Harthwin. She'd grown quite fond of the library and its four-story expanse, the shelves that seemed to go for miles stuffed with thousands upon thousands of books. She loved the wall of stained-glass that stretched from the first floor all the way to the ceiling atop the fourth floor, and the huge, always-burning fireplace and chimney that bisected it; the dozens of cozy reading and research nooks scattered throughout, where courtiers, soldiers, and scholars alike spent hours every day. Jasper could find just about any book in the library with his eyes closed, he'd spent so much time there. In lieu of their afternoon strolls, they'd taken to sitting and reading together in peaceful quiet.

It was really nice.

Jasper, ever the bookworm, was a source of endless recommendations. "What do you like to read?" he asked the first time he joined her as they strolled through the aisles. He was already carrying a small assortment of books. Kindra, however, had yet to find one that caught her eye. The sheer quantity of books at her disposal was overwhelming, and she felt like she had no idea where to even begin.

She shrugged. "I enjoyed some of the classics—Ilfris's works, Hugayn's *Fallen City*, the like."

"*Fallen City* is magnificent," he commented. "What did you like about it?"

Kindra recalled the book as best she could. It had been quite some time since she'd read it. "I liked the battles," she said, "and all the twists and turns."

"Never boring."

"Yes," Kindra agreed.

"In that case..." Jasper furrowed his brow and stopped walking, thinking hard for a moment. "Aha!" He reached for her with his free hand, lacing their fingers together. Kindra's skin warmed at the contact. He led her through the library, weaving between the shelves with expert ease. They finally came to a stop before a shelf filled with worn, well-loved tomes. Jasper scanned it until his eyes came to rest on the one he was searching for. He untangled his hand from Kindra's and grabbed it off the shelf, presenting it to her.

"Hugayn wrote several other books," he informed her. "But none ever became as popular as *Fallen City*. However, they all have similar elements— lots of battles, unpredictable plots, complex characters..." His cheeks flushed as he held out the book for her to take it. "I think you'd like this one."

Kindra took the book from him, noting his nervous stare. "*The Bone Curse*," she read aloud. She smiled. "Consider my interest piqued."

He sighed in relief. "That's very good to hear."

"Thank you for taking the time to find a book for me." It was endearing how much he loved books and even more endearing that he'd put such thought into a recommendation.

Gods above, Kindra was beginning to like him.

"I must confess, I do love helping people find books to read." Jasper looked away, a sheepish smile crossing his features. "Although I worry that sometimes I can be a bit overbearing about it. I apologize if I ever seem that way with you."

"I think it's nice that you put so much effort into it," Kindra told him honestly as they began to make their way back to the sitting area. "It shows compassion."

He reached out to take her hand in his again, but he did not reply. When they returned to the plush sofa where they planned to camp out for the afternoon, they settled into opposite ends. Kindra immediately began reading, *The Bone Curse*.

As Jasper had predicted, she did like it. It was far darker than *Fallen City*, but the tenacity of the main character—a Deathcaster—and the brutality of the world was intriguing. She read the first few chapters rather quickly.

When she finally took a break, she looked up to find Jasper watching her, his own book forgotten in his lap. "What?" she asked, squirming under his gaze.

He shook himself out of his stupor, cheeks turning red. "I just…" He looked down at his book, then back up. "I just enjoy this. Spending time with you. That's all."

"Oh." Now it was Kindra's turn to blush. "I, um, I enjoy spending time with you, too."

She was shocked by how much she meant it.

Jasper smiled, something between relief and adoration shining in his eyes. For a moment, he seemed to debate saying more but decided against it. "Enjoying the book so far?" he asked instead.

Kindra nodded. "I am."

"Good, because I already have an idea of what you should read next…"

On the third morning after her match with Ryle, the Windspinner himself appeared in the library. "My Lady," he said by way of greeting, bowing low.

Kindra looked up from the book she was reading. She'd finished *The Bone Curse* already and had taken Jasper's next recommendation eagerly. Jasper wasn't there; he'd been locked into a meeting that morning. "Hello, Lieutenant Mistron. How are you feeling?"

"I'm perfectly well, thank you. I wanted to see that you were recovered."

She smiled, flattered. "I'm nearly there. Just taking a few days to rest before returning to the training grounds."

He nodded stiffly. "Good. That's good. Um… I wanted to apologize, as well. For—"

"For what? Sparring with me? Not holding back? I wouldn't have wanted anything less. It would've been insulting to me if you'd simply let me win. Like you said after our first time, I had to learn." She sighed, closing her book. "Was it Jasper?"

Ryle's brow furrowed. "Excuse me?"

"Did he come and berate you?" She groaned. "Seriously, I thought I'd gotten through to him about this—"

"It wasn't His Highness, Lady Kindra." He focused his gaze on the wall behind her. "It was Guardswoman Orindyn."

Kindra gaped. "Tess? Really?"

"She was very upset at how injured you were, that's all. Reminded me of how important you are."

That again. Ugh. "Well, you don't have anything to apologize for, Ryle. I am healthy and healed, as are you. So all is forgiven—though there was never anything to forgive in the first place."

Satisfied with her response, Ryle bowed again and left her to her reading.

A couple hours later, Kindra was pulled from her book once more by a tap on her shoulder. She looked up to see Jasper peering down at her.

Kindra couldn't fight the small smile that bloomed as she took him in. He was wearing a black velvet jacket, embroidered with red, orange and gold leaves, atop his usual combination of a white shirt, trousers and boots. "What ever could you want?" she asked, faking exasperation.

He beamed down at her. "Close your book, Kindra. We're going into the city."

CHAPTER 30

An hour and a half later, Kindra was traveling in a carriage through the streets of Wendrith with Jasper, Helena, Emeline, and a whole squadron of guards. Sala and Cerulle had transformed her in record time, dressing her in a burnt-orange gown with billowing sleeves and leaf embroidery to match Jasper's jacket. They'd twisted her hair up into a bun, decorating it with leaf pins. Her eyelids had been brushed with kohl, her lips painted a soft red.

They were headed to the Harvest Festival. It was a three-day long event dedicated to celebrating the bountiful crops that would feed them through the winter, as well as honoring all sorts of deities, from Aspa to Yvangil to Cyrie. The whole city was decorated for it, adorned in banners and streamers in autumnal colors, but the real celebration occurred in the market district, where farmers and vendors set up stalls to sell their goods and people gathered to eat, drink and dance.

Kindra's whole body thrummed with a mix of nervousness and excitement. This would be her first time interacting with the people of Wendrith. She knew Jasper was beloved by the civilians here; she'd heard many stories of his time spent walking, talking and drinking among them. She hoped desperately they approved of her.

As they neared the market district, the streets became more crowded, though crowds were quick to clear the way for them. Cheers started up as more people saw the royal insignia on the side of the carriage and the black and gold uniforms marking the members of the Royal Guard.

Finally, the entourage came to a place where the throngs of people were so dense their party could move no further. Heinrich opened the carriage door. Helena and Emeline exited first.

The people were joyous, shouting and cheering for their princesses. The couple smiled and waved, stepping down to the ground. People tossed them flowers, streamers, bouquets of autumn leaves. Emeline, glowing in a yellow gown, draped a streamer over Helena's shoulders, presenting her with some of the flowers and placing a kiss upon her cheek. The roaring grew.

Then Jasper stepped from the carriage.

Kindra thought they had been excited for Helena and Emeline, but when the prince emerged, the cheers were nearly deafening.

Jasper, ever the charismatic prince they knew him to be, waved and smiled and accepted flowers. He held up his hand, calling wordlessly for quiet, and within seconds, the street was near-silent.

"My friends, I have someone very special for you to meet today," he announced. The air became thick with anticipation.

He held his hand out to her, the signal to come out, and he spoke again as she moved to exit. "I'd like to introduce you to Lady Kindra Bedelyn of Harthwin, my betrothed!"

As she reached out of the carriage, taking his hand and stepping down to join him, the people of Wendrith erupted once more. She smiled, bashful and overwhelmed by their response. Awkwardly, she waved, which only made them more excited.

Staring out into the crowd, she knew the moment they realized she was a Firefury, the second the gold of her eyes registered.

And she saw the fervent hope unfold across all of their faces.

"She's a Firefury!"

"Alverin is saved!"

"*Cursebreaker!*"

She did her best to keep smiling, but her stomach turned and she felt her hand grow sweaty against Jasper's cool palm. He raised it to his lips, kissing it, much to the thrill of their audience. His eyes met hers, and he murmured, just for her ears, "It'll be okay. They're just excited."

Then he turned back to the people. "Let us celebrate with you today! Give Lady Bedelyn a proper Wendrith welcome!"

More applause, more cheers, and then he was looping his arm through hers. Helena latched on to her other side, and then the four of them, their guards following very closely behind, were swallowed up into the crowd.

Not much later, Kindra was feeling much more at ease.

That was partly—or mostly—due to the fact that the first thing Jasper did was make a beeline for a tavern, where he purchased a large mug of ale for each of them. Kindra, having never had it, gagged and sputtered after her first sip, which sent her three companions into a fit of laughter.

"Come now, Kindra, you don't want to insult the brewer!" Emeline chuckled, and Kindra frowned. No, she supposed she didn't. So she gathered her courage and drank the rest of it over the next half hour as they chatted with citizens who'd flocked around them. Jasper, Emeline and Helena were extremely good at interacting with the citizens, she learned very quickly, but each in their own way. Helena had benevolence, Emeline had humor, and Jasper had charm.

And she had awkwardness.

She did her best to answer all the questions, to speak with everyone who wished to speak to her. They asked her about her family, about Harthwin, about her training. When she answered honestly that no, she'd had no formal training, most reacted with awe, but some had been bitter.

"I know a Firefury who's currently studying at Grydmarth, top ten of her class," one older man had remarked, bedecked in finery that marked him as wealthy, but not of noble rank. "I can't imagine why the king would select you over her—I mean no offense."

At this, Emeline had leaned over. "Kindra had been single-handedly defending her village from threats since before that Firefury could wield more than a torch's worth of fire. But considering you're not ever invited to court, you wouldn't know this, would you?" She grinned venomously. "I mean no offense, of course."

Huffing, the man had lurched away, and Emeline had merely shrugged, taking another drink. "He had it coming."

Now, feeling much more relaxed—and much gigglier—she leaned into Jasper's side as they walked from the tavern into the heart of the market district: a giant city square, complete with a fountain in the center. Stalls with vendors selling everything from hot food to wood carvings lined the perimeter. Tables and chairs had been set up, along with a small stage where a quartet of musicians were playing bouncy, lively jigs and beloved folk songs. Children and adults alike were dancing in front of them.

They stopped at several of the stalls, buying various snacks and trinkets. Kindra devoured a skewer of seared chicken and vegetables. Jasper bought her a necklace from a jeweler; it was a simple carnelian pendant on a gold chain that he fastened around her neck immediately. Alcohol made her bold, and she pressed a kiss to his cheek in thanks, much to the delight of onlookers. Jasper blushed a deep scarlet and didn't stop smiling for several minutes.

Across the square, near the stage of musicians, was a cart laden with differently shaped and colored tubes. "What are those?" she asked, pointing.

"They're firecrackers," Helena told her. "You light their fuse, and they shoot into the sky and explode into different colored fire."

"They're one of the latest inventions out of Laoruwen," Emeline added. "Loud as shit, but delightfully fun."

The cart was operated by a tall, well-built man clad in black. He studied the four of them, as if he could hear every word they were saying about his goods despite them being across the square.

Jasper tugged at her, his arm draped around her waist. "Let's dance," he murmured into her ear, his speech slightly slurred from his three ales. Kindra couldn't say she was much better off. Her response was to simply laugh and wrap her arms around his middle, her attention pulled away from the man and his firecracker cart. Jasper smiled and nuzzled into her neck. She sucked in a breath, her nerves singing as though she'd been struck by lightning. The people observing them cheered at their public display of affection, and even in her inebriated state she knew the whole city would be talking about them tomorrow. A true love match, she'd already overheard some calling them.

She told herself that if she wasn't drunk she'd be more upset about that.

"Gods above, they can't keep their hands off each other," Emeline giggled. Helena swatted playfully at her. She was the only one of them who remained even slightly poised, although her cheeks were flushed.

Jasper pulled her towards the stage, and the people dancing parted to make space for them. Several children spun towards them, and before Kindra could do anything, tiny hands were clasping hers, and she was being pulled away from Jasper.

Laughing, she went along with it, copying their steps as best she could. She knew some of the traditional line and group dances; she'd been to a few festivals in Mistbarrow before, and even Harthwin had its own small but lively Solstice celebrations, so she picked up the dance quickly.

She felt Jasper's presence before she saw him and then there he was, dancing alongside her. The children squealed with delight. The song ended, and they stopped to applaud. Kindra caught her breath, her brow damp with sweat, stray curls sticking to her forehead.

One of the musicians—a fiddle player—announced their next song would be a traditional love ballad. "In honor of His Highness Prince Jasper and Lady Kindra," he said. "May your union be blessed."

Jasper gathered Kindra in his arms and began to guide them in a dance she didn't know. It was slower, some type of waltz. Clumsily, she did her best to keep up with the steps. Every few beats she'd misstep or step on one of his feet, and soon the two of them were giggling messes, foreheads pressed together as they spun around.

"Are you enjoying yourself?" he asked.

"Yes," she replied, "very much so. Thank you for bringing me here."

"They love you already." He pulled her closer to him. "I knew they would."

At some point, they'd stopped dancing, completely entranced by one another. Kindra was only vaguely aware of the people still moving around them, the dozens of eyes watching their every breath.

She looked past his shoulder for a moment. The man at the firecracker cart was staring at her, and even from yards away she could feel the intensity of his gaze. It made her slightly uncomfortable, taking her out of the moment with Jasper.

"Something is wrong with that man with the firecrackers," she murmured through a tight smile. "He's looking at me strangely."

"What do you mean?" Jasper started to turn around, but she stopped him, holding him firmly in place, though to everyone else it just looked like an embrace.

She shot another quick glance at the man. He was no longer looking at her, instead fiddling with something on his cart. She shook her head. "Never mind. I think I'm just a little drunk." She laughed, but the uneasy feeling remained, even as she and Jasper began to dance again, this time to a fast tune that had him spinning her in circles.

When that song ended and she regained her center of balance, she risked another look at the cart.

The man was gone.

"Where did he—" Kindra twisted around, head still spinning, skin prickling with the feeling that something was very, very wrong. Her magic kicked at her senses.

"Kindra?" Jasper grasped at her. "What's going on?"

"I don't—something is wrong—the man—"

The next three things happened all at once.

First, Kindra spotted Tess across the square, running towards them at full speed, a wild panic she'd never seen before on the guardswoman's face.

Second, she felt a massive swell of flames, so large it nearly overwhelmed her.

And third, the firecracker cart exploded.

CHAPTER 31

Fire was everywhere.

But it wasn't just regular fire of the orange, yellow and red variety—it was green. And blue. And purple.

The firecrackers had been set off, as well as whatever other explosives had been planted on the cart, so not only was the square wrought with the screams of terrified, injured civilians, but also the constant *pop pop pop* as they detonated.

Kindra's vision refocused slowly, her ears still ringing. She and Jasper had been thrown several yards by the explosion. She groaned, pulling herself unsteadily to her feet. Quickly, she checked herself for injuries. Her dress was torn, and she had a few nasty scrapes on her arms and cheek, but she was otherwise unharmed.

The same could not be said for many of the people around her.

Kindra swayed on her feet as horror washed over her. The people who had been standing right next to the cart were dead. Some bodies were scattered in chunks, others were little more than a splatter of blood and organs.

There were children amongst those bodies. *Children*—

She stumbled backwards, nausea overwhelming her. She turned and retched, vomiting up the ale and food she'd consumed onto the bloodied, rubble-splattered cobblestones.

But where was Jasper?

Sheer, ice-cold panic coursed through her veins. She spun in a circle, desperately trying to find him among the chaos, among the bodies.

"Jas—Jasper," she croaked, then screamed. "Jasper!"

"Kindra!" A voice she knew responded—but it wasn't Jasper. It was Emeline. Her yellow dress was dirtied and torn, but she and Helena, who was clinging to her, were alive.

"Jasper," Kindra repeated as her hearing slowly returned to her, "I can't—I can't find him—"

"They'll find him, Kindra." Emeline was shockingly calm in the face of a crisis. Her voice was firm—tight, but firm. "But you need to help put out the fires."

"Put out—put out the fires…" Kindra spun around again, taking in the destruction, and yes—the fire. The rainbow of fire, burning up the tables, the stalls, the people.

She moved without thinking. Her instinct to protect could not be quelled even when she was in intense shock. She ran towards the fire, reaching out with her hands and killing the flames foot by foot, yard by yard. Kindra extinguished burning furniture, burning people. Dimly, she was aware of other Firefuries at her side: Tess, some civilians, another guardsman.

There was the sound of water swelling, and Kindra looked to see Emeline, Heinrich beside her, lifting the water from the fountain and raining it down on the fire that remained.

For a moment, there was only the sound of still-sizzling wood, the drip of water, and the final pop of the last firecracker.

And then the wailing became loud again, the whimpering of the injured and the dying threatening to overwhelm her. She staggered over to an injured child, one of the children who'd been dancing with her just minutes ago. A little boy, half his face slick with blood, eyes wide with pain and fear.

"Healer!" she shouted, kneeling down beside him, using her bare hands to try to stop the bleeding from a gash in his neck, flesh ripped open by a chunk of debris. "I need a Healer!"

But they needed Healers everywhere, because there were dying people everywhere, and there was only a handful of Healers present, and they were already busy. Distantly, she heard the city bells ringing, some kind of alarm.

"More Healers are coming," she told the child, who was drawing in short, rapid gasps. "They'll be here soon."

The boy could only look at her. He tried to speak, but the blood from his wound was gushing faster, flowing thick and hot between her fingers.

There was nothing she could do—nothing even a Healer could do at this point. Tears blurred her vision.

"Thank you for dancing with me," Kindra whispered as she felt his pulse slow and then stop. "I'm so sorry."

She remained frozen at his side for several seconds. Then—

Jasper.

Where was Jasper?

Kindra scrambled upright, panic threatening to steal the air from her lungs, but she fought through it. "Jasper!" she screamed, voice breaking. "Jasper!"

Across the square, more of the City Guard were arriving. Among them were several Healers, and they ran towards bodies, hands glowing. Some they knelt by only to rise and away from within seconds—they'd been too late. But they were able to save others.

Kindra spotted Tess again, who was helping another guardsman lift an overturned, half-burnt table off of young woman. A Healer appeared, lunging for her as soon as the table was out of the way.

Tess ran over to her. "Are you okay?"

"Jasper—I can't f-find him," was all Kindra could say between high, shallow breaths. "He was right next to me when the c-cart expl-exploded."

"They may have already found him. He may be on his way back to the castle right now. Helena just left—maybe he's with her."

Kindra shook her head rapidly. "No, no, you don't understand. *I didn't see him.* I didn't see him, Tess, *I don't know where he is*—"

She stopped herself mid-sentence when she saw him.

Not Jasper.

But the man who had been at the cart, who'd been watching her.

Kindra thought she'd felt rage before. She considered herself well-acquainted with the feeling. But what she'd felt before was nothing like the hot, murderous fury that rushed through her now.

"*You,*" she snarled, already running towards him. "*You did this!*"

A shout, and then footsteps pounded behind her: Tess was following.

The man smiled—he *smiled*—and took off, sprinting down the street. He took a hard right down an alley. Kindra was right on his heels, only seconds behind, but when she turned down the same alley, it was dark and empty.

"Where are you?" she shrieked. She wrapped her hands in fire, stalking into the darkness.

But he was gone, which made no sense, because the alley was a dead end, so there was no where he could've gone.

"Looking for someone?"

Kindra spun and saw a dark-haired woman, clad in black, step out of the shadows as if she'd materialized from thin air.

"Who are you," Kindra demanded, and the woman tsked.

"So rude. Is that really the first impression you want to make?"

"You're part of this too, aren't you? You fucking monster, you killed *children*—"

"Pot calling the kettle black, isn't it? An Alverinian angry about the murder of children." The woman raised her hand and a long, curved dagger, the blade black as night, was birthed from the shadows around her.

The woman before her was a Shadowmaster.

Where is Tess? Kindra thought, realizing that she was trapped in a dead-end alley with one of the most dangerous Wielders in existence.

"You weren't crying when it was Pryllian children. Or Breyen children. Or Laou children," she continued, another dagger forming in her other hand. Her eyes were pitch black, and as she wielded, the darkness exploded past the iris and swirled over the rest of her eyes.

"Those people had nothing to do with the crimes the Annalindis family has committed. *I* don't have anything to do with it."

"Don't you, though?" Kindra blinked and the woman was gone, having vanished into nothing. Then she felt a presence at her back, and there was a bone-chilling whisper in her ear, *"Cursebreaker."*

Kindra knew when it was time to run rather than fight.

This was one of those times. She bolted towards the end of the alley now that the way was clear. But she made it only a few steps before the Shadowmaster was in front of her again, body trailing black shadows.

"You should know better than to walk down a dark alley by yourself, little firebird." She stalked towards her, dragging her blades across the brick walls, the metal sparking against the stone.

And in that moment, as her back hit the wall behind her, Kindra accepted that she was going to die. There was nothing she could do here, not against someone as powerful and deadly as a Shadowmaster. Still, she rallied her magic, readying herself for her final stand.

"Cornering people in an alley, Vylie? Really?" Tess's voice was such a welcome relief Kindra almost burst into tears, even as she tried to process that Tess knew the Shadowmaster's name. "That's contemptible and low, even for you."

Vylie hissed, coming to a halt and spinning on her heels to face the Firefury standing at the entrance to the alley. "I can always count on you to ruin my fun, Tess." Her words dripped with venom.

"Yes, I am so sorry I keep preventing you from murdering people." Tess was striding towards them now, flames snaking their way up and down her armor. In the low light, her burns looked more severe than they actually were. "Now please leave Kindra alone."

"You got what you came for," Tess continued, speaking slowly and carefully, when Vylie didn't move. "You've started your war. That's enough for today, don't you think? All that needs to be done, right?" It was strange, watching Tess speak to a deadly Shadowmaster the way one might speak to a frightened animal. Kindra couldn't quite comprehend it.

Vylie bared her teeth. Tess stopped, holding her arms out as if in compromise. "Don't be stupid," she warned. "You know you can't possibly take us both."

The Shadowmaster hesitated, then looked back at Kindra. Teeth still bared, she twisted her lips up in a terrifying smile. "You've got a lot of eyes on you now, cursebreaker. I'd be careful if I were you."

And then she was gone.

Tess grabbed Kindra by the arm and dragged her out of the alley. Only when they were back in the sunlight and near other guards did she stop moving.

"I thought you were right behind me—" Kindra began, and Tess shook her head.

"I lost you, for a moment. You took off so fast, and there was so much happening. I'm sorry. That was my fault."

Kindra almost questioned her; she'd run in a straight shot after the man, and she could've sworn she'd heard Tess right behind her. She almost asked how Tess knew who Vylie was, but then Tess spoke again.

"They found Jasper. He's alive, but he had a pretty serious injury to his side. They've taken him back to the castle—" Kindra started to run, but Tess still held her arm. "I'll get my horse, okay?"

Kindra managed a nod. Within a few minutes, they were galloping through the streets.

As they neared the castle, Kindra could think of nothing but Jasper. He was alive. He was hurt, but alive. She could think of nothing but him and the cold fear she'd felt when she thought he was dead.

No room in her head for anything else, she told herself, pushing out the images of dead bodies and burning flesh.

Pushing out the sound of Vylie calling her *firebird*, and the distant memory of the last time somebody called her the same.

CHAPTER 32

Kindra leapt off of Tess's horse before they'd even come to a full stop at the castle gates. She stumbled, nearly losing her balance. Guards rushed for her, asking her a thousand different questions, and she pushed past them all.

"My Lady, we need to know if you are hurt—"

"Jasper," she snapped, "Where is he?"

"His Highness is all right, we need to make sure you are—"

"Oh, for fuck's sake," Kindra snarled, the shock and adrenaline still coursing through her, wearing her patience razor thin, "I'm fine. Where. Is. Jasper?"

"You should tell her." Tess dismounted from her horse and marched over to the guards. "She won't ask again."

The guards hesitated, and Kindra threw her arms out in frustration. "Send Sala after me, if you're so worried. But where is he? The infirmary? His rooms?"

"He's in his rooms, Lady Kindra," one of them finally confessed, and Kindra didn't even thank him before sprinting up the steps to the door.

The castle was in chaos. Squads of guards—more than she'd ever seen—filled the foyer. Courtiers, frenzied and panicked, were chasing them around, squawking like chickens about war and their safety and whether they should leave for their country estates. Kindra ignored all of them. She made her way through the crowd, shoving people out of her way, and took the stairs two at a time. Her body, still not fully recovered from her match with Ryle and now freshly battered from the explosion, protested her every move, but she paid it no heed. Up she went, until she reached the third floor.

Her pace didn't slow as she hurried through the halls. Servants and guards called out to her, but they might as well have said nothing at all, for she didn't hear a word.

Finally, she whipped around a corner and came to his doors. One of them was open, a few guards walking out of it.

She'd only seen the door to Jasper's rooms in passing before; she'd yet to enter his chambers. Kindra had believed the moment she did that, she would be crossing a line of some kind, entering into territory even more uncharted than the one she was currently in.

Well, regardless if that was true, she was crossing that boundary now.

Jasper's raised voice reached her all the way at the end of the hallway.

"You are not answering my question," he was shouting. "Where is Kindra?"

Somebody said something in reply, too quiet for Kindra to hear.

"Did you people just *leave her there*?"

"Your Highness," came a small voice, "you were injured, barely even conscious, when they found you—"

"Kindra might be injured as well! How does nobody in this fucking castle know if she's—"

He cut off abruptly as Kindra appeared in the doorway.

The prince stood, shirtless, as a Healer mended a gash along his side. His face was stained with dirt and ash. There was a scrape along his left cheek, but other than that and the wound currently being tended to, he was unharmed. Discarded on the table next to him were his jacket and shirt, torn and bloodied.

"You—" He started, but couldn't speak any further. His face twisted and rippled with a dozen different emotions.

Kindra stepped into the room, chest heaving. Relief, warm and heavy, threatened to make her knees buckle. He was safe. He was alive.

"Leave us," he ordered the guards and servants in the room. The Healer went to protest, still working, but he brushed her off. "I'll rest for a few days, and it will be fine. Have some poultice brought up." Again, she tried to argue, but he shook his head firmly. "There are wounded guards and civilians who still need to be seen. Don't spend any more magic on me than you have to."

Finally, after what felt like ages, the room cleared, the last person to leave shutting the door on their way out.

For a moment, Kindra and Jasper simply stared at each other.

Then, Kindra choked out, "I couldn't find you. After the explosion. You were right next to me, I thought—you should have been right next to me—"

"We got blown in separate directions, I think," he said softly. "I hit a table as I was thrown. Ended up half underneath it. Made me hard to find."

A low, pained noise tore from her throat before she could stop it. "I thought—there were people who weren't even recognizable because of the fire, I thought it could have reached you."

Jasper shook his head. His blonde hair was streaked with brown and gray. "When I came to, they didn't know where you were. Nobody knew."

"I couldn't find you," she repeated dumbly, voice haggard and torn, "I was screaming your name, and—and there were dead children, and I couldn't find you—" Her chest seized, and she sucked in a shallow, ragged gasp.

"Kindra," he murmured, reaching for her. "I'm here. I'm alive. We're safe."

She looked at him then, *really* looked at him, and something in her snapped. The final thread of restraint she'd been clinging to shredded. The sick, cold panic she'd felt today when she'd looked around and he hadn't been there; the thought of him being among the dead; the way he'd looked at her when she'd appeared in his doorway, alive; how he'd been screaming for her the same way she had been for him...

Kindra crossed the room in four strides and threw her arms around him, pressing herself as close to him as she could. He tucked her head into his shoulder and buried his face into the crook of her neck. His arms wound around her, holding her tight.

Her throat tightened and her eyes began to burn, so she shut them tightly, holding the tears back.

"I'm glad you're okay," he whispered, lips brushing against her skin as he spoke.

"I'm glad you're okay, too," she replied, nestling further into the heat of his body. Hard muscle moved beneath her hands as they stood there, swaying back and forth ever so slightly.

They pulled apart slightly, but still kept their arms wrapped around each other. Kindra stared up into his eyes, struggling to articulate what she was feeling.

So she did the next best thing.

She kissed him.

His lips tasted like smoke and blood. She knew hers did, too, but she didn't care. He made a small, startled noise, and a heartbeat later he was winding his arms tightly around her again, pulling her flush against his body. His bare skin was hot beneath her fingers as she ran her hands down his neck and chest.

One of Jasper's hands came up to cup her face, the other still twisted around her waist. He moaned softly, a tiny, delightful sound that sent a bolt of heat zipping through Kindra.

Her lips moved clumsily against his. It had been a long time since she'd last kissed someone. But he didn't mind her lack of skill or grace. Instead, he only deepened the kiss further, running his tongue along her bottom lip until she opened her mouth for him.

She pulled away first, needing to catch her breath. Jasper rested his forehead against hers, gasping. A smile danced on his lips.

"I was wondering when you might do that," he laughed breathily.

Kindra found she couldn't speak. She felt a myriad of emotions. Not regret, surprisingly enough, though she had a feeling that would come later.

Jasper drew her to him again, but not to kiss her. Instead, he pulled her back into that same tight embrace as before, his hands running up and down her back and arms, as if he was still soaking in the fact that she was alive and okay.

Kindra didn't know how long they stayed like that. But eventually, the adrenaline faded and she finally felt steady again. And as that steadiness came back, so did the acute awareness that she was pressed against Jasper's naked chest. And that she'd just kissed him.

She stepped back from him, refusing to meet his eyes. She looked at her hands—they were still stained in some spots with dried blood where her magic hadn't burned it away. A small whimper escaped her, and she shook her head. "I should—"

"Don't do that." He reached out and caught her arm. "Please don't do that."

Kindra remained silent, feeling too exposed under his pleading gaze.

"People died today," he said shakily, like he was still wrapping his head around it. "When I woke up under that table and couldn't find you, I—" He swallowed. "It was the fiercest panic I'd ever felt, when I thought you were dead."

"I know." Her voice was soft, barely audible. She took in the wound on his side; though it was now just a line of pink, healing skin, she could tell it had been a serious injury. Her hand strayed to her throat, where the necklace he'd bought her rested.

"I care about you, Kindra." He said the words freely, with no trace of reluctance. "Whether you want me to or not."

I care about you, too. But she couldn't bring herself to say it, not now— not yet. Not when she still hadn't fully reconciled that fact with herself. It had been building for days—weeks, if she was honest with herself—but saying it out loud still felt like some admission of weakness. Like she'd lost a battle.

Mercifully, Sala walked in before she had to decide what to say. "Lady Kindra, I was sent to see if you were all right." Her brown eyes flitted briefly over Jasper's unclothed torso, widening slightly, and then she turned back to focus on Kindra. "Let me examine you."

Kindra submitted without protest, silent as Sala ran her hands over the scrapes and cuts, smoothing them away with her gentle magical touch. Jasper vanished into another room, reemerging in fresh, clean clothes, including a shirt. He was still in need of a bath, though. They both were.

She was just about to ask Sala to come with her back to her rooms and give her one when Antone and Sebastian strode in.

"Oh good, you're both here," Antone said by way of greeting. He looked extremely strained: his hair was slightly ruffled, and his expression lacked its usual ire, replaced by one of tension and worry. "Come with me. We're to go to the War Chamber." He paused, grimacing, then waved a hand at Kindra. "Yes, you as well. He wants you there."

"What, not going to lock me in my rooms this time?" she snapped before she could stop herself.

Antone gave her one of his signature scathing glares. "Unfortunately, I have been overruled." He turned to leave, Sebastian following, and shot over his shoulder, "Do try not to make a fool of yourself." Kindra growled under her breath as they left the room.

Jasper gestured to the door. "Well, I suppose you got your wish. To the War Chamber we go." He looked frustrated, like he'd wanted to continue their conversation from before they'd been interrupted.

And as Kindra moved to his side and they walked into the hall, the feeling of his lips still tingling on hers, she couldn't help but think that if the cost of her getting into that room had been the violence of today, she wasn't quite sure it was worth it.

CHAPTER 33

The War Chamber, a large, looming room on the first floor, was just as chaotic as the rest of the castle, so much so that hardly anybody spared them a second glance when they entered, even in their disheveled condition. Most didn't even seem to register Kindra as an unusual presence.

King Leofric was turned away from them, hunched over the giant table, which was littered with maps and scrolls, quills and ink pots, tiny figurines and strategy books.

The Council, as well as several others Kindra didn't recognize, were dispersed throughout the room. All looked to be in various states of alarm: some paced, some drank, some sat and drummed their fingers. Others were looking at the maps and books on the table as well, debating with each other about what to do.

Kindra had never entered a space so permeated with panic.

"We're here, Father," Antone announced, he and Sebastian moving to take position on either side of their father at the table. Jasper lingered further back, by Kindra. "We brought *her*, as you requested."

If Kindra weren't so beaten down by the day's events, she would have had something sharp to say in response to the ire in Antone's voice. But as it were, she merely dipped into a low curtsy as King Leofric turned around to face her.

He looked her over first, then Jasper. "I'm glad to see you are both safe," he said by way of greeting, and Kindra actually believed he meant it. "I want to hear what happened. Every last detail."

"Right, of course," Jasper replied quickly, already nervous and uncomfortable under his father's scrutiny. "Kindra saw more than me, so..."

"They had Shadowmasters," Kindra took over, sparing the whole room from more of Jasper's awkwardness. "The man at the firecracker cart—he was one."

"Are you sure?" Councilman Avis asked.

"Yes. I didn't see him use his powers, but—I saw him. After the explosion. And I followed him." Jasper stiffened beside her. She continued, ignoring his alarm. "He turned down an alley that was a dead end, but he vanished. There were no doorways, no walls he could've climbed. Just darkness." She paused, fear gripping her as she remembered what happened next. "And then she appeared."

"Who's she?" Avis pressed.

"Does... does the name Vylie sound familiar to any of you?"

The whole room went eerily silent. Then, somebody in the back said, "Vylie Inacorro is supposed to be dead."

"That's what Tess called her. I don't know anything else. But she seemed afraid of Tess. I thought—I thought she was going to kill me. If Tess hadn't shown up, I think she would have."

For a moment, she worried she'd just revealed that Tess had lied about something. Kindra recalled Tess and Vylie's conversation. Did Tess tell the Council that she'd successfully killed the Shadowmaster, whenever they'd last encountered each other? Had something happened after that to make them think she was dead?

"Are you sure?" Avis repeated. "Perhaps she was wrong—"

Kindra barely managed to reign in her annoyance. "I know what I heard and saw. The Shadowmaster responded to the name." Hesitantly, she added, "They seemed to have a history, of some kind."

Sebastian nodded thoughtfully. "Vylie Inacorro is a Shadow Assassin from the Keep up in the Dark Blade Mountains. Guardswoman Av— Orindyn—nearly caught her some years ago. We discovered she was responsible for the murder of a city official. Sent a squad after her. Tess was the only one who even stood a chance. And she almost had her. But Vylie had an accomplice we didn't know about, and they showed up just in time to blow the whole operation." He stroked his chin. "I bet that man from today was that accomplice. Reports said it was likely a male."

"So why did we think she was dead, if she got away?" Jasper dared to ask.

"Because two years ago, we received a report from Greymont that she had been apprehended in the middle of an assassination attempt on the Lord there. The attempt to detain her had turned nasty, and she was killed because, frankly, that was better than letting her escape again." Sebastian shook his head. "I don't get it. The report had been signed and sealed by the Greymont Council."

"Greymont is awfully close to the border with Laoruwen," Antone pointed out, looking equally flabbergasted. "Is it possible—"

"That Laoruwen spies infiltrated the Greymont Council and told us one of the most dangerous individuals to set foot in this kingdom was dead, all so they could use her to launch a terrorist attack?" King Leofric spat. "Yes, I think it's possible."

"No, I'm not so sure about that," a dark-skinned woman from the back of the room spoke up. She was dressed in light armor—a general, probably, her graying hair pulled back off her face in a tight, severe manner. "That kind of conspiracy would have been revealed by now. We've spoken to many officials in Greymont about it since—they all believed Inacorro to be dead."

"Then maybe they're all traitors! Maybe they're all spies!" the king seethed.

"Your Majesty," the woman replied, voice firm and even, "have a little more faith in your people, I beg you."

For a second, Kindra thought he might cross the room and hit her, though clearly the general did not share similar concern. Sure enough, he merely turned away from her, grumbling under his breath. People around the room began to talk amongst themselves, trying to come up with an explanation.

"Is it possible there was some sort of mix up, a confusion of some sort?" Jasper suggested.

Antone snorted, rolling his eyes. But Sebastian cocked his head, and Leofric regarded Jasper with curiosity.

"Go on," the king ordered.

"Well," Jasper stammered, finding his footing, "There's no really detailed drawings of Inacorro anywhere. She's a Shadow Assassin. The whole thing that makes them so deadly is their ability to vanish into nothing. Most people that see her clearly don't survive to talk about it. Even Tess couldn't describe her fully. She was half shadow the whole time they fought."

Sebastian was nodding, and that gave Jasper the courage to speak louder. "So what if they caught another Shadow Assassin? One who vaguely fit the already vague description the guards had: dark hair, pale skin, black eyes. They catch her. They kill her. The body was burned badly in the fight, if I remember the report correctly. They think it's Vylie Inacorro—maybe they want it to be her so badly they convince themselves that it is, because what a relief it would it be if it was? They send the report."

"You have to admit, Your Majesty," the general said drily, after a moment, "that sounds a lot more plausible than the entire governing body of Greymont being traitors." She dipped her head in acknowledgment to Jasper. "Smart thinking, Your Highness."

Jasper barely managed a nod back. He smiled, but quickly stifled it.

The conversation erupted then, everyone talking over each other. Though Jasper had satisfied the question surrounding Vylie, at least for the time being, there were still dozens of others: Who had claimed responsibility for the attack? What was being done in regard to security? What kind of statement would be put out to the citizens? Was this a declaration of war?

Kindra and Jasper drifted back to a table in the corner, where a forgotten plate of crackers, fruits, and cheeses sat. They settled into a pair of chairs. Suddenly famished, Kindra began to load a plate with food, Jasper following suit.

"You didn't tell me you went after the fucking guy," Jasper hissed.

Kindra shrugged. "You were unconscious under a table, so..."

He didn't have much to say to that. Quietly, they observed the meeting. Kindra focused intensely on the conversations around her, fighting her wandering thoughts. They kept straying back to her kiss with Jasper. And they kept getting more imaginative.

She still didn't feel that punch of regret like she'd expected to. It had seemed right to do it. Neither of them could have denied what they felt for each other after today. Fear had stripped them bare, exposed their feelings plainly for everyone to see.

She supposed it was better this way. Better to grow to love him, even if she forever hated the circumstances. Better that he *was* lovable, unlike Antone or Sebastian.

Nibbling on her food, she regarded the general. Hyra Lustris was her name, the highest-ranking general of the Alverinian army, below only Antone and Sebastian. She was a Bonescribe who'd climbed the ranks with her unmatched swordsmanship skills and strategic mind. It helped, of course, that her magic gifted her the ability to see into the future—though not with the specificity or clarity an Oracle often possessed.

Right now, she was using that gift to decide the next best move. Her eyes, usually a pretty but unmagical green, were clouded over with a milky white fog as she shuffled pieces of bone in her hand. She was about to attempt to scry. Kindra leaned in to see; she'd never seen a Bonescribe wield before.

The bones fell across the table, scattering across the map. The room seemed to hold its collective breath as her gaze cleared and she studied where they'd landed.

"Pryllia will not move yet," she declared, pointing to a sharp chunk that rested along the Pryllian border. "They are biding their time, enjoying our panic." Her calloused brown hand moved to another bone, one near the southwestern border. "Breyenth holds its breath as well. But Laoruwen..." She hovered over the third piece. Her eyes clouded again, brow furrowing. "It's strange. They know, more than the others, what is to come. But they do not have armies gathered, not where I can see."

"Is Vylie under their employ?" Antone asked gruffly. "Are they responsible for today's attack?"

"If they were responsible, we would know already," General Lustris responded. Her eyes narrowed. "If any of them were responsible, we would know."

"So what does that mean, then?" Antone sounded exasperated. Kindra couldn't quite blame him; Bonescribes had a reputation for being vague and cryptic, and now was not the time for such ambiguity.

"It means that you won't see any of these kingdoms step forward to take responsibility for today's attack, Your Highness," General Lustris replied, "Because none of them did it."

Silence, thick and heavy as a winter snow, fell over the room.

"Then who did?" Councilman Epira, distinguishable by the still-healing cut on his forehead, dared to ask.

She shrugged. "I don't know."

"Oh for Scaldor's sake," King Leofric snarled, his restraint all but snapping entirely, "What good are you if you don't know?"

"Even the most powerful of Oracles cannot divine every detail, and my gifts are far more limited, as you know," General Lustris replied, the words calm but sharply edged. It was likely she'd said those words a thousand times before.

She studied the map for a moment longer before stating, "These are my thoughts, based on what I can see: these kingdoms are, at the very least, loosely working together. They don't have much in common other than their hatred of us—a warning of mine that you *all* should have heeded." She swept a stony glare around the room.

She continued, "Laoruwen has some sort of connection to this attack. I'm not sure how, but I can say with solid certainty that they did not directly order it. My guess is whatever organization this is coming from is housed within their borders. Perhaps King and Queen Umberiki know, and have a relationship with whoever's responsible, or perhaps they are entirely in the dark." The general frowned. "Ora is hiding much from me," she said quietly, frustrated with the goddess of truth.

The people in the room sat with General Lustris's words for a few moments.

King Leofric broke the silence. "I want our ships gathered in the harbor, and inspections done on all our defenses. Make sure the catapults are functional, and that the gates and walls are as reinforced as possible. Epira," he practically spat the name, "I want our Whisperers reporting daily. From every post. I don't care if they're not on a path an enemy army would take. I want to see every report. General Lustris will see them, too, as well as my sons." Jasper made a very soft noise of surprise.

"Clearly," the king declared, "We have been underestimating everyone, and we need to make up for it starting now. I want updated lists of every person in this kingdom who can fight, be it with magic or a sword. Start recruiting. We're not in need of a draft yet, but we need the people ready to fight at a moment's notice. Our army is spread too thin to handle this on its own, not if we are facing a joint attack from both the east and the west."

He sighed. "We have kept this under wraps for some time now, not wanting to stir panic. But panic has struck anyway. News of this attack will have reached even the farthest reaches of Alverin in a matter of days, of that we can be sure. We need to be ready to quell the fear that will follow with a show of strength and readiness. The people have long feared this day. We have long feared this day. Our arrogance has set us back in preparing us for what might be the greatest war of Alverin's history. We cannot let it be our downfall."

The king shook his head, anger contorting his face. "We were once hailed as the greatest kingdom in all Istreria. And we *still* are. These other kingdoms insult us with this trifling attempt to defeat us. We are Scaldor-blessed—the only kingdom on the continent who has ever received his favor. And the god of fire has continued to bless us in these troubling times." His gaze landed on Kindra. "He has brought us our cursebreaker, after all."

Kindra tried not to squirm in her seat. She held her head high because she knew it was what everyone in the room needed to see: a savior, a beacon of hope. But under the king's fierce stare, she felt a chill roll over her. That chill remained as the meeting came to an end, and she and Jasper left the room.

Perhaps, to another, the king's speech would have been heroic. It would have soothed their worried soul to see their King so confident in the face of such a threat.

But she recalled Jasper's words from before, how he'd said that his father had been waiting for this moment.

It was with those words in her head that she took one last look over her shoulder at the king. He wore a mask of stony determination, but Kindra saw through the cracks, however small they were.

She saw, just barely, the trace of his smile.

CHAPTER 34

Over the next week, Kindra desperately tried to avoid Jasper.

Well, not entirely. That, she didn't think she could bear. So she still walked with him through the gardens, still dined with him, Emeline and Helena for meals.

But she worked hard to avoid being alone with him because that would mean talking about the kiss.

After she rushed off at the end of the war meeting to her chambers to bathe and sleep, she found the last thing she wanted to do was discuss the kiss with him. The memory of it alone was enough to make her blush and stammer, so it seemed impossible that she could have a conversation about it without forgetting how to speak properly.

It wasn't that she regretted the kiss—that feeling had still yet to surface, at least not in full force. She'd felt traces of it, here and there, like when Jasper came to her door the next day with a new, expectant look on his face. The first thing he'd tried to do was bring it up, and she'd practically dragged him out of the room and into the crowded hallway to end the conversation.

But she really didn't regret it. She'd liked it. And she wanted to do it again, if she was being honest with herself.

So it wasn't regret that was the problem. It was the *lack* of it that confused her. It was the dreams that came to her every night, filled with Jasper's bare skin and soft mouth and gentle hands, that left her gasping and hot in her bed upon waking. It was the way her body seemed to reach for him subconsciously every time they were near each other, and even when they were apart.

It was the *want*.

And until she figured that out, she simply couldn't talk about it.

Luckily, both she and Jasper had plenty to do to distract themselves.

Kindra threw herself back into training. She spent hours each day at the training grounds. She not only sparred with people, she learned from them, too. She had them explain their magic to her, all the ways it was both similar and different from hers. She and Ryle spent a lot of time together as she learned the ins and outs of his wind magic. She even discovered that he and Heinrich were partners as they chatted between sessions. She liked Ryle a lot more than she liked Heinrich and didn't understand how he could stand the Wavebreaker's incessant worrying, but she kept that opinion to herself.

When she wasn't training, she was in the library reading, though she'd moved on from Jasper's fiction recommendations and was reading his favorite history texts now. Or she was in the War Chamber. Since the first meeting after the attack, she'd been invited to several more. Her attendance became a regularity, and even Antone did not begrudge her for being there anymore. She mostly stayed silent, sitting at the edge of the room with Jasper, but sometimes her opinion was sought out. King Leofric, in particular, seemed to value what she had to say, which both pleased and disturbed her. The other women in the room seemed pleased by her presence, as well. There were four of them total: her, General Lustris, an Earthwarden commander named Vitore Terberyn, and Kristaline Atmon, a Windspinner who lead the City Guard. There were but four of them among over a dozen men.

Jasper attended many meetings she was not invited to—some in the War Chamber, others with just the Council, and more still that she didn't know about, she was sure. He looked permanently exhausted despite the fact that Healers brushed away his heavy under-eyes bags each morning and brought a healthy glow to his face. Unfortunately, even they couldn't wield away the stress of a looming war. It clung to all of them. Nobody in the castle looked rested. Kindra was the same; though she collapsed into her bed each night and slipped into darkness without much effort, she still woke the next morning feeling as though she'd hardly slept at all.

But despite running herself ragged, Kindra's mind still had plenty of time to think about Jasper, and the feel of his mouth on hers, and the way he'd held her face as he'd kissed her, and the way he'd smiled at her after the fact.

It was extremely annoying.

We are preparing for war, she'd scolded herself after her traitorous mind had caused her to zone out in a meeting, distracting her with yet more thoughts about Jasper's muscled chest and arms. *We are preparing for war, so stop thinking about it!*

She did not stop thinking about it.

Day in and day out, waking and dreaming, she thought about it. Something had been unleashed within her when she'd looked up at him and pressed her lips to his. Something that she could not lock away now, however hard she tried.

So she kept Jasper at arm's length. Deflected any attempt to discuss it with a change in subject. Tried to interact with him only around others, so he couldn't trap her in an intimate conversation. And she hardly touched him, something that she saw confused and hurt him, since they'd become so comfortable doing so prior to the festival bombing. She knew she was doing what he'd asked—begged—her not to.

She also knew it was only a matter of time before he snapped.

So when, a week after the attack and the kiss, Jasper followed her back to her rooms and strode in before she could say otherwise, she was not surprised. She'd put it off as long as she could, she supposed, and gestured for Sala and Cerulle to give them some privacy.

"You kissed me," he stated bluntly once the doors were closed.

"Yes," was all she could think to say, struck stupid by the solitude they now had, the way her thoughts ran wild with that fact.

"*You* kissed *me,*" he repeated.

"Yes."

"And yet now you are farther from me than you've been in weeks. Why?"

She stared at him, unable to form the words she wanted to say.

"Why, Kindra?" He took a step towards her. "I thought we were— improving."

We were. We are. But she couldn't say it.

"You kissed me," he said again, like he still couldn't wrap his head around it, "and now you cannot even bare to touch me. You can hardly stand to be in the same room as me. Why?"

"I just—It has been a lot, these past few days. I've been very busy—"

"Don't change the subject, Kindra." He stepped closer to her. Her body screamed for her to move, to close the distance between them. But Jasper did it for her, coming to a stop less than a foot away. "You have never been afraid to tell me how you feel before. Don't be so now."

Still, the words wouldn't come, and Jasper's face crumpled further. "Kindra," he said, so soft it was almost a whisper, "please."

"I—" she started, then stopped. "Can we please—can we not talk about this right now?" Her voice fell to a shameful whisper.

Jasper misread her shame. "You regret it, don't you? Is it—is it really so repulsive? You won't even speak of it?" There was no trace of anger in his voice. Just pure, undiluted hurt.

Oh, gods. "No, Jasper, it's—"

"It's what, Kindra? What else could it possibly—"

"I do not know how to want you!" she blurted finally, and when his face rippled with confusion, she rambled on, "I was prepared to hate you, to despise you for all my days, to—to *torture* you with my hatred. And now, I—I *like* you. You are kinder than I expected, and pleasant to be around, and it is very confusing. It was easier to hate you. But now I want you, and I don't know what to do about it." She threw her hands in the air. "There! Are you satisfied?"

For a moment, Jasper was stunned into silence. Kindra felt her cheeks begin to burn and looked anywhere but him. "But you want me?" he finally said, his lips curling up in the beginnings of a smirk.

Kindra's face had never been so hot. She looked at the floor. "Don't laugh at me," she grumbled, and he placed a hand under her chin, gently turning it up so that he could see her.

"I would never," he whispered very seriously, and then kissed her hard.

Kindra had been so wound up with shock and adrenaline and terror the last time that she hadn't even fully processed the kiss until it was over. But this time... this time she felt all of it.

It was almost unbearable.

The fire that scorched her down to the bone was not her magic, but her desire. It burned through her, hotter than any flame she'd ever conjured. She was certain Jasper could feel it as he pulled her flush against him, his hands winding around her waist and into her hair. She kept herself restrained, resting her hands on his chest, afraid that if she allowed them to move, to start wandering, she'd lose herself entirely.

A small gasp of surprise slipped out of her as Jasper tugged her head back, revealing the column of her throat, and pressed his mouth there in fervent, hungry kisses. She felt her knees shake; she was as moldable as clay in his hands.

His mouth found hers again as he maneuvered the two of them backwards. Her back hit something solid—one of the bookshelves. Jasper pinned her there, one arm held above him, propping him against the shelf, the other still tangled in her hair.

Briefly, her mind cleared just enough to shoot her a question of *What are you doing?*

I am kissing my betrothed, she shot back, silencing the voice of reason—if that was what it even was.

Jasper nipped lightly at her lower lip, pulling a soft moan from her. He smiled, triumphant at her response, and was leaning back in to kiss her once more when there was a knock at the door.

The moment shattered.

Jasper took several steps back, combing his hair back into place with his fingers and rebuttoning his shirt, which Kindra had not even realized she'd been in the process of unbuttoning. His face was flushed a bright, fierce red. Kindra sagged against the bookshelf, chest heaving as she collected herself.

Whoever was outside knocked again.

"Who—" Kindra stammered, "who is it?"

"It is Princess Helena, my Lady," came Cerulle's reply, sounding strained, as if she knew exactly what had been transpiring in Kindra's chambers and was trying to stall for time.

Kindra shot Jasper a panicked look. She couldn't refuse Helena, and it wasn't like she could hide Jasper—she looked a flustered mess, and Helena would see right through any lies.

They were caught.

"Let her in," she conceded, and a second later the door opened to allow the golden-haired princess to waltz into the room.

And come abruptly to a halt as she took in the scene before her.

A taut moment of silence stretched between the three of them.

Then, Helena smirked—more like Emeline in that moment than ever—and said, "Well, it seems you two have managed to overcome any remaining animosity."

"Helena—" Jasper choked, shocked, but his sister cut him off with high, delighted giggle.

"Jasper, please, I'm happy for you two."

Kindra was horribly embarrassed. The heat of her passion was turning into shame, against her will. She felt like a teenager all over again, like when she'd been caught kissing Winona Daryn by the shabby village tavern in Harthwin at sixteen.

"Don't—make a fuss over it," Jasper muttered, clearly feeling the same way.

Helena, wisely, relented. "Anyway, I came to retrieve you both for dinner in my chambers with Em. Although," she continued, seemingly unable to help herself, "if you'd rather eat something else—"

"Dinner sounds great, thank you!" Kindra hurriedly interrupted, already exiting. Behind her, Jasper hissed something inaudible to his sister, which she only responded to with another singsong laugh.

As Jasper fell in step beside her, she couldn't help but recall the last few moments. A small smile bloomed on her lips as her heart skipped in her chest with something akin to giddiness.

And when Jasper reached out to take her hand, she didn't pull away.

CHAPTER 35

News of the refugees arrived the next day, snapping Kindra out of her well-kissed stupor.

Word had spread across the kingdom about the attack and the war that was now more inevitable than ever. Though King Leofric's show of strength had done a good job at quelling fear, panic still poisoned the air of the castle and all of Wendrith. Kindra knew it was the same throughout Alverin.

People were flocking to the larger cities because of the impending crisis, abandoning their small, defenseless villages in hopes that the walls of Dewport or Roulierne would shield them from what was to come. It had only just begun, and already lords and city officials were sending messages reflecting concerns of being overwhelmed, their streets becoming flooded with displaced people they could not house or feed.

This was the topic of the Council meeting that day. Helena had surprised Emeline, Kindra and Jasper that morning by announcing that she was going to the Council meeting, something she rarely did.

"They don't walk among the people like I do," she'd explained. "They haven't in years. Once they could get away without having to interact with the civilians, they stopped. But I'm out there, every month, sometimes every week! I talk to them. Not just those who are nobility or upper class, but all of the populace. So I need to be in there, if they're going to decide whether or not we protect our people." She'd shot Jasper a pointed look. "Besides, you're going to need all the help you can get. I imagine you'll have only Epira on your side, and that's not going to do you one damn bit of good."

But though Kindra itched to be in that meeting with them, she was instead at court, in a gown of deep brown, flowing silk rather than her nerushmyr. Jasper and Helena had both been pushing for her to make an appearance here for weeks now. The sparring and then the bombing had provided excuses to avoid it, but Kindra knew she was merely putting off the inevitable. At some point, she was going to have to interact with the courtiers

At least she had Emeline with her, who was capable of repelling the more unpleasant ones with a single glance.

Today, the Wavebreaker looked resplendent in a forest green gown cut from gossamer. It left her arms bare, and attached at her shoulders was a shimmering, sheer cape that trailed behind her as she walked. Her black hair was braided in an intricate crown around her head, her skin dusted with gold.

When Kindra had complimented her, she'd leaned in and whispered conspiratorially, "I don't often attend court. But when I do, I make sure to remind these vultures that I'm royalty, and they are not."

The gilded parlor went quiet when they entered, conversations stopping mid-sentence. Queen Cordilya was seated on a small, golden throne at the front of the room, looking as empty as always. A glass of champagne sat on a table next to her, hardly touched. As Kindra and Emeline made their way to greet her, Kindra didn't think she'd notice their presence.

But the queen gave a nearly imperceptible nod when they came to a halt, her gray eyes flitting over them. Kindra and Emeline dipped into low curtsies, bowing their heads in acknowledgment.

"Greetings, Your Majesty," Emeline said, voice softer than normal. "We've come to join your court this afternoon."

There was a beat of silence in which the whole room watched.

And then Queen Cordilya gave them yet another tiny nod, and the parlor burst back into conversation. In the corner, a musician seated at a pianoforte resumed his playing. More Rouliernien sparkling wine was poured, more violetleaf pipes were filled.

Kindra and Emeline made their way over to an open sofa in the corner of the room, hoping to be left alone. Unfortunately, they only had a few minutes to themselves before they were approached by a pair of silver-eyed twins—the Halis sisters, who had mocked Kindra behind her back when she'd first arrived. She'd also heard through the grapevine no shortage of other disparaging remarks they'd made about her since.

"Good day, Lady Kindra, Princess Emeline," the one on the left said, and they both curtsied.

"Hello, Lady Genevera." Emeline nodded to the one who'd spoken, then to her sister, "Lady Caroline."

They both had sharp, scrutinizing gazes that didn't soften as they sat on the sofa across from them. Genevera held a flute of sparkling wine in her hand, and Caroline clutched a violetleaf pipe in her long, thin fingers.

"Would you like some?" she offered, holding out the pipe.

"No, thank you," Kindra replied. She hadn't known much about the plant before she arrived in Wendrith. It didn't grow well near Harthwin; the climate was too cold for it to thrive there. She'd learned quickly, though. Violetleaf was actually a flower, though the flower itself was useless. If one crushed up the vibrant purple leaves and smoked them, however, they had a relaxing, heady effect that could help with sleep or alleviating stress. A lot of the courtiers, she'd noticed over the past few weeks, rarely went anywhere without a pipe in hand, and that was before the war closed in on them. Now, most of them spent many hours a day in a violetleaf fog.

If only everyone could simply smoke their problems away, Kindra thought bitterly as Caroline took a slow drag from the pipe. The lavender smoke floated from her mouth and into the air around them, the smell reminding Kindra of burning flowers.

"We've been waiting *so* long for you to come here, Lady Kindra," Caroline said airily.

"You've been so busy *sparring*, though, we wondered if we'd ever get the chance to talk to you," Genevera added, taking a sip of her drink.

"Well, I'm here now," Kindra said, smiling tightly and feeling very out of her element. It was so different from the training grounds; though this, she knew, was just another type of sparring match.

"Did you ever come see her? In a match?" Emeline drawled, plucking a drink off of a passing server's tray.

"Oh, no," Caroline giggled, silver eyes glassy. "I don't even think we know where the training grounds are."

"Did you not go to Grydmarth?" Kindra asked before she could stop herself. These were Windspinners of high noble rank—their uncle was Councilman Halis, in charge of the infrastructure, improvement, and construction throughout not only Wendrith, but all of Alverin. He worked with lords and city officials all over Alverin on projects like water systems and roads. So surely, his nieces were of considerable magical strength.

Genevera shrugged. "We did, because all noble children do, but..." She gestured to the ornate room they were sitting in. "Let's just say, our calling lies elsewhere."

"And what would that be, Lady Genevera? Spending your days smoking and drinking?" Emeline baited, voicing Kindra's thoughts out loud.

"Why, Princess Emeline, it's so much more than that," Genevera replied, voice syrupy. "Our calling is to serve our dear Queen Cordilya. And to marry well and continue the Halis bloodline—one of Alverin's oldest and strongest families. Second to the Annalindis family, of course." Her face gleamed with pride, but her eyes were as sharp and glinting as ever.

Caroline giggled again, leaning back into the sofa. The pipe dangled limply from her hand, the bowl nothing but ash. "Well, perhaps the Annalindis family of a hundred years—"

Genevera silenced her sister with a dangerous look and a tight squeeze on her arm. Kindra was shocked. To voice such a thing out loud was surely forbidden, wasn't it? She looked at Emeline, who was regarding Caroline as though she were prey. Genevera caught the look and shifted uncomfortably in her seat, the arrogance she'd oozed just moments ago vanishing.

"I didn't know disparaging the royal family was part of your duty to our beloved queen, Lady Caroline," Emeline observed, taking a casual sip of her drink. But every word dripped with warning. Caroline seemed to finally grasp some awareness and shrank further into her seat.

"She did not mean that, Your Highness—" Genevera interjected.

"You know, ladies," Emeline cut Genevera off as though she'd not even been speaking, "When every other kingdom on this continent comes to kill us all, your wine and your pipes will not save you. Nor will your *bloodline*, since you do fuck all with the magic you got from it. Do you even remember how to wield? Or have you drunk and smoked yourselves into uselessness?" Emeline stood, and Kindra, awestruck at the Wavebreaker's sheer ferocity, stood with her. "Perhaps you should come by the training grounds. See how somebody who's *actually* serving this kingdom spends her time." She strode away, cape flowing behind her, and Kindra practically scrambled after her. They said farewell to Queen Cordilya, who gave no indication she even knew what had transpired, and quickly made their exit.

"And that," Emeline said through clenched teeth as they made their way up the stairs to their chambers, "is why I don't go to court very often."

"I don't know," Kindra admitted, laughing softly, "That was kind of fun."

Emeline only rolled her eyes, but she couldn't hide the gleam of satisfaction in them that told Kindra she agreed.

Later that night, Jasper gave Kindra a summary of the Council meeting.

The Council was evenly split. On one side, Councilmen Terbis, Epira, and Brenlyr were for opening the gates of Wendrith to refugees immediately. On the other, Halis, Oxler and, naturally, Avis, were against it. Antone and Sebastian were also against it, though Sebastian was not so firm in his stance as his older brother. Helena and Jasper were firmly rooted against their siblings and had argued emphatically against barring people from entering the city.

"So your father is the one who decides, right?" Kindra asked, sitting cross-legged on Jasper's bed as he looked over papers at his desk. She'd only been in his room a handful of times since the day of the attack and was still taking it all in. Namely, all of the books. There were piles of them everywhere. Even the desk where he currently worked was partly covered in them.

"Yes," Jasper replied, half-distracted, "and I doubt he'll side with us."

She frowned. "I mean, surely he wouldn't abandon his people—"

He turned over a page, scanning it for something. "It'll get more people to sign up for the army. Think about it. The cities are full, but if you sign up to fight, you get a roof over your head. Three meals a day. And a small wage, which you can send back to your loved ones who may be unable to join, which can in turn help them find housing and food." He gave her a sad smile. "This is the way of it, Kindra."

She shifted, feeling uncomfortable. "Seems very manipulative," she grumbled. "Refuse to help your people so they're more likely to sign up to die for you."

"Helena and I tried to come up with a compromise. Putting out a call for people who have extra rooms in their homes to open them up. Let a family stay there in exchange for work. That way only those really capable of fighting join the army, and those who cannot fight have some place to go."

Kindra nodded. "That seems much more humane."

"It is. Unfortunately, I don't know if they'll buy it. More soldiers aren't a bad thing when we could be going up against three separate armies." He was still scouring the papers on his desk, searching for something he'd yet to find. She studied the profile of his face: the strong slope of his nose, the defined curve of his jaw, the soft swell of his lips.

She was unable to look away. *He is quite beautiful,* she thought. It was perhaps the first time she'd allowed herself to think that without feeling ashamed or angry about it.

"I can feel you staring," he said softly, lips curving upward. He turned his head, catching her eyes before she looked away, cheeks burning. "I don't mind it. I'm sure you feel me staring at you all the time."

Kindra smiled despite herself. She *did* always know when he was looking at her. He had never tried to hide it either, like she did. He'd always been completely unashamed of how he watched her.

How extraordinary, he'd said, the first time he'd seen her expel her magic. She could still picture the wonder that had shone on his face.

"Come sit with me," she blurted, suddenly needing to be close to him. "You've been working all day." He'd been hunched over that desk when she arrived half an hour ago and hadn't so much as touched her. That bothered her more than it should have. Now that she'd had a taste of it, she couldn't get enough.

Jasper straightened, turning to face her. "On my bed?"

Kindra swallowed, then nodded before she lost her courage. "Sure. Why not? You *are* my betrothed." That last sentence was more for her than him.

He nodded and made his way to the bed. "I am your betrothed," he repeated softly, settling down next to her. Hesitantly, he reached out, brushing a stray curl out of her face. The touch of his fingertips—his *fingertips*—lit a fire inside her. She let out a shaky breath, face leaning into his palm, which cupped her cheek.

"We don't—I don't expect anything from you," Jasper clarified quickly. "Just because we're sitting on my bed doesn't mean—"

"I know." She rested a hand on his chest, where she could feel his heart pounding just as quickly as hers. "But I appreciate you telling me anyway."

Then she curled her fingers into his shirt and pulled him to her until her lips met his.

It was infuriating, really, how much she enjoyed kissing him already, and this was only the third time it had happened. A small part of her wanted to be annoyed about it, whispering things about being trapped and forced into marriage and caged.

But the rest of her didn't care at all, not as Jasper reached over and grabbed her by her thighs, pulling her on to his lap so she was straddling him in one smooth maneuver.

Maybe she'd never see the freedom she'd once known ever again. But if this was the cage... well, there were far worse bars to be trapped behind.

Before she knew it, she was working to undo the buttons of his shirt. Jasper moaned, kissing her mouth, as she ran her palms down his chest and stomach, and she hummed appreciatively as she felt every solid muscle. His hands, still on her thighs, trailed up, pushing her tunic up around her hips.

And then he hesitated, even as their kisses grew wilder.

"Always such a gentleman," Kindra whispered. Her fingers slid lower on his stomach, brushing the waistband of his pants. Jasper sucked in a sharp breath.

"I'd rather be sure," he murmured back, voice strained.

"I'll tell you when to stop, Jasper." She broke their kiss long enough to meet his eyes and make that promise. "Now please, for the love of the gods, *touch me*."

He choked out a surprised laugh, and Kindra cut it off as she slammed her lips to his once again.

And finally, his hands slid up those final few inches, cupping her ass and squeezing in a way that made her whole body thrum with desire.

She moaned, pressing her hips down against his almost subconsciously. She could feel the hardness of him, and what she once thought would terrify her now only made her want more.

Jasper pushed her down against him again, grinding into her as his tongue parted her lips and rubbed against hers. One of his hands snaked up to grab her breast, and she was overwhelmed with the desperate, desperate need to get their clothes off. She hadn't felt this way in years, not since she was nineteen and had had a month-long fling with the son of a family passing through her village. She'd missed it, she realized.

It was fun.

"Kindra," Jasper sighed, pulling back to catch his breath. "We should... take... a second..."

The pause brought her back, slightly, to her senses. "Right," she managed, "right." Slowly, stiffly, she moved off of him.

His gray eyes, still heated, raked over her. "You still haven't figured it out, have you?"

"What do you mean?"

"How to want me," he said simply. When Kindra opened her mouth to protest, he shook his head. "It's okay. I'm just glad you've realized that you do."

"And what if I hadn't?"

He shrugged and stared at the ceiling. "I would have waited. It would've driven me crazy, though. I've wanted you since the second I walked into your cottage in Harthwin."

Kindra knew he was telling the truth.

"I was quite awful to you," she said quietly.

"Yes," he agreed, "but you had your reasons. I never resented you for it, even though it hurt sometimes."

She felt maybe she should apologize. But she knew, despite how far they'd come, she wouldn't mean it if she did. Her anger had been real and valid, and he'd acted in a way that deserved it.

"I'm glad you didn't," she said instead. "Most people do. Most people are frightened."

"I could never be scared of you," he whispered.

Staring into his eyes, Kindra believed him.

An hour later, Kindra slid quietly out of Jasper's chambers. The halls were dimly lit, the windows revealing the dark night sky. There was no moonlight to illuminate the dark castle; the moon was hidden behind clouds tonight.

A guard moved to escort her, but she waved him away. That was one thing that had yet to materialize for her here: the constant hovering of a squad of guards. She suspected it was Jasper's doing. She'd mentioned to him more than once how much she despised being followed everywhere she went, how restricted it made her feel, and since then, the only times guards had shadowed her was when they'd gone into Wendrith.

To be fair, she spent so much time with Emeline, Jasper and Helena that their personal guards had practically become hers. But she liked that she had the chance to have some privacy, to walk alone and feel less suffocated. She was sure her wielding skills had helped to convince them that she needed less security.

As she walked down the hall, nodding to the guards she passed, she couldn't help the smile that bloomed. *Jasper.* He wasn't so bad, was he? Indeed, he seemed to have taken his vow to treat her better very seriously. He still had his moments, of course, but then again, so did she. Besides, she found his protectiveness and sometimes overbearing nature... charming, nowadays.

You're getting comfortable, just like they want, that wicked voice whispered in her head.

And so what if I am? She shot back. The memory of Jasper's mouth on hers and his hands on her body was still so fresh. Her body still tingled where he'd touched her.

Let me have this, she told that part of herself angrily. *I'll probably be dead in a few years, anyway, so let me have this.*

Because that was still the reality, wasn't it? She could grow to care deeply for Jasper, grow to love him even, to want to bear his children, but when that first child failed to have magic...

She was only ever going to have a limited amount of time here, be it the war that kills her or the king himself.

The thought was more sobering than it usually was.

Perhaps because now the thought of fleeing and leaving Jasper behind wasn't as appealing.

Movement at the end of the hallway snapped Kindra out of her thoughts.

Ahead of her, a cloaked figure was creeping down the hall, staying in the shadows. Kindra's magic prickled in her fingers, and she looked around, only to find that in this stretch of the third floor, there were no guards. They'd rounded the corner already, continuing on their patrol. The next patrol would be coming into view in just a few minutes if Kindra's recollection about their patterns was correct.

But whoever this person was seemed to know that too, moving silently and quickly towards a door. It was plain; Kindra had never noticed it before.

Kindra ducked into the arch of a doorway and poked her head out slightly, watching as the dark figure got closer and closer to their destination.

She was only fifteen, maybe twenty feet from them, but she still hadn't been seen. What would have happened if she'd brought a guard with her, like the rest of the Annalindises? Would this person be getting arrested right now?

Distantly, Kindra heard the low murmur of voices, and by the way the figure tensed, they did too. Picking up their pace, they reached the door. As they did so, the hood of their cloak fell back an inch, revealing a flash of orange hair and a sliver of burnt skin.

Tess. It was Tess.

What the fuck? Kindra thought, alarm coursing through her as she watched Tess carefully open the door and slip inside.

Kindra waited until the door closed behind her, then moved from her hiding place just as a patrol of guards rounded the corner. She smoothed her hands over her tunic and did her best to look unconcerned, walking leisurely down the hall.

"Good evening, Lady Kindra," one of them said as they passed her.

"Good evening," she replied, hoping her voice didn't betray her nerves. As soon as their footsteps faded and they turned the corner, leaving her alone again, she turned, hurrying back to the door.

Her magic pooling just under her skin, she opened it and found—

A broom closet.

"What?" She couldn't stop herself from saying it out loud.

It was a broom closet, mostly empty. Stone walls and floors, no windows.

Lighting a small flame in her palm, she scanned the tiny space. "Tess?" she hissed.

There was no place for Tess to be hiding.
But she was still nowhere to be found.

CHAPTER 36

Two days later and there still was no sign of Tess.

Kindra hadn't breathed a word of what she'd seen to anybody. Perhaps if it was anyone else she'd seen slinking down the hall at night and vanishing, she would have. But it was *Tess*.

Tess, the first Firefury she'd ever known besides herself. Who'd brought her power to new heights. Who'd amazed Kindra with her resilience and bravery.

So no, Kindra didn't tell anybody, not even Jasper or Emeline. She respected Tess and trusted her.

Even if creeping around the castle in the dark and mysteriously disappearing from a tiny closet with only one exit was extremely suspicious.

Kindra had been training with Ryle and Terryn the past couple of days since Tess was gone. Nobody else seemed surprised by this. In fact, when she'd asked, Ryle had merely shrugged.

"Tess goes on missions to outposts all the time," he'd informed her. "That's probably where she is."

And on the surface, that made sense. Kindra tried hard to convince herself that it was really that simple. But the more she thought about it, it just didn't add up.

Why sneak out through a broom closet if she'd been on a mission ordered by the king or the Council? Why hide herself under a cloak to make sure nobody saw her?

Kindra had only two distractions from her spiraling thoughts: training and Jasper. Even late nights spent gossiping and drinking with Emeline and

Helena weren't enough. It had to be something physical, something so intense she couldn't think about anything else.

So naturally, that was either sparring with somebody like Ryle, who was still kicking her ass pretty regularly, or kissing Jasper.

If he noted her distracted air for the last few days, he didn't comment on it. He merely accepted her affection with open arms and returned it just as eagerly. The relief he felt was palpable. Kindra could feel it in every touch, every word: relief that she felt the same way for him as he did her; relief that their marriage might not be a loveless one.

So she let him be relieved, let him think the time spent learning the contour of each other's bodies was rooted purely in sheer, wild desire. It wasn't entirely false. It just wasn't entirely true, either.

These moments were pretty tame, all things considered. Neither of them wanted to take the next step into the realm of actually sleeping together, so their trysts remained, for the most part, clothed. They were both getting more handsy, though, so who knew how long they'd be able to last before they crossed that line.

Kindra knew a large reason neither of them suggested doing so was because once they started having sex, the clock started ticking. And why add *that* worry when there was already so much else to worry about?

Time passed in a blur, her concern for Tess an ever-present weight on her chest. Then finally, on the third day, Jasper presented her with something exciting: another outing into Wendrith.

"I have something to show you," he said, smiling so that his cheeks dimpled.

"Are they really letting us go out into Wendrith, so soon after the attack?" Kindra asked.

He nodded. "With an army, practically, but yes." He grabbed her hand. "We leave in an hour."

Sure enough, they were accompanied by not one, but three squads of guards. Their carriage took them to the industrial area of the city, where people worked in tanneries, smithies, and other shops, making the kinds of goods a kingdom couldn't survive without: tools, armor, weapons, and more.

They came to a halt outside a forge. Jasper helped Kindra down from the carriage, nodding and waving to some of the people who'd stopped to gawk at them.

She took in the shop before her. It was just an ordinary blacksmith shop, and so similar to Elric's that it made her heart ache. She wondered, briefly, about the Earthwarden, and those thoughts spread quickly to how all of Harthwin was faring. She'd heard nothing more about her mother or if the party from Wendrith had reached her already. Kindra tried not to think too much about that.

Jasper read all this on her face and gave her hand a comforting squeeze. "I know," he murmured. "Just trust me."

He led her into the shop, followed by an oppressive number of guards. It was already hot due to the forge burning in the open workshop, though it wouldn't have been too bad if only Jasper and she had entered. But the addition of the half-dozen heavily armed men taking up posts around the room made it hotter and more cramped.

A man—who looked nothing like Elric, thank the gods—emerged from a back room. He was younger, maybe in his early thirties, with golden tan skin and long reddish-brown hair tied back from his face. He was tall, too, towering over even Jasper, who had to be over six foot. The smith's eyes were a rich forest green, and they lit up when he saw who had entered his shop.

"Your Highness," he said, bowing low, "I was wondering when I'd see you again." His gaze turned to Kindra, and he bowed once more to her. "And Lady Kindra. Such a pleasure to have the cursebreaker herself in my humble shop."

She was glad his gaze was fixed on the floor when he said it, so he did not have to see her flinch.

"Is it finished, Master Geryn?" Jasper bounced on his toes slightly, betraying his eagerness.

"I asked you to please call me Orril, Your Highness," the blacksmith responded.

"And I told you to call me Jasper."

Orril laughed, a loud, booming sound. Then he nodded, gesturing them over to the counter. "It is done, yes. I think she will be very pleased."

"She?" Kindra's eyes widened. Surely not...

Orril vanished into the back room once more, returning a moment later with a long box. He set it on the counter and lifted the lid.

Kindra gasped.

Inside was a longsword, befit for a king or queen. The steel blade was polished and sharp, the bronze hilt was engraved with designs so intricate only an Earthwarden could achieve them: swirling flames and burning suns, wrapping up from the hilt to the base of the blade.

It was beautiful.

"It's for you," Jasper said softly. "Consider it a wedding gift."

For the first time, the mention of the wedding didn't send a chill down her spine or a shock of dread through her. Instead, it made her feel warm.

"Jasper, I... I don't even know how to use this," she started, feeling overwhelmed.

"Well, I'll teach you. We discussed doing lessons, didn't we? Of course, then you had to go break three ribs in a fight with Ryle and then the city was bombed, so it was a bit low on the priority list, but... I'd like to teach you still, if you want to." His face was flushed, and not just because of the heat from the forge.

Kindra didn't hesitate to nod. "Yes," she said. "Definitely. I just... I can barely handle the dagger."

"We'll work up to the sword. You're probably not even strong enough to swing it—" She cut him off with a haughty glare, and reached for the sword, grasping the hilt with two hands and lifting it gingerly out of the box.

Oh, shit. It *was* heavy. Her arms strained slightly at the weight, and Jasper and Orril exchanged a knowing look.

"Wielding magic requires a different type of strength than wielding a sword. You'll learn quickly, though." He clapped Orril on the shoulder. "Orril has even added the same oil tube that's in your dagger."

The blacksmith laughed. "I had no idea what he was talking about, when he came in here talking about a sword that could be lit on fire. But he showed me the dagger, and I have to say... it's a genius idea. And it's downright stupid that nobody's thought of it before."

"You stole my dagger?" she snapped, only slightly offended.

Jasper shrugged sheepishly. "I came here the day after your match with Ryle. You were still practically bedridden. It was returned before you ever knew it was missing. Besides," he added, "I wanted to do this before I lost my nerve."

She eyed the hilt and spotted a similar notch in the bottom of the hilt to the one on Elric's dagger. She pressed in, and surely enough, a thin coating of oil oozed its way down the blade. A wicked grin blossomed on her face, and she stepped back so that she was safely away from everyone. Then she touched her finger to the sword and lit it on fire.

It was even more magnificent than the dagger, which made it all the harder to control. Just holding it, it was fine, but she could tell that the act of fighting with it while controlling the flames would be taxing.

She ogled it for a few more minutes, then extinguished the sword, dipping it in a basin of water to cool it before handing it back to Orril. "It's beautiful," she complimented. "Thank you." She turned to Jasper and gave him a soft smile. "Thank you," she said again to him.

He returned her smile, looking rather proud of himself. "I was hoping you'd like it."

"I love it," she said emphatically, watching as Orril placed it back into the box, closing the lid over it. One of the guards stepped forward to take it. Jasper removed a small pouch from his pocket, setting it on the counter with a small clank. It was filled, Kindra knew, with gold. Probably enough to cover Orril's living expenses for the next few months at least.

The blacksmith's eyes grew wide and he shook his head. "Your Highness—Jasper," he corrected at the sight of Jasper's raised eyebrows, "I cannot take this. You already paid."

"Consider this my tip, then, for a job well done, Orril," Jasper said firmly, though not unkindly.

"I…" Orril seemed at a loss for words briefly. Then he nodded, blinking quickly, as if to fight away tears. "Thank you, Jasper. Thank you so much. It's an honor."

"You are this city's best blacksmith," Jasper declared. "You deserve to live comfortably for the amazing work you do." He held out his arm to Kindra. "Shall we?"

She took it and gave a wave to Orril as they made their way out of the shop. "Thank you again. It was nice to meet you."

Once in the carriage, she pressed a quick kiss to Jasper's cheek. "You really didn't have to do this."

He caught her face with one hand and kissed her lips softly. "Yes, I did. You're to be my wife. It's a requirement to shower you with gifts, is it not?"

She turned away, giggling, and looked out the window as the carriage jolted into motion.

Suddenly, her blood ran cold. There, leaning against the wall at the mouth of an alleyway, was Tess.

She tried not to go too still, so she wouldn't alert Jasper to what she saw, though why she felt the need to keep this from him, she couldn't quite put her finger on.

It was definitely Tess. Even with a cloak concealing most of her, Kindra could see the light reflecting off of a few stray strands of her hair. The way she held herself was the same. And when she looked up—straight at the carriage—she could see and feel the heat of her orange eyes from where she sat, and Kindra knew instantly that Tess was very aware that she had seen her. She leaned closer to the window, pulling away from Jasper entirely. Dimly, she was aware of him saying something, but she was too focused to listen.

A hand gripped her shoulder, pulling her away. She jerked around, annoyed.

"What is it?" Jasper asked.

Kindra looked back out the window. The alley where Tess had been standing just a second ago was now empty, save for the tail end of a dark cloak, swishing out of view.

"Nothing," she said, the lie rolling easily off her tongue. "I just thought I saw something." She turned back to him as the carriage rolled down the street. "But it was nothing. Just a little paranoid, that's all."

"Right," he replied, believing her so easily she felt a bit bad. "That makes sense."

She tucked herself into his side again. When he went to kiss her, she didn't pull away.

CHAPTER 37

Tess was back three days later, waiting for Kindra in the training ring like nothing had happened. Kindra forced herself to look casual as she approached the other Firefury.

"You're back," she noted, keeping her voice light and nonchalant.

"Indeed I am."

"Where were you?" Kindra fought to keep any note of suspicion out of her tone.

"I was sent to some of the outposts and fortresses, per the Council's request. Discussing defense plans, taking stock of what they have and don't have, that sort of thing," Tess explained. If Kindra didn't know for a fact she was lying, she would've believed her without question.

It stung to be lied to so deliberately. Kindra gritted her teeth, reminding herself to stay calm. "Of course. That's understandable." She nodded towards the ring, wanting to be done with the conversation. "Shall we?"

Tess raised an eyebrow. "Not in the mood for chatting today?"

"No," Kindra bit out, turning away and marching out into the openness of the ring.

Tess regarded her for a moment longer, eyes narrowing slightly. Then she followed suit, and she'd barely finished the countdown when Kindra unleashed herself at her.

It was an unrefined match, Kindra growing more and more wild and out of control as she grew angrier. She was hurt that her friend was lying to her but also deeply concerned. What had Tess been doing? Was it something dangerous? Her thoughts spiraled as they continued to fight.

What if she was working with one of the other kingdoms? What if she'd known about the Harvest Festival bombing? Kindra didn't feel much loyalty to the royal family, despite the fact that she was soon to be part of it, but she did care about the civilians that resided in Alverin. They would be the ones who bore the brunt of this war.

Tess kept up with her, clearly thinking at first Kindra just had some energy to release. But as the match continued, her brows furrowed with worry as it became obvious Kindra's fire was fueled by anger.

"Kindra," she shouted over the roar of fire. "Kindra, what's going on?"

Kindra didn't reply, just sent another blast of fire towards her. Tess deflected it easily.

"Kindra," she tried again, "you're letting your emotions get the better of you. I can see—" she cut off, dodging a particularly nasty blow. "I can see you're mad at me for something. Just talk to me." She dodged again, and this time her face contorted with exasperation. "Dammit, Kindra, can you use your fucking words?"

Kindra snarled, but she stopped. She stormed over to Tess and hissed, quiet enough that only the two of them would hear: "You're lying to me."

Tess betrayed nothing. "What are you talking about?"

Her refusal to admit the truth only made Kindra angrier. "Cut the bullshit, Tess. I saw you. In the hallway, when you disappeared into a—a fucking broom closet! And then, a few days ago, outside the forge. I know you saw me, and I know you know that I saw you. So stop fucking lying to me and tell me what's really going on."

Tess blinked. For a brief moment, a mere heartbeat, her composure slipped. But then her mask was back in place, and she laughed. "Oh, yes. You saw me yesterday in the worker district. I was making a stop at my favorite metalsmith before coming back to the castle, that's all. Technically, those of us on the Royal Guard aren't supposed to go to anybody but the castle smiths, but I like to slip out and get some things for myself sometimes. That's why I was trying to stay hidden from the other guards; it could be a strike against me if I'm caught. But Kindra…" She frowned. "This thing about seeing me in the hallway? I don't know what you're talking about."

Again, the lie stung. Kindra opened her mouth to argue, to rip the truth out of Tess, but then thought better of it. If Tess wanted to withhold things from her, then fine. Kindra would just figure it out herself.

She closed her mouth and offered up an awkward smile. "Right, well, that explains that, then. Sorry for all the accusations. Although I wonder who it was in the hallway... should I report it to the guard? That seems like a security risk."

Tess's eyes flashed. "You can, though I'm not sure what could be done now."

"They could post more guards in the halls at night, so there aren't as many gaps where somebody could slip by," Kindra suggested mildly. She didn't miss the slight stiffening of Tess's shoulders.

"Right. They could do that." Tess backed away from her, aiming towards the water barrel. "I have to run—I've got patrol soon. But I'll see you tomorrow?"

Another lie. Tess didn't ever have patrol at this time of day. She purposefully had requested mornings off so she could train with Kindra.

"Oh." Kindra followed her to the barrel. "Did you get reassigned?"

Tess shrugged. "I just picked up a shift for one of the others. He's sick today." She smiled at Kindra, but it was thin, wary almost, lacking its usual warmth. "See you around. Thanks for the match."

"See you—" But the Firefury was already gone, hurrying across the ring as if she couldn't wait to get as far away from Kindra as possible.

"Sala, I have a question for you," Kindra proclaimed as she entered her rooms, sweaty and aching from a match with Ryle. After Tess's abrupt departure, she'd found the Windspinner across the ring and they'd trained together for a couple of hours. Their session culminated in a sparring match, and try though she did, Kindra did not emerge victorious. This time, at least, she got closer, a small victory for what had otherwise been a very frustrating morning.

Now, as Sala helped her out of her nerushmyr and into the steaming bath, Kindra's mind spun with theories and worries. Tess's lies and half-truths had not deterred her. In fact, she was only more determined to uncover what was really going on. She'd started with Ryle as they'd been warming up: an innocent inquiry about the sickness in the guard.

"Tess had to skip out early today. She's covering a shift for one of the other guards, said they're sick. Is there some kind of bug going around?" she'd asked.

Ryle had frowned. "Not that I know of. But maybe somebody drank too much last night."

Kindra had really wanted Ryle to confirm Tess's excuse. But with no solid answer, she now moved on to her next source of information.

"What's your question, Lady Kindra?" Sala ran her hands down Kindra's back, her eyes flashing with every pulse of magic she used to soothe the worn muscles.

"I've heard there might be a sickness in the Royal Guard." Kindra sighed as the aches eased and then vanished entirely under Sala's careful touch. "Have you heard anything about it, among the other Healers? I imagine you all are kept informed about the health of all in the castle."

"Yes, we are. Healers have meetings on the mornings when there are updates, actually. We didn't have a meeting this morning, so I'm not sure if there's any sickness going around. Perhaps a bad hangover—the guards like to claim it's an illness when they're merely sick from a night of too much drinking."

Kindra barely mustered up a laugh. "That makes sense, I suppose." She sank down into the water.

Sala hummed in reply and didn't say anything more about it. Kindra didn't push any further.

After lunch, she made her way to the Great Library. The giant space was sparsely occupied. It was a nice, rather warm day for late autumn, so many had decided to take advantage of the weather before the brutal cold of winter arrived. Over the sound of her own footsteps on the polished stone floors, she could hear the crackle of the giant fireplace, the soft rustle of pages being turned, and the quiet murmur of conversation between some of the scholars and courtiers who had decided to spend their time among the books.

Perfect. She didn't need an audience right now.

As inconspicuously as possible, she made her way to the records section of the library. It was on the ground floor, spanning for what felt like miles as she peered down aisle after aisle, each stretching and curving beyond what her eyes could see. It was also restricted. Nobody was allowed except for the most high-ranking scholars and officials, and members of the royal family, which she considered herself to be, if only because it helped justify breaking the rules.

The librarian's desk was blessedly unoccupied, the only people nearby a couple of robed scholars pouring over giant texts together at one of the tables. It was easy enough to sneak around them, and they were so engrossed in their reading they didn't even look up. Her infiltration successful, she began her search.

Using the plaques at the end of each aisle, she walked until she came across one that read "Architecture and Plans." Then she squared her shoulders and started down the aisle. There weren't so many books here as there were scrolls, some faded and dusty and torn, others still crisp and clean, as though they'd just been placed on the shelves the day before. Luckily, the shelves were labeled, making her hunt considerably easier, but it was still quite some time before she came to the shelf that held what she was looking for. It seemed as if they had every blueprint every drawn in the whole kingdom of Alverin on these shelves. Kindra supposed it wouldn't be surprising if they did.

Now, standing before a towering bookshelf marked "Castle Building Plans," she began pulling scrolls off the shelves and unrolling them as she sat on the ground in the middle of the aisle. Occasionally she had to light a small flame on the tip of her finger to help read; many of the plans were obviously very old, going back centuries, and time had left its mark on them. Some she could hardly make out, others had been rolled up for so long that when she flattened them out, they threatened to break apart in her hands. She tried to move through them as gently and quickly as possible. Finally, she found the scroll that held what she was looking for: the plan for the catacombs beneath the castle.

It was a massive scroll, too wide when unrolled to lay flat all at once in the width of the aisle. Fortunately, these plans weren't too faded, though she had a hard time figuring out how exactly they lined up with the castle itself. It was hard to visualize them fitting together.

The idea had come to her last night: Tess had disappeared into the catacombs. She imagined the broom closet might hold an entrance to them, hidden behind something or opened by pressing a certain stone. It was the only thing that made sense; otherwise Tess had just vanished into thin air, which was only possible for Shadowmasters, which Tess was not. Kindra just needed to confirm her suspicions by finding the floor plan that showed there was an entrance there. It would be too risky for her to sneak into the broom closet on a theory. Plus, now that Tess was back, Kindra needed to be extra careful.

If Tess was going to conceal her activities, then Kindra was going to conceal her attempts to discover them.

Gradually, the map began to make sense to her. But it still didn't tell her what she needed. This plan showed only the main level of the catacombs, which was mostly just tombs for the Annalindis family, and she needed plans that showed connections to the third floor, to see the hidden passages and stairways that began up there.

However, to her frustration, it seemed there were no other plans for the catacombs to be found. She poured over scroll after scroll, finding detailed plans for chambers, the kitchens, even the library itself, but no other scrolls of the catacombs and where, exactly, their entrances were. There were no indicators of any secret passages on anything she looked at. In the end, she placed all the scrolls back in their spots and left the records section feeling defeated.

Logically, she supposed she could understand it. The plans she needed were probably locked up in a much safer place than the library, where on a slow day anybody could slip past some focused scholars and get their hands on them. It made sense—just as people could use the catacombs to escape the castle, enemies could use them to get in, as well. So it was best to keep them well-guarded.

But understanding the reason didn't make Kindra any less frustrated about her failure.

As she exited the library and made her way back to her chambers, where she was to meet Jasper for their afternoon walk around the gardens, she devised her plan: caution be damned. There was an entrance to the catacombs in that closet, and tonight, she was going to find it.

CHAPTER 38

"Again," came Jasper's command, and Kindra let out a snarl of frustration, sweat dripping from her brow.

She swung the sword he'd given her with a grunt. It buried itself into the dummy's shoulder—and then refused to budge. She bit back a scream as she yanked on it, stumbling back when it finally pulled free.

They'd been training for the last few nights together, working solely on Kindra's ability to use her new sword. She was abysmal. All she wanted to do was throw the blade to the ground and go up in flames.

"Can we switch to the dagger?" she asked between pants. "I think that would be a lot easier."

"Yes, it would," Jasper agreed. "That's why you need to get a handle on the sword." He flashed her a wicked smile. "Just think how easy the dagger is going to be once you build up the strength needed to use this!"

"I don't think that's a tried-and-true teaching method, Your Highness." She so badly wanted to drop the sword and lay down on the cold stone floor. They were underneath the castle—there was another, smaller, training ring in the basement of the barracks where the Royal Guard slept. Wielders rarely used it; the space was too closed in, too confined, but non-Wielders did. This late at night nobody else was in the space to disturb them.

"Trust me, your body will thank me." His grin grew more mischievous. "I could have it thanking me in more ways than one, if you'd like."

Her face grew hot. "Trust you to never miss an opportunity to make a crude joke."

She was only partly in the mood for his flirtations. Though she'd started to look forward to their nightly sessions, she wished she could have come up with an excuse to cancel tonight's. Her mind was elsewhere: on an inconspicuous broom closet door, and the mystery it held. But she didn't want to raise any suspicion. The last person she needed watching her more closely was Jasper.

So she'd train with him, and then, after she said goodnight, she'd continue her sleuthing.

"Of course I'll never miss an opportunity, not when your reactions are always so delightful." He came up behind her, grabbing her arms and putting them into the correct position. His chest pressed up against her back. She could feel his heartbeat. It was always pounding. Despite his suave facade, he was still a nervous mess around her. She'd given up trying not to find that endearing. And, despite her straying thoughts, she found her heart pounding equally as fast as Jasper pressed a soft kiss to her neck.

"Is that supposed to help my focus?" she asked, and he laughed. He pulled back, to her disappointment, though one of his hands lingered on her waist.

"Again," he repeated. "Perhaps this time you can swing it without stumbling about like a newborn foal."

She growled, stepping away from him, and shot him a glare. "You talk a lot of shit for somebody who's not holding the sword."

Within an instant, he had her disarmed, the blade now firmly in his grasp. She hadn't even registered that he'd moved, he was so fast. Her magic pulsed under her skin defensively; she had to take a deep breath to steady herself.

"Now who's holding the sword?" He strode over to the dummy and made a series of quick, brutal strikes. He handled the sword effortlessly; it was like an extension of himself. Like her magic was to her, she supposed.

"Now I see why you ranked so high at Grydmarth," she remarked. "Though I could still just set you on fire." She lit a small flame in the palm of her hand for emphasis.

Jasper tsked. "You Wielders, so brash. No refinement or finesse." His lips quirked upwards. He swung the sword around, the tip of it painting figure eights in the air.

Kindra smiled, the fire in her palm turning to a mere thread of flame. She sent it twining up her arm, then around her neck, until finally it settled around her head, a small, fiery crown.

"You know," Jasper said softly, "my ancestors used to do that. A crown of fire, instead of the ones we wear now."

She turned and regarded herself in the giant mirror across the room. Queen Cordilya's cryptic words echoed in her head. *You wore a crown of fire upon your head.* The crown made her gold eyes brighter, casting a warm glow across her skin and hair. She looked...

"So royal," he finished her thought. Then, almost tentatively, he added, "If we ever got the chance to be crowned, it would be an honor to have you by my side as queen."

Kindra held in her flinch. The crown disappeared. "To be a princess is enough," was all she said. Let Jasper figure out what she meant by that.

Judging by the look on his face, he already had: to be a princess was enough of a cage.

"Right," he amended, "of course it is." He offered her a half-hearted smile, and then held out the sword for her. She took it and faced the dummy once more.

"Again," Jasper said, and Kindra struck.

Two hours later, sweat still coating her skin and her muscles aching from hours of training, Kindra slipped out of Jasper's rooms and made her way to the broom closet.

She'd left the prince splayed out on his bed, half-dressed and asleep. Jasper had asked her to stay with him tonight, but she'd refused. Even without her mission, she still was not ready for that. Besides, she desperately needed a late-night bath.

The hallways were dark and deserted; it was past midnight. Besides the patrolling guards, she was the only one in the halls. When she rounded the corner to the stretch where the broom closet was, she was nearly giddy with relief to see that it was entirely empty.

Keeping her footsteps as light as possible, she hurried to the door, and was delighted to see that it wasn't locked, the knob turning easily. With one final look to make sure nobody was around to see her, she opened the door and slipped inside.

The door shut silently behind her. Kindra lit a small flame in her palm to illuminate the dark space. As it was before, the broom closet was empty, save for a few, well, brooms. But they were dusty, cobwebs stretched between them. Nobody had touched them in a long time, further confirming Kindra's belief that this was not really a broom closet.

She faced the stone wall before her. At first glance, it was just that: a wall. She approached it, and ran her other hand over the stones, searching for anything out of the ordinary. A loose one, perhaps. One that, when pushed or pulled, might trigger a door to be revealed.

However, she didn't find any stone even slightly out of place. She gritted her teeth in frustration and spun around to investigate the rest of the tiny closet, running her hands over the other walls. But they, too, held nothing.

Kindra closed her eyes and thought. If not a hidden lever or button, then what? Was it a trapdoor in the floor? But a few minutes of tapping her foot on various stones on the ground showed that was also a dead end.

Finally, after several minutes, it came to her.

Fire.

What else would the Annalindis family use to reveal secret passageways in their castle, especially ones meant to operate as escape routes for themselves?

Tentatively, she took the palm of her already ignited hand and pressed it, still burning, into the center of the stone wall.

The crevices between the stones began to glow as her fire threaded through them, until the shape of a door was illuminated. Kindra grinned and pushed.

The stones gave way, parting and sliding back into the surrounding wall. She marveled at it—some kind of combined feat of a Firefury and an Earthwarden, no doubt. She stepped forward into the archway the stones revealed.

Before her stretched a steep stairwell, descending into darkness.

There were no torches lining the passage's walls. She hovered at the top of the stairs, her fire only providing so much light. From what she could tell, the entire passage was built out of the same old gray stone. It was silent. The smell of stale air wafted out.

Kindra stepped onto the top stair. Her small victory at discovering the door made her confident, perhaps overly so, and she began her descent eagerly, footsteps echoing.

She came to a halt about a dozen steps down, though, when she realized she had no idea how to close the secret door behind her or what she was doing at all.

What if it shut behind her and she couldn't reopen it from the other side? What if somebody—a guard or worse, Tess—came in and found her?

Her common sense prevailed, and she turned back, returning to the broom closet. She faced the open entrance, and, not knowing what else there was to do, she simply touched the stones with her fire again.

That did the trick—the stones once again began to glow and shifted back into their places, hiding the passage once more.

She listened at the door for passing footsteps, only poking her head out when she heard none, and slipped quietly back into the hallway, feeling both victorious and defeated.

Part of her wanted to explore the catacombs, but a larger part of her knew better than to try. She had no guide. And, frankly, she had no reason to. She'd only wanted to prove that there was an entrance there, to confirm her suspicions about Tess. And now she had.

It was more trouble than it was worth, she told herself as she entered her rooms and called for Sala. As the Healer scrubbed the sweat from her skin and soothed her aching muscles, she repeated it again.

There was enough attention on her already. She didn't need people catching her sneaking around the halls at night and finding hidden entrances to the tunnels that would allow her to escape the castle.

And it didn't really impact her, what Tess was doing down there, anyway. Maybe Tess just enjoyed the privacy. Maybe she had a secret lover she met with in the catacombs. Maybe she just used it as a way to slip out of the castle and into town for some late-night fun.

Or maybe she's doing something dangerous, the suspicious voice in her head whispered. *Maybe she's not the person you think she is.*

But how is that my problem? Kindra shot back. *How is any of this my problem?*

"More trouble than it's worth," she murmured to herself that night in bed, willing sleep to come.

Far more trouble than it was worth.

CHAPTER 39

The next day, Cerulle greeted her in the morning with the news that her mother was safely on her way.

"They just passed through Bridgewood. They expect to arrive within the next fortnight."

Her relief was so intense that Kindra's knees almost gave out beneath her. She managed to stay upright but couldn't bring herself to speak. Cerulle smiled in understanding, giving Kindra's arm a squeeze. Kindra could only manage a weak nod in reply.

The second the door shut behind the Windspinner, Kindra sank to the ground, hot tears spilling down her cheeks. Things had become so distressing in Wendrith that she could no longer tell which worry revolved around her mother's safe journey and which belonged to the war, to Tess, to Jasper, to everything. But hearing her mother was safe lessened the weight she'd been carrying by a hundred pounds.

Once she steadied herself, she went to her dressing room and got ready for training. Trepidation coursed through her veins: now that she knew for certain the closet held an entrance to the catacombs, she found the task of acting normal around Tess much harder than it already was. She knew people in the castle would have their secrets and tell their lies, but she never expected Tess, of all people, to be one of them. Or at least, she hadn't expected Tess to be that way with her.

But she reminded herself, what claim did she have on Tess anyway? She'd only known the woman for a couple of months, even though it often felt she'd known her longer. Tess had been here for years, had spent most of her life in this castle under the cruel thumb of Lord Avis. So maybe she had secrets. She'd earned the right to have them.

And Kindra had not yet earned the right to know them.

As confident as possible, she made her way to the training grounds. Along the way, courtiers, guards, and servants alike stopped to acknowledge her. Their respect had grown over the last few weeks. It began when she started sparring, but it fully blossomed after the bombing. Word had spread that she was attending meetings in the War Chamber, and it became obvious she had the king's respect—or simply his interest. Those two things were considered the same by many. The same nobles that had curled their lip at her when she'd first arrived now smiled in earnest whenever she looked their way. That change was unsettling, especially because she knew that many of them still whispered about her behind her back.

Kindra's anxiety mounted with each step she took. How could she even look at Tess, much less talk to her or laugh with her? Mercifully, though, the Firefury was nowhere to be found when she arrived at the grounds. Kindra breathed a sigh of relief and hurried over to Ryle and Terryn.

"Tess gone again today?" Ryle asked, brow furrowed with confusion. Kindra nodded, already starting on her stretches, and hoped she looked unbothered.

"Trouble in paradise?" Terryn quipped, a length of vines sprouting from the pouch of seeds he kept strapped to his side.

"No," Kindra replied—too quickly, and Terryn raised his brows, his classic smirk sketching its way across his face. She leaned forward and touched her toes, using the opportunity to take a calming breath. When she popped back up, she gave him an easy smile and said, "No trouble here. She's just had her shifts changed around."

"So she's on the morning patrol block now?"

Kindra shrugged, calling her fire forward so that it danced along her hands and arms. "I guess. I may have to find a new Firefury to train with— or work out a different time with her." *Say it like it's nothing, say it like it's nothing...*

"Hm," was Terryn's reply, and Kindra gave him a curious look. He raised his hands defensively. "It's just that one of my best friends is on the morning patrol block, and he hasn't said anything about shifts being changed around. And he would've mentioned Tess—she's, um, got a reputation." He winced slightly.

She kept her face as neutral as possible. Ryle, too, watched the exchange with a blank, indifferent expression, though she knew he was taking in everything. It had been one of the first things she'd learned about him when they'd started training together. His keen eyes served him both in and out of the sparring ring, always catching even the most subtle shifts in body language, the most minuscule changes in expression or tone.

"Well," Kindra said as she turned on her heel and strode into the open space of the ring. "It's none of my concern what Tess does." She cocked her head to the side, eyes dancing with a challenge. "Now are we done talking?" Her flames wove through her fingers.

Terryn bought it, jogging over to her. He took up a position across from her, vines twisting their way around him. But she only had to glance at Ryle to know the Windspinner had seen through her easygoing facade, his eyes narrowing slightly as he looked her over. Quickly, she looked away, turning her focus to Terryn. Ryle wouldn't ask her about it, at least. He rarely meddled, but Heinrich did. She wouldn't be surprised if the guardsman peppered her with some questions about it later.

"Until first blood," Ryle directed, and they began.

Their first match was over quickly, Kindra once again victorious. If it bothered Terryn that he never beat her, he didn't show it. In fact, he was always eager to spar with her. She suspected she was the one Firefury he got a chance to train with often: He and Tess were far from friends, and Kindra rarely saw other Firefuries here at this time. He seemed to appreciate the chance to learn from her and improve his skills. Even though she beat him every time and had a habit of knocking that cocky smirk right of his face.

She went two more rounds with him, and though she remained focused enough to win, her mind strayed elsewhere. To Tess, to her mother, to Jasper. To the feeling she had that they were headed straight for some kind of calamity, and Tess was right there at the center of it.

And Kindra was, somehow, standing right there next to her.

She had lunch as she normally did these days, with Jasper. He was ecstatic for her when she told him about her mother, gathering her in his arms and spinning her around. As they waited for their meal to arrive, they sat on the sofa. Her legs folded over his lap, his hands running up and down her thighs, her arms, her waist—that was how they were now. No better than two obsessed teenagers. So far from that first time alone together in the carriage back to Wendrith, when she wouldn't so much as look at him and sat as far from him as possible.

"Oh!" Jasper exclaimed suddenly, as if just remembering something, "I have something for you." He took her hand and led her to the dining table in his room. Atop it sat a bowl, filled with small, round orange fruits.

Kindra reached for one, encircling her hand around it and feeling the pitted, tough rind. "Is this what I think it is?"

"They aren't where orange juice comes from, no," he answered, "though they are related to oranges, and taste almost the same. These are called melengeries."

She pressed her thumb gently against the side of the melengerie; it sank slightly from the pressure. "Here," Jasper said softly, taking it from her and sinking his nail into the peel, pulling it away from the fruit to reveal the plump inside. She watched his fingers work, entranced as he stripped the peel away in one spiraling motion. He gently pried the fruit in half and handed her a small section. "Eat it," he requested, so she did, sitting on the table with him standing between her legs.

It was sweeter than orange juice, she noted as she bit into it, its flavor exploding in her mouth. She made a small noise of contentment, and Jasper held out another piece for her, this time holding it directly up to her mouth. When she took it from him, her lips brushed the tips of his fingers, and his cheeks flushed. Piece by piece, he fed her, until it was gone, and she reached for another.

"For you," she said, but when she went to peel it, she pushed her nail in too far, and the juice dripped down her finger.

Jasper laughed, and placed his hands over hers, guiding her so that she peeled it correctly. She fed him this time, eyes never leaving his, feeling like she was under some kind of spell. When he took the last piece from her, he reached up and wrapped his hand around her arm, holding it in place as he kissed his way down her hand and wrist, his tongue brushing against her skin wherever juice had run. Kindra sucked in a ragged breath.

At another moment, perhaps he would have kissed her hungrily, or she him. Perhaps she would have grabbed him by his collar, his hair, his face, and pulled him onto her. But there was something so tender about this closeness, something so soft, that neither of them made a move to shatter it. Jasper pressed another kiss to her hand and reached out to brush her hair out of her face. He was looking at her in that way of his again: like she was a marvel, something not quite real.

"Thank you," she whispered, unable to speak any louder, "for the fruit."

He smiled, and his eyes didn't lose their awed glimmer. "Of course," he murmured. "Anything for you."

She did kiss him then, gently, and he made a soft noise that almost lit her on fire.

"Kindra," he said against her lips, "I—"

She felt a swell of panic at the thought of what he was going to say. She kissed him again to silence him. It could have been anything; something innocent, harmless, but she had a terrifying premonition that it wasn't going to be harmless at all. She'd seen those words painted across his face just then, before she kissed him; had seen them flit across his expression a few times in recent days.

I love you.

He couldn't say that, not yet. She didn't know what she would do. What could she do, anyway, besides say it back? And to say it back when she wasn't yet sure she felt the same… No, she couldn't do that to him. They'd come so far—for her to lie about such a monumental thing? She just couldn't.

So she kissed him harder, and as the gentleness of the moment shattered, replaced by something hungrier, she hardly gave Jasper room to catch his breath, let alone speak. And he, none the wiser, went along with it eagerly, his hands and mouth wandering over her body.

A knock on the door interrupted them, and they quickly collected themselves as servants entered with the rest of their meal. Or at least they tried to, but she was certain the servants knew exactly what it they'd been up to, judging by their barely suppressed smirks and averted eyes. Jasper winked at her from across the table, and her cheeks once again heated.

Still, though, as the servants left, and they chatted easily as they ate, the words Jasper almost said hovered in Kindra's mind.

It was more than sparing his feelings, that she knew. Because despite the tenderness between them, despite how she did sometimes feel it—that warmth in her chest when she looked at him—she just wasn't ready.

To hear it or to say it back.

There was no need to rush it. They had time.

Not enough, she thought sadly, watching him scribble in his journal as he scoured some book after lunch. She was reading a book of her own—or trying to at least. She was distracted by him. And the realization that she did, in fact, want time.

Far more time than what they were likely to be given.

CHAPTER 40

The news of the attack on Dewport came in the middle of the night a week later, nearly a month after the Harvest Festival attack.

Kindra was awoken by a frantic Jasper, who gave her little more than five minutes to change out of her nightgown before dragging her to the War Chamber. She didn't bother snapping at him for nipping at her heels—terror was written all over his face. Whatever had happened, it was bad.

Much like it had been after the first attack, the War Chamber was in chaos. None of the people present looked entirely presentable; Councilman Avis was still in his nightclothes, his red robe drawn tight around him. Even Leofric himself looked more disheveled than she'd ever seen him, and he was looking more and more unkempt with each passing day. The castle was swelling with rumors of the king's outbursts in meetings; they'd become so frequent now that Kindra had grown to expect them. Luckily, neither she nor Jasper had been on the receiving end. It was considered a miracle if they made it through a meeting without him verbally or physically accosting someone. Though nobody said it, she knew what they were all thinking: *Thank the gods he didn't have a drop of magic.*

But Leofric wasn't wrong to be stressed. They didn't have enough soldiers. Not against what was looking to be three kingdoms, as well as some rogue terrorist group none of them would lay claim to. And not when they were spread out as much as they had to be. Right now, the chance of victory was too small. And Alverin did not take *chances*.

She took up her typical spot along the edge of the room, fidgeting nervously. She reached out for Jasper, gripping his sleeve.

"What happened?" she hissed.

He leaned in close to her, lips brushing her ear as he replied, "Dewport. There was another bombing in Dewport."

Kindra rocked back on her heels, her back hitting the wall behind her. Memories of blood and smoke, broken bodies and burning wood flashed through her mind.

Distantly, she felt a burst of relief that her mother was only a few days away from reaching Wendrith. So close to being back with her and safe. As safe as she could be. "How bad?" she whispered, feeling sick.

Jasper swallowed thickly and snaked an arm around her waist, steadying her. "Bad enough."

She leaned into him, grateful for his support, and braced herself as a guard entered the room, followed closely by Councilman Epira. His brown skin was gaunt, and in his fist he gripped a scroll: the official report from Dewport.

King Leofric held out a hand, and Epira handed him the scroll without comment.

The king read the report silently. Only the tightening of his other hand on the corner of the table betrayed his distress. When he finished, he merely passed it to Antone, who held it out for Sebastian to read alongside him. The brothers swore, low and vicious, as they read.

Kindra wondered if they'd have to wait for the report to silently be passed to them, but then the king spoke.

"There has been a series of explosions in the warehouse district of Dewport. At least three confirmed in three different locations." Kindra swayed slightly, and Jasper's grip on her tightened as the king continued, his voice softer, almost pained, "The current death toll is at least fifty. At least twice that are injured."

Fifty. Kindra would be on the floor if it weren't for Jasper's arm around her.

"The targets of these explosions were strategic. The first was at the shipping harbor, specifically targeting the shipments of steel and iron that just arrived from Ciryn." This was the continent to the south, across the Oslien Sea. They were one of Alverin's biggest trade partners, especially for metals, since Alverin had yet to conquer any of the mountainous regions in Istreria. "The second," the king said, "was the stretch of workhouses where much of our nerushmyr is manufactured. And the third," his jaw twitched, "was the city's grain silos."

The room was silent.

It was strategically brilliant, to bomb supplies that were to be used to forge armor and weapons for Alverin's soldiers.

And it was unbelievably calculated and cruel to attack a city's food stores. Even though Dewport didn't have winters as cold as Wendrith's, they were still done with their harvest season. There would not be more crops for months.

Still, even though it knocked the breath from her and made her stomach turn, Kindra could not find any sense of rage about it. She did not feel a great wrong had been committed—save for the loss of innocent people's lives—or that Alverin was an innocent victim. No, she felt only sad resignation.

Alverin had forged this path itself. Alverin had shaped this future, this war. For centuries, it had planted the seeds that had now grown into *this*. It was something she'd grown up knowing, something that did not change now that she was to marry into the family that was the very cause of this rot.

She wondered just how many others in the room were secretly thinking the same.

The meeting finished nearly three hours later, the large clock in the corner chiming four. Kindra and Jasper were both slumped over in their chairs, adrenaline and shock having long faded, replaced by heavy exhaustion. Even the fear was muted by the desperate need to sleep, though Kindra knew it would return full force after they'd gotten some rest.

The last several hours were a blur. Kindra had hardly said a word the whole time; Jasper spoke only marginally more than her. Nevertheless, she was grateful they'd allowed her to come, and for the few times her opinion had been sought out, though she'd had very little to say in the end. She doubted her true feelings on the matter would be appreciated. To stand in front of King Leofric and say, *Well, this has been a long time coming, don't you think*, would've probably gotten her sent directly to the execution block, cursebreaker or not.

In the end, a statement from Leofric was prepared to be delivered across Alverin the next day. The panic caused by this attack would not be easily calmed. They would send as much as they could spare from their food stores here in Wendrith to Dewport to make up for what was lost. And more adjustments were made to their military strategy: guards increased at all warehouse districts, ships arriving in Wendrith thoroughly searched before allowing anybody to disembark, among other things she'd been too tired to fully comprehend.

But it was not enough. Kindra had been awake enough to gather that. It would involve stretching their army even thinner.

She'd think more of it tomorrow… or, seeing as it was technically the next day, in a few hours after she'd had some sleep. Now, leaning heavily against Jasper as they made it down the hall back to her rooms, she could think of nothing else but the warm bed awaiting her.

They reached her door. Jasper opened it for her, guiding her to the dressing room. He waited patiently outside as she quickly changed back into her nightgown, then took her hand and escorted her back to bed, still unmade from when he'd pulled her from sleep earlier.

Gently, he helped her under the covers, then leaned down and pressed a kiss to her forehead. It was all so tender, it made Kindra's heart twinge fondly. And perhaps it was that, mixed with the madness of the night, that caused her to reach out and grab his hand.

"Stay," she whispered, and his eyes widened with surprise. "Just to sleep," she added.

"It could be scandalous, you know," he whispered back, already taking off his shoes.

"I think there are bigger things to worry about than us spending a night together," she replied, watching as he unbuttoned his shirt and laid it over the back of a chair. Even in the low light of the oil lamp beside her bed, she could see the defined muscles of his torso rippling with every move.

He hesitated briefly before unbuttoning his pants, pushing them down his legs and tossing them aside. He was left in only his undershorts. Something heated stirred deep inside her at the sight.

Mine, she thought rather possessively, as he made his way to the other side of the bed and pulled the covers back, sliding underneath them. She twisted around to face him.

For a moment, they only stared at each other. It could have just been the exhaustion driving her into delirium, but Kindra felt strangely giddy. Something about him being half-naked in her bed made her want to giggle. Then Jasper cut through the silence. "Can I hold you?" His voice was soft, nervous. As if, even now, he was still afraid she'd recoil from him.

"Yes," she breathed, suddenly needing his arms around her more than anything. "Yes."

He reached for her, pulling her close so that her head was resting on his chest. She could hear the soft thrum of his heartbeat beneath her. He was warm and solid. Comfortable. Her eyes fluttered shut. They did not speak of the meeting, of the war. What could they say that hadn't been said already?

"This is nice," he murmured, and Kindra hummed in response.

"Goodnight, Jasper," she managed to say, snuggling closer to him.

"Goodnight, Kindra," he replied, but she hardly heard it, sleep already claiming her and pulling her into sweet nothing.

CHAPTER 41

Two days later, Kindra was sprinting down the castle stairs, her soft cream dress billowing out behind her.

Her mother was here.

For the last several weeks, she had tried to swallow how badly she missed her mother. But she'd never been separated from her before. And though she'd come to appreciate certain freedoms that came with not living together, she was desperate for the familiarity of her mother's touch, her voice, her companionship.

And she couldn't deny that she was excited for her to meet Jasper. Not the facade he'd put on when he'd come to retrieve her—the *real* Jasper. She was excited for her to meet Helena and Emeline, Ryle and Terryn, even Tess, though the Firefury had been making herself scarce recently. They'd hardly trained together in the last few weeks. When they did, it felt stiff and awkward, all work and no play.

But Kindra did not let that reminder dull her enthusiasm as she raced through the halls, her shoes smacking against the marble floors.

She reached the large doors and didn't wait for assistance from the guards to push them open, stepping out into the cold winter air. Snow was falling gently from the sky, coating the trees and ground in a dusting of white; the first of the season.

"Lady Kindra, you may need a cloak—" one of them started, but she was already out of earshot, hurling down the steps and towards the carriage that was coming to a stop. She would have hardly registered the cold anyway, but with the additional adrenaline, she couldn't feel it at all.

The carriage door swung open, and her mother had barely set her feet on the ground before Kindra threw her arms around her, happy tears streaming down her face.

"Mama," she cried, feeling like she was a small child again. Her mother held her just as tightly, and for a moment, the two of them stood there, crying into each other's arms.

"Oh, for gods' sake, let me have a look at you," Sera Bedelyn gasped, pulling away just enough so that she could look her daughter over. Her eyes grew wide as she took her in.

Kindra knew she looked different—vastly so. The past couple months of good eating and training had filled out her slender frame. Sala had smoothed away the under-eye bags that used to be a constant companion, so that even without cosmetics Kindra's skin appeared glowing and flawless. Her curls were no longer a wild, half-tangled mess thanks to the various oils Cerulle put on them each morning. But it wasn't any of those things that caused her mother to suck in a shocked breath.

It was her eyes.

They shone more brilliantly than ever. It had been so subtle and gradual a change she'd hardly noticed until she'd looked in the mirror a few days ago and was suddenly aware of the transformation. The gold in them was now almost startling, it was so bright.

With every day she trained, she grew stronger, and her golden eyes grew bolder. Now, when Sala or Cerulle lined her eyes with kohl, it made her look nearly mythical, which did not help quell the God-blessed cursebreaker whispers that followed her wherever she went—at all.

"Kindra," her mother breathed, awestruck. "You look…"

"It's the eyes, isn't it?" Jasper's voice sounded from behind them. Kindra turned to face him. A red cloak was draped over his shoulders. Snowflakes caught in his hair, his eyelashes, the cold turning his nose and cheeks a soft pink. She couldn't help the smile that spread across her face at the sight. "Makes her look rather awe-inspiring, does it not?" He returned her smile with one of his own.

Sera dipped into a deep bow as Jasper came to stand before her. "Your Highness," she murmured, and Kindra's heart twinged at the fear she saw on her mother's face.

"Please, Lady Bedelyn, none of that. We are to be family soon, after all, are we not?" He paused, and a guilty look crossed his face. "Though, I suppose our last encounter did not paint me in a very good light. For that, I must offer my deepest, sincerest apologies. If your daughter has taught me anything in her time here so far, it is that I need to be more mindful of my words. To have threatened your life—well. I am very ashamed of myself. I only hope I can make it up to you." He looked down at his feet, less a prince and more a guilty child awaiting punishment. Her mother could only gape. She looked at Kindra, searching for an indication that Jasper was sincere. Kindra gave her a small nod.

"Well," Sera said, voice still shaky, "I suppose the first way you can begin making it up to me is by pointing me in the direction of the nearest bath. And perhaps a cup of tea."

Jasper laughed, the sound wrapped in relief. "Of course. We felt much the same when we arrived." He pointed to Heinrich, who hovered only a few feet away. "Heinrich here—you remember him, yes?—will escort you to your rooms. You are just down the hall from Kindra. Figured you'd want to be nearby after the time apart."

"Thank you, Your High—Jasper." The name clearly felt strange in her mother's mouth. Kindra doubted she'd even allowed herself to think of him as anything other than *Prince Jasper*, or *Your Highness*. And why would she, when he'd been such an intimidating presence when she'd met him, coming to take her daughter away and threatening to kill her while he did?

Kindra's smile grew, and she felt a surge of true happiness. Oh, how things had changed. Jasper watched her, clearly happy that she was happy. Before he left them with Heinrich, he leaned down and kissed her cheek. His lips were cold against her skin, and the shock of it caused Kindra to giggle. "I will see you later. Enjoy your time with your mother." Sera watched the whole exchange with raised eyebrows.

"I see you've warmed up to him," she said quietly as Heinrich led them back into the castle.

Kindra blushed. "You'll be happy to know I made him work for it."

Her mother laughed, eyes bright. "I would expect nothing less."

Her mother's reaction to the castle was as awestruck as Kindra's had been, her eyes wide as Kindra led her through the halls. Kindra felt rather proud of herself that she'd come to be so familiar with such a massive place. Heinrich walked beside them, blue eyes alert but mouth mercifully shut. He seemed to have found nothing to nitpick or worry over for the time being. As they walked, Kindra pointed out where various turns and doors led. Sera was especially thrilled about the Great Library, vowing to visit it as soon as she could.

Still, underneath the excitement of their reunion, she could tell her mother was tired. The journey hadn't been easy when Kindra had made it, and it would have only been harder with the colder weather and the hovering threat of war. They'd pushed the pace as well and had arrived almost two full days sooner than originally expected. Though Kindra was glad to have her mother back with her, the accelerated travel speed had no doubt worn her out.

When they reached the rooms her mother would be staying in—indeed, just down the hallway from Kindra—they were greeted by two servants. Kindra didn't know their names but had seen both of them around the castle before. One was a dark-haired Windspinner, who introduced herself as Bella, the other a red-headed Healer named Arbigene. Heinrich bid them a hasty farewell and departed, eager to return to his post guarding Jasper.

Her mother's rooms were a bit warmer than hers, with more red and orange accents among the cream-colored furniture. Still, the layout was much the same. Sera took it all in with that same shocked expression.

When she placed her hand on the soft bed, she said, "I understand how you look so well-rested, now that I know what you're sleeping on."

Kindra smiled. "It certainly does help." She gestured to the door to the bathing room. "Please, Mama. Go take a bath. I'll be here when you're done."

Though rather unwilling to leave her side, Sera went into the bathing room with Arbigene and Bella. A moment later, she heard her mother's amazed cry through the closed door. "Oh! A toilet!"

Kindra chuckled to herself and settled down on the sofa to wait.

Her mother emerged from the bathing room half an hour later, adorned in a soft orange dress. Her hair, thick and dark like Kindra's, had been combed through and pulled back out of her face with small, bejeweled clips. Arbigene and Bella hovered by the door, and Kindra gestured for them to leave with a wave of her hand and a polite smile. When they were gone, she turned to face her mother once more.

She looked incredibly beautiful. Kindra told her so.

"You look beautiful as well, you know," her mother replied, settling down next to her. "I was so stunned by how different you look that I couldn't even speak. And then, of course, to see Pri—er, Jasper, behave so kindly…"

"Do you like it? How I look?" Kindra asked quietly, needing her mother's approval.

Sera's eyes widened, and she nodded enthusiastically. "Yes, Kindra! You not only look healthier and stronger, but you also look… well, dare I say it—you look happy." She frowned. "I don't know if I ever saw you with such light in your eyes in Harthwin."

Kindra looked down at her hands. "It is nicer here than I expected," she admitted, and her mother smirked, the way she always did when she was trying not to say *I told you so.* "And there are definitely many things about it that are better than Harthwin." At the mention of their home village, Kindra looked up at her mother anxiously. "Please tell me, is everyone there okay?"

"When I left, everyone was still alive and well. And as far as I know, Pryllia hasn't made any move to cross the border." Her mother worried her bottom lip. "But people are leaving. At least half a dozen families since you left have packed up and made for the bigger cities. Bridgewood, mainly."

Though it hurt Kindra to hear that her home was shrinking, she knew that seeking refuge in the cities was the smart choice. *Might not do them much good, in the end*, she thought glumly, but didn't speak it aloud. "I'm glad to hear it," she said instead.

"They speak of you differently now that you are gone," her mother told her, voice edged with bitterness. "Now, they are unafraid to say you were the village's guardian. Harthwin's hero, they'd say to me." She rolled her eyes. "Took everything in me not to slap them across the head."

Kindra's jaw tightened. "Well, nobody wants to admit they shunned a princess of the Annalindis family, do they?" she muttered.

Sera shook her head. "Enough of that," she said decisively. "I want to hear about you." She smiled. "You've clearly been training."

Kindra grinned as well, grateful for the subject change. "Nearly every day, Mama. There are huge training grounds here, and I've been sparring with all sorts of Wielders. There are Firefuries here as well—one of them has been training me—Tess." She faltered over the name, but she barreled on. "I've been learning so much, and there are some really great people on the Royal Guard that have been teaching me—plus, Jasper's been showing me how to use a sword." She felt overwhelmed by all she had to tell her mother, so much so that her words seemed to stumble and fall all over each other. But her mother only listened raptly, a smile on her face the whole time. So Kindra continued, "I've become quite close with Jasper's sister, Helena, and her wife Emeline, too. I'm hoping you'll get to meet them soon. And I want you to talk to Jasper more, as well. There's so much—" She paused for a moment, trying to find the right words. "There's so much about him that surprised me. He's not really at all like the nasty prince that came to get me all those weeks ago."

"Perhaps he should have led with his true self," her mother said dryly. "It certainly would've made a better impression."

Kindra nodded. "His family—well, our family now, I guess—is very complicated. Helena and Emeline are great, but..." She trailed off, unsure of how to describe the rest of the Annalindis family. "His older brothers, the king..."

"What's the king like? Have you seen much of him?"

She grimaced. "He's as terrifying as you'd expect. And from the very first day, he's made it very clear he holds me to a different standard. Even during Novon's Trial, he sent a message."

"Novon's Trial?"

So Kindra told her mother about Novon's Trial, and all the sparring she'd been doing, and all the moments in between. She talked of the king's fraying composure, of Antone and Sebastian's snobbery, and even of Queen Cordilya's emptiness.

When she got to the bombing, her words failed her briefly, and Sera went pale. "You were there?" she whispered. "They didn't—we didn't hear much of it in Harthwin, just that it had occurred. But nobody said you were *there*."

Kindra picked at her fingernails, not wanting to meet her mother's eyes. "Yeah, I was there." *I held a child as he died*, she wanted to scream, to sob, but didn't. "It was…" She cleared her throat. "It was bad." She mustered up a weak smile. "But I'm safe, and okay."

Sera glanced away, sweeping her gaze around the grand room. "And I thought you'd be safer here," she murmured, more to herself than to Kindra.

Kindra sighed. "I'm to be an Annalindis, Mother. There's no family on all of Istreria with a bloodier history than them." She reached out and grabbed her mother's hands. "War is coming. In many ways, it's already arrived. And no matter what, above all else, we will get out of it alive," she vowed. "That's all I care about. Nothing—*nothing*—else matters more than that."

Her mother looked into her eyes, and Kindra knew what she saw there: that Kindra would kill, even be killed, to keep her safe, just as she had done for the last ten years.

Sera could say nothing to that, so she simply pulled her daughter close to her chest, and for several minutes, held her as tight as she could.

CHAPTER 42

Over the next few days, Kindra and her mother spent ample time with the Helena and Emeline. The princesses had welcomed Sera warmly, showering her with compliments and regaling her with stories about their lives, and about Kindra and Jasper. Many of those had Kindra scarlet with embarrassment, but her mother loved every second of it. She was happy that Kindra was to marry a decent man. But more than that, she was overjoyed—relieved, even—that Kindra had found real, genuine friendship for the first time in years. Maybe ever.

But even as they spent their time relaxing and socializing, the castle was buzzing with excitement. On the night of the Winter Solstice, there was to be a ball, and no detail or extravagance was spared in regard to preparation. Apparently, the castle was usually the home of long, extravagant celebrations—when Helena had listed off all the different days they typically had one, it seemed as though they were an almost weekly occurrence. But the enemy armies at Alverin's borders, the bombings, and the impending sense of doom had resulted in many of those balls being forgotten. Kindra, having no clue how to dance, had no qualms with that.

But the Winter Solstice Ball was not forgotten. That one, Helena told her, she had personally fought to keep. It was good for morale, she'd claimed. Emeline had joked that she simply wanted to show off her new gown.

In the interest of gowns, the four women had spent an afternoon being fitted for the occasion. Kindra's gown was a true masterpiece: the base layer of the strapless gown was a powder blue silk, covered by a gauzy layer of midnight blue tulle. The bodice was adorned with golden jewels, some even stretching up above the plunging neckline in intricate, arching designs to better cover her exposed chest. The thin flutter sleeves were also bejeweled with tulle streaming from them down to her knees.

It was the most beautiful piece of clothing Kindra had ever worn. Her mother had teared up seeing her in it.

Kindra, too, had gotten emotional seeing Sera in her gown: a beautiful silver piece with dark blue beading. Growing up in Harthwin, there'd been little opportunity to dress up. She'd seen her mother in roughly the same clothing every day for the last twenty-two years; the same few dresses, somehow always worn thin even when she'd managed to get a new one; the same dirty apron and scuffed boots; her hair always pulled haphazardly out of her face. Even when they'd ventured to Mistbarrow for holidays or festivals, she'd only worn a less threadbare version of her usual attire. Most of the money for clothing had gone to Kindra; as a growing child, she'd needed a constant supply.

Most of everything they had had gone to Kindra.

So seeing her mother dressed in such finery was yet another moment she would always be grateful for, no matter the cost.

Two months ago, Kindra would have loathed the idea of spending a day trying on gowns with her friends. Two months ago, she didn't even *have* friends.

So much had changed. And though some of those changes still haunted her dreams at night and made her gut twist with anxiety, she grew fonder of the rest of them with each passing day.

The next two days passed in a blur. Kindra went about her regular daily routine: training in the morning after breakfast, then after her bath, lunch with some combination of Helena, Emeline, Jasper, and her mother, then doing whatever she felt like until dinner and her training session with Jasper.

There were no meetings on either day—at least none she was invited to. Jasper said nothing regarding them either. There'd been no new developments; everything was quiet since the attack in Dewport. It was as if the kingdom—the whole continent—was holding its breath. Something was coming. Though neither of them said anything about it, she knew that Jasper felt the same way. Every time she touched him, she could feel the tension coiled in every muscle. Even when he slept—almost always with her now—it seemed he never completely relaxed.

The only time he seemed to loosen up was during their nightly training sessions. Only then did his dimpled smirks return in full force, only then did she hear him really laugh. He was obviously pleased with her progress. In the month since they began, she'd gone from hardly being able to swing the sword he'd gotten her to being able to wield it with a passable amount of precision. She was still a *long* way from being able to rely on it in a battle if her magic failed her, but she at least could hit a dummy where Jasper instructed her to. Roughly.

The night before the ball, however, Jasper decided they were forgoing the dummy and instead, she was going to spar with him.

"You're joking, right?" Kindra watched him go through a series of stances and strikes within seconds. He made it look as easy as breathing. The sword was an extension of him. A couple weeks ago, he'd invited her to watch him train with other swordsmen on the Royal Guard. Even though they had just been sparring matches, with no real threat involved, he'd been a beast in that ring, his blows faster and stronger than any of his opponents. He'd won every single match.

She'd kissed him breathlessly afterwards. Even the taste of the sweat on his skin had driven her mad.

Now, as he swung his sword in strong, sweeping motions, cutting through imaginary enemies, she felt that passion for him once more.

"I'll go easy on you, of course," he replied, still swinging away. "But you should start getting a feel for what it's like to fight with a real, moving person. Not a dummy."

Kindra groaned, no more than a petulant child. Jasper laughed, halting his exercise and turning to face her. Sweat glistened on his brow, and through his half-unbuttoned shirt, she could see it beading on his chest. She swallowed thickly.

Jasper met her gaze, and the fire that burned inside her had nothing to do with her magic. His smile turned almost feral. "Of course," he murmured, walking over to stand right in front of her, so close that she could feel his breath, "I may just prove to be a distraction."

"Nope," she bit out, "not at all."

"I suppose you now know how I feel, when I watch you train," he said, reaching out with his free hand to tuck a stray curl behind her ear. She quivered at the touch.

"We should get started," she said tightly, before she lost all semblance of control and launched herself at him.

His smirk only deepened, like he knew exactly why she was so eager to begin. Thankfully, he obliged her request, stepping back from her. He gestured at the sword in her hand. "On guard, my darling."

Kindra's toes curled inside her boots. "You're not going to make this easy, are you?" She fell into the defensive position, holding the sword in front of her and widening her stance.

"I have to make this entertaining for me somehow, you know," he replied, mirroring her pose. "It's not like sparring with you is going to prove challenging."

She bared her teeth at him. "Let me light the fucking thing on fire, then." She swung at him, just like he'd had her do to the dummy a thousand times. He blocked it without even breaking their eye contact. The clash of their blades reverberated down her arms, making them shake.

"There's that temper I've come to adore so much," he purred, pulling back and striking at her from the other direction. Kindra scrambled to block it in time, and this time she couldn't hide the tremble in her limbs.

"See? You're already shaking." His eyes danced. He was baiting her. "I'm not even using my full strength."

"Maybe I'm not using my full strength either," she shot back, and he laughed, because they both knew she was. She couldn't fight the smile that blossomed at the sound. She heard it so rarely these days.

"Oh, you're not?" Jasper cocked his head to the side, a predator studying its prey. The move excited Kindra to no end. Seeing him in his element did something to her. "Then, please, unleash yourself upon me. I'm simply begging to experience the full power of Alverin's cursebreaker."

Only he could make her laugh at the title she'd unwillingly had bestowed upon her. It was, after all, a burden they both shared. Not even her mother understood how it felt as well as Jasper did.

At the end of it, it really was them against everything, wasn't it? Just the two of them, living on borrowed time.

She swung her sword at him as hard as she could, pushing that realization—and the feelings it brought—out of her mind. Jasper still blocked it easily, but his arm did falter for a second at the impact. His eyes widened with surprise and delight. Then he parried and returned the blow.

Strike, block, parry, repeat. That was the dance they fell into, moving around and around in a circle. It was ten minutes before her arms were shaking so badly she could hardly swing the sword. Another five and they buckled completely under the weight of Jasper's strike, her sword clattering to the ground.

He smiled approvingly. "You lasted quite a while."

She retorted, unable to help herself, "Fifteen minutes is a long time to you?"

Heat flared in his eyes immediately at the innuendo hidden in her words. He dropped his sword and closed the space between them. She could see every individual drop of sweat on his skin.

"For a beginner like you, it is." He leaned down, his lips almost brushing hers. "I, on the other hand, can last quite a while."

Oh, gods above.

It was moments like these when Kindra all but forgot about the curse, about the risk. Her mind was filled with thoughts of him taking her right then and there—against the wall, on the floor—

"Something on your mind, Kindra?" Jasper whispered, his hand coming up to rest on her hip. Kindra was practically quaking. "You're burning up."

"Um," was all she could manage. Struck utterly stupid. Even her quick tongue had abandoned her.

His hand slid from her hip down to her thigh. Squeezed, ever so slightly.

Kindra snapped.

Their lips met, messy and hungry. With one smooth movement, he lifted her off the ground, her legs wrapping around his hips. She was dimly aware that he was moving, and a moment later her back hit the cool stone wall. Her arms, suddenly no longer in immovable agony, moved of their own accord through his hair, down his neck, clawing at his shirt. He pressed his hips into hers, and she moaned, the sound echoing through the otherwise empty space.

She dragged her lips down the column of his throat, tasting his sweat. Her fingers started making quick work of his shirt. His hands grabbed at her thighs, her ass, and her whole body shuddered each time he ground his hips against her.

"Jasper," she choked out as he sank his teeth into her neck, biting and sucking in a way that would surely leave a mark—but Sala had become very used to smoothing those from Kindra's skin. "I need—"

"What do you need, Princess?" His voice rasped deep in his throat.

"You," she gasped. "I need—we could—right now, please—"

"Kindra," he groaned, and she could feel so clearly, even through their clothing, how badly he wanted her.

"We could lock the doors," she rambled on, barely coherent. "Nobody would be able to catch us—"

Jasper cut her off with a long, hard kiss, open-mouthed and wet and ravenous. Then he pulled away, chest heaving. "Kindra," he repeated, slightly calmer, "if you think the first time I fuck you is going to be in some smelly, damp barracks beneath the castle, you are out of your godsdamn mind."

She could only gape at him, rendered speechless by both his words and the scorching desire in his eyes.

"No," he continued, kissing his way down her jaw and neck, "when we finally reach that point, it will be in the warm, private comfort of my chambers. Or yours. You pick. And then, after that," He pressed his hips against hers again, "I'll fuck you wherever you please."

She swallowed, the thought sending lightning down her spine. *Let's go to your chambers right now*, she almost said, but her common sense—at least some of it—was returning to her.

They couldn't. At least not until the wedding. Not because of some tradition or expectation—she couldn't give a single shit about that, and she knew Jasper didn't either—but because that, the *consummation*, as they said, was when the countdown really started. When she started staring down what would likely be the last few years of her life.

If they weren't on the brink of a war that they very well might lose, perhaps she'd have more hope. But the king was losing his mind. Anybody who failed him these days was at risk. And she was going to fail him in the worst possible way.

A magical child would do little to change the outcome of the war, not unless it carried on for generations. But it wasn't the actual power that Leofric was obsessed with, necessarily.

It was what it symbolized. The message it sent, not just throughout Alverin, but to the whole continent.

To the enemies now gathered at their borders.

And when that failed to materialize...

Jasper's eyes met hers again, and he gave her a grim smile, clearly also remembering the axe over their heads. Gently, he lowered her to the ground, though his hands didn't leave her hips.

"We'll figure out how to get out of this," he whispered, as if he could sense her fear. "We can—I don't know, we could flee, if we have to. We could run away."

The words shot through her. "Jasper, you couldn't," she started, but he shook his head, silencing her.

"I would, for you. For us. We'll get your mother, and we'll go." His voice was quiet, but it nearly shook with intensity. "I don't want to face a life without you. Or a life where you're forever punished for not making some insane man's dream come true."

"You've lived most of your life without me," she said weakly, suddenly overwhelmed by the closeness of him, the earnestness on his face.

"And now that you're here, I won't live another minute of it without you by my side." He raised his hands to cup her face, pressed his forehead against hers. She closed her eyes, partly to relish the touch but also because she was unable to look at him.

"Okay," she breathed, wishing she could find some thread of hope, of safety, in his words. But all it did was fill her with icy cold fear.

Because each day, it became more and more apparent that she would have to flee in order to not be killed, either by the king or the war. And when she did, she knew she'd likely only be taking her mother.

Jasper couldn't leave. It would be hard enough to escape without him— a death wish, probably, but she still had to try, if only for her mother's sake. Even if she was caught, if her mother got away, then whatever fate she met afterwards would be worth it.

And Jasper... Jasper would have to understand, if she couldn't find a way to bring him with her. He'd have to let her go.

She was starting to worry that he wouldn't... and that part of her didn't want him to.

CHAPTER 43

The day of the ball was spent being fussed over with until every bit of her was perfect. The process this time was even more intense and ridiculous than when she was being readied to be presented to the king and queen.

The primping and preparing took hours. Kindra still didn't know the purpose of half the creams and serums they slathered on her skin, her hair, her nail beds. She could admit she saw a difference though—when she gave herself a final once-over in the mirror, she couldn't help but smile. Her skin was glowing, gold dusted onto her cheeks and over her collarbones. Her hair had been swept upwards into an elegant stack of curls and braids, every single strand shiny and soft and positioned just so, held in place by bejeweled pins. Her eyes were lined, her lashes painted, her lips a soft pink. Gold-set diamonds dangled from her ears, around her throat. And for the finishing touch...

The diadem was small, but it might as well have weighed a thousand pounds for how heavy it felt atop her head. It was little more than a gold band, save for the large ruby at the center.

When Sala had first presented it to her, Kindra had said no. She'd argued that she wasn't even a princess yet, but the Healer had shaken her head and told her the request had come directly from the king himself. So that was that.

A knock at the door pulled her away from the mirror, and she made her way out of the dressing room to find Jasper and her mother entering. They both looked stunning; her mother was breathtaking in her silver gown, her hair and cosmetics done similarly to Kindra's, and Jasper...

Clearly, his tailor had worked closely with hers while designing his outfit. The midnight blue of his pants, tucked into shining black boots, and the light blue of his jacket matched the colors of her gown exactly. And the gold detailing on his jacket collar and sleeves swirled and sparkled just as Kindra's bodice did.

He, too, wore a golden crown, but his smile faltered slightly as his eyes fell on the diadem.

"Your father requested I wear it," she explained flatly.

Jasper's mouth opened, then closed. He opted for a curt nod instead. "All right." His voice was strained, but he recovered quickly, his smile broadening again as he looked her up and down. "You look beautiful."

She decided to press him about his strange reaction to the diadem later and came over to press a gentle kiss to his lips. "And you look very handsome," she replied before turning to her mother. "You look like a queen, mama."

Sera shook her head. "I doubt I'll hold a candle to Her Majesty. You, on the other hand..." She blinked rapidly, her smile turning wobbly.

"Mama," Kindra laughed, "you have to stop crying all the time."

"Happy tears, my dear, happy tears," her mother replied as she took a deep breath and calmed herself.

Jasper held out his arms to them. Kindra and Sera, on either side, looped their arms through his, and he laughed. "I can't believe I've got the honor of escorting the two prettiest women in the castle tonight." At their answering blushes, he laughed again. "Well, my ladies, shall we?" Kindra nodded.

With the two people she cared about most, Kindra began the walk down to her very first ball.

The throne room had been transformed.

The usually dark and ominous space was now adorned with banners and flowers, the curtains pulled back on every window so the setting sun could cast its warm pink glow across those in attendance. Long buffet tables marked the edges of the room, piled high with a bounty of food. Kindra spotted one table covered in a dazzling assortment of desserts—no doubt the creations of Emeline's father. Her stomach grumbled at the sight. Throughout the grand room, there were tables bedecked in white cloth and flower arrangements where guests could relax when they grew tired from the revelry.

The center of the room had been cleared for dancing, an octet of musicians positioned off to the side. Already, they were playing, though nobody was dancing yet.

Noone had announced Kindra and her companions when they arrived, thank the gods. Her appearance drew enough attention as it was— particularly the diadem. Luckily, mentioning that the king had requested she wear it shut down any questioning, but she couldn't help but wonder what was so special about it. What about it made people's eyes widen and faces grow pale when they saw it on her head?

She had a feeling she wouldn't like the answer, so she didn't ask.

"What even is half of this?" she whispered in Jasper's ear as they heaped their plates high with food. One of the nobility, an older woman with a harsh, shrewd face, gave her a disapproving look. Kindra met her stare and willed her eyes to burn more than they already did. The woman's face flushed and she turned away, hurrying back to her seat. Kindra smirked, satisfied.

Jasper cleared his throat, and she returned her attention to the food. A good section of her plate was dedicated to the desserts: little finger cakes and truffles, miniature sticky buns and chocolate-covered strawberries. "Are you done striking fear in the hearts of your enemies?" Jasper murmured, amused.

"Depends." Kindra popped a chunk of roasted beef into her mouth, sighing as its flavor burst across her tongue. "Are they done being annoying?"

He chuckled. "Maybe you'll finally be the one who gets them to shut up for good." He took her plate from her hands, nodding to the table across the room where they'd been told to sit. "Let's sit."

Their table was at the front of the room, off to the side of the dais. The two thrones sat empty. King Leofric and Queen Cordilya had yet to arrive. Kindra hoped they wouldn't for quite some time.

Their table mates were going to be tough enough to deal with.

Antone and Celeste were already eating when Kindra and Jasper joined them. Antone gave them both a sharp nod in greeting. Kindra tried not to grimace as she nodded back. "Good evening," Jasper said, setting Kindra's plate down in front of her.

"You didn't have a server handle that for you?" was Antone's reply, eyebrows raised. His own plate was far less loaded than either of theirs—probably the acceptable amount of food.

"We have hands, don't we?" Kindra shot back, struggling to control her temper. She and Antone had come to an understanding in the War Chamber—a sort of begrudging tolerance of one another. Outside of that room there was a completely different story. Kindra still hadn't forgiven him for shutting her out of the meeting the first time, and Antone still hadn't forgiven her for trying to get in.

"I would have assumed my brother would've taught you the proper way of behaving at one of these occasions by now," Antone said. His voice was light and casual, but his eyes betrayed his malice. "I have to say, the whole uneducated-poor-girl-from-the-woods bit has gotten old."

Gods, he was such a fucking asshole.

Kindra was about to open her mouth and snap back when she felt fabric brush against her. A second later, her mother sat down in the empty chair next to her and dipped her head in acknowledgment to Antone and Celeste. "Why, that is such a lovely gown, Your Highness," she purred to Celeste, as motherly and doting as could be. But her eyes were sharp. Missing nothing, and ready to defend her daughter if necessary.

"Thank you, Lady Bedelyn," Celeste replied, who indeed looked beautiful in a white and gold gown. Her use of Sera's new title was surprising, but as Kindra studied the woman, she noted the tightness of her shoulders, and the wariness with which she watched her husband. "You also look lovely tonight. I'm sure this is all very exciting for you."

Trying to keep the peace, she thought.

"It is," Sera replied. "Quite a lot of change, to be sure, but yes, very exciting."

"Where are Sebastian and Myala?" Jasper asked.

"Not coming," Antone replied, not trying to hide his bitterness about it at all. "Myala has been put on bedrest. She's due in less than two months, now. So of course, Sebastian has to stay by her side the whole time."

Celeste's mouth twitched in the slightest of frowns, but she said nothing.

"I hope everything is all right," Kindra said sincerely. She and Sebastian were at least cordial to one another now, and she couldn't help respecting the prince for being so attentive to his wife when she was about to bear his child. It was something that Antone, clearly, had no history of doing. But she'd long since gathered that his marriage to Celeste had little to do with actual love.

"It will be," Antone replied. "This isn't the first time this has happened." Myala was pregnant with their second child. Their eldest, Eva, was a bubbly toddler no older than three.

Celeste and Antone had two children of their own, though they were nowhere to be seen tonight. Kindra had only seen them a handful of times, and only from a distance—the crown prince and princess opted to keep them out of castle affairs.

The moment of temporary peace was shattered as Antone looked over Kindra's shoulder, mouth tightening. "Oh great," he sighed. "More delightful company." He took a long drink of his wine.

Kindra didn't need to turn around to know Helena and Emeline were approaching, but she did anyway, if only to have a break from Antone's face.

The couple looked divine. Emeline was in a striking white gown, breathtaking on her against her brown skin and black hair. A thing of silken beauty, the gown clung to Emeline's every curve, pooling at her feet. Her shoulders and chest were wrapped in silver jewels that trailed down the back of the dress like a sparkling cape. It was a stunning piece and captured the attention of everyone in the room.

Helena was in a mesmerizing ball gown of deep blue. Every inch of the gauzy fabric shimmered under the light. Her hair was gathered atop her head in an extravagant, curling updo, decorated with a sparkling crown. The princess hadn't shown anybody the gown before tonight, wanting it to be a surprise instead.

She looked like a queen.

Kindra smiled at her friends. "I see now why you wanted it to be a surprise," she told Helena.

"Worth the wait, don't you think?" Helena replied with a wink, sitting down beside Sera, Emeline taking the place next to her. Kindra turned back around in time to see Antone roll his eyes. Celeste gave him an exasperated look, as if to say, *You can't be civil for one night?*

"You look beautiful, Hel," Jasper said, pointedly ignoring his older brother, who glowered. Emeline glared daggers at the eldest Annalindis, visibly leashing her temper before turning her attention elsewhere. It seemed they'd all come to an unspoken agreement, even Celeste: Antone was not going to succeed in ruining their evening.

They chatted as they ate, talking over Antone every time he made a snide comment. Celeste, however, was sociable, practically downright friendly. It surprised Kindra, but the others were unfazed, gladly welcoming her into their conversation. Perhaps she'd misjudged the woman. She was, after all, married to a nasty, mean-spirited man. And though Jasper swore none of his family ever behaved violently against their spouses—that even his father, for all his cruelty, would not allow it—she doubted Celeste's marriage was a peaceful partnership. It certainly wasn't an affectionate one.

As Kindra watched the princess laugh with Helena about something, scooting her chair further from her husband and closer to their side of the table, she realized that it was probably a very lonely marriage as well. Maybe Celeste's aloofness regarding Jasper and her before hadn't been out of cruelty but of self-preservation, to keep Antone's malicious attention elsewhere.

Throughout the conversation, Kindra noticed several glances at the diadem she wore. She didn't miss the alarm in their eyes. Even Antone paled slightly as he observed it.

What the fuck had the king had her wear?

Finally, their plates were cleared, and their glasses were filled for the third time. People started trickling into the center of the room. The musicians began to play a lilting waltz, and Kindra watched as couples moved as one, their skirts and coats swirling around them as they danced.

Antone stood, rather abruptly, and held his hand out to his wife. An innocent enough gesture, but there was anger burning in his eyes. "Dance with me," he practically snarled, and everyone at the table went deathly still, their laughter dying instantly.

Celeste rose slowly, no fear on her face as she took her husband's hand. "Of course, dear," she said, her attempt at a sweet smile looking more like a grimace. The pair locked eyes, having some sort of silent argument, judging by the way Antone's eyes flashed and Celeste's jaw clenched. But then Antone relaxed, rolling his shoulders back, an easy-going grin playing on his lips. Celeste, too, donned a cheerful expression. A mask for the people. She looked over her shoulder at the rest of them, dipping her head. "Thank you for the lovely conversation." There was true gratitude there. Yes, the princess was lonely.

"Anytime, Celeste," Helena replied softly, eyes gentle. "You're welcome anytime." Celeste managed to nod in reply before Antone tugged at her hand again and pulled her out onto the dance floor.

They all loosed a breath of relief as the tension dissipated. "Well," her mother murmured, "he is certainly—"

"The worst," Jasper finished for her, taking a long drink of wine. "He is the absolute worst."

"At least Sebastian has been mellowed out by Myala," Emeline mused. "It's made him a bit more tolerable."

"I feel bad for her," Kindra said, watching the crown prince whisk his wife across the dance floor: the picture of an elegant, perfect couple. "She's clearly very lonely."

"She is," Helena agreed. "She's been married to Antone for nearly a decade now. I don't think there's ever been a spark of true feeling between the two of them. Not for lack of trying, at least on her part. She wanted the marriage to be a loving one. During her first few years here, she tried. But Antone is…"

"Not capable of loving anybody," Jasper grumbled.

"I think he loves his children," Helena replied, "as much as he can. They're his blood, after all. But," she sighed, "neither of them have magic. And apparently, their attempt to conceive another is not going well."

In fact, their youngest was nearly four. They were running out of time, if Kindra remembered the marriage contract correctly. They were obligated to have a child at least every four years. "What happens if they can't conceive?" she asked.

"She'll be evaluated by the Head Healer, although I'm sure she's already been to see her, if they've been struggling for this long. In fact, that may be why she's suddenly… reaching out, more. Actually talking to us. She may already know she won't be able to conceive another child. And with the

Head Healer's signed agreement, she's spared any sort of punishment. Her duty is fulfilled."

"She no longer has to share his bed," Emeline said, chuckling. "So she's done putting up with his bullshit."

"Yes, if that is indeed what's happened." Helena stood. "I suppose we'll only know for sure if she tells us, or if little Amie turns four and Celeste doesn't get her head cut off." Blunt, brutal words from the princess.

Her mother blanched. "Would they—would they do that?"

"Oh, yes." She offered a hand to her wife, bringing the Wavebreaker to her feet. "Our great-aunt was executed when she'd failed to fall pregnant after four years. She went to the Head Healer, swearing she was barren after the dangerous delivery of her first-born. But the Healer found she was still fertile. So she was executed." Helena sighed. "Never mind that conceiving can be quite hard, even for the most fertile of couples." The princess plastered a smile on her face. "Enough doom and gloom. This is a ball! Let's dance." And with that, she and Emeline strode out to the dance floor, the people parting to make room for them.

"Do you want to dance?" Jasper asked her.

"Oh, I don't know," Kindra stammered. "I don't really know how, and besides, my mother—"

"Do not use me as an excuse, Kindra," her mother chided. "Go dance."

"I'll show you the steps," Jasper said, grasping her hands. "You just have to follow me."

She had no choice but to allow him to lead her out into the crowd, wrapping an arm around her waist, keeping his other hand clasped in hers. She placed her free hand on his shoulder; she knew that much, at least. "Feel the beat," he murmured in her ear, lips brushing against her skin. Lightning zipped down her spine, but she managed to focus on the music, indeed feeling the beat in her body like a second pulse. Gently, Jasper began to guide her through the steps, and though she stumbled a few times, even stepping on his toes once, she had a handle on it by the end of the piece.

"See?" Jasper smiled at her, and for a moment, it felt like it was just the two of them in that giant room. "Not so hard, is it?"

Kindra opened her mouth to reply, but before she could speak, the doors to the throne room opened, and a hush fell.

"Presenting Their Royal Majesties, King and Queen Annalindis," a voice boomed.

Every person in the room dipped into low bows as Leofric and Cordilya walked into the room. Leofric wore his usual black and gold formal attire, but Cordilya was dressed in a glimmering blue gown, looking so much like her daughter that Kindra had to fight the urge to twist her head and find Helena to see her reaction.

Slowly, they processed towards the dais. Nobody dared rise before the king gave permission. So Kindra remained bowing, her eyes fixed on the floor.

Until a pair of shoes, polished black, came into view.

"Rise, cursebreaker," King Leofric ordered.

She fought the wave of nausea as she did so, not daring to look him in the eye. His gaze fell on the diadem, sparking with approval.

His next words shocked her.

"A dance, Lady Kindra," the king requested, holding out his hand to her. "If you please."

CHAPTER 44

Kindra stared at King Leofric's outstretched hand, head spinning from his invitation.

The weight of dozens of stares rested on her shoulders, heavy and expectant. Jasper stepped back from her side, leaving her alone.

A dance with the king.

Though she wanted to say no, she didn't have any other option, did she? So she smiled as brightly as she could despite the knots twisting in her stomach and placed her hand in his.

He smiled approvingly, a terrifying thing, and swiftly pulled her into position. A second later, the musicians resumed their playing, and the music quickly swelled into a lush waltz. Leofric began to lead, and she could do nothing but try her best to keep up as he spun them across the dance floor.

The first minute of the dance was nearly unbearable, as neither of them spoke. Kindra did her best to not look terrified under his gaze. He regarded her with his usual sharp intensity, as if even this dance was some sort of test.

Then he began to talk, and that was far worse than the silence.

"If I may, Lady Kindra," he began, "I must say that you have become quite a beacon of hope for Alverin during this time."

"Oh," she breathed, trying to focus on dancing and speaking at the same time, which was not quite as easy as it was with Jasper. "Thank you, Your Majesty."

"I'm greatly anticipating all of the ways you will continue to instill that strength in our kingdom," he continued, his smile lupine.

"Yes," she managed, nearly missing a step and crushing his toes. "I am as well."

His eyes drifted to the crown she wore. "I'm very pleased to see you heeded my request."

She dipped her head in a small nod. "I was happy to do so," she replied, choosing her words carefully. "Though, I am curious about its origins. I've gotten no shortage of strange looks tonight for wearing it." She gave him what she hoped was an innocent smile.

King Leofric's mouth twisted in what she assumed was a smirk. "Yes, I imagine you would have. I'm surprised you do not know it—do you not recall?"

Baffled, Kindra shook her head. "No, Your Majesty, I don't."

"I suppose you wouldn't know to look for it unless you were told," he admitted. "The diadem you wear is ancient—one of Alverin's most prized artifacts. It belonged to Queen Scalya Annalindis. The first Queen of Alverin."

Kindra couldn't hide her stumble then, though the king recovered them both smoothly. Vaguely, she remembered seeing the diadem before: the painting of the queen, in the king's chambers. She'd been wearing it. "Your Majesty—" she stammered. "Your Majesty, surely I am not worthy of such an honor."

"It was Queen Scalya who carried the greatest portion of our power, actually," Leofric told her, ignoring her protests. "King Novon was powerful, yes, an extraordinary Wielder, but Queen Scalya was... well, it's in her name, is it not? Scalya."

"Scaldor," Kindra murmured. "She was the one who was God-blessed?"

"Yes," the king replied. "He came to her frequently. Over time, that detail was forgotten. It did not matter so much, after all. She was as equal a founder of our kingdom as King Novon—if not more so. King Novon established our place on this continent, but our history of expansion did not really begin until she joined him on the throne. It was her vision that pushed Alverin to greatness."

"To never-ending war?" she said, unable to stop herself. A foolish retort, and she braced herself for his rebuke. But Leofric only tilted his head thoughtfully, his grip on her tightening slightly.

"It was not supposed to be this way, Lady Kindra." His voice was so soft, she had to lean closer just to hear him over the music. "Novon and Scalya dreamed of a unified continent. That was what Alverin aimed for—has always aimed for, even though the rest of this land reviles us for it."

She remained silent, biting her tongue. He spun her out in a circle, her dress billowing around her. When he pulled her back to him, he said, "You may voice your thoughts. I will not cart you to the dungeons." He chuckled, as if that wasn't a very real outcome he often threatened and saw through.

But Kindra took advantage of the opportunity, though each word felt like another shovel of dirt dug for her grave. "With all due respect, Your Majesty, I think the concept of a unified continent, ruled by one family, when multiple kingdoms already existed there... there was no way it wouldn't have gone badly. We have taken miles upon miles of land, and millions of people from all kingdoms have died because of the wars we have fought in our efforts to expand. It doesn't matter that Alverin is a great kingdom; it doesn't matter what dreams we might have for Istreria. To them, we are nothing more than brutal conquerors." She cleared her throat, looking down. "Your Majesty."

King Leofric didn't speak for a few moments, and they danced in silence. As they spun, she saw Jasper dancing with her mother, the two of them each keeping one eye on her the whole time.

Kindra dared to look at the king. He did not appear angry—no murderous intent glowed in his eyes, no grimace or snarl on his features. Still, she felt her knees shake slightly.

"It has been a long time since somebody dared be so honest with me about their thoughts on our kingdom's history," he finally said.

"I apologize, Your Maje—" she began quickly, but he cut her off.

"Your eyes—they are so brilliantly gold." He blinked, and awe briefly crossed his face, as if he was just now really seeing her, for the first time. But as quickly as it had appeared, the expression vanished, replaced by one far more thoughtful. Calculating.

"It's my training," she replied, unsure of what, exactly, to say.

"They say Queen Scalya's eyes burned like molten gold, that they glowed and swirled when she wielded her fire. Even the greatest of painters could not capture it." He spoke more to himself than her, but the words rocked through her regardless. The musicians were still playing, their feet still moving across the dance floor, but she hardly registered any of it.

"I'm just a girl from Harthwin, Your Majesty," she murmured, hating his expression: one of awe and hope and greed—and just a kernel of fear. Of wariness.

It was that tiny kernel that scared her the most. Helena had warned her of it months ago, after she bested Ryle in front of him and the Council. Jasper had, too, the night before she was introduced to his parents. *My family isn't exactly rational when faced with something they don't know how to control,* he'd said. And when did she become that? When did she change from a marvel to a threat? Was she already too close to the line? Had she already, unknowingly, crossed it?

"Don't play those bashful games with me. We both know you are far more than that, Lady Kindra." There was a coldness in his voice now that had alarm bells ringing in Kindra's head. Yes, she was indeed dangerous close to crossing that line.

The waltz, mercifully, came to an end. How long had that dance lasted? It felt as though she'd been trapped with the king for hours. Leofric stepped back from her, dropping his hands. He bowed his head to her, and she dipped into a low curtsy. "Thank you for the dance, Your Majesty," she said.

King Leofric hummed, deep in his throat. "And thank you." His eyes glanced past her shoulder, where she knew Jasper hovered. "You may return to my son. Enjoy the rest of your evening." With that, he made his way to the dais, where Queen Cordilya already sat. He took his place upon his gilded throne, and laid a hand on his wife's arm, stroking her bare skin softly.

Jasper was at her side immediately. "What did he say to you? You look sick."

Kindra shook her head. "Later. I'll tell you later." She turned to him, and offered what she hoped was a passable smile. "Dance with me?"

Gently, he gathered her into his arms as the music began again, a fast-paced tune that had Kindra nervous. "Try and keep up," her betrothed said with a grin, and then they were flying across the dance floor.

And though she danced and drank and laughed the rest of the evening, she felt the king's gaze searing into her more than once. His dance with her had been a test of some kind, she knew that much.

But she had no idea if it was a test she'd passed or failed.

CHAPTER 45

"What did he say to you?" Jasper demanded as soon as Cerulle shut the door behind her, leaving the two of them alone for the night. The Windspinner had made quick work unlacing Kindra out of her gown, placing Scalya's diadem in a velvet-lined box and taking it with her when she left. Now, her hair down and her face washed of all cosmetics, Kindra sat on her bed and recounted her dance with the king.

Jasper paced in front of her while she talked. When she finished, he came to sit next to her. He ran his hands through his hair.

"I didn't want to tell you. About the diadem," he said finally. "I just— I knew it would freak you out—"

Kindra bristled. "I could have handled it," she retorted.

"You were white as a ghost after you finished dancing with him," Jasper shot back, though not unkindly. "And you were already nervous about the ball. I didn't want to make it worse—"

"You don't get to make those decisions for me," she snapped. It wasn't quite anger she felt. It was more alarm than anything that he now knew her well enough to pick up on her tells. She hadn't told him she'd been nervous for the ball, but she had been, and he'd known, and he been considerate of it when deciding what to tell her.

It was moments like these where she felt her walls fighting to go back up, when she couldn't hide from the fact that they were more than two people who simply were attracted to one another. It had been more than that, so much more, for a long time. She knew that was why she resorted to bristling and snapping in that moment, and she hated herself for it.

"If you had asked about the diadem, I would have told you," he said firmly, capturing her glare with his own and holding it. "But you didn't ask, so I decided to not say anything until you did. If you did at all."

Kindra glowered for a moment longer, then sighed. "Okay," she relented, and Jasper visibly relaxed. Then she asked, "Could you really tell I was nervous?"

He laughed quietly, wrapping his arm around her and pulling her closer to him. They leaned back against the pillows. "You always feel hotter when you're nervous," he told her. "Or angry or scared. It's like your magic is coiling right under your skin, ready to spring out and protect you. The last couple days, when I'd touch you... you were burning up. Like a fever." He smiled down at her. "Plus, you're so much quicker to snap at me when you've got something worrying you."

She sighed again. "I suppose I'll always be burning up now," she mused grimly. She looked up at him. "He's afraid of me, Jasper. Just a little bit, but..." She trailed off.

"He thinks you're God-blessed," Jasper said bluntly, and Kindra shuddered. But it was the truth, though the king himself might never say it. What he'd said tonight, about her eyes... Whether he'd intended to reveal what he believed or not, she wasn't sure, but he'd revealed it all the same.

"I'm not God-blessed. Scaldor has never appeared before me. Cyrie hasn't either."

"You know," Jasper mused, "We have some of Scalya's journals. You could read them. They're in the restricted section behind lock and key, but you'd be able to get access. Especially now that you've been seen wearing her crown. They would likely hold her first-hand accounts of her experiences with Scaldor."

She mulled it over. "Do I even want to know?" she murmured, thinking aloud.

He gave her a knowing look. "Of course you do."

Kindra rolled her eyes. "You pick up on too much." But he was right— she was curious.

"I just pay attention, that's all." His voice had gone soft. "I enjoy watching you. Learning you."

"Learning me?" She scoffed, face heating. She didn't dare look up at him. She knew he'd have that look on his face—the one he got these days when she could tell he was fighting to hold back those three little words.

"Yes, learning you. Is that not what love is?" His breath hitched.

She stiffened, just a bit. "I suppose," she replied, trying and failing to make her voice light.

Danger! The voice in her head screamed. *Danger, danger, danger!*

But why? Why did she still freeze whenever he brought it up—the love between them? Why did she prickle and snap when he showed how well he knew her, how much attention he paid her every move? She was no fool; she knew what this was, what this had been for a while now.

It should be easy to hear it from this man, to say it back to him. He was to be her husband. He had proven, again and again, how he cared for her. He listened to her—he had *learned* her, yes, to put it in his own words. And yet—

"Kindra," Jasper breathed.

"Don't," she gasped. "Don't say it." Shame, cold and heavy, quaked through her.

He pulled away from her, and she dared a glance up at his face. Hurt was written plainly across it.

"Why not?" It was more a demand for honesty than a question.

"Because," she said, looking anywhere else but him, "I just—I can't say it back."

"I don't care if you can't say it back yet, Kindra," Jasper said roughly. He turned her face towards his, holding her chin firmly so she couldn't turn away. "Don't say it if you don't want to. We don't have to—we don't have to be on the same timeline." He huffed a soft laugh. "Gods know we rarely ever have been." He grew serious again. "I don't mind. If you don't—love me."

He did mind. Kindra forced herself to meet his gaze. "It's not that I don't—" She choked on the words and took a steadying breath. "It's hard to accept. That I…" She trailed off again.

"Because you had been determined to hate me forever and you're having a hard time accepting that you don't?"

She nodded, relieved to the point of tears that he'd said it for her. "Yes," she breathed, "and I hate it. Not that—not that it's changed. But that I'm struggling. It's hurting you."

He leaned down and pressed a kiss, feather soft, to her mouth. "It does not hurt me, Kindra," he whispered against her lips. "It's enough to know that your heart has changed and that you are trying." He kissed her again, harder this time. "It's enough," he repeated. Another kiss, his hands pulling her flush against him. "It's enough."

The tension fled her body, and she went pliant in his arms, snaking her hands into his hair. He kissed her long and slow, his tongue brushing against hers, stoking the fire that had begun to burn within her.

His hands drifted to her thighs, bare thanks to the short nightgown she was wearing. She whimpered into his mouth; his grip tightened as he raised himself over her to slide between her legs, one hand moving to the pillow to prop himself up.

They'd done this dozens of times before; they'd played this game, come close to the edge. Just the other night, he'd pressed her into the mattress just like this, grinding against her until they were both writhing and panting. It had been a feat of god-like strength from both of them to resist the temptation.

This felt different, though. Some final wall between them had crumbled—a wall Kindra hadn't even known existed until she'd heard him say that it was enough.

She was doing enough.

As if sensing she needed to hear it again, Jasper breathed, "It's enough, Kindra." His hand began snaking its way up her thigh, underneath the fabric of her nightgown. His fingers danced across the soft skin of her stomach, the underside of her breasts.

"Take it off," she demanded, and he froze.

This was the threshold they'd never crossed, because they both knew if they did, there'd be no stopping what would happen next.

"I'm sure," she said before he could ask. When he still hesitated, she placed her own hands on the hem of her gown and began pulling it off. Tossing it to the side, she didn't allow her nerves to slow her as she tugged off her underwear, too. A second later, she was completely naked beneath him.

He simply stared at her, jaw slightly slack, his gray eyes wild. "Kindra," he choked out, her name a plea, an oath, on his lips.

"Do you want to join me, or do you want to sit and stare?" She put a bit of playful snap in her voice, though the words shook slightly.

Jasper snapped out of his stupor then, and he was upon her, mouth and hands everywhere, touching all the places they'd yet to explore. Kindra clawed at his clothing, practically ripping his shirt from his body before tearing at the buttons of his pants.

Finally, they were both entirely bare. Kindra swept her gaze across his body. She'd seen him shirtless countless times, but what his *pants* had been hiding from her... She eyed him hungrily. He was doing the same to her, his stare halting first on her breasts and then on the apex of her thighs. His breath hitched, uneven and rough.

"Are you sure?" he asked. "I just... I need to hear it again."

"Yes," she replied simply. "Are you?"

He nodded rapidly. "Yes. Gods, yes."

"Then have your way with me, Your Highness," she purred, and her head fell back against the pillows as he slid a hand between her legs and finally touched her.

He moaned at the hot slickness of her, his fingers sliding into her slowly, gently. She squirmed underneath him, bucking her hips into his hand. He grinned, pure carnal delight lighting his features, his thumb brushing against *that* spot—

Kindra's back arched off the mattress, pleasure shooting up her spine, down her legs as he stroked her. More, she needed more, she needed *him*—

The warmth of his hand vanished, and she bared her teeth, only to have her frustration vanish when she felt the hard press of him against her.

"Please, Jasper," she gasped, nails already digging into his back, his shoulders. She was practically shaking with want. "Please."

Jasper swallowed her pleas with a wet, hungry kiss as he slid into her, moving so carefully she could feel him trembling with restraint. But she was grateful for his care. It had been years since she'd last done this. She whimpered softly as she adjusted to the size of him.

"Kindra," he panted. "Holy fucking gods."

"Move," she begged. She rolled her hips into his for emphasis.

He did not need any further instruction, pulling out and thrusting back into her with one tantalizingly slow movement. With each thrust, he picked up speed, the stretch of him so perfect that Kindra was rendered almost speechless, her nails ripping up and down his back as she nearly sobbed with ecstasy.

Why had they waited to do this? Stupid, utterly stupid.

Not stupid, a voice reminded her. *You were waiting for a reason.*

Right. Because a pregnancy—

"You can't," she started, managing to find the words, and Jasper nodded, already ahead of her.

"I know." His voice was low, ragged. "I won't."

He reached a hand between them and stroked her while he moved, the sensation so overwhelming that Kindra had to sink her teeth into his shoulder to avoid screaming. He moaned in her ear, and she knew he was close, too.

Her release barreled through her, and she thrashed against him, crying out his name. A moment later, he slid out of her, catching himself in his hand as he shook with the intensity of his pleasure.

For a few heartbeats, there was only the silence of their heavy, gasping breaths. Then Jasper looked up at her, his eyes glassy. "Wow," was all he could manage.

Kindra could only nod her agreement, still recovering. He leaned down and pressed a kiss to the hollow of her throat, and she was vaguely aware of him getting off the bed and vanishing into the bathing room. She heard the sound of running water a moment later.

When he reemerged, she was a bit more collected, and she gave him a soft, sated smile as he prowled towards her. Noting the hungry glint in his eyes, she tensed, desire already pooling within her again.

"You didn't think I wasn't going to taste you, did you?" He growled, spreading her thighs and lowering himself down between them. He ran his tongue up her center and they both moaned. "I've been dreaming about *this* for months."

Kindra let every other worry, every other concern, fade to the background as he pressed his mouth against her. And as they lost themselves in each other again and again that night, she didn't spare a single thought for anything else.

CHAPTER 46

She was loathed to leave her bed the next morning.

Partly because she was exhausted, having spent much of the night tangled up with Jasper instead of sleeping, but also because she didn't want to come back to reality.

It was so easy to forget about the pressure, the expectations, when they were busy doing such *delicious* things to each other.

But they couldn't lock themselves in her room all day, though Jasper had suggested it after they awoke, his hands and mouth roaming over her body. They had duties to attend to—Jasper had a day full of meetings with his father and the Council, and Kindra had her morning training, followed by a much more daunting task:

Getting her hands on Queen Scalya's journals.

So she'd reluctantly batted him away, rolling out of his grasp and sauntering into the bathing room.

"You have one minute to make yourself presentable before I call for Sala and Cerulle to bring breakfast," she'd threatened. When she'd reemerged, dressed in her nerushmyr for training, Jasper was mercifully clothed, already seated at the dining table.

His eyes devoured her as she approached. "Have I ever told you just how delectable you look when you're dressed like that?"

She rolled her eyes, but heat coursed through her at the words. "You're going to be insufferable now, aren't you?"

Jasper grinned. "If by insufferable you mean showering you with twice as many compliments as usual, then of course."

Kindra sat down next to him and couldn't fight the blush that bloomed on her cheeks. "Well, that's fine, I suppose."

"Glad to hear it." He reached over and took her hand in his, then pressed a kiss to the back of it. Then her palm. Then her wrist.

She yanked her hand away. "Do *not* start," she hissed, but she was smiling.

"Whatever could you mean?" He stared at her with wide, innocent eyes, the corners of his mouth twitching in a barely suppressed smirk.

There was a knock at the door, and Sala and Cerulle entered, carrying breakfast. Kindra's stomach rumbled. The night's activities had left her famished. Jasper seemed to feel the same, eyeing the food hungrily.

They ate in silence, too focused on their food to speak. Kindra was grateful for it—without the distraction of Jasper's flirtations, she could actually think about her day.

"So, you plan to go to the library today?" Jasper broke the silence.

She nodded. "Yes, this afternoon. Are you sure they'll let me access the records?"

He hesitated, which wasn't reassuring. "Honestly, I'm not sure. I've never been permitted access, at least, and I don't know if my siblings have, either. But I also don't think any of them have ever asked—I'm the history buff, after all. But surely, considering your status you should be able to convince them." He shrugged. "Don't be afraid to throw your weight around a little bit, Kindra."

She grimaced. "I don't like that idea very much."

He stared at her, suddenly very serious. "My father has read those accounts backwards and forwards, I can tell you that much. If he believes you are God-blessed, then I guarantee he's read something that supports that theory. You need to know what that is. If only so you can know for sure that you're not what he thinks you are." He paused. "Or, so you can find out that you actually—"

"I'm not," she bit out, but she didn't feel entirely certain of that claim. Something about it all nagged at her.

Jasper studied her, then shrugged again. "It would still be worthwhile."

"I know," she agreed quietly, and they returned to their food.

When Jasper left to prepare for his meetings, he gave her a long, searing kiss that contained a hundred promises for later.

But even that was not enough to quiet the worries that now swirled inside her head.

Surprisingly, Tess showed herself at training that day, and the women sparred for the first time in weeks. Though their conversation was still lukewarm at best, at least the other Firefury wasn't icing Kindra out anymore. Whatever Tess's motives were for spending time with her again, Kindra was glad to have Tess back with her in the ring. She'd missed the woman's blunt criticism and helpful suggestions about her wielding.

"You danced with the king at the Solstice Ball," Tess remarked as they took a water break.

Kindra nodded. "He's quite the dancer."

Tess hummed. "Any interesting conversation?" Her tone was suspiciously light.

But Kindra decided some honesty would be good for them. So she replied, "Oh, yes. The man thinks I'm God-blessed."

Tess blinked, clearly surprised that she was telling her. Kindra continued, shaking her head, "It's crazy, isn't it? I mean, Scaldor's never appeared to me once."

"I don't think it's that crazy," Tess admitted softly, watching her carefully. "Your eyes—"

"I know, I know," she sighed. "But just because my eyes are more gold these days doesn't mean I'm God-blessed. It just means I've gotten stronger. I mean, your eyes are quite brilliant, too." It was true. Tess's orange eyes were striking.

Tess shook her head. "Nobody's power grows the way yours has in such a short time, Kindra."

"I'm not God-blessed," she snapped, exasperated.

"Would it be such a bad thing if you were?" Tess argued. "Think of what you could do with that kind of power." Her eyes took on a fanatical gleam. "You could *transform* this kingdom—"

"I do not want to do *anything* like that," Kindra hissed. "I already have the unwanted attention of the king on me. I do not need the attention of a god as well."

A taut silence stretched between them. "Then I hope the king is wrong," Tess finally said. She cleared her throat awkwardly. "Look, I'm sorry I've been distant these last few weeks. There've been some things going on that I... well, regardless, I'm glad to spend some time with you. You can tell me anything, you know that, right?"

Kindra regarded her carefully. "You can tell me anything too, Tess." A plea.

Tess smiled, though it was rather sad. "I know," she replied, but it didn't sound like she meant it.

CHAPTER 47

Trepidation pooled in Kindra's veins when she walked into the library a couple of hours later. Though the sweat from the morning's training session had been thoroughly scrubbed away, her skin still felt sticky and itchy, like it had been pulled taut over her bones. Her nerves were trying to get the better of her.

She did her best to swallow them down as she approached the large desk at the front of the restricted section. One of the many librarians, a silver-haired older woman, looked up from her reading at her approach and dipped her head in acknowledgement. Kindra fixed a pleasant smile on her face.

"Hello, Lady Kindra," she said, voice withered and soft.

Kindra scrambled to recall her name. "Good afternoon, Iris," she replied, and prayed she had gotten it right. She'd been trying to learn the names of as many castle staff as possible, but there were hundreds of them. She'd hardly made a dent, and already their names were mixing up in her head.

But the librarian smiled, pleased, and Kindra bit back her sigh of relief. "What can I do for you?"

Now came the hard part.

She held her head high and hoped her nervousness wasn't obvious as she said, "I need to access some documents from the restricted section." Iris nodded. Good. At least she could enter the restricted section at all. That made what came next marginally easier.

She leaned forward, indicating a need for secrecy. Iris leaned in, too, watery blue eyes alight with curiosity. "The journals of Queen Scalya. I need to read them."

To her credit, the librarian covered her shock quickly. "Oh, Lady Kindra, those are... those are quite restricted. I'm not sure if you're permitted."

Don't be afraid to throw your weight around, Jasper had said. Kindra didn't quite feel ready to start doing that yet.

But she could throw around the king's.

"Ah," she said, making a good show of looking disappointed. Then, "That's understandable. It's just—well, the king honored me with Queen Scalya's diadem at the Solstice Ball, and when we were dancing, he mentioned her journals and said I might find them of interest." A lie, but she was banking on Iris being too afraid of defying the king to say anything to him about it. She shrugged. "Does he need to come give permission himself for me to see them? I could ask, though he's so busy these days—"

"No need, my Lady," Iris interrupted, terrified by the suggestion. "If he said you should read them, then read them you shall."

"Oh, thank you so much," Kindra gushed, reaching over and squeezing one of her wrinkled hands. Iris beamed.

"Come with me." She walked out from behind the desk and began to lead Kindra down one of the aisles. Upon reaching a locked iron door, Iris took a key from the pocket of her robes. She unlocked the door and it swung open to reveal a whole other library.

Kindra gaped as she walked in. It was far smaller than the Great Library—only one story, and considerably less cozy with its lack of windows and sofas. Rather, every wall was lined with shelves laden with books and scrolls, save for one tiny hearth in the corner of the room. There were a few desks placed throughout the center of the room, adorned with oil lamps and ink pots and quills.

"The king and the Council are typically the only ones who use this room," Iris told her. "Sometimes the crown prince. We keep the most valuable and secret documents here." She strode over to a shelf and pulled off several books. No, not books, Kindra realized as she took a closer look—journals.

Iris set them on a table, gesturing for Kindra to come sit. "Here you are," the librarian said. "I hope you find what you're looking for. The door will lock behind you when you leave—so if you need to come back, don't hesitate to find me."

And then she was gone, leaving Kindra with a stack of almost a dozen journals and no clue where to start.

Unfortunately, it seemed that Queen Scalya did not just document her encounters with Scaldor; she was the type who had wanted to document *everything*.

The first journal was dated prior to her marriage to Novon by several years. If the records of her birthdate were accurate, the future queen was fifteen at the time of the first entry.

Though Kindra had at first been tempted to skim through the pages, searching for words like *Scaldor* and *gods*, the young girl's entries were not only interesting, but entertaining.

Scalya, like her, had grown up poor, in a small village. Her upbringing had been nothing but war and other hardships as the fight to establish the various kingdoms of the continent was underway. Alverin's history had been bloody from the start; it took years to unify the various lords and their small lands under one banner, and that was not achieved without violence. And then, of course, came the wars with the other budding kingdoms as they each tried to conquer the best lands for themselves. It had been a decades-long struggle that had begun long before Scalya had been born.

But still, Scalya had maintained a rather raunchy sense of humor, often interjecting it into otherwise dark entries. Kindra actually found herself chuckling as she read certain passages.

Her magic had come to her when she was only six, which was extremely young. Though there were indicators of magic that appeared from birth— eye color being the primary one—the actual power to wield usually did not manifest until one was well into childhood, typically between ages nine and twelve. Kindra's had appeared just a few months shy of her ninth birthday. It didn't really mean anything about how powerful one would be, though people liked to pretend it did. There were plenty of great Wielders whose magic didn't show up until they were eleven or twelve; some had been even older than that. And there were plenty of early bloomers who turned out to be entirely mediocre.

But to be only six years old… Kindra had never heard of that happening. At first she thought maybe it used to be more common, but based on Scalya's writings, it was just as rare then as it would be now.

Scalya wrote of her training, of discovering new ways to manipulate her fire. The similarities to Kindra's own development both warmed her heart and chilled her to the bone. She hated the way she felt a kind of kinship to the long-dead queen; hated anything that might connect the two of them. But she couldn't look away, devouring every word.

Two hours later, she wasn't done with even the first journal. As intriguing as Scalya's entries were, Kindra's patience was beginning to wear thin. Scalya was sixteen now—there'd been an ample entry about the celebration her family had thrown her. But at least she wasn't making an entry every day; there were jumps in the dates spanning anywhere from a few days to a few weeks.

Kindra had just finished reading through an entry detailing some drama with a boy in Scalya's village. She huffed a laugh, wondering how the boy had felt when he later learned he'd fumbled the God-blessed Queen of Alverin. *If he survived long enough to see it,* she thought grimly.

She turned the page and sat up straight as she noted the date at the top. Nearly six weeks later—longer than any other jump between entries.

Scalya's handwriting was different. It was still obviously hers, but it was more slanted. Frantic.

Kindra's insides twisted as she read the passage:

I feel as though I am going insane, Scalya wrote. *I thought it impossible. To be visited by a god. I did not believe they ever deigned to grace anyone with their presence. But there I was, in that clearing those weeks ago, surrounded by my enemies, and I felt him.*

"No," Kindra breathed.

Nobody will listen to me when I tell them how it happened, how I alone took on two dozen soldiers and left them in ashes. They have always thought me powerful; they believe that is all it was. But this was different. This was not my fire in my veins—not mine alone, at least. It was joined by another's. When I needed it most, when I called for aid that would save me, my family, he answered.

I have no other explanation for it. The flames that came out of me acted of their own accord. They spread further and quicker than I have ever been able to control. They burned so hot they were blue at points. When have I ever done that? Never, not once. I did not feel as though I was in my own body; I felt cast out, used, watching it all happen but not having any ability to stop it.

A memory pushed at the corner of Kindra's mind. Her breathing quickened; she tried desperately to block it out.

When it was over, and he mercifully left me, I was strangely empty. My magic had not been worn down, though my veins, my very bones, felt stretched and battered, as if they'd been overexerted. A conduit for his power, that's what I had become.

But nobody here believes me. I am a hero. I saved my home. When I came to them screaming, they did not understand that my horror was not from the carnage I had enacted but from the possession I had just experienced. The gods do not come to us in that way, the priests and priestesses told me gently. Your power is great, and that is all that Scaldor has given you. That is his blessing.

But I know what—who—it was that came to me that day. He did not speak— though I fear if he comes to me again, he will. But the force that brushed against me, as though he were touching the very kernel of my soul, that was no adrenaline rush. That was a god. Scaldor. For whatever reason, he chose to answer my call.

I am grateful. I am terrified. And nobody will believe me, so I am writing it here, so the truth is in the world, somehow. Perhaps one day somebody will discover this and they'll believe me.

Kindra pushed the journal away from her, feeling sick. The memory she had fought so hard to bury broke free and flooded through her mind.

She'd repressed much about the first time she'd defended Harthwin all those years ago. She couldn't forget how she'd killed one of those men; she couldn't forget how close she came to dying.

And she couldn't forget how she'd survived it, though she'd certainly tried.

For years, she'd been able to convince herself it was nothing more than a power surge. Her survival instincts had kicked in; that was all it had been. She'd never been visited by a god. That was what she had told herself, over and over again. Scaldor had never appeared in front of her, not while she was dreaming, not while she was awake. And that was what they meant when they spoke of being God-blessed, right? When they talked of the Annalindis family. So it had simply been an adrenaline rush, that's all.

Kindra whimpered, biting back a sob. Ten years later, and she could still remember how it felt. It was exactly as Scalya had described; like something touching the deepest core of her, some ancient force asking a silent question.

And she'd said yes, because it was that or face something worse than death at the hands of those men.

The fire that had surged through her had not been her own. It was the most rageful, burning power she'd ever experienced. That remained true. And the emptiness Scalya described… she'd felt that too, when it was over.

For several moments, she simply sat with her head in her hands, torn between wanting to cry or vomit. Slowly, she steadied her breathing. She bottled up her terror and placed it on a shelf to be dealt with later. There was more to learn, and she didn't know for certain if she'd get access to these journals again.

With shaking hands, she pulled the journal back to her.

She kept reading.

CHAPTER 48

Kindra read for the rest of the day, scribbling notes about what she was discovering. After the initial passage about Scaldor, she started to skim, flipping desperately through page after page, journal after journal. She made it through five—not nearly as many as she would've liked, but it would have to be enough for now. Possibly enough forever if she never got access to this room again.

Scalya had suffered a years-long internal conflict about Scaldor, about her kinship with him, as she called it. He did not come to her again for quite some time, during which Scalya both hoped and feared that the first encounter would also be the last. It was interesting: in some entries, the young queen would express gratitude that he had not reappeared; in others, she would be frustrated, slighted by his absence.

I hope he leaves me be and never returns, she wrote once.

Did he not find me worthy after all? she wrote furiously another time.

But he did return to her when she was freshly eighteen. The fighting Scalya had grown up with had increased tenfold, and her village had unfortunately fallen right along what would be the original border between Laoruwen and Alverin. Many in her village had signed up to fight for a young man named Novon. He was the son of one of the fierce leaders who'd helped unify the various lords under one cause: to establish a kingdom. Upon his father's death, Novon took up the banner. He was only a few years Scalya's senior—maybe twenty-three, twenty-four—but his youth only rallied those around him. A powerful and skilled Firefury, he'd been fighting on the battlefields since he was fifteen.

Does Scaldor come to this Novon, too? Scalya scribbled jealously in one entry. Kindra laughed. *Did he find someone else more worthy of his attention?*

Perhaps it would make sense, she had conceded. *After all, he is leading an army, fighting to build a real kingdom. And what am I doing?*

Nothing. I am doing nothing.

That incessant worry that Scaldor had abandoned her for somebody more worthwhile was what pushed Scalya to officially join the fighting. She insisted in her journal that it was her desire to defend her home, but Kindra recognized someone convincing herself of a lie when she saw it.

Regardless of Scalya's motivations, though, she made a difference in battle. Her power, even without Scaldor at her side, was ruinous for their enemies. She wrote often of how it felt to be the cause of so many deaths, and though sometimes she seemed remorseful about what she'd done, she did not seem to be haunted by the lives she'd taken the way Kindra was.

The second time Scaldor came to her was also the first time she saw Novon.

She'd become a well-respected figure in her modest division of the army. They fought under Novon's banner, had for years, but Novon hadn't fought alongside them before. He'd sent generals or lieutenants in his stead, too busy fighting on other fronts to spare time for the journey.

But the border with a budding kingdom called Breyenth had been secured in the last few months, according to the rumors. The fighting had ceased there, both sides coming to an agreement. So Novon was able to journey to other battlefields where the fighting still raged, lending his fire to his armies, who in turn bowed to him like a king.

Exactly as the young man wanted.

The battlefield was a disaster when Novon finally arrived. The enemy— Laoruwen, a kingdom newly founded and eager to establish its territory— was relentless. It was never-ending carnage, both sides enduring massive losses. Nobody knew who would emerge as the victor.

So Novon came to give his people the push they needed.

I assumed he would ask for me, Scalya wrote furiously. *I am the most powerful fighter here, and everyone knows it. Surely, he has heard of me. I've held the line for us nearly single-handedly. He owes me his gratitude, at the very least.*

Kindra wasn't sure how much of that was truth and how much was Scalya's arrogance. Regardless, she could feel Scalya's indignation rippling off the page as she read.

When Novon gave no indication he knew of her at all, Scalya vowed to change that. *He will know me soon enough,* she promised her journal.

But her plan was contingent on Scaldor answering her call, something he hadn't done in nearly a year.

So Scalya had to do something bold to get the god's attention: she had to walk directly into the mouth of death.

When the fighting resumed the next day, she strode onto the battlefield wreathed in fire, as she often did. But this time, she kept walking when the rest of the army stopped. She let the enemy surround her; they did so gladly, eager to defeat their opponent's greatest weapon. Then, in a situation where even her powerful magic could not save her, she reached for Scaldor.

Later, after it was over, she confessed in her journal that she did not truly believe it would work. *A large part of me believed I was going to my death. I vowed to take as many of them with me as I could before I fell and hoped that my fellow fighters would forgive me for what would seem a foolish sacrifice.*

But Scaldor did not fail her. *I'd forgotten how horrible, and beautiful, it was,* Scalya wrote, *to look certain death in the face and be able to laugh as you burn it to ash.*

She described how it was different this time; she'd been able to shape Scaldor's power, intertwine it with her own. He did not treat her like a vessel for his power. He gifted it to her, it seemed. When she'd incinerated a quarter of the opposing army, she made her way to where Novon had been fighting—had been, because he and most other soldiers had frozen mid-battle to observe her destruction. Their enemies were fleeing; the battle was won.

I let him see me. I let him look me in my eyes and see that the power I held was not entirely mortal. And then, Scalya continued, *Scaldor vanished, and I fainted. By the time I woke up, two days later, Novon had left, moving to the next battlefield that needed him. He left a note, though, expressing his gratitude—and his interest in my 'remarkable' gifts. Good enough, I suppose.*

After that, Scaldor came to Scalya more frequently, never less than a few months apart, but only when he deemed it necessary. If the god had been at her beck and call, she would have been channeling his power daily. But Scalya knew when she needed him and when she could handle it on her own. Though she wanted to call for him more, she was smart, and didn't abuse her connection to him.

It still sometimes terrified the young woman—the sheer scale of what she could do with him beside her, the devastation she could unleash. But what scared her more than the power itself was the fact that she'd come to crave it, had started to despise wielding without it. But over time, her terror faded to the background.

Is it possible to become addicted to a god? she wrote at twenty-one, over four years since he'd first come to her. She'd called upon him successfully dozens of times now, had traveled far and wide winning battles because of it. Even without Scaldor, her power was unmatched. He left traces within her, she claimed. Each time he came, he left a piece of his power behind. It allowed for her magic to grow past what was thought possible.

That, too, felt terrifyingly familiar to Kindra.

They called Scalya, "Scaldor's Chosen," and "Scalya the God-blessed," but more than anything, they whispered of her becoming the bride of Novon—King Novon officially by then, Alverin now truly established.

And though Scalya had at first hated the idea, she'd grown hungry. Power—through magic, through title, through marriage—she hungered for all of it.

So, when word spread of Novon's Trial, she made the journey to Wendrith.

I know he will not choose another, she had scribbled in her journal, her writing shaky from the rocking of the carriage she was riding in as she wrote it. *I saw how he looked at me that day three years ago. There is no other in this realm that he truly desires by his side.*

The traces of the queen that Kindra had read about were starting to appear now: her irrational desire to win, to conquer; her infuriating arrogance and sense of importance. The history texts had framed these traits nobly, but Kindra had always thought differently. She had hoped that these journals would reframe her perspective, and at the beginning, they had. But Scalya was a different person now than she had been on that first page. If anything, having direct insight into the young woman's mind only made the stories Kindra already knew of her *worse*.

Such fantastic qualities she's passed down through her lineage, Kindra thought drily as she read.

But Scalya's arrogance wasn't foolish. She did walk away from Novon's Trial as his bride and the future queen. She had been right—the first thing he told her when they were alone was that he had never forgotten about her, and he'd been hoping she would come.

The love that grew between them was as fiery and passionate as they were, and their first child very well might have been conceived before the wedding. Kindra grimaced and skipped through the sordid details of their physical affairs.

And then her stomach growled, bring her back to the present.

She blinked, pulling away from the pages. She cleared her throat and coughed, her throat dry. Only then did she glance at the clock. It was nine at night; she'd spent the entire day in the library.

Slowly, as if she was waking from a dream, she came back to her senses. She was hungry and thirsty, and, wincing as she shifted in her seat, desperately needed to pee.

Jasper would be expecting her soon. She'd already missed the dinner hour; she'd have to ask Sala or Cerulle to bring something up from the kitchens.

As tempting as it was, she couldn't hide in this room forever, putting off actually thinking about what she'd discovered.

Kindra was God-blessed.

Just thinking the words made her stomach turn. She rose quickly, putting the journals back in their place on the shelves. Then she gathered up her notes, tucking them into the belt of her tunic.

The library was dark when she slid out of the room, closing the door softly behind her. Only a few people remained, curled up on sofas reading by lantern light. Iris was long gone, the librarian's desk vacant. On silent feet, she crept out and back to her rooms, mercifully reaching them without being stopped.

"Lady Kindra," Sala said as she approached the doors. "You're back." The Healer scanned her, no doubt noting her pallid complexion and tense muscles. "Prince Jasper said you were in the Great Library today, are you all right?"

"Yes, Sala," Kindra replied hurriedly, stepping into her chambers. "It was a most enlightening afternoon. I just got swept caught up in the texts I was reading. The day got away from me; I forgot to eat. Could you go down to the kitchens and make me a plate of whatever is left over from dinner? And could you send for Jasper? Immediately, please." She tried and failed to keep the urgency out of her voice, and Sala's eyes widened as she noted that, too.

But the other woman said nothing, simply bowing her head before she turned on her heels and was gone.

Kindra practically sprinted to the bathing room. When she emerged, she was dressed in one of her night gowns. She grabbed the notes she'd taken while reading and sat down on the sofa, intending to go over them while she waited for the arrival of her food and Jasper.

But she found it impossible to do anything other than stare into the fireplace. Her head ached from the hours spent reading, her world spun with the knowledge she'd learned about herself.

Well, she supposed she hadn't learned anything. Rather, she'd confirmed something she'd long fought to deny and ignore.

Jasper burst into the room without knocking. He hurried to her side.

"What is it?" he asked, reaching for her. "Sala said to come immediately." He froze as he took in the look on her face.

"I read the journals," Kindra said, voice thin and shaking. She kept staring into the hearth, unable to look at him.

"What did they say?"

She opened and closed her mouth as though she were a fish tossed on land. The flames in the fireplace swelled with her rising panic.

"Kindra." Jasper's voice was gentle but urging. "Kindra, what did they say?"

"I can't—I can't say it," she whispered. "I don't want it to be true."

"Then don't say it," he breathed, gathering her into his arms and holding her close to him. "You don't need to say anything right now."

She crumpled in his embrace, the sobs that tore from her shaking her entire body. Jasper cradled her, ran his fingers through her hair, pressed soft kisses to her head.

"I don't *want* this," she sobbed. "I never wanted *any* of this."

He stiffened slightly at her words but said nothing. She knew he understood by now that regardless of their relationship, this was not the path she would have ever chosen for herself. That would always be true, no matter how much happiness she found with him.

Sala's knock snapped Kindra out of her distress. Jasper gently disentangled himself from her, retrieving the food the Healer had brought.

Kindra, despite her turmoil, still devoured the meal, though every bite tasted like dust.

The food steadied her, however. She gulped down glass after glass of water. The pain in her head eased from a pulsing throb to a dull ache. Jasper watched in silence, waiting.

Finally, she said, voice raw, "Do you remember when I told you about the first time I killed somebody?"

Jasper's eyes flashed with recollection. "Yes."

She took another long gulp of water. "I should have died that day." Her eyes slid to his face. "I *would* have died that day."

He went very still next to her.

"In the last seconds before I lost consciousness, I prayed to the gods. To Scaldor, to Cyrie, to Yvangil and Aspa—I prayed to all of them. I didn't need the god of fire in particular to save me, but I did need some act of divine intervention." She closed her eyes. "Scalya said that the first time Scaldor came to her, it was as though some ancient power touched her soul. She said that it asked for permission, and in her desperation to survive, to save her loved ones, she granted it." She shuddered as she remembered, all these years later, how it had felt. "I granted it permission, too."

"Kindra." Her name on Jasper's lips was little more than an exhale.

"I thought I had imagined it," she confessed, staring once again into the fireplace. "When it was over, and I was safe, I thought it had been an adrenaline rush or a power surge." She swallowed. "I think... I think I always knew it was something else, though. I tried to ignore it, but... reading Scalya's journals made it abundantly clear that it wasn't *just* something else."

"It was Scaldor," Jasper said for her.

She nodded, taking a shuddering breath. "Yes."

"So, you're really...?" He trailed off—he would not say it before she did, before he knew she could handle hearing the words.

Kindra wrenched her gaze from the fire. She looked her betrothed in the eyes. And then she said it, for the first time, though the words felt like stones in her mouth.

"I'm God-blessed."

She stiffened. She forced herself to say it again. And then, on the third time, when her body began to shake with the force of her sobs renewed, Jasper held her for as long as she needed him to.

CHAPTER 49

They did not breathe a word of what they'd discovered to anybody.

Nobody could know. Not Helena or Emeline. Not even her mother, who Kindra could tell knew something was amiss but had wisely learned a long time ago not to press her daughter about such things.

It was bad enough—catastrophic, really—that the king already knew or at least strongly suspected. But Kindra had no doubt he'd poured over those journals more than once since she arrived in Wendrith. He'd likely figured it out months ago.

At the very least, wedding preparations were in full swing. The wedding was little more than two weeks after the Solstice Ball. Kindra hadn't realized how soon it was, but two days after the ball—the day after her discovery—her daily schedule was completely changed. Gone were the hours-long morning training sessions and leisurely afternoons. Her days were now filled with all things wedding-related. From cake tastings with Emeline's father to dress fittings with Mabyl, every hour from dusk to dawn was booked. All the while, more nobility than she'd ever seen descended upon the castle, hailing from cities all across the kingdom. The place was filled to the rafters.

Kindra was lucky if she got an hour at the training grounds every few days. Even her nightly sword fighting lessons with Jasper had ground to halt, the two of them choosing instead to collapse into bed each evening after supper and do other things with their nights.

Lots of other things.

Oh, they were dignified enough during the day, but behind closed doors, they couldn't keep their hands off each other. Kindra didn't know what was wrong with her; it was like some part of her had gone completely feral. She spent each day counting down to when she'd get him alone again.

But their time together was more than that. It was also what grounded her, what reminded her that all the lessons and fittings and tastings she was enduring would be worth it.

At the end of it, he would be hers, and she his, officially.

She looked forward to her wedding day for that reason only. At least she had that; at least she had him by her side. Sometimes, when she looked at him, she felt that no matter what happened in the years to come, if she had him next to her, together, they could conquer all of it.

That was love, she knew. But she still hadn't even uttered the words.

She and Jasper didn't speak about her being God-blessed. There was nothing to be done about it. They hadn't even truly discussed not telling anybody else—they just knew, without a doubt, that nobody else could know.

And so, the days passed. And so, they kept their secret.

"No, no, no. It is *one*, two, three, not one, *two*, three!"

Gregory's voice cut over the quartet of musicians, who halted their playing. Kindra and Jasper stopped mid-waltz, and Kindra had to inhale deeply to keep herself from scorching the etiquette master's head off. Jasper gave her waist a gentle squeeze.

There was a week left until the wedding, and the powers that be had started scheduling etiquette lessons for the marital couple. She had no idea if it had been the king, the Council, or some other official who'd ordered it. Regardless, the two-hour daily sessions left Kindra fuming.

Gregory was fucking insufferable. Like Cerulle, he hailed from Roulierne, and had a similar accent to the Windspinner. Unlike Cerulle, however, his voice was grating and snobbish. If it were any more nasal, he'd probably start talking out his nose.

Gregory was an older man, probably in his sixties. Not a Wielder, but Kindra learned quickly that the etiquette master did not need magic as a weapon—no, he was quite gifted enough with his words.

The first session with him had been more humiliating than any defeat she'd experienced while training. Through subtle verbal jabs and scathing critiques, he'd reduced her to a quivering, demoralized bundle of misery in the span of an hour. She'd ended the lesson early. Jasper had been mortified.

"Your Highness, I offered to help with her when she arrived," Gregory had told Jasper as she'd stormed out. "Now we are pressed for time with much to do. I will not apologize for being thorough."

Everything she did marked her as poor and uneducated, apparently. The way she held her silverware. The way she sat in a chair. The way she fucking chewed.

She'd thought she'd been doing a good job. How hard was it to sit up straight, after all? But nothing she did was good enough for Gregory.

"Maybe you should have had me take lessons with him when I first got here like he said, Jasper," she pouted one night. "Then at least I could've gotten this humiliation over with."

"Kindra, do you think you could have sat through one of those sessions back then?" Jasper all but laughed in her face at the thought. "You would have killed him." He reached across the bed and ran his fingers through her hair. "Nobody would have blamed you, though. Pretty much everybody hates Gregory."

"Why is he still here, then?"

"Well, darling," he sighed. "We all hate him, but nobody can say that he's not good at his job."

And he *was* good at his job. Within a matter of days Kindra was carrying herself in a manner he deemed satisfactory. Gregory's snide commentary subsided. But then they moved on to the dancing, and his brutal scrutiny returned.

She knew the dancing would be rough; she hardly had any experience. Her dancing at the Solstice Ball hadn't been anything extraordinary—a fact Gregory wasted no time reminding her of.

"Did you see how Antone and Celeste danced? *That* is my work. You will create art in that ballroom on your wedding day." That had been his promise at the start of their first dance lesson.

But now, three days in, even Gregory was starting to accept that passable was the best he was going to get out of the couple, though his idea of passable was still unreasonable.

"Do you not feel the pulse of the waltz in your body?" he snapped at them.

"We were on beat," Kindra retorted, patience wearing thin.

"On beat, sure, but you do not *feel* it. There is no swell and ebb in your moves, no musicality." Gregory tsked and leveled a disapproving glare at Jasper. "I trained you to dance myself, Your Highness. Her lack of artistry I can understand, but you? I expected better."

"Is this a wedding or a talent show?" she huffed. "The waltz is fine."

Gregory was unmoved. "Lady Kindra, it seems you still do not understand. I may appear to you as scrutinous and excessive, but I am here for a reason. In less than a week, you are to be a princess. More than that, you are renowned as the cursebreaker, and, as I've heard it, rumored to be God-blessed." She barely managed to stifle her wince. He continued, though now his voice was a touch gentler, "Whether you like it or not, you have a reputation to uphold now. You must appear to the people as invincible, in every sense. You cannot do that if you can't hold your own against the nobility. Even now, though they respect your power, they mock you behind closed doors. You are still a commoner to them—a powerful one, yes, but common, nonetheless. The lords and ladies who are traveling from the other cities in Alverin have not been witness to your sparring matches. They do not know you. So, your wedding is indeed a pageant of some sort. If you swallow your pride and allow me to do my job, we can quiet their whispers in a single evening. Hate me all you want, but I *am* on your side."

Kindra blinked, stunned. "Have they still not accepted me?"

Gregory gave her a sympathetic grimace. "They regard you the same way they regard Alverin's fiercest warriors. But it will take more than great displays of power to get them to fully embrace you as their princess, unfortunately."

"Superficial," she muttered.

"Yes," he agreed. "Very much so. But you must learn to play the game, my Lady. I did."

The next time he corrected her steps, Kindra bit her tongue. And she continued to bite it as the etiquette master used his own, unique kind of magic, honing her into a weapon of a different sort.

A kind of weapon she'd never had to be, but a weapon nonetheless.

The night before the wedding, Jasper and Kindra spent the night apart. It was tradition. They shared an intimate dinner together, and after a couple hours spent tangled up in each other, he kissed her goodnight.

"Tomorrow, you become my wife," he whispered against her lips. Despite her many anxieties surrounding the occasion, she smiled at his words.

After he departed, she visited her mother, who'd been just as busy the last few weeks with her own schedule of lessons and fittings. Her wedding to Kindra's father had been a simple affair—both of them were the last of their families at the time, so it had been a small event with little fanfare. A royal wedding, however, was the opposite of that in every sense. She'd spent a lot of time learning the ins and outs of the ceremony.

"Are you excited?" Sera asked her daughter, relaxing on the sofa in her chambers.

Kindra nodded. "I am. I'm still frightened about a lot of things, but I'm excited to marry him."

Her mother smiled. "If you have love, you can conquer anything."

Kindra's throat grew tight at the words. She was keeping so much from her. It was for her mother's safety, but still.

"I hope so," she replied, opting for a bit of honesty. "With the war and the curse, sometimes I worry it won't be."

Her mother squeezed Kindra's hand. "Don't worry about such things tonight. What's important is that you get a good night's sleep. Tomorrow is going to be a long day. A beautiful day, but a long one."

Kindra chuckled. "Long is right. The rehearsal this morning made that very clear." The ceremony alone was over an hour. Most of it didn't even directly involve Kindra or Jasper—the exchanging of their vows took a mere fifteen minutes—but the processions, the prayers… it all added up.

She left her mother's rooms and headed back to her own. When she arrived, however, she was greeted by a familiar face.

"Tess," she said by way of greeting, unable to hide her surprise. "Is something wrong?"

The Firefury smirked. "Is it that unusual for one to pay her friend a visit the night before her wedding?"

Kindra laughed. "No, I suppose not. Would you like to come in? I need to go to sleep soon, but I can talk for a while."

Tess nodded. "That would be lovely. I won't bother you for long. But I like to have a drink with my friends on the eve of their wedding. As a token of my well wishes, of sorts."

The two Firefuries entered Kindra's rooms and headed for the fireplace. Kindra went to a table and poured them each a glass of wine while Tess took in her chambers.

"These are certainly something," she commented, taking a glass from Kindra as they settled into the chairs by the hearth.

"I know." They clinked their glasses, and Kindra took a sip. "It took me a while to adjust to waking up in here every morning." She frowned. "Have you really never been in here?" For a second, she couldn't believe it. But Tess had been distant and outright missing for much of the recent months. Only in the last few weeks had they begun to rekindle any type of real friendship.

Tess shook her head, eyes flashing. She was clearly thinking the same thing. Rather than commenting on it, though, she took a long drink of her wine. They sat in a comfortable silence.

"Do you truly care for him?" Tess asked suddenly.

Kindra turned to face her. "Jasper?"

"Who else?"

Her brow furrowed. "Yes. I do." What a strange, abrupt question.

"Is it enough?"

Kindra laughed nervously. "What do you mean?"

Tess shrugged, swirling her wine in her glass before taking another drink. "I mean, is it enough to make up for what you've lost? What you could've had?"

"Oh." She was quiet for a minute. Then, "I don't know. Sometimes, when it's just the two of us, it feels like it is. But outside of that, when we can't ignore everything..." She shook her head. "I suppose a part of me will always wish it was different. Jasper understands."

Tess nodded. "I'm sure he does."

Again, another stretch of silence, this one less comfortable than the first. Tess broke it once more. "You could be so much more, Kindra." She met Kindra's gaze unflinchingly. Her orange eyes glowed in the light of the fire.

"What more could I be?" Kindra tried for humor, but she was starting to feel uneasy. Tess was always bringing this up, whatever it meant. "I'm already a princess and a cursebreaker. I doubt I could juggle much else."

Tess didn't take the bait. "You could be a true savior of this realm, if you wished to be."

Kindra shook her head and drained her glass. "You overestimate my power." She wanted to stop talking about this.

"I think you underestimate it, actually."

"This doesn't feel like a friendly pre-wedding drink," Kindra commented lightly, but her voice had taken on a dangerous edge.

Tess noted the warning but did not heed it. "If you knew, beyond a doubt, that you could change the fate of not only this kingdom, but this entire continent, would you do it? Or would you still deny who you are? Would you still hide?"

"I'm not sure what you mean," she replied, growing more unsettled. "And I know exactly who I am, Tess."

"Do you? Because I look at you, and I see a once-in-millennia power." Kindra tried to interrupt her, but Tess barreled on fervently. "I see the first God-blessed Firefury since Queen Scalya herself." Kindra couldn't help it—she recoiled, and Tess smirked triumphantly. "So, I'm right after all."

"Please stop," Kindra whispered, head spinning. "This isn't a conversation I want to have right now." Or ever.

"I was in the library the day you spent holed up in the king's little secret room. I saw the look on your face as you left that night, too stricken by whatever it was you'd learned to even notice you were being watched. Figured I'd take a guess at what it might have been, given the conversation we'd had that morning." A vicious grin slashed across her face. "I'm so glad I guessed correctly."

"Tess, please," Kindra begged. "You can't tell anybody."

"Do you take me for a fool? I would never do such a thing. Gods know what the king would do with this kind of knowledge."

"He already knows," she confessed, and Tess's eyes widened. "He figured it out long before any of us did."

Tess shook her head. "It doesn't matter. You could still change everything if you just use your power—"

"I will *never* call on Scaldor," Kindra snarled, patience finally snapping. She stood and glared down at the other woman. "I've had enough of this. I need to rest." She reached down and all but yanked Tess's glass out of her hand, not caring that it wasn't yet empty.

Thankfully, Tess didn't argue further. She only gave Kindra a long, remorseful look as she rose and headed to the door.

"Well, I can't say I didn't try. I won't bother you with this any longer, Kindra." She paused, hand on the doorknob. "Best wishes for tomorrow. Good night."

And then she let herself out, leaving Kindra irritated and unsettled, her words hanging like a heavy, ominous cloud over the room.

CHAPTER 50

Unsettling as it had been, her conversation with Tess nearly faded entirely the next morning as her room became a bustling hive of activity.

It was her wedding day.

She was up before dawn, not because she had to be but because she'd awoken and had been unable to fall back to sleep. Instead of calling for Sala and Cerulle, however, she took a few moments to herself, lying there in her bed.

This was the official start of the rest of her life.

After today, she would no longer be Kindra Bedelyn of Harthwin.

She would be Kindra Annalindis, Princess of Alverin.

She said the name aloud, rolled it around in her mouth.

"Kindra Annalindis," she whispered to herself. "Princess of Alverin." Then, "Cursebreaker."

And then, quieter than the rest, "God-blessed."

She took a deep breath, brushing off the strange feeling the title gave her.

Today was not the day to let her anxieties get the best of her. That could come later. Today she had to swallow down every bit of fear. She had to be strong, for the sake of her kingdom. And herself.

There was a knock on the door, and she took another deep breath. She steeled herself and allowed the mask Gregory had helped her craft slide into place.

When the servants entered, none of them saw through its cracks.

Kindra's wedding gown was a triumph of extravagance in every sense.

She'd seen dress already, of course, in the numerous fittings she'd had over the last couple weeks. Every inch of fabric had to be perfect, no thread too loose or too tight. But still, seeing it paired with the long veil and plentiful number of jeweled accessories, it was no doubt a thing of beauty. She was glad that she was able to appreciate it.

The gown was a deep blood red—the same shade as the dress she'd worn to meet the royal family all those weeks ago. The bodice was adorned with gold accents; there were several gemstones sewn along the neckline and waist that glittered in the light. Some were as large as coins—one of them alone could feed a family for years. She tried not to think too much about the outrageous wealth she carried on her body.

The skirt fell in flowing layers all around her, the silk decorated with swirling golden thread. It was by far the largest dress she'd ever seen, much less worn. It was also extremely heavy. Already, she was anticipating getting to take it off. At least she had a different gown for the celebration ball tonight.

Her hair had been arranged into an intricate updo, sparkling pins holding the shimmering golden veil in place. When it was time, the veil would be brought down to cover her face—it would remain that way until the very end of the ceremony. For now, though, it remained pulled back so Cerulle could apply the last of her cosmetics.

Her makeup was simple for the ceremony, but she'd been told that for the ball tonight, a much more dramatic look was expected. Her dress for the occasion was sure to be a conversation-starter, and Cerulle would undoubtedly match its boldness.

Cerulle pulled back, examining her work. She and Sala wore matching black gowns. They were long-sleeved and plain, but elegant in their own right. The two women were to walk with her down the aisle, making sure her dress and veil fell just right when she got to the altar, so their attire was designed to prevent any attention from being pulled away from the bride. They were to be her shadows.

"You look beautiful, my Lady," Cerulle said softly. "I believe you are ready." She glanced at the clock. "And not a moment too soon; we are to head to the temple in just a few minutes."

The wedding ceremony would take place in the fire temple. All royal weddings occurred there, but her and Jasper's was the first time in decades that it felt like there was a deeper reason for it besides stubborn family tradition.

Kindra nodded, taking a deep breath. "All right, then."

Sala came to stand beside her. After a moment of hesitation, the Healer reached over and grabbed Kindra's hand, squeezing it reassuringly. "It is just a ceremony, Lady Kindra. It changes nothing. You and His Highness's love is true."

It changes everything, Kindra wanted to say, but she knew the Healer would not understand, not when she didn't know what was at stake. So, she opted for a demure smile instead. "Thank you, Sala."

They brought the veil down over her face and the world was cast in a golden haze. She was grateful to have the two women there to guide her out of her rooms, where the guards were waiting to escort her to the temple.

The castle was essentially empty. All the nobility and a good portion of the Royal Guard would be at the wedding and were already at the temple. Only a few guards remained, the ones who likely drew the short stick and were having to miss out on the ceremony to patrol.

Still, the guards surrounded Kindra so that she was entirely hidden as they made their way out of the castle and across the grounds to the fire temple. Every foot of the gardens had been decorated, the bright red and gold streamers and ornaments popping against the barren trees. The sky was slightly overcast; it was likely going to snow soon. She'd always thought she'd marry in the summer, when Cyrie's power was at its peak, but here she was, in the dead of winter, walking to her wedding. Hopefully, that wasn't an omen of some kind.

The outside of the fire temple was quiet, save for the few dozen guards stationed around it, but Kindra knew the inside was packed. She could hear the distant hum of the crowd gathered outside the castle walls, waiting to catch a glimpse of their new princess. After the ceremony, she and Jasper were to walk the walls, so people arrived as early as dawn to get as close as possible.

As soon as it was relayed that she had arrived, the grand doors to the temple swung open, and the sound of a choir flowed out. Still hidden behind the swarm of guards, she heard more than saw the crowd inside rising to their feet. From the side of the temple entrance, the rest of the royal family appeared, along with her mother, ready to process in.

She tried to catch a better glimpse of Jasper, but he, too, was surrounded by guards. She caught the bobbing of his head, though, and giggled, knowing that he was trying to see her as well.

Helena turned her head to snap at him. "Quit it! It's bad luck! You'll see her in just a few moments." The chastisement got a chuckle out of a few of the guards. Helena turned and rose up on her tiptoes to peer over at Kindra. "I can look at her though. And I have to say, she looks *beautiful*."

Kindra smiled. "I better," she replied, "considering this dress weighs three times as much as I do!"

More laughter. Even the king's mouth twitched in a fleeting smile. Their chuckles were silenced, however, as a guard began to usher the king and queen forward into the temple, starting the processional.

The order was simple: the king and queen, followed by the royal family in order of their right to the throne. At the guard's signal, Antone and Celeste made their way down the aisle. Sebastian and Myala were next. Kindra had been surprised when she'd learned the other princess was to attend, given her bed rest order. But Myala walked with her head high, her steps slow but even, one hand curved under her full belly. Sebastian was a steady presence at her side. Kindra heard the gasps from the crowd in the temple—they had not expected to see Myala today, either.

After Helena and Emeline, it was her mother. She looked radiant in her golden gown—all the family was wearing gold today, save for Kindra and Jasper, who were both dressed in red. Kindra tried to find a space between the guards to watch as her mother walked down the aisle alone, looking every bit as regal as the queen herself.

Jasper was next. The guards around him dispersed so he could process alone, and Kindra finally got a good look at him. As usual, his jacket matched her gown, though it was far more detailed than any one she'd seen him in before. He wore his crown on his head. She would receive a crown of her own at the end of the ceremony, something she didn't like thinking too much about. That was the one element of her attire she hadn't seen yet.

Before she knew it, she was moving up the steps to the entrance, and every pair of eyes in the temple were on her.

For a moment, the sheer amount of attention on her was overwhelming, and she felt her hands begin to shake. But then she locked onto Jasper. Even through the veil, she could make out the softness of his expression as he beheld her. It steadied her, and she began to move.

Cerulle and Sala took up their places behind her, holding the ends of her skirts. Her hands clutched the front, hoisting the heavy fabric up just enough so she wouldn't trip. Through the veil, Jasper's face was blurry, seemingly a mile away at the end of the aisle.

This is who you're marrying, she told herself. *He is a good man. He is a kind man.*

He loves you.

And you love him.

Yes, she loved him, and she had never been so sure as she was in that moment, walking towards him to the ornate golden altar where the fire priest awaited. She felt no fear, not as she reached the steps and slowly climbed them to stand by Jasper's side.

More than anything, she wanted to turn to him, to grab his hand, to at least look at him, but that was not permitted, not yet. First, they had to recite their prayers, a monotonous ritual that was made even more so by the priest's monotonous recitations. But the couple drank from their chalices and made all the appropriate gestures with the rest of the royal family. The final bow to the statues of Scaldor and Cyrie—one hand over their heart and the other placed over their stomachs, where it was said that fire magic was stored—signaled the beginning of the next portion of the ceremony.

The king and queen stepped forward from their spots on the dais. Kindra had made a point to not look at them once so far, but now she was unable to avoid it.

King Leofric took the place of the fire priest. Clad in white and gold today rather than his usual black and red, he looked every bit the hero he believed himself to be; the savior of Alverin, standing before his God-blessed cursebreaker who would help lead his kingdom through war.

"Today is a historic day for our kingdom," he began, voice booming through the temple. "For more than a century, the Annalindis family has been wrongfully punished, our God-blessed magic ripped from us by the actions of an ignorant child." Malice dripped from his words, and Kindra was grateful the veil concealed her face. "For generations, our family—our kingdom—has not seen a Firefury Annalindis. But today, that changes." He looked down at Kindra, and if she didn't know any better, she would've sworn there was something akin to affection on his face. "Kindra has dedicated much of her life to protecting her home. Most of you have heard the stories by now; many of you have seen her great power on display. You have witnessed her dedication to strengthening her magic and serving Alverin—something she has been doing before she ever became Prince Jasper's betrothed. She is our burning hope: our cursebreaker." Then he spoke the simple words of the royal blessing: "The Crown blesses you."

She heard the warning, meant just for her, behind every single word. Every syllable was an expectation being set: she was indeed to be Alverin's beacon of hope during this time, and if that meant she had to actually serve Alverin on a battlefield, she would have to do so or risk his fury.

Leofric looked to his son now, and Kindra braced herself for whatever half-hearted and backhanded blessing he was about to bestow upon him. But to her surprise—and Jasper's, judging by the slight widening of his eyes—the king was kind. He spoke to Jasper's scholarly pursuits, to his masterful swordsmanship, and even to his compassion. She didn't know how much of the praise the king truly meant, but he delivered it with a convincing earnestness that had even Jasper moved. Kindra thought she glimpsed silver lining her betrothed's eyes. How long had he been waiting to hear this kind of praise from his father? How much did it hurt that he was only hearing it because it now served Leofric's best interests?

"The Crown blesses you, my son." Kindra blinked at the added endearment; she felt the shock ripple off Jasper.

Part of her wished the king was really turning over a new leaf because he'd improved as a person; the rest of her knew better than to even dream of such a thing. It was now necessary to make nice with his youngest son, whom he'd disregarded since birth but was to be married to the one he believed could save his kingdom. He was no fool; if he was to have Kindra's support, he had to stop shitting all over her husband.

He would never truly have Kindra's support, but she wasn't going to be the one to let him know that.

Finally, the king stepped back, and he and the queen once again moved off to the side. The fire priest took his position in front of them again.

The priest began rattling off the many tenants of marriage. Kindra was barely listening; half of the tenants were archaic and hardly even acknowledged anymore, but tradition was tradition. She and Jasper both gave their affirmation to uphold them with little enthusiasm.

"You may turn to one another and join hands." They did so, and Kindra once again locked onto Jasper's gaze. She felt the world around her blur and fade, until it was just them and the priest. Just a man and a woman exchanging vows because they loved each other.

The priest began the promises. Jasper went first, proclaiming a loud, "I do," at the end of each one. He never once looked away from her.

When it was her turn, she said every, "I do," just as loudly. She meant each one—she did promise to love him, to protect him, to stand by him.

"As you have made your promises," the fire priest said when they finished, "it is now time to present this union to the gods. May they bless you."

This was their cue to kneel. It was a tricky feat in her giant dress, but she managed it. They each bowed their heads and waited.

This was the part of the ceremony that Kindra was the most nervous about. At the end of the promises, the gods were supposed to either bless their union or ignore them. To be ignored wasn't a condemnation, exactly—none of Jasper's siblings had been blessed on their wedding days, nor had Leofric and Cordilya, but none of them were Firefuries. None of them were God-blessed.

So, if Scaldor and Cyrie did not send them a blessing… well, that would not look very good at all, even to the people who had no idea she was God-blessed.

It was only a few seconds before it came, though it felt like an eternity. The crowd collectively exclaimed in awe as the sun burst through the overcast sky, sending a beam of light down through the stained-glass windows to illuminate the pair. Kindra's skin warmed—it was too powerful to be a simple act of nature. Around them, the firelit sconces flared in unison.

Kindra let out a relieved exhale, only to stiffen a moment later when she felt an ancient, yet frighteningly familiar power brush against her own.

Scaldor's presence danced around her for a second longer before vanishing, the sun drifting away behind the clouds once more. Kindra swallowed, throat tightening, and hoped nobody had detected the shift in her demeanor. But everyone was smiling and applauding. The king observed her with an approving grin. Her mother wiped tears from her eyes.

The fire priest laughed gleefully, stunned to witness such a phenomenon for the first time in his life—for the first time in a century. When he presented Kindra with her crown, he did so with a hopeful smile.

The crown looked suspiciously like Scalya's, though more decorated. She had little doubt the king had overseen its design. Yet another message, another expectation.

Jasper lifted the veil from her face, pushing it up and over her head.

"Let the gods bear witness." The priest crowned her. Everyone seemed to hold their breath before he lifted his hands into the air. "Rise, Prince Jasper Annalindis. Rise, Princess Kindra Annalindis. You are bound, in life and in eternity. Look upon your people."

And so, the couple rose to the applause of the crowd. Jasper drew her close to him; he wasn't supposed to kiss her, but he did so anyway, his hands cupping her face.

"Wife," he murmured against her lips.

"Husband," she replied breathily.

The fire priest coughed awkwardly behind them. They were supposed to lead the processional out.

"We're going, we're going," Jasper said, and Kindra giggled. He interlaced their fingers, and they made their way out of the temple.

Outside, they could hear the excited clammer of the civilians, eagerly waiting to catch a glimpse of the married couple. The guards led them to the walls, where they climbed—slowly, given Kindra's gown—up a watchtower staircase to emerge on the broad stone walkway overlooking Wendrith.

The applause in the fire temple had been enthusiastic. But it was nothing compared to the deafening roar of the crowd as Kindra and Jasper appeared.

Kindra couldn't help it; an overwhelmed laugh escaped her at the sight. Thousands of people flooded the streets, all the way down the sloping hills of the capital. Many were too far away to see much of anything, but they cheered and waved streamers and threw flowers with the rest of the crowd. Jasper kissed her again, and the resounding cries left her ears ringing.

But as they began their walk along the walls, waving and smiling and looking every bit the happy, royal newlyweds the people wanted them to be—that they were—Kindra couldn't shake the feeling of Scaldor's power wrapped around hers; that it had served as a warning of some kind and they were cresting the top of a hill, about to begin an unstoppable, dangerous descent.

CHAPTER 51

After the walk, Kindra and Jasper returned to the castle, where a luncheon had been prepared. The newlyweds had to greet a line of nobility a mile long before they could begin their meal, which meant they didn't get to eat much at all. Each courtier wanted to offer their congratulations and support. People who'd turned their noses up at Kindra when she'd first arrived now pandered; people who'd whispered rotten things behind her back now clasped her hands like they were old friends. Although some of her duties as princess would have her crossing paths with them on occasion, she was grateful she'd found a circle of true friends here.

Those true friends made their way over to them after the nobility were done with their cooing and fawning. Ryle and Heinrich—the latter there mostly for Jasper—came over first, each offering well wishes that felt far more heartfelt than any of the hundred they'd previously received.

Ryle smiled at her and promised that her official title as princess would not make him go easy on her in the ring.

"I would never expect such a thing," Kindra replied. "I'd only tell you to cut it out if you did."

Next was Terryn, who appeared humbler than Kindra had ever seen him. "It's easy to forget who you are when we're just training, and you're dressed the same as us," the Earthwarden admitted. "But, seeing you now... I..."

"I'm just Kindra," she said, reaching out and squeezing Terryn's shoulder.

Terryn gave her an incredulous look, his green eyes disbelieving. "No, you're not."

Kindra laughed it off, but it made her a bit worried. Part of the reason she enjoyed Terryn's company was that he didn't treat her any differently from anybody else. Yes, he respected and admired her, but it was never in the reverent way others did. She had always appreciated that with him—with many of the guards she'd trained with over the last few months—she could just be herself. She hoped that wouldn't change now that she was officially a princess.

She certainly didn't plan on changing.

A few other guards stepped away from their posts around the throne room to come over and speak with the couple, and then Tess walked up to her.

Kindra swallowed, still shaken by the strange turn of their conversation the night before. But Tess was nothing but friendly, if a little distant, though that was nothing new these days. Kindra embraced her when the guardswoman offered her congratulations.

"I'm happy for you," Tess said, and Kindra bit back her retort of *Are you?* She opted to thank her and smile instead.

Kindra's mother, who'd been seated beside her the whole time, reached over and squeezed her hand. "At some point, you're going to tell me what the deal is between you two," she whispered in her daughter's ear.

"You noticed?" Her mother had never shown any indication that she suspected something was wrong between them.

Sera nodded. "Of course I did, from the moment you said her name. But I didn't want to arrive and immediately thrust myself into your business. I figured you'd tell me on your own time." She gave Kindra a stern look. "And you will."

You don't want to know, she almost said, but left it alone as Helena and Emeline ambled over, pulling Jasper and her into a group hug.

Finally, hours later, Kindra was able to relax. She'd been carefully undressed, her wedding gown carried away to gods knew where. She wondered if she'd ever see the beautiful garment again. There would at least be a painting of Jasper and her to remember it by—there'd been a painter present during the ceremony, capturing the day. But she'd certainly never get another chance to wear it. If it hadn't been so cumbersome and heavy, she'd be a bit sadder about that.

She lay on her bed in her robe. No point in getting dressed again, not when Sala and Cerulle would be arriving shortly to begin her transformation for the celebration ball. Exhaustion already pulled at her eyelids, but she knew better than to succumb to it. If she fell asleep now she'd only be groggier for the night's activities.

Kindra stared at her right hand, at the gold, flame-embossed band that encircled her middle finger. A simple wedding ring, made to stay on even when she was wielding. She'd been assured it wouldn't melt—it was a ring worn by one of the ancient Annalindises, one who'd been a Firefury. How much bloodshed had this ring seen, she wondered.

Still, the sight of the ring brought a warmth to her chest that drowned out her trepidation. When she got the letter announcing her fate so many months ago, she never imagined that she would walk down the aisle willingly, with hope for the future and love for the man before her in her heart. Honestly, there was a part of her that once would have rather died— she'd said as much, once upon a time.

But that was before she knew Jasper—the real Jasper. Before she met Helena and Emeline, Ryle and Terryn, and Tess. Before she realized that though there was much to fear in the coming months, that letter had brought her to things she had once believed she'd never really have, outside of her mother: love.

Yes, she had love now. She was surrounded by people who loved her.

And what would you do to save them? Would you be the king's cursebreaker? Would you harness your God-blessed power? Would you fight in Alverin's armies to keep them safe?

Kindra pushed the thoughts out of her head. She didn't want to think about that now. She had a ball to prepare for, and then finally, finally, some time alone with her husband. It wasn't the time to consider what to do if it came down to sacrificing herself for a king she didn't believe in so she could save the people she cared about most.

When Kindra and Jasper strode into the ball, gasps were heard around the room.

It had been the king's idea to wear the gown. It made her grimace when she realized she loved it.

She loved it a lot.

Despite the festive air, nobody could forget that a declaration of war could come at any moment. The king didn't want to ignore that; rather, he wanted to embrace it. And who better to signal that than his esteemed cursebreaker?

So, Kindra did not just wear an ordinary ballgown tonight.

Her gown's bodice was plated in golden armor. It was, of course, adorned with sparkling gems, but it was armor, nonetheless. It covered her shoulders, her upper chest, even stretched down to the sides of her hips. The skirt was white, billowing fabric, true to Alverinian fashion, but if the skirt had been replaced with pants, she could theoretically fight in it.

Combat was even in the gown's details: underneath the armored bodice lay not stiff corset boning, but nerushmyr, which reflected the way the guards' armor worked. So not only did she feel powerful—she was comfortable, too. The metal armor wasn't the strongest—it was thin, not truly designed for a battle, but it was the aesthetic that mattered.

It was designed for a warrior. Someone who'd spent hours training, who'd taught herself the ins and outs of her powers, who'd been fighting since childhood.

Someone like her.

The king had relayed that it was a wedding gift, but that did little to make her feel any better.

She wore her new crown, but no other jewelry. Even her shoes were simple flats, though that was less of a statement than a necessity, as her feet would have fallen off after the whole morning and afternoon spent in heeled shoes. Her hair was in a low bun: a deceptively simple-looking hairstyle that had in fact not been simple at all, as Kindra had sat for nearly an hour while Sala had twisted and braided back individual pieces of hair, arranging each one just so.

But it was her cosmetics, Cerulle's masterpiece, that completed the look and made her look like something straight out of a painting. Her eyes were thickly lined with kohl that swept out and upward, making her gaze that of liquid fire. Her eyelids and cheeks were painted with that shimmering golden powder. Under the light of the chandeliers, she looked radiant.

Jasper had gone still upon seeing her when they'd arrived to walk in together. He hadn't said a word, just kissed her deeply. His eyes had danced with all sorts of promises for later, sending a zap of heat down her spine.

He, though not clad in armor, still looked every bit the warrior she knew he was. His jacket was cut of a thinner, more breathable fabric, not like the stiff material he usually wore, and it showcased his muscular frame in a way that made Kindra's blood heat. Belted to his hip was his sword.

"Father's orders," he explained, and she gestured to her gown.

"Me, too," she replied. "Guess I better get used to that."

"Unfortunately," was all her husband got out before they were ushered into the room—they were the last to arrive, as it was a ball thrown for them. Even the king and queen were already present, seated in their thrones. Leofric took them both in, and he nodded his approval, lips spreading in that wolfish smile of his.

Nobody was dancing yet. The first dance of the evening was reserved for them, so their first stop was the center of the room. The musicians began playing, and Jasper and Kindra bowed to each other. This was the dance that Gregory had meticulously choreographed and nitpicked for days. She could feel the etiquette master's eyes on her from somewhere in the room, and she took a steadying breath before she and Jasper stepped forward and into each other's arms.

They moved across the floor as one. Kindra's dress floated out around her with every sweeping turn and graceful spin. She and Jasper never glanced away from another except when they had to. She didn't look down at the floor to check her footing once. And when she caught the surprised and cowed stares of some of the courtiers, she couldn't help but admit that Gregory had been right.

They will see me as their princess after this. She'd have to take a moment tonight to thank Gregory, and maybe apologize for her sullenness in their sessions.

When the dance ended, the room erupted into applause. They bowed together, hands joined, and before the chittering courtiers could swarm them once again, Jasper spirited them over to where Helena and Emeline sat with Kindra's mother.

"Please protect us," Jasper whispered, faking panic.

"You have to walk among them at some point, brother," Helena chided. "They expect it of you and will be appalled if you don't."

"But we spent all day talking to them!" he protested, stomping his foot childishly and getting a laugh out of Kindra. "We know they don't really like us."

"Oh, but you know what they say about appearances," Emeline remarked. Kindra frowned. The Wavebreaker looked beautiful as always, but there was a restlessness in her that Kindra hadn't seen before. She shifted back and forth, eyes darting nervously around the room, not entirely present in the conversation at hand.

"Something wrong, Em?" Kindra asked.

Emeline started, as if unaware she'd even been behaving strangely. "No, no," she said, "I just, ah, am a bit eager to be done with this very long day. The food at lunch didn't sit well with me."

"It wasn't the cake, was it?" Her mother asked. Emeline's father had baked it. It had been about the only thing Kindra got more than a couple bites of at the luncheon. It had been exquisitely decorated tower of chocolatey goodness. Kindra's mouth watered just thinking about it.

Emeline huffed a laugh. "Gods, no. Father's never underbaked something in his life. It was probably the duck. That never settles in my stomach well."

Helena nodded along, clearly having already heard it. Kindra smiled at her friend. "Well, I hope you don't feel so poorly that you end the night early. If you two leave the ball before we do we'll basically have no other friends here. That is, besides the guards. And none of them can drink."

Emeline gave her a weak smile that didn't meet her eyes. She must really feel bad if she was this mellow. "We wouldn't dare abandon you, Kindra," she vowed.

Kindra and Jasper eventually had to abandon *them*, though. Helena was right: they could hide for only so long. So, they gritted their teeth and ventured back out into the crowd, dancing and talking with the now-drunken courtiers.

The one highlight was Gregory, who didn't so much offer praise as he simply just restrained himself from being critical. Kindra thanked him genuinely for his guidance, and he gave her a knowing smirk. "We are not finished, Your Highness," he said before drifting away, the promise of more lessons sounding like a threat.

"Oh, joy," Kindra muttered, and beside her, Jasper laughed. He pressed a kiss to her temple and her body hummed.

"You look absolutely breathtaking tonight, by the way," he said softly. "I didn't tell you earlier because I was rendered speechless."

"Good to know the compliments don't stop now that we're married." Sparks flickered under her skin.

"Never, darling. I intend to spend the rest of my days worshipping you." Another kiss, this one to the side of her jaw.

"Worshipping, eh? How so?" Her heart fluttered in her chest, and her magic buzzed, as if roused by his touch.

"Oh, so many ways. With my words, my hands, my mouth—"

"Hey, lovebirds!" A familiar voice cut Jasper off mid-sentence. Tess closed the gap between them in a few strides. "Their Majesties would like to see you now, if you don't mind saving the debauchery for your bedroom." She wore her classic smirk, but there was a sense of urgency in her orange gaze.

"I suppose we can do that," Jasper replied smoothly, but Kindra didn't bother to respond. She was too busy trying to calm the rising thrum of fire in her veins. Did Jasper really have this much of an effect on her? He normally made her hot and bothered, and sometimes it did rile up her magic, but this was different.

She tried to shake it off as they followed Tess to the dais where the king and queen sat. It must be the alcohol—she'd had several glasses of that Rouliernien wine tonight, so it must have gone to her head. Indeed, as they walked, she swayed slightly on her feet; Jasper's arm came up around her waist to support her.

Tess peeled off before they reached the dais, swallowed up by the throng of dancers within seconds. Jasper and Kindra approached the king and queen, sinking into respectful bows.

"We were told you wanted to see us, Your Majesty," Jasper said to his father.

But instead of nodding or launching into a conversation, the king merely blinked. "I did not give such an order." He tilted his head to the side. "Though I appreciate you coming to greet your king and queen."

Again, that respect with which he spoke to Jasper now jarred her. It was so unlike the exasperated, disdainful tone he used to have when talking to his son. She felt Jasper's body stiffen against hers; he, too, was finding the change unnerving.

"Of course, Father." Jasper cleared his throat, now on less sure footing. Kindra would have spoken up, but her magic was still acting strangely, straining and kicking under her skin. She blinked and shook her head, but the feeling only grew.

"Princess Kindra," the king said, genuine concern furrowing his brow. "Is something the matter?"

"I—" She shook her head again, unable to speak. A roaring grew in her ears. "I'm not sure, honestly. My magic is—it just feels—"

She didn't get a chance to finish. For in that very moment, Queen Cordilya shot to her feet, eyes nothing but milky white. Leofric was at her side instantly. "Cordilya, what is it?"

The queen was shaking. Kindra's eyes began to water from the pressure building under her skin. Jasper was asking her something, but she could hardly make out the words; not when she was focused on Cordilya, who stared at nothing, mouth opening and closing without sound. The king began to say her name louder, drawing the attention of the courtiers. His other children began making their way across the room to their parents.

When the queen finally spoke, she said only two words.

"Darkness comes," the Oracle rasped, and then collapsed into the king's arms as the corner of the room where Jasper and Kindra had been standing mere moments ago exploded.

CHAPTER 52

Someone threw up a shield of wind around the royal family before the impact of the explosion could reach them. Shards of debris and bodies slammed against the wall of air as thick, black smoke rippled into the room.

The pressure under Kindra's skin subsided immediately.

She hadn't been riled up by Jasper or too drunk.

Her magic had been sensing a bomb, right where she and Jasper had just been standing—

And Tess had gotten them away.

Had the other Firefury sensed it too? Had she felt something and lured them away, thus saving their lives?

Another possibility floated through her mind, but it was so horrifying Kindra did not even entertain for a second. Her magic back under control, she wrapped her arms in flames and surveyed the room, picking out faces among the chaos.

The smoke was so thick, shrouding half the room in darkness.

Darkness comes. The queen had seen it.

Helena and Emeline were behind the shield of air, along with Antone and Celeste. Sebastian and Myala hadn't come tonight, though she had no idea how safe they were if the castle was under attack. Even her mother, thank the gods, had found sanctuary behind it.

No sign of Tess.

She desperately tried to find her amidst the crowd of people fleeing for the doors, only to be pushed back by another cloud of rolling black smoke.

Not smoke, she realized as she watched people try to penetrate it and be stopped as though it were made of stone.

A bolt of terror so severe it nearly brought her to her knees shot through her.

The wall of blackness blocking the way out wasn't smoke at all.

It was shadows, which meant—

The first Shadow Assassin stepped out of the darkness. Not even fully formed, he swung his blades towards whoever was nearest.

It happened to be Caroline Halis, too drunk and cloudy with violetleaf smoke to fully understand what was happening. Genevieve Halis grabbed for her, but a guardsman pulled her back.

She screamed as her sister was stabbed clean through the heart.

Beside her, Helena and Celeste were screaming. Emeline stood defensively in front of her wife, having drawn water from somewhere to fight with. Jasper and Antone had their swords drawn.

Kindra looked at her husband. "I'm going out there," she told him, simply and matter-of-factly. He looked sick about it but didn't protest. "Guard my mother."

He nodded, and for a second, she really looked at him. *Oh, how I love you,* she thought, and she, despite the circumstances, gave him a soft smile.

He didn't return it, but he reached out and cupped her face. "Come back to me," he told her. "I love you, Kindra." And then he kissed her hard on the mouth.

She didn't even get a chance to reply before he was gone, racing over to stand in front of her mother, who was sobbing.

"Let me through the shield, Ryle," she demanded as she strode down the steps of the dais. A dozen more assassins stepped out of the shadows, attacking anybody unfortunate enough to be near them. Nobody stood a chance. Guards and courtiers alike fell at their feet. Whenever they found themselves at a disadvantage, they simply vanished and reappeared in another place, resuming their carnage on the other side of the room. The guards were overpowered—most people could not face a Shadowmaster one-on-one, and with the door blocked, no more could get in to help them.

"Kindra, we cannot protect you if you do this," Ryle said, sweating from the exertion of maintaining the shield. "Our priority is the king and queen."

"I know," she replied. "But what kind of cursebreaker would I be if I stood by and did nothing?"

When she stepped through the shield, she realized it had muffled some of the sounds, too. Suddenly, all she could hear were the screams of terrified people, the shouted orders from the guards trying to form a plan, and the never-ending cacophony of battle.

It nearly overwhelmed her, and she stumbled.

But then Tess was there. "Kindra, what are you doing? Get the fuck behind the shield!"

"No," Kindra retorted, flames licking up her skin. "I'm not a *coward*, despite what you may think."

Tess looked at her, utterly distraught. "That's not—I didn't mean that you should do this."

"And that's what you don't understand about me, Tess," she yelled above the noise. "I may not want to be a savior or a cursebreaker, but I will *always* protect the people I love."

And then she was running across the room, straight towards the Shadow Assassin who'd killed Caroline.

It was the same Shadow Assassin from the Harvest Festival, she realized as she drew closer, and a deadly calm settled over her.

He grinned as she approached, as if he'd been hoping for this. His black eyes glinted with violent delight.

You might've escaped me once before, but not this time. She launched herself at him.

They circled each other as they fought, trading blows. Where his darkness rose to swallow her, her fire flared, blasting it back. Where her blasts aimed, his blades deflected. When he vanished only to reappear behind her, she was already twisting to meet him.

There were no Shadowmasters in the castle to train with, so she'd spent the months since the Harvest Festival reading about them. She'd read all there was about their fighting style, their magic. And though it wasn't anything compared to actual fighting experience, it allowed her to hold her own.

If her ability to keep up surprised him, he didn't show it. Rather, he seemed bored as they dueled, like this was a waste of time.

Or a waste of hers.

The realization came too late.

She felt the shield quake behind her. She risked a glance over her shoulder just in time to see Ryle narrowly dodge a dark blade. The guard who'd been maintaining the shield with him already lay dead, blood pouring from his sliced throat.

The second assassin was a blur behind the Windspinner, and Kindra could only watch in horror as the Shadow Assassin aimed for Ryle's side, still fending off her own attacker.

Ryle spun out of the way, but in doing so, he lost control of his magic. The assassins attacked again, and he became entirely focused on keeping himself alive.

The shield fell.

Darkness rippled near her, and when she looked, the assassin she'd been fighting was gone.

He was halfway across the room, a dark blur as he teleported his way directly towards the royal family.

Kindra began running, eyes only on Jasper and her mother.

Vylie Inacorro got there first.

She materialized out of nothing, pulling herself from thin wisps of darkness. It was such a magnificent feat of magic it would have impressed Kindra under nearly any other circumstance.

Vylie swung for Jasper, and Kindra screamed. Too far, she was still too far—

Jasper did not hesitate. He attacked Vylie with such vigor and strength even the assassin herself was caught off guard. Within seconds, he had her on the defensive, pushing her back, away from Kindra's mother. But Vylie was a master in her own right. She disappeared and reappeared in quick succession, hopping around him so that he was spinning to keep up.

Kindra was a few yards away when he stumbled, too dizzy, and Vylie brought her blades down.

Time seemed to slow down as she watched Jasper swing his blade to parry the blow. Too slow. Tears blurred her vision as she continued to run, rallying her magic to protect him. She hadn't said it back. *She hadn't said it back—*

Fire slammed into Vylie, but it wasn't Kindra's. No, it was Tess, who was charging towards the assassin with a murderous look on her face. "No!" the guardswoman screamed, launching herself at the assassin.

Jasper managed to avoid the death blow, Vylie now locked in battle with Tess. Relief set the tears gathered in Kindra's eyes streaming, but it was short-lived.

The man she'd been fighting was now attacking Antone.

It was more like a cat toying with its prey—Antone was nowhere near the swordsman Jasper was, and only a true master could hold his own against a Shadowmaster. Spotting Vylie and Tess, though, he grew tired of playing, and a second later his blade pierced Antone's stomach.

The king, guarding a still-unconscious Cordilya, bellowed. Celeste screamed. Even Jasper cried out.

Kindra was upon the Shadowmaster within seconds, but the steadiness she'd felt when she'd first attacked had faded as the violence around them only grew. Jasper tried to fight with her, but she shoved him back towards her mother. "Do not leave her," she snapped as she deflected a swath of darkness.

The assassin shifted into shadow; his next blow came from her left side, slamming her onto the floor. She struggled to rise, but the darkness had a solidness to it, pressing her into the ground.

Jasper started screaming, but he did not move from her mother's side.

"You were supposed to be off limits," the man crowed as he stood above her, shadows wrapping around them and blocking everything else out. "But every Annalindis is as guilty as the next. *All of you deserve to die.*" Her fire illuminated the space around her, and she saw him raise his blade, grinning like a maniac.

In her last moments, Kindra thought of Jasper. Of her mother. Of Helena and Emeline. Of Tess. Of Harthwin, and her small cottage. Of the children she danced with at the Harvest Festival. The one she held as he died.

There has to be more than this, she thought. *I have to be more than this.*

And then, facing her own death, panic ripped opened her soul. "No," she gasped, fighting against the shadows, against herself.

But she couldn't stop it as it reached for that ancient, furious power that had once saved her life all those years ago. She could not keep from calling it to her.

And as Scaldor answered, as his power flooded her senses, scorching her from within, as the fury and might and never-ending fire of him filled her completely, she ignited, the force of her power blasting away any trace of darkness.

Enveloped in flame, she rose.

And then she slammed a fist of pure blue flame straight through the assassin's chest and incinerated him from the inside out.

CHAPTER 53

It was worse than she remembered it being.

So, so much worse.

Every sense was overwhelmed. Her bones seemed to scream, her skin stretched taut and burning.

But as the man who'd bombed children, who'd murdered dozens of innocents, disintegrated into ash in her fist, she felt just a small pulse of satisfaction at the sheer power—hers, but not—thrumming through her veins.

Vylie screamed, teleporting away from Tess to stand before the charred, crumbling husk of her fellow assassin. The look she gave Kindra was one of pure hatred.

"You fucking bitch," she spat.

Kindra replied, in a voice that was not quite her own, "You're next." And then she was upon her.

The other shadow assassins flocked to the woman who was clearly their leader. They would have stood a chance had Kindra not had the literal power of a god coursing through her. One by one, they fell, eaten alive by gold and blue fire blasts that scorched the ground and the ceiling, that ate up debris and bodies alike. Somewhere inside her, something seemed to laugh, delighted by the carnage.

Scaldor was enjoying himself, it seemed.

Kindra couldn't tell if she was. She felt only the fire, only the rage, only the need to *burn burn burn* through anybody who opposed her. Her previous reluctance was forgotten, her prior fears about giving into this power devoured.

Nearly half a dozen she killed, cut down like blades of grass. Some of the deadliest Wielders were nothing compared to her. A crazed laugh escaped her—or was it Scaldor's? She began to feel as if she was outside of her own body, dangerously out of control. *Too much,* some part of her whispered. *This is too much.*

The guards rallied behind her, and they launched themselves at the remaining Shadowmasters. She spotted Terryn, Tess, and Ryle among them, all of them battered but alive.

Kindra was so caught up in the sheer vastness of the inferno inside her that she didn't see Vylie vanish. She didn't see her appear behind Jasper until it was too late, until she heard his pained cry.

She whirled. Jasper slumped to his knees, Vylie's blade sticking out of his side. The woman gave Kindra such a hateful, furious look as she withdrew her bloodied blade that she knew, instantly, this was Vylie's revenge for murdering that man. An eye for an eye. A lover for a lover.

Her connection to Scaldor faltered and then snapped under the sweeping wave of panic, his power vanishing with Kindra's gut-wrenching scream. Kindra fell to the ground, her body giving out on her. Her own magic guttered, weakly beating beneath her hot, agonized skin. She reached for Scaldor again, she *begged,* but the god did not reply.

No. *No, no, no.* Stupid, horrified anger raced through her and she staggered to her feet. So foolish to rely on a god, to not expect the fickleness that all deities enjoyed. She stumbled for Jasper, who was trying and failing to stop the blood pouring out his side. His father, who'd watched Kindra with something akin to terrified satisfaction on his face now reached for his son, but Vylie still stood there. She raised her blade for the death blow.

"Please," Kindra sobbed, reaching for her fire. It slipped through her fingers. Oh gods, it was all over. "Please don't." But Vylie wasn't even looking at her, staring down at Jasper with a vicious, murderous snarl. Kindra's mother cowered against the wall, too terrified to even scream.

And Jasper just looked at her, clutching his wound with one hand and straining for her with the other. His mouth moved—her name falling from his lips, over and over again, like he wanted her to be the last thought he had before the end.

Something metal glinted at her feet. A guard's forgotten sword. Kindra grabbed it. Her head swam with the motion.

Terryn was by her side in a heartbeat.

"I got you," he panted. "I'll distract her."

She managed a nod. Terryn wrapped his torso and arms in thorned vines and leaped at Vylie. The surprise attack worked, and she stepped back before transporting to Terryn's other side. The Earthwarden blocked her blow and sent her staggering with a swing of his long, thorned arm. The assassin hissed as the thorns sliced open her arm.

Kindra saw her opening and lunged. She swung the blade down, just as Jasper had taught her. The sword cut deep into Vylie's thigh, and she howled.

She stumbled back, falling to the ground as Vylie jerked her bleeding thigh away from her, the sword wrenching free and clattering to the ground. She sent Terryn reeling with a blast of shadow, and then she limped over to Kindra.

Agony and vitriol gleamed in her all-black eyes as she closed her hand around Kindra's throat and lifted her from the ground. Kindra scratched and kicked at her, but she knew this time no god was coming to help her. No, she'd already played that card. Distantly, she heard Helena and Emeline screaming. Out of the corner of her eye, she saw Tess sprinting towards her from across the room, but one of the few remaining assassins intercepted her.

Vylie put her lips against her ear.

"You stupid, little bitch," she hissed as Kindra struggled. "There are greater things at work here than your selfish pride." She reared back, looking at Kindra with almost pity. "Some things are not up to me, firebird. Remember that. If they were, I would do more than slice your precious prince open for what you've taken from me tonight—I would have cleaved him in two. Consider *this* an act of mercy."

And then her blade sliced through Kindra's torso like it was paper, sliding through a gap in the thin metal Kindra had foolishly thought of as armor earlier in the evening.

Vylie sneered as she let go of Kindra. She fell limply to the ground, choking on her own blood and grasping at her ripped stomach. "Don't worry, I didn't hit anything vital. You should live—probably." She nodded towards Terryn, who was once again on his feet and barreling towards her, fury written plainly across his face. "He won't, though."

Kindra could only watch as Vylie, bleeding leg and all, turned to face the Earthwarden. Even in the assassin's wounded state, Terryn was outmatched by her. He brought his vines up in a shield that she cut through in a heartbeat, she slashed down every stalk he sent towards her. She saw the dread on his face, the pained resignation, a second before it happened.

Vylie's blade cut clean through his neck. Kindra's mouth opened in a silent scream as his head tumbled to the floor.

Dead.

Vylie gave Kindra one last scornful look before letting out a shrill whistle. The remaining assassins—a measly four—stepped back from their battles and vanished. A beat later, and Vylie was gone too.

Mere seconds after they disappeared, the wall of shadow blocking the doors disappeared too, finally allowing a flood of guards and Healers inside. The Healers raced first for the royal family. Kindra looked at Jasper, who lay unconscious mere feet away in a pool of his blood.

Warm hands brushed against her skin, but Kindra didn't look away from her husband until a Healer was by his side, not even when her mother grabbed at her face, her quaking sobs shaking her body. Not until they confirmed that he was still breathing.

Only then did she allow agony and exhaustion to overcome her and slipped away into nothing.

CHAPTER 54

It was dark out when Kindra woke.

She was in her chambers, cocooned in her bed. A fire was blazing in the hearth. She breathed in its life, feeling her magic crackle weakly under her skin. Her whole body was devastatingly sore, and for a moment, she was confused as to why, but then she remembered.

The ball. The attack.

Scaldor. She called on him, the one thing she had said she'd never do—

The Shadow Assassins—

Vylie. Rage rushed through her. That bitch had nearly killed Jasper. Had nearly killed *her.*

Her memory was clearing ever so slowly, as if it had been hidden behind fog. She recalled the Shadowmaster's blade slicing through her stomach like her skin was mere paper after she'd reduced half a dozen other Shadow Assassins to ash; the hatred in the other woman's black eyes. The vastness of power that burned through her when Scaldor answered her; the emptiness inside her when he left. She remembered trying to hold the wound closed as blood poured down her front, trying to crawl to Jasper, unconscious and bleeding out on the ground. Watching Caroline Halis get stabbed straight through the heart, watching Terryn get decapitated—

Terryn. Oh gods, Terryn was *dead.* How many others were, too? There had been so many bodies, so many bloodied faces she couldn't put a name to amid all the chaos. The assassins had blocked off the doors to the throne room, trapping everyone inside—and keeping reinforcements out. They would've been completely outmatched, if it hadn't been for—

For her.

She didn't want to think about it, didn't want to accept it, but she knew it was true. When she had opened herself up to that burning, angry god, it had saved them. When she let her fear get the best of her and lost control, she became Alverin's savior, not just in name or hope, but in truth.

She groaned, both at the realization and her aching body. She had been sapped of all her energy and spirit. The wound Vylie had given her plus the aftermath of Scaldor's presence within her was taking its toll. She wondered if Jasper was feeling similarly.

Panic rushed through her then. Was Jasper even alive? The Healers had reached him by the time she lost consciousness; the last thing she'd seen had been a Healer crouched by his side. But what if he'd been too wounded? What if it had been too late? Further terror grabbed her by the throat. Where was her mother? Emeline? Helena? Tess?

She tried to sit up, only to let out a scream as agony ripped through her abdomen. Frantic, tears pricking in her eyes, she pushed back the blankets and yanked her nightgown up.

Vaguely, she was aware of the door opening, and the sound of hurried footsteps coming towards her. But all she could do was stare at the new jagged scar that stretched from under her right breast all the way down to the top of her left hip. Not quite fully healed, it was still a bright pink, and it fucking *hurt*.

"Kindra," came her mother's voice, wrenching her gaze up and away from her stomach.

She took in her mother—haggard, but unharmed—and burst into tears. Sera Bedelyn crawled onto the bed and gathered her daughter gently in her arms, careful to avoid hurting her.

"You're safe, sweetheart," she whispered into Kindra's hair, which was growing damp with her own tears. "It's over. The castle is under control. You're safe."

"Jasper—"

She didn't realize Cerulle had entered as well until the Windspinner spoke. "Is alive. Helena is alive. Emeline is alive. Tess is alive." Every name clanged through her like a bell, and she could only sob harder with relief.

"How many are dead?" She had to know.

Cerulle swallowed thickly, but answered, "Over two dozen dead, most of them guards." Her voice wavered slightly, and Kindra knew she was bogged down with grief. "A few of the nobility, too." Caroline Halis's face flashed through Kindra's head.

"How many injured?"

"At least thrice the number that were killed."

Such devastation, unleashed by just a handful of Shadowmasters. Dread pooled in Kindra's bones. How were they to survive if the other kingdoms had managed to get the Shadow Assassins on their side?

"All in the royal family are alive." Cerulle continued her reporting. "Antone and Jasper were gravely injured but are expected to make full recoveries. Queen Cordilya is…" The Windspinner swallowed, shaken. "Queen Cordilya has yet to awaken after collapsing at the ball."

Kindra nodded shakily, her body still rippling with pain. She had little love for Antone, but she was glad he had survived. The queen's state disturbed her, though she didn't know what there was to do except wait. Her mother tightened her arms around her. "Is Sala—is she all right?"

"Yes. Exhausted—she has healed many more than just you over the last day—but all right. Alive."

"Last day? Have I really been out for a whole day?"

"Yes," her mother said, "you needed the time to recover." Given how worn Sera looked, the time Kindra had been unconscious hadn't been easy on her.

"Jasper is still sleeping," Cerulle said, as if she knew exactly what Kindra was about to ask next. "He's been drifting in and out of consciousness. Healers say he probably won't wake fully until the morning."

"Which gives you more time to rest," her mother said sternly. She looked to Cerulle. "And eat. Would it be possible to send for some food? Something light—a soup, perhaps."

"Of course," Cerulle replied, dipping her head in a respectful nod to them both. "I'll be back shortly." And with that, she was gone.

Kindra looked up at her mother. "You don't need to do that, you know."

"What, take care of you? Please, you may now be a princess, but you're still my daughter," Sera chuckled softly, hand still stroking Kindra's hair.

Princess. The title made her stomach flutter. Jasper's wife. Not betrothed, not anymore. His *wife.*

"I suppose I am a princess, now," she murmured. Princess Kindra Annalindis. No commoner surname anymore. She looked down to her right hand, where that little golden band of fire sat.

"How do you feel?"

"I'm not quite sure," she confessed. "I'd come to terms with being married, but I think I spent so much time on that I didn't give enough thought to what it would feel like to officially…"

"Be a part of the royal family?" Sera finished for her. Kindra nodded mutely, suddenly overwhelmed by all that lay before her, all the obstacles she'd pushed to the back of her mind as she'd gotten swept up in Jasper, in her love for him. It had been so easy to forget it, to say *we can worry about that later.*

But later was *here*, now that she and Jasper were officially wed. And with the disdain between them thoroughly and publicly obliterated, there would be no reason in the eyes of the king why they couldn't get right to their true, only purpose: breaking the curse, especially now that he knew she was God-blessed.

Kindra shuddered as the king's face flashed through her mind. The victorious gleam in his eyes, even as he held his unconscious wife and reached for his injured son.

But she had not missed the fear that lurked in his gaze by the end, when she'd burned through Shadowmaster after Shadowmaster, when he had seemed to realize that the power he'd long hoped she possessed was something even he might not be able to control.

When he had understood that she was not just his potential savior, but his biggest threat.

Tears welled as everything seemed to crash down around her. Reality came rushing back in. Her chest began to rise and fall rapidly, and she tried to focus on her breathing, but the panic—and the grief—was too great.

"Oh, sweetheart, you're going to be okay." Her mother held her close, rocking her slightly as if she were still a child. "You've already done so well—I can't imagine it will be that hard." Then, softly, "Do you want to talk about it?"

She was silent for a few heartbeats. Part of her still wanted to shield her mother somehow, but there was no use now. Not when she was certain the whole castle knew what she'd done, if not half the city.

"I'm God-blessed," she said slowly, still struggling not to choke on the words. "Scaldor can use me as a channel for his power, if I allow it—or I use him. I'm not sure which one it is. It only happened once before, when I was young. The first time I—" She cut herself off, not wanting to relive that memory again. "The king said something about Queen Scalya that made me curious when he danced with me at the Solstice Ball. I got a hold of her journals and read about her experience. It's... it's the same, Mama."

Her mother did not respond. Kindra continued, needing her mother to understand, "I didn't mean to do it. I had promised myself that I wouldn't, because of what it would mean to the king. How it would change everything even more. But I just—I thought the assassin was about to kill me and I... I just did it. I don't know. I just felt that I'd do anything to stay alive, so I could keep fighting, even the one thing I'd vowed to never do again."

"I don't blame you, Kindra," her mother replied finally, surprisingly calm. Kindra suspected that the shock of the last day had yet to wear off, and she was merely grateful her daughter was alive. "You saved people's lives, mine and Jasper's included. I would never blame you for that. And you saved the crown prince's life, as well. The king will be grateful to you, I'm sure."

He's going to kill me, Mama, she screamed in her head, unable to voice the words. Some things she could protect her mother from just a little bit longer.

"Terryn is dead," she murmured instead. "I saw him die. I couldn't—I couldn't stop it." Then, the words she could hardly stomach saying because they filled her with such shame: "He was trying to save me. Save Jasper."

Her head filled with memories of the snarky Earthwarden she'd come to call her friend. His cocky introduction to her, all those months ago; him, damp with sweat after losing to her again but eager to go just one more time; his wielding, which had grown so much since he'd started training with her. How magnificent it had been, in his final moments—how beautiful it had been as he'd fought his way across the ballroom by her side, his face empty of all his usual arrogance and humor, replaced with fierce determination.

And terror—especially in those last few seconds when Vylie closed in, her blade still dripping with Kindra's blood, and he realized he was alone, that nobody, not even her, was coming to save him.

And Kindra could do nothing but watch from her place on the bloodied floor, one hand straining for Jasper and the other holding her stomach together, mouth open in a silent scream.

It was as if Vylie knew exactly what would hurt her the most.

She remembered, then, what the Shadowmaster had snarled in her ear as she ran her sword through Kindra's torso.

Some things are not up to me, firebird.

At that moment, Kindra had hardly registered the words. But now that she was safe, she finally thought about them, as much as she could with her battered mind.

What did she mean by that? Who was really pulling the strings?

And why did she keep calling her firebird?

Cerulle returned with a tray laden with bowls of hot soup. Kindra allowed her mother to feed her, too weak to protest or do it herself. She was too exhausted to even register the taste as it slid down her throat. When she was finished, she had her mother and Cerulle help her to the bathing room, where she relieved herself before crawling back into her bed. Her mother laid down next to her and pulled her daughter back into her arms, as if she couldn't bear to let her go.

Kindra's mind was racing, but her head felt so heavy on her mother's chest. She had to see Jasper, but she reluctantly accepted that that would have to wait—though there was so much to be said to her husband once he awoke and she was able to stay conscious for longer than a half hour. And then there was the matter of everything else—the king, her power, the war—but she could think about that after she saw Jasper. After she said everything she had been holding back.

She didn't remember falling asleep, but blackness swooped in, and she drifted into nothingness.

CHAPTER 55

While Kindra had planned to see Jasper before she did anything else the next day, King Leofric had different plans.

When she'd awoken that morning, Cerulle had delivered the news that Jasper was awake and asking for her. Within an hour, she was being rolled down the castle halls in a wheeled chair. She didn't feel as unsteady as she had yesterday, but Sala and her mother had been insistent that she continue to rest as much as possible.

But halfway to Jasper's rooms, the king intercepted them.

"Princess Kindra," he greeted her. He'd looked as though he'd seen better days; but then again, everyone in the castle did. While before, the atmosphere had been fraught with tension, now there was a haunted, terrified air wherever she went, every person she passed wearing the same grief-stricken, stunned expression.

Kindra did her best to hide her dread, bowing her head. "Your Majesty."

"I'm glad to see you are recovering." He sounded like he meant it; she knew better than to take his desire for her well-being as compassion. "I assume you are on your way to see Prince Jasper?"

She nodded. "Yes. I was told he is awake and asking for me."

The king nodded. "Yes. But he will understand if I divert your attention for a moment." Her displeasure must have shown briefly on her face, for he said, "Just a brief conversation." He didn't wait for an answer. He jerked his head at Cerulle. "I will escort her from here." The Windspinner bowed and left without so much as a glance at Kindra, but she didn't miss the stiffness in her shoulders as she walked away.

King Leofric came behind her and took hold of the handles of her chair, pushing her forward. They didn't speak.

He wheeled her down the hall, taking a left turn where he should've taken a right and leading her instead to a stone balcony that overlooked the front of the castle. It was empty, save for a lone statue and a few benches.

The snow that had fallen the morning of her wedding was starting to melt, leaving the landscape gray and muddy. The air was crisp; she called some of her magic up to just under her skin, warming her. Much to her relief, it felt less sluggish and weak than it did yesterday.

The king pushed her over to the edge of the balcony. For a brief, paranoid moment, she wondered if he planned to toss her over—just kill her right then and there and get it over with.

But he did no such thing. Rather, he came to stand beside her, overlooking his kingdom. Before them, the city of Wendrith sprawled, smoke billowing up into the air from chimneys.

Kindra broke the silence. "How is Queen Cordilya?"

"She has still not awoken," the king replied stiffly. "The Healers are not sure why she has continued to sleep." It was clearly causing him a great amount of distress, his shoulders slumping ever so slightly as he spoke.

"I hope she wakes up soon," she said, and he merely grunted in response.

Another taut silence stretched between them.

When Leofric finally spoke, he said, "Breyenth, Laoruwen and Pryllia have officially declared war against Alverin." His voice was flat, as if he were simply reporting the weather.

Kindra nodded, not surprised. "I take it they were responsible for the attack at the ball?"

"Surprisingly, they claim they had no part in the planning or execution of it. But they made it very clear in their *joint* declaration that they fully support any and all attempts to achieve *justice*. They intend to slaughter us. They've made that much clear." Now, his voice grew bitter, mocking. "I suppose you have more empathy for them than I do."

She risked looking up at him and found he was still gazing outward. "I never claimed to have any empathy for them," she said. "Only that I could understand how history might have led them to this point."

"Is that not empathy, Princess?"

"I would say it's less empathy and more logic, Your Majesty," she replied with a bit more bite than she intended. "It has nothing to do with my loyalty towards Alverin."

She could've sworn the king's body flared with heat at the retort. "You are God-blessed," he said, changing the subject.

"Yes." No use in denying it.

"It was quite the feat, what you accomplished when you called upon Scaldor. So many Shadowmasters, gone in moments." He cast a sideways glance at her. "It would be a boon to have in battle."

Kindra understood very plainly what this conversation was then. "Your Majesty, the cost of using such power—"

"Yes, yes, I know. It exhausts you; it can drive you to madness—I read those journals, too. Many more times than you have." At Kindra's blink, he continued, now facing her fully. "Did you think I was a fool, bringing up Queen Scalya to you, alluding to the fact that I believed you to be like her?" He laughed, as if amused that she'd think him so indiscreet. "You may curl your lip at how I treat my son, but I've always paid attention. I knew he'd tried to access those journals many times, being the scholar he is. I knew he'd point you in that direction, and I knew you would go. I knew you'd figure that you could use my name to get access to them, because nobody would dare go against one of my requests."

He leaned down so he was eye-to-eye with her, face merely inches away. Kindra resisted the urge to shrink down in her chair. She hated how helpless she was.

"So, I ask you, Kindra, are you daring to go against one of my requests?"

"You want me to fight for you," she breathed. "You want me to risk my life on the battlefield?" Desperately, she asked, "What about the curse?"

"Why would I focus on a hypothetical magical child when I have a God-blessed Firefury right now?" The king scoffed, like he found the very notion ridiculous. "A child is necessary to continue the bloodline, but it would be an offense to the gods—to Scaldor—if I let you waste away producing children instead of using you to your full potential."

"Which is to be your weapon." Kindra managed to shake her head. "Your Majesty, it's not as if I can call upon this power on a whim. It's up to Scaldor. I cannot make demands of a god. Even you should know that."

"Oh, I do. I've been screaming at them my whole life and they've never listened. But in bringing you to me... perhaps they've finally tossed me a bone." He smiled, and Kindra's stomach turned.

"What if I am killed before I can produce an heir?" How horrifying, to now be using one of the ideas she used to hate the most as a way to avoid a far worse fate.

"You will not be killed, dear girl. You are too gifted for that, even without Scaldor's power blasting through you. And I am not an idiot—I would not send you to every front line. You will be used sparingly, only when the people need to see you the most. So, you don't have to worry about that." His smile vanished. "Unless you let foolishness take the lead. And then, well." He clicked his tongue. "I cannot save you."

Because I will be the one who kills you. She heard the unspoken threat loud and clear.

She also knew quite plainly what this was: the king was making a quick move to exert control over her. He was making his authority known: God-blessed or not, she still had to bow to him.

But that was how it was always going to be. She'd known for a while: she would obey, bending until she finally snapped, and even then, the alternative was not to outright refuse, it was to simply flee.

"When would you have me go?" she asked, and he grinned in earnest now, pleased that she'd relented.

"Oh, it will be months yet. We'll let them expend their energy in their initial assault. They'll be aggressive in their attack strategy—they've no choice but to be if they want a chance at defeating us. But it will wear their armies out, especially during the winter. And then you will walk onto the field, call upon your god, and burn them to ash. And even if he decides not to show up, you will still deliver a devastating blow. Soon, just your presence alone will be enough to stoke terror and sway battles in our favor."

She hated him; hated how she was being backed even further into this cage, forced to become some murderous weapon she never wanted to be.

Leofric stood back up to his full height. "Scaldor abandoned us long ago. I'll never understand why he did not save us from that curse—what is some mortal girl's power against that of a god?" He shook his head, turning once again to survey his kingdom. "Everything we did, we did in his name. His image. But it was not enough for him." He looked down his nose at her. "But for whatever reason, he has decided to gift you with an ability he once reserved for this family. One that you are now a part of. So, you will do your duty, as Scalya did, and you will defend this kingdom in its time of need."

There was no question. No promise of consequences—that was unnecessary, for she already knew them.

So she turned out to face the horizon. "Yes, Your Majesty." She hated how tired and defeated she sounded.

The king went behind her again and began wheeling her inside. "I'm glad we had this talk, Princess Kindra." At her silence, he said, "And do not be mistaken—I am immensely grateful for your actions during the attack. You saved many lives. That act will not be forgotten."

He pushed her down the halls until they reached Jasper's rooms. He handed her chair to Tomas, who was posted outside the doors.

"My apologies to my son for keeping him waiting. It was of utmost importance that Kindra and I speak." Before he left, Leofric met her gaze one last time. His eyes narrowed ever so slightly. Kindra read the warning there.

Tomas grabbed hold of her chair as the king vanished around the corner. The guard noted her weary expression. "Are you all right, Your Highness?" His eyes flicked briefly to where the king had been.

Kindra swallowed. "Who is, right now?" She offered him a weak smile. "I'd just like to see Jasper, please."

Tomas studied her, and then nodded. Before he opened the doors, he said softly, "You stopped an assassin from running me clean through with a blade at the attack. Thank you. Your power—it's extraordinary. A true gift."

"So I've been told," she sighed as he wheeled her into Jasper's chambers.

CHAPTER 56

Despite his obvious pain and discomfort, Jasper smiled at her when she entered.

Cocooned in his bed, her husband's face was pale and gaunt, his eyes bleary. He looked terrible. Judging by the way his gaze flashed with concern, so did she. Tomas left them with a swift bow.

The two silently regarded each other for a few seconds, as if they were both processing that the other was alive.

"Well," Jasper spoke first, voice hoarse, "how's that for a wedding night?"

Kindra could not even bring herself to fake a chuckle. "Your father just told me he wants me to fight in the war."

Any humor drained abruptly from his expression. "What?"

She nodded and rose from her chair. Her knees wobbled slightly, but she slowly limped her way over to his bed and crawled onto it, settling down next to him. She stared up at the ceiling, unable to look directly at him as she spoke. "He says he wants to use me sparingly. But he expects me to use it. My... power."

"But it doesn't work like that."

"He knows, Jasper. He set it all up. He mentioned Scalya on purpose to me at the ball because he knew you'd suggest the journals, and he knew I'd read them." A tear rolled down her cheek and she didn't bother to wipe it away. "He essentially told me the only thing that could get me killed is my own foolishness, and we both know what he meant by that."

She felt Jasper's eyes on her. "We'll find a way to get you out of this. You're not a weapon, Kindra."

She turned to look at him then and smiled sadly. "Yes, I am, Jasper. I always have been. But I was a weapon I could control." She let out a shaky breath. "But I'm not the one in control anymore. Since the second you came to get me, I haven't been in control. Those days are over."

"Hey." Jasper reached out a hand and touched her cheek. It was cold and clammy against her skin. "That's not true."

"I thought we were past you trying to sell me bullshit." No bite in her voice. Just defeat. Exhaustion.

He was silent; there was nothing to really say, after all.

"I'll come with you, obviously," he finally said. "I don't want to hear any arguments."

But Kindra only nodded fervently, her face crumpling under the weight of her relief. She hadn't wanted to ask him outright, but she'd known from the second the king demanded this of her that the only way she'd survive it would be with Jasper at her side.

He tugged her closer to him, holding her as tightly as he could without hurting either of them.

She pulled away from him after a few moments, raising her head to look him in the eyes. "I love you," she said—finally. *Finally*. She felt a weight ease from her as she did. "I should have said it before I raced off to fight. I should have—I should have said it weeks ago."

"You're saying it now," Jasper said hoarsely, looking as if he might cry. "Oh, how I've dreamed of hearing those words." He pulled in and kissed her, feather soft. "I love you, my beautiful, brave wife. We'll get through this together, Kindra."

"Even if we have to run?" she asked, needing to know if what he'd told her a few weeks ago was still true. "Because Jasper, I don't—I don't think I can be what he wants me to be. I can't walk onto a battlefield and just call on Scaldor to win this war. I wouldn't want to do that even if I could. The brutality, the *murder* he's asking—forcing—me to commit—"

Jasper's hands cupped her face, snapping her out of her spiral. "Yes. Even if we have to run, Kindra. At the ball, watching you use that power…" A shudder ran through him. "You are right. It is an awful, awful thing. I don't understand how my father saw that and felt anything other than terror."

"I think terror is exactly what he felt," she replied, "and that's why he is doing this now. Fire is only useful when it can be controlled, Jasper. If you allow it to go unchecked..." She shrugged. "You said it yourself, remember?"

He nodded as he recalled his warning to her, that first night in the castle. "I shouldn't have expected anything different. I guess I just didn't think he'd do this when we still have the curse to think about."

"He doesn't give a damn about the curse. He said as much. I don't think he believes I can break it any more than we do, honestly. At least, not through the bloodline." She grimaced, feeling sick.

"Does a curse really matter if all your enemies are dead? If Alverin wins, once and for all?" Jasper murmured, voicing her thoughts aloud. Because Kindra knew what the king was thinking. She'd read those journals. They'd both read Scalya's passages on the mass destruction she caused when channeling Scaldor.

Kindra's panic swelled again. "I will not be a tool for mass murder, Jasper. I just won't. I love the people of this kingdom, and I don't want them to suffer, but..."

"I know," Jasper said, cradling her. He pressed a kiss to her forehead. "And I would never ask that of you. Hel and Em wouldn't, your mother wouldn't. I don't think even the people of Alverin would. So, we will go, if we have to." She grabbed hold of his promise and tucked it away in her heart.

"You are the brightest light in my life, Kindra," he said. "I'll do anything I can to keep you from burning out."

Three days later, Emeline appeared at Kindra's door, alone.

"May I speak with you?" Emeline asked, unusually hesitant.

"Oh, I suppose I could spare the time," Kindra replied drily, waving her hand to indicate just how busy she was, which was to say, not at all. She'd been practically bedridden since her initial waking. Even her brief visit with the king and Jasper had drained her for an entire day. Her body still ached horribly. Even the simplest of movements were agonizing.

At least tonight, the Head Healer had cleared her to sleep with Jasper in his chambers. The two of them were finally recovered enough that the

Head Healer was not worried about them hurting themselves with whatever activities they might get up to. But as much as Kindra wanted to lose herself in Jasper, she was still not feeling physically up to it, and it didn't seem like Jasper was, either.

Her joke did not bring a smile to Emeline's eyes like she thought it would. The Wavebreaker gave nothing more than a small, stiff smile, and came to sit at Kindra's bedside.

"Emeline, what's wrong?" Kindra asked, concerned at the lack of her friend's usual spark.

Emeline did not answer. "I'm very glad to see you are recovering smoothly," she said instead.

Kindra reached for humor again. "Oh, I don't know if you could call this a smooth recovery," she joked lightly. "I practically cry every time I have to get out of bed." Again, nothing more than a twitch of Emeline's lips. "And I'm glad to see that you and Helena were unharmed in the attack," she added seriously.

Emeline nodded, looking away. "I'm very relieved as well. It was horrible enough to witness you and Jasper and Antone getting injured. I don't know what I would have done if Hel had been injured as well." Something akin to guilt flashed across her face.

Kindra studied her closely. "Emeline, what is it? This isn't like you." It was making her uneasy.

There was a brief silence, where Emeline appeared to be searching for the courage to speak. When she found it, what she said rocked Kindra to her core. If she were not already sitting, it would have knocked the world out from under her.

"What if I told you there was a way to break the curse? One that doesn't involve heirs?"

For a moment, Kindra could only stare. Then she said, slowly, "What do you mean?"

"Exactly what I just said. That there's a way to break it, and you wouldn't have to do any of this bullshit."

"What is it, then?" Kindra pressed, feeling hopeful for the first time in days.

"Ah," Emeline looked away. "I can't tell you right now."

"Em. Come on."

"I'm serious. It's not—it's not safe, right now." There was fear—real fear—in Emeline's blue eyes when she looked back at her. Telling this to her was clearly a huge risk, though what exactly she was risking, Kindra wasn't sure.

"Okay." Kindra took a deep breath, wincing as she did so. "So when can you tell me?"

Emeline relaxed slightly, some of the tension bleeding from her shoulders. "In two days. Midnight. Tess will be waiting for you outside of your chambers. Or Jasper's, if you decide to move to his."

"I have to wait two whole days?"

Emeline nodded. "Yes. I'm sorry, but we just—things have to be arranged, that's all."

Gods. What was this? "Who's we? You and Tess?" She tried to ignore the stab of betrayal she felt; how long had Tess and Emeline been hiding this? Something she'd hoped so much for these last few months? How long had they known there was another way? She tried to remind herself that she didn't know what the other way was; it could be something impossible.

"Yes, and—well, you'll see. It's—" Emeline took another deep, stabilizing breath. "It's the only way, Kindra. Know that." Again, that flash of guilt and apology.

"Okay," Kindra said softly, feeling like she was speaking to a frightened child. "I can wait."

"Great." Emeline stood; her mission accomplished. "I have to tell Tess that you've agreed. I will stop by again soon; perhaps we can share a meal together? Get some semblance of normalcy back." She smiled at Kindra, some of the light returning to her eyes.

Kindra tried to return it, but her head was spinning with all the new information. "Yes, that would be nice."

Emeline's exit was swift, and Kindra was left wondering how, in such a brief conversation, everything had been turned completely upside down.

She knew one thing for certain: if there was even a chance of there being another way, a chance for her to regain her freedom, a chance for her to not be the king's personal weapon—she would at least hear them out. It would kill her to not know.

She hoped this discovery wouldn't tear her away from the person she loved, but she had a feeling there was no way it could be that simple.

CHAPTER 57

Two days later, Kindra slipped out of bed at precisely quarter to midnight. Jasper, ever the deep sleeper, did not stir from his place beside her. His chest rose and fell evenly in deep, heavy breaths. For a moment, she just watched him breathe and felt a swell of love for him. Her prince— her husband.

She hoped that whatever Tess and Emeline were about to reveal to her would be enough to save them both.

She padded silently into the dressing room and changed from her nightgown into a set of nerushmyr. She would not be caught unprepared this time, even taking an extra moment to equip Elric's dagger.

When the clock on the mantle struck midnight, she was ready. Ever so quietly, she snuck out of the room and into the hall.

Tess was there, as promised. Her eyes flashed with relief when she saw Kindra. She glanced at the dagger sheathed at her waist and frowned. "We're not going into battle," she whispered, and Kindra shrugged.

"Nobody thought the ball would turn into a bloodbath either," she hissed back, and Tess stiffened slightly, but said nothing in reply as she began to walk down the hallway, Kindra following closely at her heel.

"Em will meet us there," Tess murmured, barely loud enough for her to hear. She halted at the sound of approaching footsteps, pushing Kindra behind a thick velvet curtain before she could protest.

The sound of guards drew closer, and Kindra didn't dare to breathe as they paused briefly to greet Tess.

Only when they'd disappeared around the corner did Tess pull Kindra out of her hiding spot.

"You may have to tolerate doing that a couple more times," the guardswoman told her as they began moving again.

It was only then that the feeling that she was probably about to commit treason took root.

That feeling only grew as they turned down a familiar corridor with an all-too familiar door. They slipped inside the broom closet without being seen, closing the door silently behind them. Tess walked over to the wall, a flame already lit in her palm, and pressed it to the stone, like she'd done it a thousand times.

And she probably had, Kindra thought as she watched the catacomb entrance illuminate and then slide open. The stale dusty air of the tunnels drifted out and enveloped her.

Wordlessly, Tess began to descend down the steps. Kindra had no choice but to follow, feeling increasingly wary with every passing second. Once in the tunnel, Tess turned around and closed the entrance behind them.

"We can get back out," she assured her, speaking at a louder volume now that they were sealed within the catacombs. The fire in her hand grew to light up the space around them, and they began to make their way down the stairs. "You know," Tess continued, "I was surprised that you didn't push this with me. When you found the entrance and confronted me about it—I was expecting you to not let it go."

"I didn't let it go," Kindra admitted. "I was angry with you for a long time for keeping secrets from me and lying to my face about it." *I still am*, she finished silently. But at least it seemed like she was finally going to know the truth.

"You will understand very soon," Tess replied, voice deadly quiet, "why we had to keep this from you."

We. "So, Emeline has known the whole time, too?" She couldn't fight the note of hurt in her voice.

"A lot of people have known," Tess said, and gave Kindra a burning look. "A lot of people have died for this, too. It was a choice—to wait to tell you. You have already almost died twice because of—" She cut herself off abruptly, turning her head away and focusing intently on the stairs, which were still taking them down, down, down in a winding, twisting path.

"Because of what?" Kindra pressed, but Tess did not give an answer. "I'm getting really tired of this cryptic shit." Again, no reply. Kindra held her tongue. She'd find out soon enough, she supposed.

For several minutes, they continued to walk in silence, the air growing colder and staler with every step. They had to be deep into the cliffside by now. Finally, the stairs ended, and they came to a small landing. There were three directions they could go. Tess directed them to the passage on their left. Again, stairs took them further into the earth. The smell of salt hit Kindra's nose; there must be an exit that led out to the ocean ahead of them.

Eventually, the sound of other voices, hushed and tense, floated up from about two dozen steps down, where the stairs ended. She could see the dim glow of torches seeping out from underneath a closed door. Kindra's body stiffened, and fire sparked in her palms. "Calm," Tess hissed. The other Firefury took a deep breath, and grabbed Kindra by the shoulders, forcing her to look at her. When she spoke, she was more intense than Kindra had ever heard her sound. "Kindra, when we walk into that room, you are going to have a lot of questions. Knowing you, you are going to be very angry—and I can't blame you for that, considering all we've put you through. But just know this: it's all for Alverin's future. For Istreria's future."

Before Kindra had a chance to respond, Tess pulled away from her and quickly descended the last few steps. She gave the door a series of knocks, some long, some short, and the conversation occurring behind it ceased immediately. Kindra, still registering Tess's words, hovered a handful of steps behind her, still on her guard despite Tess's assurance that she was safe.

And she was glad to be farther back when the door opened; glad to have the space to rally her magic.

Because when the door opened, it was Vylie Inacorro standing in the entryway.

CHAPTER 58

Kindra's fire acted upon instinct at the sight of the Shadowmaster.

It shot from her like an arrow, soaring through the air straight for Vylie's heart.

"Oh, godsdammit," somebody shouted, and she heard other people rushing to the door, felt Tess's power reaching for hers—

Water, cold as ice, splashed over her, and the shock of it shattered her concentration long enough for Tess to successfully squash her blast.

Shivering and furious, Kindra stumbled back, falling against the stairs. Vylie had, of course, vanished the second Kindra attacked, though she could see the assassin hovering in the back of the room, more shadow than person. Emeline had replaced her in the doorway, her hands hovering over her head, a mass of water stretched out above her.

"Wh-what the fuck?" Kindra sputtered, her magic fighting to warm her against the cold.

"Are you going to do that again?" Emeline asked. "Because we have barrels of water in here, specifically for you. I can keep you drenched so you can't even light a spark, but I really don't want to have to."

"S-she—what the fuck is *she* doing here?"

"I told you that you would be confused," Tess said calmly, but there was a tension in her stance that betrayed her nerves. "And I was right to assume you would be angry. But we can't answer your questions if you're busy attacking us."

Confusion and fury rippled through Kindra at the same time, and though every part of her screamed to fight, to attack, her hands remained at her sides as she climbed to her feet. "Are you forgetting what she has done? She killed Terryn! She almost killed *me*. She—she almost killed

Jasper." Some nasty, hungry part of her reached for Scaldor, begging her to call for him. She shoved it down.

"We aren't forgetting," Emeline said quickly, "but it's far more complicated than you think it is. You were never in any real danger—"

"I wasn't aware getting my stomach sliced open didn't count as real danger, Emeline," Kindra snapped, then shot Vylie a burning glare. "Besides, her *lover* definitely intended to kill me. Luckily, I incinerated him before he got the chance."

Vylie bared her teeth, her fists clenching. But she didn't move, though the shadows around her rippled.

"Mattias shouldn't have done that," Tess admitted. When Vylie growled, she shot the Shadowmaster a stern look. "He disobeyed orders, and that kind of recklessness endangers what we're trying to accomplish here. It's his own fault he got killed. He should've known better than to let his personal vendetta cloud his judgement."

"And what, exactly, are you trying to accomplish here?" Kindra breathed, seething, body shaking with the effort to contain her emotions.

"We will tell you if you fucking *cool* it," Emeline shot back.

"Fine," Kindra snarled, not bothering to hide her anger. "But you keep that bitch as far away from me as possible. And you'd better have a damn good reason for why she's here."

Emeline nodded, and stepped aside to let her enter, lowering her hands and allowing the water to float back into an open barrel as Kindra stalked into the room.

Sure enough, there were at least a dozen barrels spread through the space, open and ready to go. Kindra bristled at the thought of these people preparing to contain her. She scanned the low-lit room, taking in the people scattered throughout, including Vylie, who had half-melted into the shadows of a dark corner—indeed, as far away from her as possible. The woman's black eyes glinted as she glared at Kindra. Kindra returned the glare with equal vitriol. All she could picture was Terryn's face as Vylie dragged her sword through his neck—

"Watch it, Kindra," Emeline snapped, and Kindra wrenched her gaze away from the Shadowmaster. Slowly, she surveyed the others.

Most she didn't recognize, but there was a handful from the Royal Guard present. A couple she'd even sparred with, once or twice, and they gave her tight nods of acknowledgment. But there were three new faces she'd never seen before. All crammed into what really wasn't that big of a space. It would be extremely hard to wield here, unless she accepted the fact that she might hurt somebody accidentally.

The point, most likely.

"So, is somebody going to start talking?" she breathed, getting a grip on her rage.

Tess glanced at Emeline, who gave her a nod. The Firefury seemed to steady herself, then said, as though she were just trying to get it over with:

"We are going to oust the Annalindis family and place a new bloodline on the throne."

Silence, thick and crackling, surrounded them.

Then, when Kindra could find her voice, she replied, "Is this a joke?"

"Not at all."

"It's the only way to break the curse, Kindra," Emeline added, and Kindra's blood chilled.

"So that's your grand plan," she said softly, hardly able to believe what she was hearing. "Your plan is to overthrow the fucking Annalindis family?" *My family*, some small part of her cried. "The family that birthed this kingdom, that grew it from the ground up over centuries? Revolution—that's your big idea?" She shook her head. "That's—"

"Impossible?" Tess finished for her. She nodded, her orange eyes bright, borderline fanatical. "Yes, it is. And that's why it's the only way."

"Where the fuck do you think you're going to get support for this?" Kindra spat, feeling like the ground was tilting underneath her. "You stand on the same side as the monster who killed Terryn and bombed *children*! And," she continued, panic swelling in her at the thought, "what do you plan to do with everyone—with the king? With—with Jasper? With your *wife*?" She shot at Emeline, who remained unmoved. "How do you think these revolutions go for the people deposed, Emeline? Have you fucking thought about that? Because typically, the people in power get *executed*—" The Wavebreaker did flinch at that, even as somebody interrupted Kindra's tirade.

"We plan to give them the choice," an older woman said, her watery gray eyes hard. "They either peacefully abdicate, or we execute them. Helena and your Jasper will choose to abdicate, we are sure."

"Peacefully abdicate," Kindra repeated slowly, and actually laughed. "You think the Annalindis family is capable of peacefully abdicating the throne they created—"

"For the good of their people, we hope so," the woman retorted.

She felt like she was going crazy. "Am I the only one who realizes this is insane? And Helena, she doesn't know, does she, that you're plotting to overthrow her family—*our* family, Emeline!"

"I didn't realize you'd become so attached to that," Emeline snapped back, blue eyes like chips of ice. "I thought you'd be all for it! After all, this saves you, doesn't it? Absolves you of your *cursebreaker* duty. You don't have worry about bearing children anymore, about being Jasper's wife, you can be free—" She paused, taking in the expression on Kindra's face, what was so plainly written there. "Unless you don't want that anymore."

Kindra swallowed. "I do want to be free of my-my duty," she said, hating how her voice shook, how it felt, somehow, not entirely true. "But Jasper—I…" She squared her shoulders. "He is my husband, and I love him," she declared, and someone in the room gasped. "I will not see him harmed. Not even by those who claim to have the best of intentions." She stepped back, towards the door. "Do what you want with this—this revolution. I won't say a word, I won't stand in your way—but I cannot— I just can't be part of this, Emeline." *I am so tired,* she finished in her head. The still-fresh scar on her torso pulsed dully with pain from the exertion it took to come down here. Her head ached from lack of sleep. She wished, desperately, that she hadn't come.

It was so foolish of her to believe that this was even worth learning. It only made everything worse. "I already have a target on my back—from the king, from the war… I will not place additional ones on those I love by being involved with this. Not Jasper. And certainly," she choked, "not my mother. So I will pretend this never happened, I swear on my life, but please, leave me out of it."

Tess went to reach for her but snapped her hand back at the look on Kindra's face. "Think about it," she said, pleadingly. "The bloodline is *cursed,* Kindra. There is no fucking loophole—no potion or true love's kiss that can undo it. The way to break it is so simple: a new bloodline. A new family on the throne. But the Annalindis family would never do it. Their arrogance, their God-blessed *right*, would not let them. And Eija Cursebringer knew that—"

"And she still got herself killed. All the rebels did. They still failed," Kindra shot back. It was a childish response. It all made sense, honestly, as insane as it was. Of course it would be something so simple. The royal family would never step down. They'd walk headfirst into their kingdom's doom as long as it meant they got to lead the charge.

"I didn't expect her to have such weak morals," one of the newcomers remarked, his green eyes glinting. Kindra went still. Emeline winced.

"You dare insult *my* morals?" she said with lethal quiet. "You dare call me weak, when you have killed innocent civilians and *children*?" She swept a dark glare around the room. "I have dedicated my life to protecting innocent people. I have risked myself again and again for them, I have sacrificed my *childhood* to keep those I love safe—and yet you, who slaughtered dozens at the Harvest Festival, and dozens in Dewport— possibly hundreds, if you count those that starved when you bombed their food supply, and dozens at *my wedding*—you act as though you are better than me?" She leveled her scorching gaze at Tess and Emeline. "You assumed I would be willing to get myself killed for this notion you have— an idea you cannot even prove will work. And I am weak for wanting to survive?" Again, she shook her head and made for the door.

"We are going to war," the same man snapped.

"Yeah, I fucking know, thanks," Kindra snarled. "The king has made me well aware of what I am to do about it."

"So, you will fight for him? For that monster?"

"I will do what I have to do to keep my mother and Jasper safe. He has made it very clear what is to happen to me and the people I love—people *you* love," a glare at Emeline and Tess, "if I disobey him. I do not want to fight," she confessed, "and I plan to do my best to get out of it, but I will not risk their lives. Nor will I risk mine for this foolish, impossible idea."

"You are blessed with the power of a god—"

"*Do not speak to me about that.*" Flames sparked in palms. The man stepped back, eyes turning wary. And she realized then that they, too, wanted to use her, just as the king did. They wanted her to fight with them, to spill blood and take lives for their cause.

Did they even know her at all?

Her eyes filled with tears from the hurt and frustration that they had so blindly misunderstood her. *I thought you understood me*, she wanted to scream at Emeline, at Tess. But she felt like she'd been played for a fool, used as a pawn.

"I am leaving," she declared, leaving no room for argument. She reached the doorway. Nobody moved to stop her. "I will not tell a soul," she vowed, "but I am no revolutionary. I have only—" Her voice cracked; she cleared her throat before continuing. "I have only ever done what I needed to do to protect my home and my family and myself. That's all. You should have never—you should have never believed otherwise." *Coward*, some part of her whispered, but she was so tired.

She wrenched open the door, ready to escape the suffocating room, only to find the space beyond it occupied.

Her soul knew who the man standing before her was before the rest of her did. Her soul only had to take in the broadness of his shoulders; the freckles dusting his face; the dark curls atop his head, not yet quite faded to gray.

"Do you mind staying for just a bit longer, firebird?" the man before her asked. And she only had to hear his voice—the voice that still floated through her dreams sometimes—for her once-clouded memory to clear.

And as he looked at her with burning, golden eyes lined with silver—identical to her own—Kindra fell to her knees before her father.

END OF BOOK ONE

TERMS TO KNOW

Magic Wielders

Elemental Wielders: these Wielders control one of the natural elements and make up the majority of the Wielder population. Their eyes are permanently a vibrant shade associated with their magic, though the brilliance of their eyes can vary based on how active or powerful their magic is.

Earthwarden: an Elemental Wielder who possesses the ability to manipulate plant life, and to a limited extent, metals/minerals. They cannot produce these on their own, so they must have some form of plant or mineral on hand to use. As far as their ability to manipulate metals/minerals goes, they are often used in smithing and engineering rather than combat. Naturally, they are also quite gifted at farming, botany, and alchemy. They are the most common type of Elemental Wielder. Typically have eyes that are a shade of green, though occasionally hazel or even brown.

Firefury: an Elemental Wielder who possesses the ability to produce and control fire. They are most frequently used for combat and make up most of the front lines of the army. While no class of Elemental Wielder is technically rare, they are the least common. Typically have warm eye colors: gold, orange, yellow, even red.

Wavebreaker: an Elemental Wielder who can control water. They cannot create water, so they must have a source nearby to use, and many Wavebreakers carry small cases of water with them. They can also freeze water and Wield it as ice, was well as controlling steam or mist. Their ability to sense the quality of the water they Wield was a major reason running water is as successful as it has been in Alverin, as they man the sanitation centers. Their eyes are typically a shade of blue.

Windspinner: an Elemental Wielder who can manipulate the air around them. Like Firefuries, they are best used in positions associated with combat. The fact that they are always surrounded by their element, as well as their ability to form shields, makes them extremely valuable as guards. Their eyes are usually a shade of silver, gray, or even white.

Illuminated Wielders: this class of Wielders are primarily known for their gifts in healing and divination. Their eyes can be any color but will change when they are actively wielding.

Healers: these Wielders possess the ability to heal both internal and external ailments. The more serious the injury or illness, the more magic they use to heal it. One of the most common types of Illuminated Wielder. Their eyes flash gold/glow brightly when they are wielding.

Whisperers: these Wielders have the ability to communicate across great distances using items such as paired mirrors. They are the main way communication works in most kingdoms, especially for the military. They also have the ability to communicate telepathically with others when they are in close enough proximity, though they cannot read minds. Their eyes turn milky white when they are wielding.

Oracles: other than Luckbringers, this is the rarest type of Illuminated Wielder. They are capable of receiving and deciphering prophecies/visions of the future. The only known Oracle currently in Alverin is Queen Cordilya, who reportedly had a vision so terrible it rendered her near-mute. This is not uncommon with Oracles. Their magic is deeply unpredictable and the visions can have varying degrees of frequency, detail, and severity. Even Oracles who manage to get some semblance of control over their abilities struggle with symptoms of insanity. Their eyes turn milky white when they are receiving a vision.

Bonescribes: Bonescribes are the most common Illuminated Wielders with divination magic. Through the act of scrying, they can discern some aspects of the future—though their visions are never as clear as Oracles can be. It is more of a "vibe" reading than a specific vision. Their eyes also turn milky white when they are wielding.

Luckbringers: Luckbringers are the rarest type of Illuminated Wielder. They can grant wishes, or "good luck," but at the expense of their own life force. The greater the wish or luck, the greater toll it takes on them. Their eyes glow gold when wielding.

Darkened Wielders: these Wielders are known for their abilities to manipulate all things death and darkness. They are the rarest class of Wielder. Their eyes can be any color, but are typically dark, and typically turn black or milky white when they are wielding.

Shadowmasters: the most common type of Darkened Wielder, these Wielders can create and manipulate shadows, or darkness, into physical, tangible forces or weapons. They can also use the shadows to teleport, though not very long distances. Their eyes turn completely black when wielding.

Cursebringers: the opposite of a Luckbringer, these Wielders can cast curses at the expense of their own life. Eija Cursebringer is the most well-known Cursebringer as the source of the Annalindis family curse. Their eyes turn milky white when wielding.

Deathcasters: The rarest type of Wielder across all classes. They can drain beings of their life force and take it for themselves, commune with and even raise the dead. This type of magic typically drives most who are cursed with it to insanity by a very young age. Their eyes turn black when wielding.

Deities

Fire Deities:
Cyrie: goddess of the sun
Scaldor: god of flame

Water Deities:
Bevare: goddess of water
Tempra: goddess of storms
Cylina: goddess of the moon

Air Deities:
Zefrynos: god of wind
Selestrine: goddess of the sky

Earth Deities:
Aspa: goddess of the forest
Dovon: god of animals

Evronis: god of stone

Illuminated Deities:
Israla: goddess of healing
Yvangil: god of luck
Ora: goddess of truth

Darkened Deities:
Morta: goddess of death
Keros: god of misfortune
Osulon: god of shadow

ACKNOWLEDGEMENTS

The spark for this story came to me in a dream back in December 2020. It was over winter break, and I was home for Christmas. I had a dream that I had written a fantasy romance book. When I woke up, I could not stop thinking about it. It wasn't that the dream gave me any plot ideas. It was just the question: If I did write a fantasy book, what would it be about? What story would I tell? An idea took root, and I wrote the first few pages—some of which still exist in chapter two—that day.

It took nearly four years to finish. When I started, I was finishing up my senior year of my undergraduate degree. Almost immediately after receiving my diploma, I went to a summer program in Arkansas for the summer, and then I moved to Indiana to start graduate school. I tried my hardest to sit down and work on it as much as I could, but I had no experience writing a novel, and pursuing a master's in music was extremely time-consuming. To put it plainly, I spent probably the first two and a half years of this process fucking around. I did not sit down and make a proper outline. I knew the major beats, but I had no idea how to bridge the gaps between them. I thought the story would just flow out of me, the way poetry often has. With my poetry collections, I don't need in-depth outlines or plot structures. I simply say, "I'm writing a collection with this theme," and the poems fall together like a puzzle. I can stitch them together over the course of months, quickly typing out a poem on my notes app in between classes or before bed.

Call me crazy, but I really thought that writing this book would kind of be like that. And in some ways, it was: I'd spend an hour writing the bones of a scene during lunch, 30 minutes cleaning up some dialogue before work. But in other ways—most ways—it very much was not.

So finally, I sat down and I made an outline. That was in 2023. I had been setting deadlines for myself that I was continuously failing to meet: *I'm gonna release this in 2022. Fine, spring 2023. Okay, nevermind, fall 2023. Shit, maybe 2024?*

I was so frustrated with myself because I believed in this story. I believed in the world I'd created and the characters that lived there. I *lived* in this book. More often than not, I was thinking about it. I made playlists to listen to on my walks and on my drives. I dreamed of the day I'd get to hold it in my hands, of seeing it in bookstores, of being a New York Times Bestseller. I can't really explain it, but I've always had a feeling about it. Like it could change my life. Like it's maybe the key to everything I've ever wanted.

So I made the outline, and guess what! There's a reason authors say you should use them, because they really work. It still took longer than expected, because life tends to get in the way, but in July of this year, I finished it. And now that I've done it, I feel far more confident in my ability to do it again. Which is good, because this is going to be a four-book series and I really can't wait 4 years before releasing the next one.

Anyway, there are some people I want to thank, starting first and foremost with my family, specifically my mom, who copy-edited this book for me and did a wonderful job. Turns out I am really bad at semicolons. She never got to edit these acknowledgements, so I'm sure I've brutalized something here that everyone's going to see, and I'll receive a text about it. Seriously though, the cost of editing is a major financial barrier for indie authors and I'm really lucky to have an English teacher for a mom who will do it for free. Thank you to my dad, who gave me my love of fantasy in the first place when he showed me Lord of the Rings (Extended Edition) for the first time. Thank you to my brother, who rewatches LOTR with me annually, played Legos with me when we were little and let me come up with all sorts of insane storylines, and has been my best friend for 22 years.

Thank you to my partner, Matt, who developmentally edited this book for me as well as being my dream come true. Thank you for being such a steadfast and supportive person, for being a soundboard as I talk through ideas, and for being such a gentle soul. I guess I should thank the bookstore for hiring both of us and ensuring our paths crossed, too.

Thank you to my cover designer, Miriam Schwardt. I feel like I struck gold when I discovered you, and you were such a delight to work with. I could not have dreamed of a more perfect cover.

Thank you to my beta readers: Wiktoria, Abby, Alex, Hunter, Kat, Mahin, Rebekah and Regan. Your feedback was unbelievably important, and I know this book would not feel as complete if it weren't for the perspective you offered. Additionally, you are all some of my dearest friends. Some of us—Mahin, Rebekah and Kat, I'm looking at you—have known each other for a very long time. I am very lucky to have such supportive friends.

Thank you to Ashley, who was one of the first people I told about this book back when it was still a tiny seed of an idea. Thank you for being my best friend, no matter how many miles are between us.

Thank you to *all* of my friends. I was not always surrounded by the most supportive people. In high school, my writing was mocked by several who claimed to be my friends but ridiculed me behind my back. It took a long time for me to feel comfortable talking about my writing so openly with people. Sometimes, I still don't feel totally comfortable doing it, like I'm still waiting to become the butt of the joke. But over the last few years that has changed, and that's largely due to you all, who have embraced me and lifted me up instead of tearing me down.

Thank you to my poetry family, the first community who believed in my writing and what it could do. It's because of you that I am doing this. I have felt so much love and support from you these last 11 years. It has made me believe in myself and my writing, even when the algorithms were making me frustrated. Especially then. Thank you to Michelle Halket at Central Avenue Publishing for taking a chance on my books and making a young writer's dream come true.

And finally, thank you, my readers. Whether you've read my poetry collections and are following me on this new adventure, or you just picked up this book today with no idea who I am: thank you. I get to do this because of you.

Much love,
Catarine

i gave myself the world

"what is it that you want?"

i want all this world can give me.

"then you're going to have to give it to yourself."

i gave myself the world showcases the beauty of introspection and exploring personal conflict. Through a conversation with an inner voice, Catarine Hancock portrays and symbolizes the peaks, valleys, and plateaus of the journey toward recognizing self-worth. This collection of uplifting verse is a balm for the soul in need of peace and will help the reader grow into the person they're meant to be.

shades of lovers

love comes in many colors.

this is a story of breaking and healing, of forgiving but not forgetting, of understanding and balance.

it is not only something to enjoy, but something to learn from.

here are the things i did right, and the many things i did wrong.

i give them to you, so that when love comes knocking, you will have a sense of what to do when you open the door.

Explore the experience of six different relationships in this moving collection that dives into the highs and lows of love.

sometimes i fall asleep thinking about you

A look into the process of recovering after a particularly bad love, *sometimes i fall asleep thinking about you* is a collection of poetry on the feeling of never getting closure, that lingering longing you still get even when you know you shouldn't, and how it feels to finally be able to say, "I have finally let you go," after years of struggling to find the words.

holy ground

do you think this longing will haunt us for a lifetime?

Split into five different sections, *holy ground* covers the sensation of falling in love and discovering one's sexuality, the anxieties and fears that accompany being in a relationship, the inevitable way life pulls people apart, unique heartbreak and grief one experiences when a good love comes to an end, and the gratitude you feel that you ever got to know it at all. Tender, reflective, and understanding, this collection is for anyone who has ever loved a person that finally showed them how beautiful love could really be. A person that they had to let go of, anyway. A person that, in another life, they'd be with forever.

sprout: selected poems

sprout: selected poems is a collection of pieces written between the years of 2013 and 2021. Beginning with the very first poem she ever posted on social media, *sprout* features over 250 poems, prose pieces, and truisms written by Catarine as she grew up. Sorted by year in chronological order, this collection showcases the evolution her writing has undergone since she began writing poetry when she was 13.

This collection was created as a gift to her readers, to whom Catarine owes so much.

Catarine Hancock is a poet, author and opera singer from Lexington, Kentucky, currently living in Chicago. She holds a bachelor of music from the University of Kentucky and a master of music from Indiana University. Aside from music, writing is her other great love. Since 2013, she has been sharing her poetry online. Over the last decade, she's garnered an audience of over 300,000 for her work.

She is the author of several poetry bestselling collections, including "shades of lovers" (2020), "sometimes i fall asleep thinking about you" (2021), and "i gave myself the world" (2023), all published with Central Avenue Publishing.

When she is not singing or writing, Catarine can be found curled up with a good fantasy novel, wandering the aisles of the local bookstore, or adding a weird décor item she found at the Goodwill to her already too-cluttered apartment. This is her debut novel.

Where to Find Catarine
Website: catarinehancock.com
Instagram: @catarinehancock
PoetryTok: @catarinehanc0ck
BookTok: @bookchatswithcat

www.ingramcontent.com/pod-product-compliance
Lightning Source LLC
Chambersburg PA
CBHW060243030726
47493CB00025B/1586